"I APOLOGIZE FOR THE ABRUPTNESS OF OUR WEDDING."

"I had to wed you quickly to seal my claim. In all the haste, I forgot to give you this." Fawkes reached for the gilt money pouch on his belt and withdrew the ring he'd carried all the way from Jaffa. Although Nicola did not know it, it was not booty. He'd had it made especially for her, guessing at the size.

He motioned and she held out her hand. "Nay, the other one," he said. He took her left hand in his and slid the ring onto the third finger. "They say that the blood in this hand flows directly to the heart."

The ring fit perfectly, gold filigree and rubies glinting in the candlelight. Fawkes stared at her hand resting in his. The hand of a lady. Smooth, unblemished skin, long, slender fingers, pale oval, perfect fingernails. The contrast against his own tanned, battle-scarred, rough-nailed hand was startling.

Nicola stared at the ring in astonishment. He'd given her a bride gift, one he'd seemingly chosen just for her. She'd been thinking of him as a brutal, ambitious warrior, yet the graceful beauty of the ring bespoke another kind of man, one of taste and subtlety. Had she not misjudged him once before? The squire she'd thought to order to do her bidding had ended up seducing her. The loutish soldier she'd expected had turned out to be a lover of great finesse and skill . . .

BOOK YOUR PLACE ON OUR WEBSITE AND MAKE THE READING CONNECTION!

We've created a customized website just for our very special readers, where you can get the inside scoop on everything that's going on with Zebra, Pinnacle and Kensington books.

When you come online, you'll have the exciting opportunity to:

- View covers of upcoming books

- Read sample chapters

- Learn about our future publishing schedule (listed by publication month *and author*)

- Find out when your favorite authors will be visiting a city near you

- Search for and order backlist books from our online catalog

- Check out author bios and background information

- Send e-mail to your favorite authors

- Meet the Kensington staff online

- Join us in weekly chats with authors, readers and other guests

- Get writing guidelines

- AND MUCH MORE!

Visit our website at
http://www.kensingtonbooks.com

NO SURRENDER

Nikki Donovan

ZEBRA BOOKS
Kensington Publishing Corp.
http://www.kensingtonbooks.com

ZEBRA BOOKS are published by

Kensington Publishing Corp.
850 Third Avenue
New York, NY 10022

All Kensington titles, imprints, and distributed lines are available at special quantity discounts for bulk purchases for sales promotion, premiums, fund-raising, educational or institutional use.

Special book excerpts or customized printings can also be created to fit specific needs. For details, write or phone the office of the Kensington Special Sales Manager: Kensington Publishing Corp., 850 Third Avenue, New York, NY 10022. Attn. Special Sales Department. Phone: 1-800-221-2647.

Zebra and the Z logo Reg. U.S. Pat. & TM Off.

First Printing: July 2002
10 9 8 7 6 5 4 3 2 1

Printed in the United States of America

One

The room was dark. He could not see her.

"Lady?" he whispered. There was no answer. He breathed a sharp, uneven breath. He could sense her. Smell her rich, elegant perfume. It heated his blood, aroused him. He'd never had a woman like this, pampered, refined, a lady. For a short while, she would be his. He would not think about why.

Swiftly, he removed his clothes. The ropes supporting the bed groaned as he climbed in. He reached out and felt warm, smooth skin. Her shoulder was silk, her arm lithe and gracefully shaped. With cautious fingers, he groped upward and grasped a thick braid.

"By the saints!" Her voice was a taut whisper. "Will you hurry and finish!"

He went rigid. Half with surprise, half with resentment. Clearly, she dreaded what was to come and wished to have it over with. Very well. He would do his duty. Then he would leave.

He released her hair and moved his hand lower. The feel of a lush, pliant breast made his breathing quicken. So far, her body was a soldier's wet dream. He would be damned if he would waste it.

He caressed her nipples. "Don't," she murmured. He ignored her. She tensed beneath him, as if she would push him away, but then she arched upward and the nipple he was fondling peaked tight and hard against his fingers. His own desire grew. His cock was aching hard. But there was so much yet to explore. He was beguiled by this woman. The scent of her, the sleek, slender feel of her body.

He moved his hand to touch her face. He could tell that she was beautiful, her features fine and perfect. Delicate bones, flawless skin. He wondered what color her hair was. Her eyes. He wanted to go to the window and throw open the shutters so he could see her, but he worried that she would grow impatient once again. Besides, even in the darkness she was exquisite, with a face and form to haunt a man's dreams. And for this moment, she was his. He could not believe his good fortune. He had intended to make it good for the woman, but now his urge to please her had grown even more compelling. She was the embodiment of his fantasies, his most heated, lustful thoughts made real. He would not fail her; he would pleasure her well. She would never forget this bedding.

Shifting his body, he leaned down to press his lips to hers.

She should be repelled. Disgusted. But she was not. His mouth felt wet and hot. The pressure of his lips against hers made them tingle, and he tasted like something indefinable, warm and faintly sweet. Eager. Alive. His body against hers was big and muscular. She smelled the scent of him, wild and male. It astonished her that the gorge did not rise in her throat. But it was not repugnance that she felt. Intrigued, that's what she was.

Coupling was supposed to be enjoyable, but she could not imagine how. Yet there was something about the way he touched her, callused fingers gentle and slow. Something about having his mouth pressed against hers, rubbing against her lips so skillfully, sensually. It ignited a strange yearning inside her, and she forgot she meant to lie motionless and furious while he performed his task. Forgot that she was going to insist that he get it over with quickly.

He stopped kissing her, and, absurdly, she wanted to protest. Then he mouthed her neck and she knew that was even better. Little pricks of longing traveled down her body. He moved to her ear, and she dissolved. He nipped her earlobe with his teeth, then used his tongue to lick. She shivered, shocked at the feelings welling up inside her. Her groin ached. Her nipples hurt. She wanted him to keep doing what he was doing.

He kissed her again, slow and coaxing. She was not certain what he wanted. But when she parted her lips, he thrust his tongue inside, like a sweet, spiced plum filling her mouth. She went rigid at the invasion, but the throbbing hunger inside her grew. His tongue thrust boldly, a pulsing rhythm that mimicked the motion of coupling.

His free hand worked loose her braid and smoothed the strands over her body. His hand cupped her breast, then played expertly with the nipple. Her other nipple rose tight and hard, eager for the same attention. She moaned. As if that were some signal, he stopped kissing her. Fierce need made her want to reach for him. But then she felt him move downward. He blew on her breasts, and like a flame fanned by bellows, her body caught fire.

Jesu, her breasts were perfection. Shaped to fit his hand. The nipples delicious, hard peaks. The feel of liquid flesh against his mouth. The hot, wet nipple tightening against his tongue. When she moaned, he increased the pressure.

She felt a ripple of desire strike like lightning between her thighs. Her hips arched upward, wanting, wanting. . . . His hand slid down her belly.

Her maidenhair was so fine and silky. He twined his fingers in it, excruciatingly aware of the place of even greater softness and magic between her thighs. A thought came to him. He'd heard of kissing a woman there, but had never tried it. This was a lady, clean, pampered, perfumed. He knew her cunny would taste good, as warm and female and lovely as the rest of her. But first, he would make it drip with love juice.

He was teasing her, dandling his fingers so close to the burning center of her. At last, she felt the longed-for touch. Delicate pressure. Not quite enough. She squirmed. So lightly, so tenderly did he explore her, as if he were a blind man memorizing her flesh, discovering that secret place she hardly understood herself, possessed of mysterious folds and contours and a damp slit between. She felt him open her as if unfurling the petals of a flower. He dipped one big finger into the center of the blossom. Her body clenched and tightened, then melted to allow him entrance. He left his finger there, pressing slightly upward, and began to kiss her again. The strange throb inside her grew incessant. She arched her hips, seeking deeper pressure.

When he withdrew his finger, she wanted to cry out at the loss, but before she could gather her breath, there was a waft of warm breath against her belly, then lower. When she realized what he was going to do, she froze in shock. God in heaven, she'd never guessed a man might kiss a woman *there,* the place the serving women referred to as a quim or coun, men, the coarser term of cunny.

Pure molten pleasure filled her insides as he licked her, and her fingers clawed the bed linens. When his teeth rasped lightly against the tender folds, she gasped in breathless ecstasy. The sensation of his tongue inside her caused her to writhe wildly, and when he sucked on some hidden place at the top of her cleft, she shrieked. It was too much. She felt as if she were losing her wits. His attentions left her weak, limp, shaking. "Please," she whispered.

She was ready for him now, he thought. Time to fill her deep and hard and make her scream some more. He adjusted his body, holding himself over her, then brushed her belly with his cock. He traced a path downward, stroking softly. Her body opened. Legs splayed wide. Hips lifted. Yea, she was ready.

She delighted in the feel of his shaft pressed against her impatient swollen flesh. But then came a stinging thrust of heat and pressure, and a startling moment of pain. She clutched at his shoulders, clawing him with her nails. By the saints, he was too big. She would die!

He had not expected this. For a moment, he was still, stunned by the undeniable sensation of thrusting through the barrier of her maidenhead. He experienced a keen sense of regret. Despite all his attempts to make it good for her, he had hurt her, this paragon of beauty and womanhood. But there was no way to change things. All he could do was try to make it up to her. "Shhhh," he soothed. "I'm sorry. I didn't know this was your first time."

He moved his hand between them, where coarse hair meshed with coarse hair and taut skin stretched around solid flesh. Using all his skill, every trick every woman he'd bedded had taught him, he stroked, coaxed, soothed, trying to relax and arouse her.

Gradually her tension eased. He felt a quivering pressure as she yielded to him. Then she wriggled a little, and he knew it was safe to move. A slow subtle rhythm, although it was torture to hold back. He had thought once they reached this point, he could ease his own need, thrusting deep and urgent. But he would not hurt her any more than he already had. He would make her reach her peak, so she could take him.

She felt his fingers search for some precise spot hidden between them. He found it, and like a door opened by a key in the lock, her whole being seemed to open up and turn inside out. Fierce sensation coursed through her body, making it buck and jump. She cried out. He removed his hand and thrust into her. Deep. Deep. The whole unbearable length of him. He moved faster. Harder. They were as one, struggling, heaving, fighting toward the same goal. Stinging pleasure-pain tore through her, and then a kind of light. She heard his shuddering groan.

Two

England, July 1193

Fawkes de Cressy pushed back his helm and stared across the valley at the gray bulk of Mordeaux Castle. But he did not see weathered stone. Instead, his vision was filled with perfect, milk-white skin. A fall of hair like liquid night. Eyes like moonstones. A mouth of petal-like softness.

The odors of sweat and horse and oiled armor also vanished, replaced by a scent so rich and intoxicating, it took his breath away. He'd never been able to decide what kind of petals and spices comprised the rare perfume that filled his dreams. It was the sublime essence of the woman herself—mysterious, untouchable, holding the promise of almost unbearable delights.

But soon, very soon he would have a chance to once again breathe the exalted air that surrounded her exquisite flesh. To touch her, to hold her, to—

"Fawkes, damn it! Where are you? I've asked you three times what our orders are, and you just sit there on your horse like a rotted tree stump!" Reynard de Gautier wheeled his destrier around beside Fawkes and swore emphatically. "Jesu! It's *her*, isn't it? We're on the verge of attack and all you can think about is the three-year ache in your balls. If you don't pull yourself together, you're not like to live long enough see Lady Mortimer again in this lifetime—"

"Don't call her Lady Mortimer!" Fawkes exploded at the mention of his deadly enemy. "By rights, she's not even his wife!"

Reynard snorted in disgust. "I forgot there's no reasoning with you on this. Well, if you won't worry for your own neck, at least consider everyone else's. If we wait too long, one of the wall guards will see us and sound the alarm. Either lead the charge or let's come back another day. I don't fancy risking good men because you're a lovesick fool!"

Reynard's words sent a sting of warning through Fawkes. They had both seen too much of death and suffering these past years. He could not let anything distract him now. There was much besides his own dream at stake.

He raised his arm and brought it down. The troop of knights surged forward, racing down the slope and into the valley. A cloud of dust surrounded them and the clink and clatter of their heavy armor rattled in their ears.

Fawkes considered how many times he'd experienced this moment, the pulse-pounding and terrifying sense that he might well die this day. Yet the worst dangers he'd faced in his life had not come as a knight on horseback. He thought of the very walls of Acre collapsing upon him, the only tunnel leading to air and life blocked by an assassin sent by Mortimer. He thought of watching men die of fever, moaning and out of their wits. Of the long march down the coast of Palestine, when men roasted to death in their armor or fell prey to the devil Saracens, who flayed their victims alive.

He had survived those things, by the grace of God. Now there was only this, one last battle, the last link in the chain that would render unto him all that he had dreamed of. Mordeaux, claimed as his very own. Mortimer, dead. Lady Nicola, in his arms, safe forever.

He still could not believe that this day was upon him. The writ from the king was tucked away under his gambeson, the ornate lettering of the monarch's clerk clearly identifying him as the new lord of Mordeaux. But words on parchment meant nothing unless he could seize control of the keep. Richard was in Germany, his formidable muscles wasting away in the prison of the emperor, who was no doubt in the pay of Prince John himself.

If he wanted this castle, he must seize it on his own. At least he had the element of surprise on his side. Mortimer would believe him long dead, and few of the inhabitants of either Mordeaux or Valmar were likely to remember him, a lowly squire in Mortimer's retinue.

And her. Would she remember him?

How could she not? He'd held her in his arms. Come inside her body. He'd been her first lover. Hopefully, her *only* lover.

The way he'd left her gnawed him. He'd been powerless then, unable to say or do anything against her cruel, depraved husband. Mortimer was his lord, and he'd had no choice but to do his bidding, to go with the rest of his troops when they left for London and then on Crusade with King Richard. He'd had no choice but to leave her.

But he'd vowed to himself on that journey that someday he would return and free her. That vow, that destiny, had kept him alive through all the suffering and misery of the Crusade. It compelled him to risk his life many times, to impress and astound his liege, so that the king would knight him, and then, finally, offer him a reward for his bravery and valor.

"What would you ask of me?" Richard the Lionhearted had inquired, sitting back on a stool in his tent, his fierce predator eyes narrowed and his bulky, restless form filling the small space like the regal beast he was named for. "What ambition compels you? Do you, like me, desire to free the Holy Sepulcher above all things in this world? Or are you driven by less noble motivations? Wealth? Power? Revenge?"

Fawkes's mouth had been so dry he could hardly speak. Finally, he forced the words out, wondering if the truth would cost him everything. "All of those things, Your Highness. And one other—a woman."

Silence had followed, an eternity of silence. Then the king had laughed. "You reveal yourself too eagerly, de Cressy. Most men would have lied and said that my quest was theirs. But I admire your honesty, and you do deserve some reward. Name something within my power to give, and you shall have it."

"The honor of Mordeaux Castle in Worcestershire," he'd answered. The king had motioned for his clerk and that had been the end of it.

Except, there was plenty of struggle and suffering ahead of him. He'd still had to survive the rest of the campaign and the long journey back to England. Then he'd had to use persuasion, as well as much of his hard-won booty, to convince this group of war-weary crusaders to join his mensie and travel with him to Mordeaux. And now he must survive the coming battle, the confrontation with Walter Mortimer—

"Something's wrong!" Once again, his friend's nagging jerked him back to awareness. "See the village." Reynard gestured to the cluster of daub-and-wattle structures directly ahead of them. "It's been abandoned."

Alarm prickled along Fawkes's spine. There should be chickens pecking in the dirt around the huts, smoke rising above the thatched roofs, dogs barking. "Jesu," he breathed. "Have they been warned? Did they know we were coming?"

His worst fears were confirmed as they neared the castle. The portcullis was down, the bridge over the ditch deserted, and on the ramparts, he could make out the forms of archers in the crenels.

He held up his hand to call a halt and jerked on the reins of his own mount.

"What are we going to do?" Reynard dragged his destrier to a stop beside Fawkes. "There's no point attacking if they're waiting for us."

"I know that," Fawkes grated out. "This means we're going to have to camp here and build siege engines. The keep can still be taken. It's just going to take time."

"And cause a lot of damage. By rights, the castle is yours. You have the king's writ. Do you really want to undermine the walls and half burn the place down in order to take possession?"

Reynard's words evoked a grim picture. By the time they conquered Mordeaux, it might little resemble the secure, prosperous keep it was now. Fawkes imagined the stone walls blackened by fire and half collapsed by missiles from a mangonel. He envisioned the fields surrounding the castle trampled by his men's horses, the neat village plundered. Fighting men tended to pillage and despoil, to assume their right to take whatever they found in their path. He could order his men to leave the fields and the village alone, but it would cause ill feeling and grumbling. He might near his goal of conquest, only to find his fighting force depleted as knights drifted away to seek employ elsewhere.

"God's bones," Reynard muttered. "Who could have told them? No one knew we were here. No one except the messenger you sent to Lady Nicola and the woman herself. Do you suppose *she* warned them?"

"Why would she?" Fawkes asked incredulously. "I wrote her that I'd come to rescue her. That I intended to kill Mortimer and free her from the hellish life he's forced upon her. Why would a prisoner warn her captor? It makes no sense."

"Maybe not. But someone has spread word of our arrival. Look!"

Fawkes swore as he turned and saw a mounted force approaching from the other end of the valley, a distinctive red and gold banner in their midst. *"Merde!* It's Mortimer. I had hoped not to have to deal with him until I had Mordeaux safely in my possession."

"It might be for the best," Reynard said. "We'll fight a pitched battle for Mordeaux, along with the rest of Mortimer's lands and the lady herself. Whoever is the victor will have it all."

Fawkes nodded, his jaw so tight with determination and hatred, he could not speak. Although not how he'd planned it, this confrontation was the ultimate answer to his prayers. Finally, he would deal with his enemy face to face.

The small army slowed as they neared Fawkes and his men, and a knight on a black destrier rode forward. He wore a red surcoat emblazoned with a gold lion rampant, a device clearly intended to show that he was the Lionheart's own man.

What would Mortimer think, Fawkes thought with grim satisfaction, when he discovered that his opponent had also risen high in the king's favor, high enough to make Richard forget he had previously given the honor of Mordeaux Castle to *him?*

The knight pulled his mount to a halt a few paces away and raised his helm. Although he recognized the hated face, Fawkes also knew a moment of shock. Mortimer's face was ruddy with unhealthy color and so bloated his eyes appeared as mere slits in the puffy flesh. What had happened to the vigorous and formidable warrior he remembered?

"It's you!" Mortimer bellowed, his expression one of genuine surprise.

"Yea, it is I, Fawkes de Cressy. Your assassin failed. I left his body to rot beneath the walls of Acre." He took a step forward and drew his sword. "Now I have returned to repay you for your treachery."

"You?" Mortimer made a hoarse, derisive sound. "You're naught but a puling squire, a stable boy. You're not worthy of the effort of killing."

Fawkes gripped the sword with all his strength, lest his body leap forward of its own accord and strike off his opponent's ugly head before the terms of combat could be discussed. "I'm a knight now, exalted by the king of England himself. Richard also gave me the writ to Mordeaux." With his head, Fawkes motioned toward the castle. "I challenge you to a fight to the death. For Mordeaux. And for Valmar and the lady who rightfully possesses the property."

"You're still mooning over my bitch of a wife?" Mortimer's smile widened, giving his face a grotesque, toadlike appearance. "Well, the slut hardly recalls you with fondness. She's the one who warned me of your arrival."

For a moment, Fawkes stood stunned, disbelieving the words he had heard. Then reason returned. He smiled back. "Nay. She would not. Even if she cares naught for me, she hates you enough that she would never try to save you."

"Oh, you think not? Do these words sound familiar?" Mortimer clasped his hands and quoted in a gleeful falsetto, " 'My dearest lady. At last I've come to save you. My forces will reach Mordeaux Castle in a fortnight. . . .' "

Fawkes's gut wrenched with shock as his own words rang out mockingly. No. She would not. It was a trick. Somehow Mortimer had found the missive. Or perhaps he had intercepted it before it even reached Nicola.

"Ah, it's gratifying to see the poisonous viper strike another victim." Mortimer's voice rang out, rich and mocking. "For too long she has reserved her torments solely for me. I vow, my wife is the devil's handmaiden, an evil, cunning Eve, a witch from hell. I would say you could have her, with my blessing, but unfortunately, the lands are hers. To maintain my claim, I must endure her foul presence in my household." Mortimer straightened and his gaze appeared to clear. "I accept your challenge. I will kill you and carry your heart back to my wife. Perhaps the sight of it will please her, heathen sorceress that she is."

Mortimer replaced his helm, drew his sword and advanced toward Fawkes, moving with a stealthy grace that belied his corpulent form. Fawkes shook himself. Mortimer's words were a trick. The bastard meant to demoralize him. A common battle tactic, and one to which he would not succumb.

They circled and parried, assessing each other. Fawkes felt

the battle fever surge through him. He'd waited nearly four years for this moment. During that time, every man he'd killed, every opponent he'd struck down, had worn Mortimer's ugly visage. Now, at last, he faced his true enemy. Mortimer had tried to murder him. He had humiliated him and mocked him. But even worse, this man had hurt and debased Nicola. He had treated her like a piece of property, used her as a pawn in his greedy schemes.

His blade slashed forward and caught Mortimer's arm. Mortimer retreated and then parried the next blow. Cold steel grated against cold steel. Fawkes felt no fatigue, no fear, nothing but exhilaration. His body, honed to a hard, keen edge by dozens of bouts of combat, sang with speed and strength. His legs easily carried him out of reach of Mortimer's gleaming blade, and his sword arm struck out with deadly precision.

His opponent was weakening, the movements of his bulky body growing sluggish. His breath came in harsh rasps. As if he were watching it from far away, Fawkes observed his blade striking nearer and nearer to Mortimer's mail-clad body. Blood dripped from a wound on Mortimer's left arm and another at his hip. Any moment he would falter and Fawkes would land the killing blow. Victory was so near he could almost taste it.

"Is she worth it, you fool?" Mortimer panted. "If you kill me, you'll have to face Richard someday and tell him why. Do you think he'll accept that you took my life over a woman, and a perfidious, scheming slut at that?"

"She was never a slut, you bastard!" Fawkes pressed his advantage, feeling his hatred grow even fiercer and more consuming. *"You* sent me to her! *You* used her like a broodmare!" Mortimer lost his balance and fell. Fawkes loomed over him and drew back his arm, panting in rage. "Whatever she has done, you'll not defame her . . . ever again." With a savage thrust he drove the sword into Mortimer's neck.

He sat back on his heels and surveyed his handiwork.

Mortimer's bright blue eyes stared up at the sky, bearing a look of surprise. The wound spouted blood, reminding Fawkes too vividly of other deaths, deaths that had come by his hand. He felt vaguely queasy.

Gradually, Reynard's voice penetrated his haze of shock. "It's over. You've done it. Now all that is left is to claim everything that was Mortimer's. First, Mordeaux, then Valmar and your new wife. How does it feel, my friend? You'll be able to share Lady Nicola's bed this very night. And you're a wealthy man now. A real lord. Mordeaux appears prosperous, and Valmar is an even richer desmense. You'll have to pay some sort of fine to the king, I'm guessing. That is, if Richard ever makes it back to England. . . ."

Reynard prattled on as he helped Fawkes up, picked up his sword and cleaned off his blade on the grass. Fawkes stood numbly, barely hearing his friend or the other cheering soldiers gathered around. None of it seemed real. He had dreamed of this moment for so long. Now it was here, and it seemed utterly strange and fantastic.

He pulled off his helm, then looked down at his blood-spattered hands. "I need to wash. There must be a well in the village." He started off.

Reynard grabbed his surcoat. "What are you doing? Aren't you going to speak to them? The men are all waiting to congratulate you. What's wrong? Are you wounded?"

Fawkes shook his head. "None of the blood is mine."

"Then, what's the matter with you? You aren't acting like a man who's just won two castles and the right to wed the woman he loves."

Nicola was his now. Nothing stood in the way of claiming her. He should feel happy, jubilant. So, why was there a cold emptiness in the pit of his stomach? Mortimer's taunts. What if it was true? What if she hadn't wanted him to prevail? What if—

"Here now. Shake it off," Reynard said. "You're certain

you didn't get hit in the head? You seem dazed." Reynard reached out, as if to examine his temple.

Fawkes pulled away. "I'm well enough."

"Well, then, act like it!" Reynard slapped him hard on the shoulder. "Smile. Acknowledge your men."

For the first time, Fawkes looked around. The other knights were cheering loudly, their faces flushed with anticipation and excitement, his triumph mirrored in their eyes. They'd sworn fealty to him because they believed he offered them an opportunity for a comfortable and settled future. As knights in the garrison of a prosperous keep, they would have a roof over their head at night, food in their belly, perhaps fresh-faced serving maids to warm their beds. To men returning from the miseries of the Crusade, it sounded very like paradise.

He raised his arm in a gesture of victory. These knights were his brothers, his comrades. They'd been through so much together, to hell and back.

The men cheered more loudly. Fawkes took a deep breath. He'd won Mordeaux and Valmar Castles, but the real prize was not yet his. Nicola.

What did she feel for him? Did she even remember him making love to her over three years ago? For him, it had been the most splendid, stirring experience of his life. But for her . . . He'd agonized over every detail of their coupling a thousand times, and he had to admit that except for her sighs and moans and her body's response, he had no idea what those hours meant to her. He told himself that she would be grateful to him for saving her, and that should be enough to get her to wed with him. Once he got her in bed, he planned to entice her, make her rapturous with ecstasy. All the things he would do to her. Touch every part of her beautiful body. Kiss her everywhere. Suckle her breasts. Fill her deep and hard. . . .

At the thought, his cock hardened to bursting and a tremor of white-hot lust shook his body. He took a deep breath,

trying to shake off the mind-numbing desire. Three years of
abstinence had driven him almost mad, and his obsession
with Nicola had become so consuming, he could scarce think
of anything else. But he could not afford to lose what little
control he yet possessed. He still had to win her. And there
were Mortimer's gloating words to worry over. What if, God
help him, they were true?

Three

Simon. She had to think of Simon. Nicola conjured the image of her son, recalling the way he had looked the last time she saw him. His solemn, round blue eyes. The tousle of golden curls. His sweet cherub's face.

By the time she saw him again, the flaxen hair would have darkened slightly. His face become thinner, his chubby legs grown straighter and more agile. He was turning into a little boy, leaving the innocent perfection of babyhood behind.

He's growing so fast. Will he remember me? Does he ever think about me? Will I someday be able to tell him the truth, that I am his mother? That I have sacrificed everything for him, including, God help me, his father's life?

Nausea rose up inside her at the thought, and she went to the chest in the corner of the bedchamber and opened it. Inside, beneath the piles of clothing was a folded piece of parchment. She took it out, but did not read it. She knew the words by heart.

Mortimer had laughed at her when she wrested it from his hands. "Keep it," he'd taunted. "It's all you'll ever have of your lover. After I've killed him, I'll throw his corpse in a ditch to rot. He deserves no better. The worthless whelp couldn't even give you a healthy babe."

Nicola closed her eyes, her breath coming in shallow gasps. She had not meant for this to happen. Her intention in warning Mortimer had been to make certain the garrison at Mordeaux was prepared. At most, she had expected Mortimer to rouse himself from his drunken stupor and order a small force sent to aid the defenders. Never had she dreamed he would don his armor, climb on his horse and lead nearly his whole army out of the gates of Valmar.

For the last few years, Mortimer had done little but drink and rave, shouting vile oaths at anyone who got near him. How could she have known that the mention of Fawkes de Cressy would cause her husband to regain his wits and that ruthless ambition that had once made her life a living hell?

But the transformation had taken place. And although Mortimer was now corpulent and dissipated, he commanded a formidable force. Fawkes's troops would be outnumbered. He would be defeated, and Mortimer would kill him.

Heaven help me, what have I done?

The latch to the door rattled and Old Emma came waddling in, her plump cheeks flushed as red as apples. "There's news," she panted.

Nicola froze. She stared hard at the pattern of the wall tapestry, dreading what the servant would say.

"The two armies met at Mordeaux, but they did not engage in battle. De Cressy challenged Mortimer. They fought. Yer husband was killed."

At first, she could not believe what she'd heard, then her relief was so intense she wanted to weep. Mortimer was dead. Her foul tormentor would never trouble her again. Simon was safe. Fawkes could take control of Mordeaux by peaceful means. She could not have hoped for a better outcome.

Except . . . what about Fawkes? She looked down at the piece of parchment in her hands. Would he know that she had warned Mortimer? A new dread filled her.

"Always the stone face, aren't ye?" the servant chided. "That evil bastard's dead and ye scarce move a muscle. Aren't ye pleased? Isn't this what ye have dreamed of every day for the past three years?"

"Yea," Nicola whispered. Fawkes was alive. The man who

had once given her rapture was returning to Valmar. But, this time, would he offer her cold anger and the sting of his fists instead of his skilled, tender mouth and the pleasure of his entrancing body?

"What is that ye've not told me?" the servant persisted. Although they called her "Old Emma," Nicola always wondered how "old" the servant actually was. She had not a tooth in her head, but her skin was smooth and unlined, her wits as sharp as newly cast nails.

Nicola paced across the room, the missive gripped tightly in her hands. "I'm the one who warned Mortimer. I told him that de Cressy was coming."

"You? You warned that devil!" Old Emma shrieked. "Why? What madness has overtaken ye now?"

"Because of Simon! Anything can happen when a castle is taken by an enemy force. Fire, bombardment, rape and pillage. People die. And a little boy with the fair hair and blue eyes of the former lord would be an easy target for rowdy soldiers!"

"Ye could have sent a message to de Cressy. Ye could have warned him to be careful of the boy."

"And whom could I trust to send that message?" Nicola asked bitterly. "Everyone but you and I and a few people at Mordeaux believe Simon is dead. I could not risk that the truth might find it's way to Mortimer."

Old Emma shook her head. "It's a fine coil ye've wound for yerself. If Fawkes thinks ye betrayed him, he'll not look so kindly on ye now." The old woman crossed the room and touched Nicola's arm. "But ye could make it up to him. Tell him about Simon. Tell him that he has a son, and I vow, he'll forget everything else."

Nicola laughed, feeling slightly hysterical. "You think he'll believe me? Simon's fair hair and angel's face are his curse. He looks nothing like Fawkes, nor me either. Anyone would say that he is Mortimer's child."

"Not if they know anything about milord's taste in bed partners. He could never sire a child."

"They'll say he managed somehow. And he could have, I believe, if he'd not despised me so much. He loathed my 'witch's black hair,' as he called it, and my pale skin."

Old Emma snorted. "I doubt he would be capable, unless yer tits fell off and ye grew a cock."

"It does not matter what you think," Nicola said in exasperation. "What matters is what everyone else believes. And what de Cressy will think when he sees a child who looks nothing like him, and I try to convince him that the boy is his!"

"Then, what are ye going to tell him? Ye have to give some excuse for warning Mortimer."

Nicola shook her head. She had no idea what she would say. With luck, Fawkes would be content to stay at Mordeaux and leave Valmar alone.

No, no man would ignore a rich prize like Valmar.

"Maybe he doesn't know the truth. He may think that Mortimer got wind of the impending attack by other means."

"So we can hope," Old Emma said.

"How long?" Reynard demanded. "How long before you decide that Mordeaux is secure and go to claim the true prize—Valmar."

"There are things to do here," Fawkes retorted as the two men sat eating bread and drinking ale in the castle hall. "I must make certain that the people have truly accepted me as lord. And my men need a rest, to have a full belly and sleep on a bench in a warm keep for a few nights."

"Lame excuses, both of them. Everyone at Mordeaux is delighted you have killed Mortimer. The man was not well-liked. His taste for boys particularly distressed people. And the fact that he apparently spent the last two years in a state of near constant drunkenness does not aid his reputation, either. What could have happened to the bastard? I recall him as a vigorous leader and a strong fighter. *That* man would never have been so foolish as to accept your challenge. He was more cunning than that."

"I don't give a damn what happened to Mortimer. I'm only glad that he's dead and I finally have my revenge."

"Does it feel as sweet as you anticipated?"

"Yea, it's all I had hoped for." Not true. It had all happened too quickly. He'd never had a chance to say the things to Mortimer that he wanted to. To make him suffer for what he had done. To make him beg for mercy.

"Then why don't you go and savor the fruits of your success?" Reynard winked broadly. "You could share her bed this very night."

But what if she doesn't want me? The thought popped up, unbidden, unwelcome. How little he really knew the Lady Nicola. Despite the fact that they'd made love, he'd spoken only a few terse words to her, and she to him. They were strangers of everything but each other's bodies.

"We will stay here this night and go to Valmar on the morrow," he said. "We'll wear full battle attire and be prepared to fight. It's possible that the garrison there will refuse to open the gates for us."

"And who would order the gates closed?" Reynard demanded. "Do you truly believe that any of Mortimer's men will remain loyal now that he is dead? You saw our reception here at Mordeaux. They almost seemed relieved to see you take command."

Fawkes fought the urge to tell Reynard of Mortimer's taunts. What if Nicola *had* warned Mortimer? She might well refuse to surrender the castle.

He shook off the thought. Mortimer was dead. He would not let the foul bastard's lies weaken him. Setting his pewter cup down with a clatter, Fawkes said, "Tomorrow. We'll go tomorrow."

* * *

Adam FitzSaer, Valmar's castellan, entered the solar. He gave a faint bow, then approached Nicola where she sat by the glazed green window. "My lady. If I could speak with you a moment."

Nicola put aside the altar cloth she was embroidering. She disliked needlework, but the tedious activity helped calm her nerves. "What is it?"

"De Cressy has sent word that he means to claim Valmar. He should arrive in a few candle notches. What do you want us to do? Do we draw up the bridge and man the walls? Or do we welcome him and his army?"

It surprised her that FitzSaer had come to her, since he had always disliked her and complained she overstepped her authority. But then, he probably had no choice. With Mortimer dead, there was no one else to give orders.

For a brief moment, she considered barring the gates. If Fawkes had learned of her betrayal, he must hate her. There was no telling what he would do to her, how he would punish her. But even as her fear urged her to refuse to relinquish the castle, reason told her how foolish defiance would be. If they resisted, men would die. Women and children suffer. And in the end, she had no doubt that Fawkes would prevail anyway.

She shook her head. "There's no purpose to fighting de Cressy. If not him, some other lord will claim the place. These are lawless times, when men take what they can by force. With King Richard imprisoned in Regensburg, there is no one to petition for justice."

Justice. What was that? Nicola well knew that even if he were free, Richard would not mete out justice, but sell the honor of Valmar to whoever offered him the most coin or the most advantageous political alliance. Or, perhaps, as he had the first time, he would marry her off her to one of his "favorites."

Four years ago, the king had given her to Walter Mortimer,

an ambitious young knight who'd fought beside him at Chinon. Her mind traveled back in time.

She'd been locked in her bedchamber for days, since first arriving at Valmar after their wedding. Finally, Mortimer had come to her. He was drunk, slurring his words and reeking of wine. She'd been terrified that he was going to rape her, hold her down and thrust into her with his big, brutal body. But although he'd used his hand to try to arouse himself, he had not been capable. He'd bellowed and raged at her, calling her an "ugly, repulsive slut." Then he'd struck her, his ring cutting into her face and making her cheek bleed.

Finally, his mood had changed, becoming thoughtful. "I'm going to send a man to you," he'd said, "to get you with child. My heir. As soon as it's born, my right to your property will be secured."

He'd approached her again, his blue eyes cold and pitiless, like a snake's. "You will not resist him. You will lie willingly for him. If you do not, I will beat you, then tie you to the bed and watch him take you. . . ."

Across the solar, Adam breathed out in obvious relief. "I think you have made a sound decision, milady. From what I've heard of him, de Cressy would make a dangerous opponent. I'm certain he learned much of siege warfare at Acre." His gaze moved to Nicola's person. "But be aware, milady, de Cressy will not only take possession of Valmar, he will also take you for his wife. It's the easiest way for him to enforce his claim." He cleared his throat. "I'll leave you now. I'll tell the garrison that you wish to make de Cressy and his men welcome." He turned and left.

Nicola gazed after the castellan, seeing not him, but another man, her lover of three years ago. Although they'd coupled in darkness, afterward Fawkes had gone to the window and thrown open the shutters. She'd finally had a glimpse of the bold, enticing man who'd explored and aroused her body so ruthlessly. He was young, only a few years older than her, with roughly cut black hair and dark eyes that seemed to look into her very soul.

At the thought, she shivered and wrapped her arms around herself, then rose to call for Old Emma.

"What should ye wear, ye ask?" Old Emma examined the gowns hanging on the clothing pole in Nicola's bedchamber, then pulled down a plain wine-colored bliaut. "Well, by rights, ye're a widow and should dress in somber attire to mourn your husband." Nicola gave the servant an incredulous look, and Old Emma turned her attention back to the pole, cackling gleefully. "But then, that likely would not please de Cressy, and I think it best that ye try to cosset him. The rose sarcenet would be a fine choice." She pulled down the garment and began to smooth the wrinkles from it. "The color sets off yer hair and skin. Then, with luck, he won't notice what a skinny wench ye are."

"He liked me well enough years ago—" Nicola broke off and flushed furiously. Although she resented the servant's criticism of her slenderness, she had not meant to speak of what had happened between her and Fawkes in the past.

Old Emma cackled again. "Aye, so he did. So, he did."

Nicola moved to the unlatched window and took a deep breath of rain-freshened air. Never would she forget the day Fawkes came to her bedchamber. To a woman expecting rape, or at least clumsiness, his deft touch had been astounding, his skillful use of his fingers and lips and big, hard shaft a revelation. He had taught her so much in a few short hours, all the mysteries of her body, the magic, earth-shattering power of a man and woman joined in ecstasy. . . .

"Here now, come away from the window and let me help ye dress," Old Emma's voice intruded. Sighing, Nicola let the servant help her out of the serviceable wool and into the rose silk bliaut. It fit snugly through the bodice and the sleeves, then widened to a long, full skirt with a train. Embroidery done in silver thread glistened at the neck and along the sleeves.

Old Emma fastened the laces underneath Nicola's arms, then stepped back to squint at the effect. "Yer breasts are fuller from bearing the babe, but it fits tolerably well. Now for yer hair. I think ye should wear it down. It's most becoming that way."

"Unbound hair is for maids," Nicola said. Fawkes, of all men, knew she was a virgin no longer. "It would be unseemly to wear it loose."

"Ye'll need every advantage to make the new lord forget what ye've done," Old Emma chided. She drew the boar-bristle brush through Nicola's hair, making the sleek black strands crackle.

Nicola took a deep breath. "Sir Adam says that to secure his claim to Valmar, de Cressy must marry me."

"Aye, he'll wed ye. Then he'll have every right to beat ye."

Cold dread shivered down her spine. She remembered how Mortimer had dealt with her in the early days of their marriage. She recalled the numbing pain of his blows, the terror she felt whenever he was in the room. A woman was mere property of her husband. He could do nearly anything he wished with her. Exactly how would Fawkes decide to punish her for betraying him?

Old Emma finished brushing out Nicola's waist-length hair and stepped back. "Ye're a vision ye are. Mayhap yer beauty will bring ye some advantage this time, instead of yer husband wishing ye were a boy, like Mortimer did." The servant guffawed. "Now, if only ye could learn to act meek and dutiful like a proper wife." She shook her head. "But I suppose that's not likely. Ye were always proud and defiant. That's what set Mortimer against ye."

"Don't you dare insinuate that his treatment of me was my fault!" Nicola cried in outrage. "He was a monster! A cruel bastard who used me for his own ends! What sort of man sends a stranger—a squire from his stables—to service his wife?"

"Aye, he was a devil," Old Emma agreed. "But more often than not, ye made things worse by openly defying him. If ye had used your feminine wiles a bit, ye might have won him over. As it was, yer viper's tongue nearly got ye killed."

With a shudder, Nicola recalled that terrible day when she had pushed Mortimer too far. If she had not been carrying the babe that was to be his heir, he would surely have beaten her to death.

"Ach, lady, I didn't mean to frighten ye." Old Emma smoothed a strand of hair away from Nicola's face and arranged a ruby circlet around her brow. "I'm certain de Cressy is not such a beast as Mortimer was."

Nicola closed her eyes. A beast. Yea, Fawkes had been a kind of beast when he entered her, a rutting animal. But then he'd made her like it. Revel in every pulsing inch of his shaft inside her. The thought made her knees go weak.

She opened her eyes. Old Emma was referring to another kind of savagery. The violent cruelty of a man determined to terrify a woman into obedience. What did she know of Fawkes de Cressy now? He'd gone off to war, survived the dangers of a Crusade. Such experiences hardened a man, made him ruthless and cold, perhaps vengeful.

Another shiver afflicted her, but this one was not caused by desire.

The day was dazzling. Sunlight winked and glinted off the polished mail of the army moving through the lush green valley. At the head of the force, Fawkes felt sweat soak the linen shirt he wore beneath his gambeson. The heat was stifling, but even worse was the tension building inside him. He'd dreamed of this day for so long. Now he worried that it would all go awry.

He glanced up at the ramparts of the castle, searching for

archers. The drawbridge was down, the portcullis raised. But that did not mean they would be allowed safe entry.

Fool, he told himself, there was no treachery here. He'd become too suspicious, too wary. Years of warfare did that to a man.

The castle seemed slightly smaller than he remembered. Probably because he'd seen much grander fortresses, whole walled cities, the splendid palace of King Tancred of Sicily. But it was a fine enough castle. Stout walls, solid defenses, several turreted towers that added a touch of grace to the sprawling structure.

His gaze went to one of the towers. In the very top portion of it was Nicola's bedchamber. He'd spent not more than two candle hours in that room, yet the memory of what had transpired there seemed lodged in his soul.

He felt another twinge of warning. Could any mortal woman live up to his impassioned dreams? His image of Nicola had become a kind of grail, a shining vision of beauty and grace in a world of atrocity and evil. Had he built up things too much? Well over three years had passed since he'd seen her. What if Mortimer's abuse had damaged her beauty? What is she were no longer slender and elegant and perfect?

He set his jaw as he urged his destrier onto the bridge. There was nothing to do but pass through the gates and find out what awaited him.

Nicola watched from the ramparts as Fawkes and his army swarmed into the bailey of the castle. She was surprised at how many knights there were, how well-equipped, how fine their horses. She'd heard the tales of warriors who went off on Crusade in hopes of winning glory and wealth, only to die ignominiously of one of the fevers that ran rampant in the hellish climate of the East or to be killed in battle with the Saracens. For every man who returned in triumph, it seemed that two or more had perished. Yet Fawkes had apparently thrived. She guessed at the sum it would require to pay for this many knights, and was impressed anew. Not only had Fawkes earned his spurs, he must have won an enormous amount of booty. How many men had he killed to amass this fortune?

The breathless anxiety again surrounded her. It increased as her gaze picked out the army's leader. He appeared bigger than she remembered, but perhaps that was the effect of his armor and the huge, glossy chestnut destrier he rode. Over his mail he wore a crimson surcoat, emblazoned with the white cross of a crusader. He wore no helm, and his long dark hair riffled in the breeze. His coloring was the reason Mortimer had chosen him to father her babe. His near-black hair was a close enough match for hers that Mortimer believed any child Fawkes sired would be said to favor its mother.

She'd always found it satisfyingly ironic that Simon was as blond as a Saxon, but now the jest had turned sour. A raven-tressed child she might present to Fawkes as his son, but gilt-haired Simon he would never accept.

For a moment Fawkes was caught up in the chaotic mass of horses, shouting servants, barking dogs. The arrival of a troop of knights was always a disordered affair, with the knights struggling to dismount in close quarters, squires and hostlers trying to calm the horses and lead them off to the stables, and other servants unloading supply wains.

Eventually, she caught sight of Fawkes on foot. Adam was hurrying to meet him. Valmar's castellan bowed low in the muck of the yard, formally relinquishing Valmar to the new lord. She saw Fawkes motion for Adam to rise, then he glanced around, as if looking for someone. Her apprehension became a palpable thing, squeezing her chest so tight she could hardly breathe. Although he did not look up at the tower walk where she stood, she could feel his piercing gaze as he searched the yard for the lady of the keep.

Old Emma had urged her to meet him and throw herself

at his mercy, to wring her hands and weep to show her fear and sense of helplessness. "Tell him that Mortimer found ye reading the missive and bullied ye so badly that you had no choice but to hand it over," the servant had urged. "If ye appear meek and terrified, he'll take pity on ye, I know it."

Nicola was not so certain of his mercy. She had decided it was better to pretend that nothing was amiss and to hope that he had not found out what she had done. Still, she could not quite bear to face him until she'd had a chance to observe him from a distance. But what she had seen so far told her nothing, except that he was now a powerful and wealthy man, and a formidable warrior. Much as her first husband had been.

Her heart sank at the thought, but she could delay no longer. If she did not go down and greet him soon, he might take offense and despise her all the more.

With more than a little trepidation, she started down the stairs to the bailey.

Where was she? Fawkes scanned the castle yard. His nervousness was increasing by the moment. Was Nicola deliberately avoiding him? Did she consider him not worthy of greeting? His jaw clenched at the thought.

Reynard came up beside him. "She's probably in the hall, waiting for you. Or maybe she's seeing to the preparations for the evening meal."

Fawkes shot him an incredulous look.

Reynard shrugged. "Well, I don't know. If she doesn't appear soon, we'll ask someone to fetch her." Then he turned and said, "Fawkes. There she is."

The knights and servants drew back as she walked across the yard. She was a vision in rose and silver and midnight black hair. Her face was a perfect oval. Her eyes shone like raindrops glimmering in the sun. Her mouth was a berry-tinted jewel. She was even more beautiful than he remembered. Her youthful body had ripened slightly, her exquisite features refined with maturity. Three years ago, he had coupled with a maid. This was a woman.

But what sort of woman? There was no hint of emotion in her countenance. Her face might have been carved of marble. She was very near. He should say something. But a loathsome weakness rendered him unable to speak.

She paused a few feet away from him and bowed, so faintly that her heavy tresses, secured by a ruby-studded silver circlet around her brow, barely fell forward. "My lord," she said, and straightened.

The scent of her perfume reached him at the same moment. It curled around him, rubbing against his senses like a languorous, silky cat. Heat and woman, rare crushed flowers, tangy spices, wild herbs. His balls tightened and his cock grew hard, even as the rest of him seemed to dissolve.

"Lady Nicola." His voice came out harsh and strained, but at least it was not the adolescent croak he feared it would be.

The tension between them seemed to vibrate through the air. Everyone in the yard was watching them. His men, the garrison knights, servants and squires as well as kitchen knaves and pages—the most insignificant inhabitants of the castle.

Jesu, if they guessed at how he really felt, no one in this hall would ever respect him again! He could not let them see what she did to him, how she turned him back into a callow, adoring squire, ready to kiss the hem of her skirts and beg her for the honor of being her champion.

He took a steadying breath and spoke in a commanding voice that rang up to the rafters. "I claim Valmar Keep and all the surrounding lands by right of conquest. And I claim you, Lady Nicola, as my wife."

Four

"Milord." She bowed faintly. "If you would wish to bathe, I have had the bathing chamber prepared. Thomas will direct you there." She motioned to a young, golden-haired page. "After you have refreshed yourself, we will celebrate your arrival at Valmar with a banquet."

Fawkes turned and started after the page, feeling stunned. Her response to his announcement seemed very odd. He had just told her that he intended to make her his wife, to bind his life with hers, share her bed, beget children of her body, and she coolly sent him off to bathe.

It angered him a little, that she could deal with the matter so impersonally. Then he reminded himself that she was probably in a state of shock. In less than two days, her circumstances had completely changed. She probably could not believe her good fortune in being rid of Mortimer. And now she was to wed another man, a man she did not really know. It must be unnerving for her, and so, good chatelaine that she was, she fell back upon the formal gesture of offering a noble guest the opportunity to bathe.

But the tradition also usually included the lady of the household helping with the bathing, and he saw no sign she intended to do so. That rankled a little. Did she consider him unworthy of her personal attention? Was he still no more than a squire to her, a man beneath her?

The muscles in his jaw tightened as he followed the boy

into the bathing chamber. A fire burned in the hearth, despite the summer heat, and buckets for fetching water were stacked nearby. In the center of the chamber stood a large tub, the scents of meadowsweet, bay and rosemary wafting from its steaming depths. Two giggling maids waited with towels and a bowl of soap.

Nicola's absence here probably meant nothing, he told himself. She was probably busy seeing to the banquet, as Reynard had said.

The two maidservants put down the bathing supplies and moved to divest him of his armor and garments. Fawkes finally had to call a squire to help them, as his height and the weight of his mail made it an impossible task for a woman, or even two of them. They were more efficient in removing his clothing, their soft hands moving over him with tantalizing skill. It was clear from their coy demeanor that they hoped to service him in more ways than simply helping him bathe.

That startled him. Why would Nicola send these wenches to him when he was supposed to lie with her tonight? Of course, she might not know that her serving maids would behave so suggestively. She was a lady and probably sheltered from such things.

He climbed into the tub and sighed as his body relaxed in the sweetly scented water. What luxury. In his life he'd had few baths in a proper bathing tub. Usually it was a cold wash by the castle well, or a dip in a river or stream.

The warmth felt soothing, yet tantalizing at the same time. The pleasant scent of the herbs reminded him of Nicola and her exotic, haunting perfume. Indeed, that was the first memory he had of her, that bewitching odor he'd smelled as soon as he'd entered her bedchamber. But for all its promise, even her provoking scent had not prepared him for the woman waiting in the bed. Everything about her had been more arousing than even his wildest fantasies. Her breasts, high and firm and petal-soft. It seemed to him from the glimpse of her in the yard that they were fuller now, like roses that had blossomed into even headier splendor. Her waist was still tiny, her belly flat as a maid's. Maybe her hips had widened slightly, her buttocks rounded—the better for him to grip their soft warmth in the throes of passion.

And then there was her cunny. He remembered how it tasted of salty, musky passion. How tightly it squeezed his cock, with wet, slippery heat. He wondered if any other man had known her there . . . then quickly forced the thought away. He would cling to his memories and think about what he would do to her as soon as he got her alone in a bedchamber. How he would spread her legs wide and suck the juices from her, put his mouth upon her soft, delicious slit and tease her with his tongue and then—

"Don't fall asleep, you worthless whoreson! I'm to be next in the bathing tub and I don't want the water to be completely cold!"

Fawkes jerked upward and opened his eyes. Reynard stood near the tub, his perpetually ruddy face widened by a grin.

"Jesu, you startled me," Fawkes gasped. He took a deep breath, trying to drag himself from his intense, gripping reverie.

"What were you dreaming of, I wonder," Reynard teased. "Could it be the fair Lady Nicola?"

"None of your business." Fawkes hastily ducked his head to rinse his hair, then started to rise from the tub. Abruptly, he realized that his prodigious erection would be obvious to everyone. "Fetch me a towel," he told Reynard.

Reynard smirked, then stepped back and gestured to the serving maids, who were waiting near the hearth. "Milord requires your services," he told them.

Fawkes shot Reynard an annoyed glance, then gritted his teeth as the two serving women approached carrying towels. Damn Reynard! There was no way he could get out of the tub without them seeing his arousal! He tried to turn away as he climbed out, but they saw anyway.

"My lord, your lance is a fearsome thing," one of them teased.

"Aye," the other responded. "I would surrender easily to such a show of might."

Fawkes grabbed a towel and covered himself. The women backed away, giggling at his glowering expression.

"Milord is saving himself for his lady wife," Reynard said as he began to remove his own clothing. "Don't you think that is noble of him? Why, did you know that he has not had a woman in over three years, that he has—"

"Shut your mouth," Fawkes warned. "Or I'll throw you in the tub and drown you here and now."

Reynard's grin widened as he settled himself on the seat in the tub. "But as monklike and pure as milord is, I more than make up for him." He motioned for the serving maids to come near. With coos of delight, they began to soap him.

Fawkes shook his head as he dried himself. He was not certain how Reynard did it. Few would call him attractive. His hair was red as the fox he was named for and he had slightly bulging blue eyes and an overlarge nose and mouth. But despite his lack of pulchritude, his friend did always seem to manage to have a woman, or two or three, eager to bed him.

Finishing drying, Fawkes looked around for his clothes. Not seeing them, he called out to the women. "Where are the garments I took off?"

"Thomas carried them to the laundry," one of them answered.

"Now, what am I supposed to wear?" Fawkes complained.

"I brought your saddle pack," Reynard said. "It's by the door. You might as well don your court tunic. The wedding ceremony is scheduled to take place at nones."

"Today?" Fawkes approached the tub, the towel draped around his hips.

"Today—of course today. You said you intended to take Lady Nicola to wife. If you want to have the lawful right to take her to bed tonight, the ceremony has to be performed right away."

"But I—" Fawkes stopped. Why was he protesting? Everything Reynard said was perfectly logical. But somehow he did not feel prepared. What if she didn't want to wed him? Shouldn't she have some say in the matter? Despite his commanding words earlier, he'd really didn't want to coerce her. She'd had no choice in marrying Mortimer. Now she must feel that she'd once again been pushed into marrying a man she scarcely knew.

But, then again, she did not really have a choice. In order to secure his right to Valmar, he had to marry her, and the sooner the better.

He started toward where his saddle pack lay. "I suppose the damned thing is hopelessly crushed," he muttered.

The chapel was stifling. Knights and villagers and tradesmen filled the small church. Squires, hostlers, scullery boys, milkmaids, villeins and their families spilled out into the yard around the tiny structure. Everyone was eager to catch a glimpse of the new lord as he said his vows with the heiress of Valmar.

As he sweated in his formal attire of blue samite tunic, Fawkes wondered why he'd even bothered to bathe. But the heat did not seem to affect the woman beside him. She looked cool and regal, an ice princess. Her hair, held away from her face with the circlet, flowed over her shoulders like a blue-black river. Her skin was the palest, finest alabaster. Against its creamy purity, her lips appeared as rich and red as the rubies in her headpiece. In the soft light filtering in through the chapel's rose-tinted windows, her eyes were clear and silvery.

Every time he looked at her, it seemed as if a jolt of fire raged down his cock. And there was her perfume. Despite the pungency of the holy incense and the stale odor of his less fastidious knights, he was able to detect its faint, beguiling scent. It drifted to his nose, seducing him with the promise of sensual delights—delights he had experienced and never forgotten. She was female enchantment incarnate, the essence of mystery and sex.

The priest's voice droned on, and Fawkes struggled to remind himself that this was a religious ceremony. He should not be indulging in lustful thoughts in a chapel.

Perhaps it was the need to ignore his aching loins that made him feel so tense. He still had this vague sense of uneasiness, of being caught up in a whirlwind. As soon as the ceremony was over, they would go to the hall and sit down to a banquet. He would have a few hours to sit beside Nicola and converse with her, then they would climb up to her tower room and go to bed. As much as his body looked forward to that moment, his mind worried that it would not be all he expected.

He'd thought about this night so often, fantasized about it, imagined it a dozen, nay a thousand, different ways. He took her slowly, making it last, savoring every kiss, every caress. He took her fast and hard, scarcely taking time to remove their clothing before coupling in a violent fury that left them both drained and breathless.

In other versions, the room was filled with candles, illuminating it near as bright as day. He watched her take off her clothing. But she was not wearing the modest attire of a lady, but the scandalous, near obscene attire of a Syrian dancing girl. Beneath the sheer fabric, he glimpsed the dark shadow of her maiden's hair. She approached him and thrust her hips forward . . .

With effort, he forced away the tantalizing image. Another came to him. This one, the most provocative, the most forbidden. He disrobed for her, feeling her gaze upon him, hot as fire, as he pulled down his braies and revealed his enormous swollen cock. She stared at him in awe and reverence, then moved to take him in her mouth—

"Milord?"

With a shock, he realized that mass was over, and the priest was prompting him to move toward the altar. Nicola said her vows in a soft, refined voice, promising to love, honor and obey. His own voice rang out in response, sounding loud and harsh in the small chapel. Fawkes wondered how he must appear to Nicola. All he had done since arriving at Valmar was act like a conqueror claiming his conquest. Did she even guess how much he cared for her, how much he had suffered and endured for her sake?

The priest pronounced them man and wife, and they gradually made their way out of the chapel. Outside in the sunlight, the women showered them with flower petals and the men shouted crude innuendos regarding Lady Nicola's fertility and his sexual prowess. Fawkes endured the bawdy remarks grimly, wishing that Nicola did not have to be subjected to such coarseness. She was a lady and should not have to endure the leering comments of other men. He wanted all the white-hot passion burning beneath her cool, regal façade to be his secret, reserved for his pleasure alone.

As they started toward the hall, Fawkes felt a tug on his arm. He turned and saw a plainly dressed woman with a scattering of freckles on her cheeks and coppery brown eyes that matched her ruddy curls. "I'm pleased for you, milord." She dipped into a deep curtsy. Fawkes nodded faintly and prepared to move away, but the woman caught his arm again. "Don't you remember me?" she asked breathily. "It's Alys." She winked. Fawkes was struck by the memory of a plump, full-breasted body, soft and yielding beneath his.

"I must say, I barely recognized you," the woman continued. "You've changed much, Fawkes. Now you're a fine knight and ruler of the keep where once you were merely a squire, albeit a very handsome one." She winked again, and her voice dipped to a smoky whisper. " Do you still remember what you did to make me scream?"

He exhaled sharply, then looked around to see who was

watching. Nicola stood a short distance away. He turned and removed Alys's hand from his arm. "Things have changed," he said meaningfully. "I'm now married to Lady Nicola."

"Hah, to the biggest bitch in creation, you mean," Alys said. "You won't get any good of her. She poisoned Mortimer, you know. Fed him something that made his ballocks wither and his cock shrivel."

He didn't wait to hear any more. He moved away, then saw Nicola walking off, not toward the hall, but in another direction. What did she think? he wondered. Did she care if he'd fucked the serving maids? Did she care at all?

Nicola's head ached as she made her way across the bailey. The wedding had been a strain, reminding her far too much of her marriage to Mortimer. That day, she had also stood next to a handsome, imposing knight and said her vows. She remembered feeling pleased that Mortimer was young and comely. So often when a woman was married by the king's decree, her new husband was a hoary old warrior, with a thick belly and a breath that stank. Although massively muscled, Mortimer was not fat, and his teeth looked white and strong. But her enchantment with her fair-haired, blue-eyed bridegroom had not lasted long. All too soon, he had revealed what a monster he truly was.

She sighed as she neared the kitchens. Would Fawkes be any different as a husband? The man who had made love to her three long years ago had been young and rather boyish, and she would have been delighted to wed him. But this Fawkes was a powerful knight, who had survived untold horrors and somehow managed to return to England and avenge himself against Mortimer. Only a man who was very ruthless and determined could have accomplished all that, and she knew, all too bitterly, about ruthless, determined men.

The kitchen was crowded and chaotic. Nicola started to make her way toward the burly Saxon cook, then she was distracted by a strange flurry of movement to her right. A bunch of pages were gathered around the wine tuns, but instead of filling pitchers, they were watching one of the squires, who held a kitchen knife like a sword and gestured wildly. "You should have seen him," the youth enthused. "Fast as lightning he was. Feinting this way and that. No way could fat Mortimer keep up with him. Fought hard, Mortimer did, but he was simply overmatched. And then de Cressy got him down and thrust his sword clean through his throat. Blood everywhere, there was. I vow, the bastard bled like a pig at butchering time." The youth paused and gazed around at his audience with bright, excited eyes. "You should have seen it. I'd never seen a knight fight so fiercely and with so much skill."

"They say he was a hero in the Holy Land and admired by even the king himself," another page chimed in.

"And I heard that he killed a hundred men at Acre," one of the other pages exclaimed. "That's why Richard knighted him."

"A hundred men?" The squire gave a snort of disgust. "That's not possible."

"Yea, it is," the page protested. "You see, they were Saracen prisoners, and they were all lined up, bound and trussed. The king had commanded that they be killed to show Saladin how Normans deal with men who fail to honor their oaths. The knights moved down the line of Saracens, cutting their throats. There was so much blood it reached up to the knights' ankles."

As the image painted by the page's words filled her mind, Nicola swayed. A serving man entering the kitchen grabbed her arm. "Milady, are you well? Let me help you to a bench."

With the aid of the kitchen knave, Nicola staggered over to a bench and sat down. She closed her eyes and breathed deeply through her mouth. Pages and squires often exaggerated. Besides, she'd grown up knowing that the life of a knight was all about killing and being merciless. Still, the cold savagery of the tale she'd just heard disturbed her. What sort of man had she wed? Exactly how ferocious was Fawkes de Cressy?

"Milady?" She opened her eyes and saw the cook holding out a wooden dipper of water. "Drink," he said. "And don't worry about the food, milady. Everything is well in hand. Go to the hall and sit beside your husband. I promise he will be pleased with the banquet we have prepared."

Nicola took a drink of cool water and thanked Agelwulf. She rose slowly. By now the pages had returned to their duties and were busily filling pitchers and baskets of dried cheat bread to be used as trenchers.

She smoothed her veil and skirts, then left the kitchen and started toward the hall.

The hall was sweltering, the air dense from the perspiring flesh of the many people gathered inside. But Fawkes forgot his discomfort as he gazed upon the brilliant whitewashed walls with their bright weavings of hunting scenes and religious vignettes, the polished trestle tables, the snowy linen cloth and the jeweled plates, cups, bowls and candlesticks arraying the high table.

Reynard came up beside him. "Holy Mother, I've not seen such splendor since King Richard's coronation banquet in London. When we served Mortimer as squires, he never put on such a spread. This must be Lady Nicola's doing."

Fawkes nodded. "I certainly cannot complain about how the keep is run."

"Ah, but skill in managing a castle is not the reason you wed Lady Nicola." Reynard poked him playfully in the ribs. "How do you bear it, to know you must endure a tedious formal banquet before taking her to bed?"

"It would be good of me to talk to her a little first, don't you think?" Fawkes said. "I've not seen her in well over three years, and even then, well, let us say that we did not talk much when we were together. It may be my right to bed her, but I'd rather share at least a few pleasantries before I pursue such intimacy."

"You're a more patient man than I would be under such circumstances," Reynard said. "If you'd occasionally seen fit to slake your lust with a whore or serving wench, I could understand it, but you've gone three years without—"

"There are other ways to relieve yourself," Fawkes interrupted. "The Church may abhor onanism, but most men have done it under some circumstances."

Reynard shook his head. "I don't understand it, if there be a willing woman available."

"I didn't want *any* woman, I wanted Nicola. And if the only way I could have her was in my fantasies, then that poor substitute has had to suffice."

"Of course, there was the one dancing girl . . ." Reynard smirked.

"Yea, there was," Fawkes agreed. He had not bedded her either, but he'd never revealed that to Reynard.

"But now your long wait is over. Look, here she comes."

They both watched Nicola enter the hall. She seemed paler than ever, but no less beautiful. She held her spine straight as an arrow, and her whole bearing was so queenly and composed, it took Fawkes's breath away. It did not seem possible that tonight he would have the right to touch such perfection. To hold her in his arms, to stroke her silken skin and kiss those rose-petal lips.

He'd made up his mind. His approach in the bedchamber this night would be one of slow, elegant seduction, to match the refinement and beauty of the woman herself. He would make certain there was wine and plenty of candles. Thankfully, he'd had a bath and did not reek of the stables. And it was well he wore his fine court tunic and looked like a lord rather than a rank, crude soldier.

He exhaled deeply, imagining the moment when they were finally together in the bedchamber and all that dazzling love-

liness was his and his alone. Then he started forward to take
her arm and lead her to the dais.

Fawkes helped Nicola sit down at the head table, then took
his own place in the lord's seat. The tall chair was carved
with the silhouette of a hawk, the device of Valmar castle.
How fitting, she thought, that this man had earned the right
to carry that fierce, bold symbol on his shield. He did so
remind her of a cunning, unpredictable bird of prey.

She perused him from under her lashes, observing the way
his newly washed hair shone like polished ebony, the hard
shape of his freshly shaved jaw, his dark onyx eyes, hooded
like a hawk's, the incipient power in his body, clad now in
a tunic of deep blue velvet banded with gold. He was beautiful the way a wild animal was beautiful. Grace mixed with
deadliness.

She sought to steady herself. She dare not reveal her apprehension. With Mortimer, that had been nearly fatal. He
had thrived on the weakness and fear of others. As she took
a sip of wine, she tried not to let her hands tremble.

Potent emotions of dread and desire mingled inside her.
Her body remembered this man, her lover. Remembered the
feel of his mouth, the touch of his callused fingers, the sleek
hard fullness of his shaft inside her. Her womanhood
clenched with longing at the thought, but as much as her
body desired this man, there was too much at stake to let
those thrilling memories guide her actions. Simon's safety
depended upon her remaining on her guard. She dare not
give in to her yearning for this man. She must be shrewd,
cautious.

Recalling the tale she'd heard in the kitchen, she repressed
a shudder. She hadn't wanted to believe it was true, that
Fawkes had been part of such systematic slaughter. But on
the way to the hall she'd encountered one of the de Cressy
knights and asked him if Lord de Cressy had really killed a

hundred Saracen prisoners at Acre. The man had regarded her with narrowed eyes, then said, "They were naught but filthy infidels, milady. They deserved to die."

She told herself that what he had done was perfectly normal. Knights killed; it was the way of the world. But it bothered her that they were helpless prisoners . . . and all that blood. . . . She thought of Simon, so small and fragile. Fawkes had hated Mortimer so much. What if he believed Simon was his enemy's son? The thoughts that followed terrified her so badly she had to take a deep breath to keep her wine down.

The servants began to bring out the food—a whole boar's head, roast duck and capon, platters of trout and eel in sauce, trays of cheeses, baskets of warm, freshly baked bread, berry tarts and spiced pasties. They poured more of the wine, the finest vintage in Valmar's cellars. A warm, lazy murmur seemed to fill the hall, the sounds of people eating and drinking, smacking their lips and making contented comments to their companions.

Nicola ate carefully, all her concentration on the man beside her. Now they were wed, he had complete power over her, the right to beat her, imprison her, all the things that Mortimer had done. But—the thought tantalized her—he also had the right, the *duty,* to bed her.

Ah, Fawkes the lover; what delicious memories he'd given her. She thought of their bodies entwined, the intimacy they had shared. As she watched his mouth, she remembered how firm and demanding those lips had felt as they suckled her nipples. *Mmmm.*

For a moment, just a moment, she would put her fears aside and dare to indulge her fantasies. She'd thought him dead these past three years, but that had not stopped her from daydreaming about him. About what it would be like to have him come back and take her to bed. The delights he could show her, the feel of his body against hers. His smell. The urgent, intense pressure of his shaft inside her, guiding her to the heavens. . . . Heady, intoxicating stuff, made all the more so by the realization that the object of her dreams was actually beside her, flesh and blood, real and alive.

He turned toward her and her breath caught. The years had only heightened the aura of virility and power that surrounded him. He seemed even more male, more magnificent. He spoke. It took a moment for her to get past the thought of how sensual his mouth appeared, how white his teeth. Then his words registered in her brain—*The food is delicious. My compliments to you and to your cook.*

"Thank you, milord." Her automatic reply came out breathless, strained. She wanted to tell him not to break the spell by speaking, but only let her look at him.

He took another sip of wine. She wondered what other banal pleasantries he would utter, at this moment when her whole body felt as taut as a bowstring, aching for his touch. A faint frown crossed his face. "Valmar seems like a prosperous, well-defended keep. I am pleased with what I've seen here." He put down the goblet and it made a dull thud despite the linen tablecloth. "Now Mordeaux—I have to say that Valmar's sister castle appears much less secure. In fact, I was thinking of sending some of my men back there in a day or two."

Five

Nicola froze. Mordeaux, he'd mentioned Mordeaux. Why? What was his purpose in keeping soldiers there? Had the garrison resisted him in some way? Ridiculous. Gilbert de Vescy, the Mordeaux seneschal, would not be so foolish as to defy a man like Fawkes, who had an army of crusader-trained knights at his back.

She relaxed fractionally. Fawkes's tone was casual, as if he merely spoke his thoughts aloud. As long as no one knew who he was, Simon was in no danger. And who would betray her son? Not Gilbert's wife, Hilary, who was raising him as her own. Not Glennyth, the midwife who had made the deception possible. And certainly not Old Emma. The serving woman had been with Nicola ever since she could remember. As meddlesome and outspoken as she was, the old crone was utterly loyal.

"Tomorrow, I'm going to tour all of the castle and see what needs to be done," Fawkes said. "Although the defenses look solid, you never can tell. And I want to find out how deep the main well is, if we could survive a siege."

Maybe this was the source of his concern, not any suspicion of defiance from within, but from without. He might well have enemies that had followed him here and would try to wrest away his newly won properties. Her anxiety returned. If Mordeaux were attacked by some other army, Simon would be in as great a danger as ever. "Do you expect Mordeaux to be attacked?" she asked.

"Mordeaux?" He paused, looking at her strangely. "A good commander always expects attack, is always prepared for treachery."

Treachery? Was he referring to what she had done in warning Mortimer? Did he know the truth and play some sort of game with her, treating her gently, with velvet gloves, to see if she would give herself away? Mortimer had sometimes found sport in doing things like that.

She dared another glance at the man beside her. Although his voice was even and calm, she could sense the tension in his body. There was no reason he should be uneasy around her. He had all the power. As her husband, the law gave him the right to beat her, lock her away or punish by other means. And as a man, he had the physical power to kill her with one blow. All she had to use against him were her wits. She must carefully weigh everything she said, everything she did. Her life, and Simon's, might depend upon it.

He was bungling things, Fawkes thought sinkingly, talking about defenses and battle tactics. She probably thought him a crude fighting man, little different than her first husband. When had he lost the skill of cosseting a woman? He'd once done it a half dozen times a day, cajoling the kitchen wenches to give him a fresh loaf or a drink of buttermilk, stealing a kiss from one of the dairymaids, enticing one of the village girls into a hay mound for a quick, exuberant tumble.

But none of them had been like Nicola, a lady, born and bred, with the manners and the aloofness of a queen. Only in the bedchamber had he known what to do with her, how to win her over. But he could not wait until then. He must find some means of thawing the ice between them.

"I apologize for the abruptness of our wedding," he said. "I had to wed you quickly to seal my claim. In all the haste, I forgot to give you this." He reached for the gilt money pouch on his belt and withdrew the ring he'd carried all the way from

Jaffa. Although she did not know it, it was not booty. He'd had it made especially for her, guessing at the size.

He motioned and she held out her hand. "Nay, the other one," he said. He took her left hand in his and slid the ring onto the third finger. "They say that the blood in this hand flows directly to the heart."

The ring fit perfectly, gold filigree and rubies glinting in the candlelight. Fawkes stared at her hand resting in his. The hand of a lady. Smooth, unblemished skin, long, slender fingers, pale oval, perfect fingernails. The contrast against his own tanned, battle-scarred, rough-nailed hand was startling.

Nicola stared at the ring in astonishment. He'd given her a bride gift, one he'd seemingly chosen just for her. She'd been thinking of him as a brutal, ambitious warrior, yet the graceful beauty of the ring bespoke another kind of man, one of taste and subtlety. Had she not misjudged him once before? The squire she'd thought to order to do her bidding had ended up seducing her. The loutish soldier she'd expected had turned out to be a lover of great finesse and skill.

Seeing his hand over hers brought back tantalizing memories. Those long, strong fingers squeezing her buttocks and pressing her against him, then deftly stroking her as they were joined, making her wetter and wetter, searching for a precise secret spot that when touched would catapult her to paradise.

"Thank you," she said, "it's beautiful." She looked at him and he smiled at her, a warm beguiling smile that made the skin crinkle around his eyes. Her heart began to thud in her chest, but she fought the longing stealing over her. There was more to think of than herself and her own carnal desires. If she made a mistake, Simon would suffer as well as her.

Fawkes took a deep draft of wine, feeling much better about himself. She liked the ring. He'd seen the surprise and pleasure in her eyes. And for a moment, he'd almost thought he'd glimpsed a hint of the passion he knew was there behind the demure mask. The passion that had made her scream as she found her release. Yea, she was a hot-blooded wench beneath that cool exterior. He would find that lusty maid and make her moan and cry out for him.

But first, he must find a garderobe. He rose. "Pray, excuse me, madam. I will return anon."

There was a spring in his step as he started toward the back of the hall, and he had to quell the urge to grin like a fool. Then, he met Reynard. Seeing the troubled look on his friend's face immediately dampened his cheerful mood. "What's wrong?" he asked.

Reynard shook his head, then shot a look toward the high table. "Come," he said, "let's go out in the bailey."

"God's teeth, spit it out!" Fawkes said as soon as they were away from the hall.

Reynard shook his head again. "It's hard to believe, but I've heard the same from two different men."

"Heard what?"

"You remember when we arrived at Mordeaux and found the village deserted and the castle manned with archers?"

"Yea, I do. What of it?"

"Remember when we speculated who could have warned them? Well, I was right. It was Lady Nicola."

Fawkes glanced back at the hall. "How do you know?"

"Mortimer's men told me. And I had the same from the castellan here at Valmar, Adam FitzSaer. They said that Mortimer went on and on about what a fool you were to trust a devious witch like his wife. He apparently knew by heart the message you had sent her and quoted it to show what a lovesick, ball-less whelp you were."

Fawkes swallowed the fury that threatened to engulf him. Even dead, Mortimer had the power to provoke him into a murderous rage. "He might have servants who spied on her. They could have found the message and taken it to him. For that matter, the message might not even have reached her. If she were Mortimer's prisoner . . ."

Reynard shook his head. "There's more. The helpless

damsel you thought to rescue does not exist. For the past two years, Lady Nicola has roamed freely about Valmar, directing the household."

"I'm pleased that he finally came to his senses and released her. I was half afraid that she might have lost her wits from his mistreatment."

"It seems that it was Mortimer who lost his wits. They say that Nicola poisoned him, or cursed him, or maybe both. He went from being a strong, virile man to a worthless tosspot muttering to himself in a corner of the hall."

Fawkes recalled his shock when he first beheld Mortimer two days before, the puffiness of his face, the glazed, bloodshot eyes. "If she cursed or poisoned him, then it was with good reason," he said. "Mortimer treated her most cruelly. I have no sympathy for him."

"Don't you understand what I'm trying to tell you? Lady Nicola is no meek, helpless victim. Mortimer may have deserved whatever fate befell him. But if she is capable of such things, you need to beware. And the fact that she warned Mortimer makes it seem likely that she has no fondness for you. What I'm trying to say is"—Reynard put his hand on Fawkes's arm—"you have made this woman into some sort of goddess, a saintly creature worthy of any sacrifice. But what if she is really all too mortal and flawed? I don't want to see you ruined as Mortimer was."

"Mortimer was a corrupt, hateful bastard! He deserved the fate that befell him!"

"Yea, but you do not."

Fawkes stood stunned. The idea that Nicola had poisoned or cursed or otherwise done something to Mortimer did not distress him. But that she had seen fit to warn his deadly enemy of his arrival at Mordeaux was another matter. He'd sought to block out Mortimer's words, to believe they were lies meant to demoralize him. But he could not deny the fact that someone had warned Mortimer. It seemed most logical that it was Nicola.

He turned and stared toward the hall. Why had she done it? What did it mean? He was going to have to ask her these things. The question was, did he ask her after he bedded her or before?

Expectation coursed through Nicola as she followed Fawkes up the stairway to her bedchamber. She glanced at the ring glinting on her hand. Perhaps beneath the façade of hardened warrior, Fawkes was still the man she remembered. It might be possible to entice him, to make him feel so much desire for her that he would forget about her betrayal. If she could satisfy him in bed, that might be enough.

Her body thrilled at the thought, and as the light from the cresset torch silhouetted his tall form ahead of her, potent, visceral memories struck her in waves. The feel of his strong body pressed against hers. The force of his muscular hips thrusting his shaft inside her. That magnificent torso arched above her as he drove into her with that magic, stirring rhythm. He glanced back, and all she could think of was his well-shaped lips hot and burning against her quim.

Longing shimmered through her. So many years she'd waited for this. So many nights had she went over and over every detail of that afternoon long ago, while her body burned with unquenchable desire. Now, at last, he had returned to end her torment.

They reached the top of the stairs, and he started down the short passageway. He remembered the way to her bedchamber, she realized. Would he also remember what they had done there? Did he, like her, obsess about it every night?

His leather boots struck the stone floor with soft thuds. Her own calfskin slippers made a faint scuffling noise. He paused in front of the door to her bedchamber. She had followed so close she nearly fell into him. As he fumbled with the latch, another memory slashed through her.

His smell. Dark and male. Animal warmth and sexual

musk. It overrode the other faint odors surrounding him, the acrid smell of the burning cresset, the food they'd eaten that night, the lingering essence of the herbs she'd chosen to scent his bath. The scent she smelled was him, Fawkes. Time and events had not altered its evocative power.

The door creaked open. He turned to let her enter first.

Did he know that this was the same bed, the same mattress they'd lain upon together? The straw stuffing and supporting ropes had been changed, and the linen bedclothes were new, but the frame of the bed was the same. A narrow bed, too narrow for two people, especially when one was as large and as long-limbed as he was.

He went to the window. She thought he would close the shutters and block out the deep blue of the midsummer night sky. Instead, he turned to face her. The light from the cresset torch played over his face, highlighting the graceful planes and casting his deep-set eyes into unfathomable shadow. "Undress for me," he said.

Her heart seemed to beat so fast and loud she feared he would hear it. This was the moment when she would discover if perhaps she had some power in this thing after all. After removing the silver circlet and her gossamer veil, she set them on the clothing coffer. The gown she wore was fastened under the arms by lacing and was nearly impossible for her to undo it by herself. "If you please," she said, "I need your help."

He used the cresset torch to light the night candle by the bed, then, after placing the cresset in a bracket on the wall, approached her. He found the laces and began to undo them. Standing close, Nicola inhaled his male smell and admired the graceful cast of his features as he bent near, his expression intent. Her throat was dry, her body weak with anticipation. His hands were deft as he undid the lacing, surprisingly so considering their size. But then, she knew how delicately he could use those long fingers, with such breathtaking precision and expertise.

As soon as the laces were undone, he stepped back.

"I still cannot do it by myself," she murmured. In the normal way of things, she would have a servant undress her before he came. "I could call for a maidservant if you wish it."

"Nay." He shook his head, looking angry, then stepped forward, and helped her gather up her long skirts and pull them over her head. The bliaut fell to the floor in a pool of rose. Was he as impatient as she was? Her whole body was taut, her nipples and quim aching. Underneath, she wore a thin linen shift. He nodded to her and she took it off, dragging it over her head, then smoothing her hair afterward.

She stood before him and realized that despite the intimacy they had shared, he'd never seen her like this, utterly naked in a well-lit chamber. Her nipples seemed to tighten even more at the thought, contracting as though cold, although it was a warm, breezeless night. Her skin tingled, every inch of it. She'd waited three years for this moment. For him to do to her the things she dreamed of.

Simon. In the back of her mind the warning echoed, but she did not heed it. She had a plan. She would give Fawkes what he wanted, please him well. And in doing so, she would both soften his mood toward her and ease her own desperate need.

But something about Fawkes suddenly seemed different. She noticed a wariness in his expression, a hint of hostility that had not been there earlier. It made her uneasy, yet did not dampen her desire. If anything, the dark emotion in his eyes heightened her craving to fever pitch.

She could feel the tension in his body as he put his arms around her and kissed her. It wasn't a skillful kiss, but a hungry, possessive one. She sensed the banked fire of his passion, the hot urgency. *Yea,* she thought, *that is what I want, too. Give me your passion. Don't hold back.*

She opened her mouth for him, for the sublime sensation of his tongue filling her as his shaft would fill her other wet,

yearning opening. She melted in his arms, weak and bone-
less, ignoring her fear, telling herself that she could do this,
yield to her desire and at the same time find a means of
controlling him.

He moved his hands over her body, caressing her breasts,
her waist, then lower. Hard fingers sought her pulsing quim
and stroked. She felt her body convulse and shudder, burning
with unbearable yearning. The tension in him also seemed
to intensify, as if he were a bow drawn back, ready to unleash
an arrow.

He released her a moment to fumble with his clothing.
She caught a glimpse of his shaft, huge and purplish, then
he pushed her onto the bed and entered her. Her body
clenched around his as he thrust into her violently. Once.
Twice. Then he collapsed against her.

Fierce disappointment struck her. She had expected him
to soothe the yearning inside her, but it was still there. He
pulled out and rolled over with a groan. She wanted to
scream with frustration. Her body ached with furious hunger.

She waited, breathing hard. Her quim felt so tight and
engorged it was painful. She wanted to beg him, to demand
he do something to relieve her feverish craving. He sat up
and straightened his clothing, then he looked at her with cold
onyx eyes and said, "Tell me now. Tell me why you betrayed
me to Mortimer."

The passion drained out of her, replaced by fear, then a
sudden anger. He'd done this deliberately. Brought her near
her climax, then withheld the dazzling prize she'd expected.
The skillful lover knew how to use his abilities for purposes
other than offering satisfaction. What a fool she had been,
to think that this man was different, that he would not manipulate her and use her as Mortimer had.

She fought for composure as she covered herself. What
should she say? How should she answer? Old Emma had
urged her to weep and act pitiful, to arouse his sympathy.
But she could not do that. Not now, not when she knew what

sort of power this man had over her. She had to be strong and cunning and not let her guard down for a moment.

"I told Mortimer you were coming not to warn him, but to taunt him. I thought him too far gone to field an army. I could not resist telling him that he was about to lose all of it—Mordeaux, Valmar, all the rich prizes he'd been given by the king."

Fawkes took a deep breath. "What if he had defeated me? Your plan could have turned on you most cruelly."

"Mortimer could do nothing to me that he had not already done."

Fawkes stared at the woman in the bed, the bedcovers clutched around her. There was a ring of truth to her story. She'd hated Mortimer enough to do anything to hurt him, even if she risked destroying the man who had come to rescue her. It bespoke a woman who had been driven to become as ruthless and cruel as her foul tormentor had been to her.

It disturbed him to think of her being so pitiless. In her own attempt at revenge, she could have caused his death. Had she not thought of that? Did she care so little for him that she gambled his life on an opportunity to torment her enemy?

He stood up. He had to get out of this room and go someplace away from her, somewhere he could think. Adjusting his clothing, he strode to the door.

He went up on the ramparts and stared out at the northern lights, transparent green, blue and red blossoms flaring in the heavens. Maybe the balmy night air would help clear his head, but he doubted it. A dozen emotions roiled inside him.

Jesu, what sort of woman had he married? He had imagined her as Mortimer's helpless victim, but that was far from the reality. She was complicated, even dangerous. The things she made him feel. . . . Even now, despite her cold admission that she had betrayed him, he wanted to go back to her, to love her, kiss her, bury his body deep in hers. Regret gnawed at him. He'd wanted things to be perfect this night, their first time back together. Such dreams he'd had, such dazzling, heated visions of this coupling. But then Reynard's revelation had soured everything. He'd gone to the bedchamber intending to hurt her, to use her body quickly to find his own release, then when she was unsettled and vulnerable, ask her the fatal question about Mortimer.

In truth, he did not know if he could have held back anyway. She had looked so beautiful, her body perfection, alive and glowing before his eyes, and he had wanted her with a need bred of three years of longing. He'd barely been able to ready her even as much as he had. The feel of her lips, her smell, the lithe, silky shape of her in his arms—he was on the verge of exploding with each new, exquisite sensation. And explode he had, with a draining climax that made him feel as if he had been transported to the heavens where he burst forth like a shooting star.

At the thought, another wave of desire washed over him. God help him, he was ready to go back to her. Despite the fact that she'd almost gotten him killed. Despite the fact that her explanation for her betrayal failed to satisfy him. Who knew but that it was a lie, that she'd really intended for him to die. Dread dampened his arousal, but only a little. His need was great, so strong that it was a struggle to concentrate on anything else. Perhaps that was the problem. He hadn't half quenched the raging desire inside him. Maybe if he took her again, eased himself a bit more, he would be able to deal with her better.

He started toward the stairway.

Nicola squirmed on the bed, trying to sleep. What a fool she was, she thought grimly. She'd said the wrong thing. Made him hate her. Old Emma's scheme would have been much more likely to satisfy him. But she'd resisted the idea of letting him see her weak and desperate. How could she dare to appear so vulnerable to a man she scarcely knew, a man who had such provocative, stirring power over her body?

Even now, despite everything, it still throbbed with tension, in an agony of unrelieved lust. She touched herself between her thighs, feeling the wetness of his seed. Her body felt hot and hard, miserable. Mixed with her regrets was a kind of fury. He'd left her to ache with need, as she had the last three years. Found his own pleasure, then pulled out before she could know any sort of satisfaction.

Tears of frustration pricked her eyelids and she began to caress herself, to do what she wished he had done to her. Stroking the soft folds of her quim, feeling her body clench deep inside, as if to draw in the thick, hard shaft that was not there.

She threw off the covers, then lay back on the bed and arched her hips, imagining what might have been. The delicious fullness of his body within hers, the deep, rhythmic thrusts, stroking against her womb. She thought of the feel of his big body holding her down, his mouth warm and sweet, his tongue delicately exploring hers. She tried to think of how he had smelled and tasted, the heat of him.

Desperate, she pushed a finger inside herself. Too small, far too small. She tried another one, but it hurt. Despite the firmness of his shaft, it had felt velvety and smooth inside her, not bumpy and hard like her fingers were.

She removed her finger from her slippery passageway. How had he touched her that time long ago? Gentle, teasing, running a finger down the slick cleft, then back up again. Finding that special place buried in the folds of her quim. A tiny nub of flesh, but with such astounding sensitivity. To touch it almost hurt, especially now, when she was swollen and engorged. She flicked her finger over it, as he had when he flung her into the precipice, the whirling maelstrom of her desire.

Her eyes were closed as she concentrated, struggling to find the right spot, the right rhythm, the pathway to release.

But then some warning sense made her eyes snap open and she saw Fawkes standing in the doorway, watching her. She thought how she must look—naked, legs splayed wide, soothing her need with her own hand. She froze, mortified.

His gaze was hooded and cold, as he said, "Don't let me interrupt you."

Six

She snatched her hand from between her thighs and rose from the bed with as much dignity as she could muster. "I didn't hear you knock, milord."

"I am your husband now. I don't need to announce my presence."

His words angered her, but she shrugged into her shift and faced him as calmly as she could. "Of course you are. You can do anything you wish. Perhaps, like Mortimer, you will lock me away or punish me with your fists."

Her words horrified him. Of all things, he did not want to be like Mortimer.

He turned away from her, fighting all the conflicting urges tearing him apart. He wanted to push her down on the bed and fuck her senseless. But if he did that, she would think him as brutal as Mortimer. He wanted to beg her pardon, to tell her that he would make it all up to her and love her with all the finesse and skill he had sought to use those years ago. But then she would think him weak. And cool and bewitching as she was, he dare not let her know how he felt about her.

He hesitated another moment, then left her without speaking.

Once again, he made his way up to the ramparts. Jesu, to see her like that, her beautiful body bared, her thighs spread, her fingers on her cunny, stroking and playing. . . . It aroused him unbearably. It also startled him, made him see her in a new light. All these years he'd imagined her as some shining, perfect icon of womanhood. But she was not that. The last few hours had made that clear. She was real and complex and . . . lusty. A woman who believed in satisfying her own desires.

He began to pace. Of course he'd known that, sensed the passion inside her. But to see it revealed so blatantly. . . . It shocked him. Made him think. Three years ago, he'd taught her the pleasures of lovemaking. *Three years*. In that time, his own sexual hunger had near driven him mad. What had she done to ease the cravings of her body? Had she pleasured herself as he'd just seen her do? Or had she found some other man to satisfy her?

He jerked to a halt, rigid with jealous rage. Had she taken a lover? Is that why she did not care if Mortimer killed him? He took a deep breath. He had to go back there and force her to tell him the truth. This time he would not be put off.

Once again, he started toward the stairs. There was a sound behind him, and he whirled instinctively, reaching for the sword that was not there.

"De Cressy? Is that you?"

Fawkes relaxed as he realized the voice belonged to the castellan of Valmar.

"FitzSaer."

"Yea, milord. What are you doing up here? That is not to imply that you should not be here, but that—"

"I'm thinking," Fawkes said sharply, cutting him off. "Tell me, Sir Adam, how long have you served at Valmar?"

"Near three years. I hired on with Mortimer after so many of his men went off on Crusade with the king."

Three years. The man might still feel some loyalty to Mortimer. He would have to deal with him carefully. "And what did you think of Mortimer?" Fawkes asked.

The man hesitated. "He had his faults, of course. I never did come to terms with his taste for boys, but that does not mean he deserved what happened to him."

"You mean his death at my hands."

"Nay, I do not mean that. You killed him in fair combat and it was he who issued the challenge. Nay, I mean before that, how he came to such a sorry state. I might not have cared much for the man in some ways, but he was my lord. To see him rot away and become a pathetic thing before my very eyes. . . ." He shook his head. "Lady Nicola, now your wife, be wary of her. She is no natural woman."

Fawkes felt warning sting through him. "What do you mean?"

Again, the man hesitated. "I'm not saying that she used witchcraft, although she does keep company with Glennyth the healer, who is said to dabble in sorcery. But she did do something to Mortimer, fed him poison or something that disordered his wits and made him less than a man." Fawkes started to ask about Nicola, whether she might have had a lover, but FitzSaer went on, "And then there is the matter of the babe. It may be rumor, but I thought she behaved strangely myself."

"Babe, what babe?" The blood in Fawkes's veins seemed to have turned to ice water.

"She said it was stillborn, but I have heard otherwise. They say she strangled the babe in its cradle in order to foil Mortimer's ambitions. And the fact is, she has never appeared to mourn it. The child—it was a boy—is buried in the garden by the chapel. There is no marker or effigy to mark its passing."

"Take me there," Fawkes said.

"Now, my lord?"

"Yea, now."

Fawkes stared down at the grave in the torchlight, at the rounded mound of grass unadorned by marker or memento. FitzSaer cleared his throat. "What are you thinking, milord? Do you worry that if you get her with child, she will kill it also? I do not think she would. I think she did it because she hated Mortimer so much, and it was her chance to rob him of what he wanted most. Losing his heir was part of the reason he lost his wits. In fact, that is when he began to change, to guzzle his wine . . ."

FitzSaer droned on about Mortimer, but Fawkes was too caught up in his own thoughts to listen anymore. *Did the babe look like me? Or Nicola? He must have had black hair, and all babes had blue eyes. If he died at birth it would be too soon to know if they were going to darken or turn a pure, shining silver. Had he even opened them? Drawn a breath? My babe. And she had killed it.* The numbness began to fade, replaced by anger. How could she do such a thing? What kind of woman was she?

"To be fair to Lady Nicola," the castellan went on, "I suppose it's true that Mortimer must have done something to her to make her hate him so. I have heard a tale that he sent a man to rape her and get her with child because he could not. I guess something like that would harden a woman, make her capable of killing the babe that was so begotten. But still, to kill a child she'd just given birth to, it boggles the imagination, to think a woman capable of that."

Fawkes drew a deep breath. If he heard any more, he'd go mad. "Leave me," he said in as calm a voice as he could manage. "I have some thinking to do."

FitzSaer started to move off. "Sorry to roil the waters between you and your new wife. But I thought it best that you know."

Best that he know that the love of his life was a foul murderess, that she had killed a child—his son. Fawkes exhaled a ravaged breath into the darkness.

"You told him *what?* Where are yer wits?" Old Emma screeched. "Like as not, he's planning to come back here and beat ye within an inch of yer life!"

"Yea, he may," Nicola said grimly.

Soon after Fawkes had left, the servant had knocked on the door and asked slyly if she could bring anything. When she entered and realized Nicola was alone, Old Emma had demanded the whole tale. Nicola had told her of her conversation with Fawkes, but nothing else.

"Oh, the folly, the sheer stupidity of my mistress." Old Emma shook her head sadly. "Why didn't ye explain how terrified ye were of Lord Mortimer? If ye'd acted pathetic and helpless, I vow de Cressy would take pity on ye. 'Tis clear he still has a *tendre* for ye."

"And if I told him that I was in dread of Mortimer, what do you think he would do when he learned the truth?" Nicola paced across the bedchamber. "Anyone at Valmar will tell him that it was Mortimer who avoided my company these past years, not the other way around. At least the explanation I gave him is something he can understand. He hated Mortimer, too."

"Ye could have thrown yerself on his mercy, begged for his forgiveness."

Nicola tried to fight her growing panic. The servant was right. She should have tried to appear meek and terrified. She should not have lost her temper and provoked him. That was what nearly got her killed by Mortimer. But she could not change things now. She sighed. "I have so little power in this marriage. I don't want him to think me weak and helpless."

"Why not? It seems to me that men like their women weak and helpless."

Nicola's mouth twitched in grim recognition of the truth of Old Emma's words. The stubborn will that had enabled her to endure Mortimer's cruelties and finally get the best of him had probably served her ill with Fawkes. No doubt he thought her a coldhearted, calculating bitch. And there were certainly those at Valmar who would reinforce that opinion. Many of Mortimer's men blamed her for his deterioration and had come close to openly accusing her of witchcraft.

"Well, what's done is done," she said. "I can't take back my words."

Old Emma clucked her tongue.

A sense of doom swept through Nicola as she sat down on the stool and let the servant brush her hair. Maybe she should flee. Go to Mordeaux and claim Simon, then vanish into the countryside. But even if she took all the coin in the strongbox buried under the solar floor, she would not be safe. An unattached noblewoman was prey to the ambitions and lust of any man who could seize her. And Simon, poor Simon. How could she care for a child under such circumstances?

Better to stay here and take her chances. She did not think Fawkes would murder her. After all, she was the heiress of Valmar. He needed her alive, as his wife, to reinforce his claim. Surely he'd realize killing her might well cost him everything he'd won. She shivered, realizing that her life might depend on how well she'd judged Fawkes's character.

"I just don't know what to do with ye," Old Emma clucked. "Ye're your own worst enemy, ye are."

Nicola had to agree. So many poor choices she'd made, one leading up to another, until she was caught in a terrible trap of her own making. *I did it for you, Simon,* she thought. *If he kills me or locks me away and I never see you again, I hope someday you will know that I did it all for you.*

She conjured the sweet baby face in her mind and clung to the rush of love that flowed through her body. Some things were worth any pain, any misery. Verily, they were more important than life itself.

Fawkes climbed the stairs leading to Nicola's chamber. He'd spent a long, sleepless night. His stomach churned with distress, and his steps were leaden. But he could not wait any longer to confront Nicola.

Furious thoughts roiled through his mind. *She did not have to give the child life and then kill it. If she didn't want the babe, she should have asked a wisewoman for some potion to make her lose it before it quickened. Women knew of such things, even if the Church and most men abhorred the practice.*

But if she had done that, her revenge against Mortimer would not have been so complete, so satisfying. Fawkes fought the urge to retch. Could it really be true, that the woman he'd loved and almost idolized had murdered his son?

But he would not condemn her yet, he decided. He would give her a chance to tell him what happened to the babe she bore near three years ago. But, he thought bitterly, her explanation had better be convincing. He'd reached her bedchamber. With grim determination, he grasped the leather door handle and jerked it open.

She sat on a stool beside the bed while a servant brushed her hair. She was dressed, and in donning her clothing, she had regained her mantle of cool composure and queenliness. If she was surprised to see him, she did not show it. Her expression was wary, but distant. Did her guilty conscience gnaw at her? he wondered. Or was her hatred for Mortimer so strong she felt she could use it to justify anything?

"Leave us," Fawkes told the servant. The older woman placed the brush on a coffer by the bed and moved past him. Something about her triggered a memory. Had it not been this same plump-bodied servant he'd passed in the hallway years before? He recalled her waddling, goose-shaped body, her bright, dark eyes.

He turned back to the woman on the stool. "I have some questions to ask you." He moved nearer, wanting to intimidate her, to make her afraid. "Your castellan, he told me that some two years ago, you gave birth to a babe."

She did not speak, but something changed in her face. Her pupils became black pools surrounded by silver rims. He watched her carefully. "FitzSaer said the babe died." He took a breath. "Surely that is true, for I see no sign of it." He gave an exaggerated look around the room, as if she might have a cradle hidden under the bed or behind the clothing pole.

Still, she did not speak, and he realized that he must ask the question directly if he wished her to respond.

"How did . . . the babe die?" He almost said "my son." But he did not know that for certain; it was another question he must ask her.

She looked startled. Finally, she spoke. "He was born dead. The cord was wrapped around his neck. The midwife said he strangled in the womb."

"And if I bring the midwife here and ask her how the babe died, will she tell me the same?"

He watched her, ruthlessly assessing her expression. He saw wariness, a faint hint of fear. "Of course," she said. "Go to the village and ask her."

If they had conspired together to cover up the murder, they would certainly tell the same tale. "And the child," he pressed on, "was it mine, or some other man's?"

She stared at him, then said, "It was yours. I felt it quicken ere Mortimer returned from London."

"What did he look like?"

She rose from the stool, the movement giving away her agitation. "He was . . . good-sized. I carried him a full nine months. If not for the cord, he would have thrived."

"What color was his hair?" He could tell she did not like these questions. Her unease made him fear the worst.

"His hair was dark. What would you expect of a child begat of the two of us?"

"What did you name him?"

Again, that hesitation, as if she were deciding how to answer. "Simon. I named him Simon."

Simon. Not what he would have chosen, but then he'd been little consulted in any of this.

"Was he blessed by a priest before he was buried?"

"Of course."

Fawkes felt a surge of relief. In this, at least, he hoped she told the truth.

She stood facing him, looking like a bird poised for flight.

"There are rumors you killed the child." He could barely say the words. "Is it true?"

She turned away from him. He could sense her mind working as she struggled over how to answer him. It did not bode well, that she did not exclaim "Nay!" immediately.

"I saw an opportunity to torment Mortimer and I took it," she said. "I pointed at the dead child in the cradle and taunted him that he would never have an heir of my body. I don't know what he made of my words, how he twisted them. He was a cruel man. Although I was yet weak and bleeding from my travail, he beat me brutally. I nearly died that day as well."

Her response aroused the familiar loathing of Mortimer, yet it did not satisfy Fawkes. She did not say she had not killed the child. And in all of the exchange, she seemed to be choosing her words with care.

There is a secret here, his mind told him. *At the very least, she has not told you all of the truth.* He moved toward the door, more disturbed than ever.

Nicola paced across the small chamber after Fawkes left. A shiver of fear raced down her spine. Every time she was in the same room with her husband, she became aware how powerful he was, how volatile. He'd mentioned the tale that she had killed the babe—had he also heard rumors that the babe had not died after all, but was being raised in secret? Beneath her clothing, her skin prickled with alarm.

She'd kept her ears open these past years, listening for every bit of gossip, every whispered rumor, and although she'd heard herself defamed and vilified in every way imaginable, never had she heard anything about Simon. She'd believed their ruse had gone perfectly.

Her mind traveled back to those nerve-racking days. It had been only a fortnight before her babe was due when Glennyth had arrived in the middle of the night carrying a bundle. Nicola still remembered the horror she'd felt when the wisewoman unwrapped the blanket to reveal a tiny blue infant, the birth cord encircling its neck. Stillborn, the woman said, and the mother died a few hours later. But what was a tragedy for one village family was the greatest good luck for them. The babe's father had been too sick with grief to take note of what Glennyth had done with his dead son. Now, all they needed was for Nicola's babe to arrive. Then they could spirit it away and leave the dead infant in its place.

It was no easy matter to make a babe be born before it was ready. Glennyth had prepared a potion for Nicola to drink, warning there was some risk. If the contractions were too intense, Nicola could die. But she offered no alternative. They could not wait the dozen days until the babe decided to come on its own.

Just remembering the pain made Nicola grit her teeth. It had seemed as if a beast were inside her belly, devouring her from the inside. She had endured wave after wave of agony, and she was so certain she would die that she made Glennyth promise that even if she perished, she would carry out their plan. She would cheat Mortimer of his hoped-for heir even if it cost her own life.

But then it was finally over and she'd heard the babe cry. For the first time, she wondered if she could do it. How could she give up this beguiling, perfect creature who nestled on her breast with such heart-rending sweetness? Only the dark terror that Mortimer might someday change his mind and lash out at the son that was not his kept her determination strong.

Everything had gone perfectly. Placid, cheerful Simon had made not a peep after his first birth throes. She had tearfully kissed his tiny face, then Glennyth had put him in her herb basket, covered him up and carried him out of the castle.

Meanwhile, Old Emma had fetched Mortimer to Nicola's chamber. He glanced briefly at the still, pathetic form in the cradle, then his already florid face turned a violent red and he stalked to the bed. She had not been able to help taunting him, telling him that he would never have what he wished of her.

He struck her repeatedly, and she thought he meant to kill her. She'd swooned from the pain. When she regained awareness, she had wept with triumph—and despair. Her son was safe, but other women would have the joy of raising him. Her swollen breasts would never suckle him. She would not see his first step, nor hear the first word he spoke. Her darling love. And to save his life, she must give him up.

Nicola went to the window and closed the shutters. Her life was fraught with difficult choices, secrets that threatened to break her heart. And now Fawkes had come, bringing with him more turmoil. Just a moment ago, she'd felt his anger, his banked-down turmoil. Yet, he'd held back. Unlike Mortimer, he did not shout and strike out with his fists. No, he was subtler than that—and more dangerous.

Fawkes walked across the yard, his mind going over and over his conversation with Nicola. She had been hiding something, he was sure of it. Was it her guilt over the babe, or something else? A lover, perhaps?

God, how little he knew of her. He had fallen in love with an exquisite face and the memory of sexual pleasure so intense it seemed burned into his soul, but he truly had little knowledge of the woman he had idolized and dreamed of for years. He thought back to his recent encounters with her. In one, she'd made him almost mindless with lust. In another, she had aroused and shocked him. And finally, just moments before, he'd had the sense that he was dealing with a clever and yet desperate liar. What a puzzle she was. Was she a cold-blooded monster who had killed her own babe for vengeance? Or a weak-natured creature who was driven mad by Mortimer's torture, her mind so deranged by his abuse that she did not know what she was doing when she crushed the life from the body of a tiny, helpless infant?

Or was she somehow innocent of it all?

But she was not innocent of betraying him to Mortimer. She'd admitted to that, and her reason for doing it was hardly noble. To torture Mortimer, she'd said. If her hatred was so consuming, then it might be enough to drive her to murder.

He shook his head. He had to stop thinking of these things. But what else was he to think of? For the past three years he'd soothed himself to sleep with the fantasy of making love to Nicola. Now that blissful image was tainted by the thought that she might not be the perfect paragon of his dreams, but a murderess.

Fawkes entered the knights' barracks and met Henry de Brionne. "Where's Reynard?"

"Not up yet," Henry answered. He grinned. "You might try the stables."

In light of his own unsatisfactory night, the idea of Reynard sleeping late in the arms of an obliging wench was almost more than Fawkes could bear.

He entered the long, low building set against the curtain wall and walked past the stalls, redolent with the odors of horse and freshly cut hay. "Reynard, you lustful whoreson," he called out, "where are you?"

"Fawkes? Fawkes?" a voice responded. "Is that you? What the devil are you doing out of bed already. I thought you would be—"

"Never mind that!" Fawkes bellowed. "I have need of you. Get down here."

There was the sound of whispering, then soft noises as Reynard dressed. A creak of a ladder and Reynard suddenly appeared beside him.

"Why aren't you with Lady Nicola?" Reynard asked. "You can't tell me you've slaked three years of lust that quickly."

"I'll thank you not to announce my business to the entire keep," Fawkes growled. "Come outside with me and I'll tell you what's come to pass."

They ventured out under the still star-studded sky. "Well," Reynard asked, "how did it go?"

"I took her to bed, but that's not the half of it. Afterward, I asked her why she warned Mortimer. To taunt him, she said." Fawkes shook his head. "It chilled me to hear the hatred in her voice. I hated Mortimer as well, but I'm a man, I'm supposed to be hard and vengeful."

"But it's a believable answer," Reynard said. "If she'd played the terrified damsel, you might well have reason to doubt her, based upon castle gossip that says she is no helpless victim."

Fawkes took a deep breath. "There's more. After I left her, I spoke with the castellan, Adam FitzSaer, and he told me a horrifying tale. Some two years ago Nicola bore a child."

"Yours?" Reynard asked.

"Yea, she confirmed it. But that is where her tale and FitzSaer's diverge. She says the babe was dead at birth. He says that there are rumors that she strangled it herself to thwart Mortimer of his goal of having an heir to seal his claim to Valmar."

"Rumors, he said rumors," Reynard said. "I don't think any woman would do such a thing to her own child, no matter how much she despised the father."

"My instincts tell me the same, but there are other things. . . ." Fawkes took a deep breath. "I have been to the grave. It is barren and deserted. She does not seem to mourn the child. And I questioned her this morning, and although she said at first that the child was born dead, when I asked directly about killing it, she acted strange, uneasy. I felt she was hiding something."

"Jesu, I suppose such a story would make a man think twice about a woman."

"Twice and twice again."

"What will you do?" Reynard asked.

Fawkes shook his head.

Seven

"Ye must come, lady! The whole castle is in an uproar. Lord de Cressy, he's turning the place on its head!"

Nicola moved away from the window as Old Emma burst into the bedchamber. All morning she'd been pacing and agonizing, trying to figure out a plan for dealing with this unpredictable and dangerous man she'd married. How was she going to protect herself—and Simon?

"Lady, ye must listen!" Old Emma screeched. "He's making a real mess of things! The cook and the kitchen girls are in fits. His own knights grumbling fiercely. Why, he roused them all first thing and ordered them to appear in the yard, dressed in all their gear, weapons ready. 'Course, half of them have aching heads, or a wench in their bedroll they had to get rid of first. Dressed 'em down right sharply, he did. Said they were a shameful lot, the poorest excuse for soldiers he'd ever seen. Then he told his captain—the redheaded fellow—to put them through their paces, and started on the rest of us!"

Nicola ignored the servant's ranting. She was thinking about the confrontation with Fawkes that morning. He'd implied that she had killed their child. Although it was distressing to have him believe such a terrible thing of her, maybe it was just as well if he did. If he thought the babe was dead, then maybe he would not ask so many questions.

"Just everywhere, he was," Old Emma continued with her

tirade. "In the kitchens, demanding the keys to the storerooms, saying he wanted to see what sort of food stores we had in case of a siege. Then he's after the reeve, asking him about the tally sticks that show amounts of produce and grain still owed—"

"The reeve!" Nicola was suddenly jerked back into the present. What was Fawkes doing? Questioning all the servants about her? Searching for clues about the babe she'd birthed?

"Aye, he's in a foul mood," Old Emma continued as she helped Nicola arrange her veil. "Shouted at the cook when he wouldn't give him the keys at first. Ordering everyone about and bellowing like a maddened bull when they don't move fast enough for his taste. A foul mood, and ye're the cause of it, milady."

Nicola shook her head. What was Fawkes thinking? Did he believe that by bullying the servants he could get to her?

"A fine thing when the rest of us must suffer for yer mistakes," the servant grumbled. "Why he does not simply beat ye and have done with it, I'll never know."

Nicola started toward the door. Old Emma was right. She had to put a stop to this. She could not allow him to harass the kitchen staff or her serving maids.

When she reached the hall, she found the place deserted. No one had scrubbed down the trestles from the last evening's meal or tended the main hearth fire, which was smoking badly. She went to the kitchen and found it also abandoned and in disarray. Bunches of vegetables and the half-plucked carcasses of several capons lay on the wooden worktables and the fire was smoldering. She shouted for a page and after a moment, a boy crawled out from behind a basket of leeks.

"Tend the fire," she ordered him. "And tell me, where are the others?"

"The lord sent them down to the cellars to make a tally of supplies," the boy answered.

"All of them?"

The page nodded. Nicola sighed. Old Emma was right. Fawkes was so angry he was striking out at anyone near. She remembered his cold voice asking her about the babe, about why she had betrayed him. He had not liked her answers; now he would make others suffer.

"Where is Lord de Cressy?"

The boy shook his head and put more wood on the cooking fire.

She attempted to restore some semblance of order to the kitchen and the hall. First she got the cook and the scullery maids and the rest of them back to their usual tasks, then went looking for the other castle servants. She found them in the armory, polishing mail and weapons. They hesitated when she told them to return to their normal duties, but she reassured them that she would deal with de Cressy.

"Only she can give him what he wishes, anyway," she heard one of the women say to another as they started toward the hall. "If milady would try to please him in the bedchamber, I vow all our lives would be much easier."

"Mayhap she thinks herself too haughty and fine for him," the other retorted.

Nicola repressed the urge to pursue the serving women and give them a tongue-lashing for gossiping about their betters. But what would that accomplish? They were right. If Fawkes didn't mistrust her so violently, he would not be doing these things.

She made her usual rounds, locating servants and getting them back to their normal duties. As she left the weaving shed, she heard a jarring crash outside the castle, like a giant tree being felled. Fear swept through her. Were they being attacked? What if Fawkes had known an assault was coming and been trying to prepare for it? Had some unknown enemy already overrun Mordeaux? *Simon!*—she invoked his name in a silent prayer. *Please, God, let him be safe!*

Her legs would not seem to move fast enough as she ran

to the gate and shouted up to the guards in the tower, "What is it? Are we being attacked?"

One of the guards called down, "It's Lord Fawkes and his captain fighting."

Her relief was so intense, she felt weak. She leaned against the tower for a moment, then climbed the stairs to the gate tower and stared out. In the common pasture below the castle, two knights on horseback, garbed in full armor, rode to different ends of the open space. They were both holding heavy lances.

Nicola recognized Fawkes by his armor and the chestnut destrier caparisoned in tattered crimson. The other man must be the red-haired knight, who served as his second in command. Turning, the two men began to spur their mounts, heading directly for each other.

Nicola held her breath as the mounted men neared each other. Their lances collided, making a thunderous sound, but neither of them was unhorsed. They pulled in their mounts, then circled around for another go at each other. "Are they mad?" Nicola asked. "They could be killed!"

The guard standing near shook his head.

Again, the two knights charged. This time, Fawkes leaned in hard as their lances met. The other knight went flying off his horse and landed in a heap on the ground. As Nicola watched, gaping, he scrambled to his feet and drew his sword. The mounted knight turned his mount and started to ride him down.

"Good Lord!" she said. "Is it a mock battle or a real fight?"

Again the knight shook his head. "They were friendly enough with each other as they rode out. Now they act as if they mean to kill each other."

The chestnut horse's broad hooves dug into the ground, scattering clots of earth and grass. Beneath its glossy brown coat, the muscles bunched and stretched in sleek rhythm. Silver mail glinted in the sun and the lance thrust forth like

a streak of light. Horse and man and weapon moved in perfect deadly harmony.

At the last moment, the knight turned his horse, and the
huge lance pierced thin air instead of solid flesh. She gave
a gasp of relief. He circled back to the other man and shouted
something down to him. From the ramparts the watching
knights shouted and cheered.

Nicola knew she had seen something incredible, a remarkable display of skill and strength and lightning-quick reflexes. It took her breath away. Fawkes de Cressy was not
only a master in the bedchamber but on the battlefield, as
well. She thought of his body, so powerful and mighty, yet
capable of such gentleness and deftness when he wished to
use it that way. She wanted it all—the strength and domi-
nance of his fleshly lance inside her and the exquisite, subtle
caress of his mouth and hands.

Fawkes dismounted and a squire rushed up to take the
head of the lathered destrier. Then both men pulled off their
helmets, and holding them cradled under their arms, started
to walk toward the castle. Following behind were squires
with the weapons and equipment and hostlers with the
horses. Nicola watched avidly, letting the fantasy wash over
her. Fawkes striding across the courtyard to meet her, that
curving, sensual smile on his lips. He would lean near, smelling of sweat and horse and raw, heated male, and whisper in
her ear what he wished to do to her as soon as they were
alone in the bedchamber.

She swallowed thickly. It had been like that once between
them; what was to say that she couldn't find a way to make
it like that once again, to entice him and arouse that harsh,
raw passion that was inside him? Since arriving at Valmar,
he'd mostly behaved as the controlled, disciplined warrior,
but that did not mean his defenses could not be breached.
Like Mortimer, he had his weaknesses. If she could only find
them and exploit them.

He drew near the gate. His face was flushed; his hair plastered to his head in wet, inky-black strands. He talked animatedly to his companion. His dark eyes gleamed, and his mouth turned up at the corners in a pleased expression. The rush of hunger that went through her was almost unbearable. She climbed down from the gate tower and hurried into the keep, thinking that somehow she must find a way to make him desire her as he once had.

"My lord." The castellan, Adam FitzSaer, approached as Fawkes entered the gate. "That was an awesome display. I've never seen the like."

Fawkes nodded in satisfaction.

Reynard struck him hard on his mailed back "You see, you have not grown fat and slow. And now that you have proved you are the fiercest, most valiant knight, mayhap you will not have to act the bad-tempered slave driver with the castle garrison."

Fawkes gave his friend a look. It had felt good to challenge himself, to test his strength and skill against another man's. He was soaked with sweat; his muscles throbbed with a pleasant sort of soreness. Some of the impotent frustration had left him. But he could hardly risk his neck and Reynard's like this every day. He would have to find some other sort of release.

As they moved into the bailey, he instinctively looked around for Nicola, then cursed himself. No matter how he tried to banish her from his thoughts, she was always there.

"Let's get this blasted armor off." He started for the barracks. Inside, the two men helped each other out of their long mail shirts, then hung them on pegs on the wall, along with their shields and gauntlets. Fawkes pulled open the padded gambeson he wore under his armor and flapped it to cool himself. "I was thinking of going to Mordeaux in a few days. Taking a few hand-picked knights with me to lead the garrison there."

"You act as if you are expecting trouble."

Fawkes hesitated. He'd decided he should get away from Nicola for a time so he could better figure out how to deal with her, but he had no intention of telling that to Reynard. "I always expect trouble. Besides, it stands to reason that if I could seize control at Mordeaux so easily, some other man might try it as well."

"But you have the writ from the king."

"The king who is now rotting in a German prison. What if Richard never makes it back to England? There are many who hope for that outcome. And some, like King Philip of France and Prince John, have the power to influence his captors to that end."

"What will happen if John becomes king?"

"It'll be every man for himself. And I intend to make certain I have the means to hold on to what I've won, whether it be the supplies to hold off a siege, or the coin to pay off the new king, lest he try to sell my property to some other man."

"I guess I didn't think about these things," Reynard said, sighing. "I guess I thought that once you seized Valmar, we would all have a life of ease."

"That you'd spend every day dicing and drinking and every night wenching?"

"Something like that." Reynard smiled ruefully. "It seems we are both to be disappointed in our dreams, does it not?"

Fawkes stiffened. Reynard's words brought the sense of anger and disappointment rushing back. "I'm not disappointed," he said harshly. "I've won two castles. And as for my wife, things are not yet settled between us."

Reynard gave him a look, then said, "About Mordeaux, rather than you going, why don't we send FitzSaer? If we are here, we do not need him. We can defend Valmar ourselves."

Fawkes considered the idea. The very sight of FitzSaer reminded him of Nicola's betrayal and the dead babe. It would be good to be rid of him. But that also meant he had no excuse to go to Mordeaux himself. Yet, perhaps that was for the best. If he left Valmar, he would not have to deal with his wife's bedeviling presence, but he also would not be around to watch her. And knowing how cunning and deceitful she was, leaving her alone might be the worst thing he could do. "You're right," he told Reynard. "We'll send FitzSaer."

From her tower room, Nicola leaned from the unshuttered window and watched the two men cross the yard. No one would ever have guessed that a short while ago they had charged each other with weapons drawn, as if they were deadly enemies. Now, they talked easily together, like playful boys.

She observed that they had removed their armor and strode about in their gambesons and hose. They wore their quilted jackets open at the neck, and watching Fawkes, she caught a glimpse of sun-browned skin and black chest hair. At the sight, her quim grew wet and clenched with longing.

The two men walked back to the gate tower. She heard them call up, then Adam FitzSaer came down to join them. She watched the three men walk to the keep. An uneasy sense came over her.

She moved away from the window, wishing she had stayed in the hall where she might overhear their conversation. She had no idea what Fawkes meant to do next. Would he beat her as she'd mockingly incited him to do? Ignore her? And then there was the matter of the babe. She did not think he would let the thing go. He would keep asking questions.

That thought decided her, and she hurried to the door and went out. In the kitchen, she found Gillian. The slender, fair-haired maid had an irritating giggle, but she was biddable and comely enough for Nicola's purposes. "The lord and some other knights are in the hall," she told the girl. "I want you to take them wine and bread and cheese. Then, wait around to see what they are speaking of."

The girl's eyes widened. "You want me to spy on them, milady?"

"Not spy. I merely seek information of my lord husband's plans. How can I strive to please him if I do not know his wishes?" She smiled at the girl, trying to appear the dutiful wife.

"Of course, milady." Gillian dipped into a curtsy.

"This is a reward for your loyal service to Valmar, FitzSaer," Fawkes said. "At Mordeaux, you will have complete authority to order the castle garrison as you see fit. Whatever you need to rebuild the castle defenses, I will make certain it's provided. Whether it be masons to rebuild the curtain wall, or a day's labor from the villeins to clean out the ditch, you shall have it."

"Of course, my lord." FitzSaer's face was expressionless. Fawkes could not tell if he was pleased with his new duties or not.

"Have you a wife or family that you would want to take with you?" He should have taken time to learn the personal circumstances of the castle garrison when he first arrived. But he had been too obsessed with Nicola to note which men were wed.

FitzSaer shook his head. "I've never had time to woo a woman. With my lord Mortimer spending his days drinking as much wine as he could hold, the burden of the castle defense rested upon me."

"And you've done a commendable job, FitzSaer," Reynard said. "That's why Lord de Cressy has put his trust in you to see to Mordeaux's fortifications."

FitzSaer looked from one of them to the other. "The thing I don't understand is why you are so concerned with these matters. Do you expect an attack on Mordeaux? Or Valmar, or both?"

Fawkes gave the castellan the same explanation that he had given Reynard. That with the king imprisoned in Germany, anything could happen.

FitzSaer listened attentively, then rose. "I suppose it shows foresight on your part to plan for these things, my lord. You have years of battle experience, and you learned strategy from the Lionheart himself. By the way, that jousting match between the two of you—a magnificent display, simply breathtaking. I wish all the garrison could have seen it. Not to mention the men who will be under my command at Mordeaux."

"The Mordeaux troops saw him fight Mortimer," Reynard said. "I think that will be enough to instill in them a healthy respect for his battle prowess."

FitzSaer nodded, then excused himself.

"A hard man to read." Fawkes stared after the castellan. "I mislike his loyalty to Mortimer."

"Well, if he'd not been loyal to Mortimer, you could never trust him to be loyal to you, either," Reynard said reasonably. "Don't be so grim and suspicious, expecting treachery in everyone around you."

Fawkes snorted. "How else should I behave, under the circumstances?"

"I know what you need," Reynard said. "You need to forget your troubles in the arms of a willing woman."

"Nicola was not unwilling, in fact she . . ." Fawkes paused. He did not want to speak of these things with Reynard. Just the memory of seeing Nicola naked and aroused, her hand touching the swollen jewel that he longed to caress, was enough to make him painfully hard. Still, he was not ready to go to her. He hadn't sorted out his feelings yet, nor decided on a plan.

"What I mean is, you need some simple, honest fucking,"

Reynard said. "No secrets or expectations. Just a satisfying tumble."

Fawkes grunted. He'd begun to think the same thing himself. He was tense and irritable with unrelieved lust. Under the circumstances, there seemed no point to remaining faithful to Nicola.

Reynard cocked an auburn brow. "You're not immediately saying nay. So, what's the question, then? Who the lucky maid will be? I know more than a few that are willing. Alys, for instance."

Fawkes shook his head. "I want nothing to do with the past. Any of it."

"Ah, so you wish to start out fresh. With someone young. Innocent." Reynard nodded to the blonde serving maid who stood a few paces away, waiting to fill their wine cups. "Why not her? She's probably a Saxon from the village, sent here by her parents to seek a better future than marrying a red-faced, loutish villein. Probably not a virgin, but little used anyway."

Fawkes forced himself to glance at the girl. Thin, with long, rather scraggly hair the color of ripened wheat. But she did seem genuinely naive and uncalculating.

"Why not?" he said, then shook his head. "But how do I go about it? I'm so out of practice, I don't remember the way of it."

"You're the lord now. You don't even have to ask. Just order her to come with you."

Fawkes stood, deciding he must do the thing before he thought about it too much. He took a step toward the girl, then abruptly met Reynard's gaze. "But how will I know if she's willing?"

"Oh, she's willing." Reynard smiled knowingly. "For the lord of the castle, they're always willing."

Fawkes approached the girl and smiled at her. "What's your name?"

Her round blue eyes grew rounder still, then she giggled. "Gillian," she answered.

He took her arm. She did not resist as he led her across the hall. "Gillian," he said, "are you from the village?"

He exchanged pleasantries with the girl, then fell silent as they climbed the narrow stairs to the upper floors of the castle. He could not help remembering the day he'd gone to Nicola's room three years ago. He'd been nervous and anxious then, wondering if the woman was ugly or repulsive, if he'd be able to perform if she was. That was the irony. He'd worried about getting hard for a homely wench, when he should have been concerned about losing his heart to the fairest woman in creation.

"Milord, should I have brought the wine?" The serving maid's high, thin voice interrupted his thoughts. They were standing in front of the doorway to the bedchamber he'd chosen for his own.

"Nay, we don't need wine," he said, then knew immediately that he'd lied. In the dim light of the hallway, lit only by a cresset torch on the far end, the girl appeared pale and nervous. Was she a virgin? he wondered. By the rood, that was all he needed!

He opened the door and held it for her. As she moved past him, her scent came to him. Sweat and cooking grease. A far cry from Nicola's bewitching perfume. He sighed and sat down on a stool to remove his boots. Without speaking, she pulled her stained kirtle over her head. Underneath, she wore no undergarments.

She was slender with high breasts, a flat belly and narrow hips. A maid, as Nicola had been when he first came to her. The memory of Nicola's almost unbearably tight sheath made his cock rise in anticipation. That part of him was easily fooled. But his eyes, his nose, his thoughts, they knew that this pale, unprepossessing female was a poor substitute.

He shrugged out of his gambeson, then stood to pull his braies down. The girl looked at him. Her lips parted and her

eyes widened, in fear rather than anticipation. If she'd had
men before him, they had not been as large as he was.

"Are you a maid?"

She nodded.

He could not go through with this. It would be a miserable
disappointment, totally unsatisfying. "I've changed my
mind," he said. "Go back to the hall."

She gave him a startled look, then grabbed her balled-up
kirtle and fled.

Eight

Nicola entered the kitchen and looked around. "Have you seen Gillian?" she asked one of the potboys.

When he shook his head, Nicola frowned in puzzlement. A short time ago, she'd peeked into the hall and seen no sign of Fawkes or his captain. Assuming that Gillian had returned to the kitchen, she'd come in search of her.

At that moment, Gillian came in carrying the wine and wine cups. She gave Nicola a startled look and started to leave. "Gillian, stop," Nicola called. "Where are you going? Come speak to me."

Reluctantly, the young woman came back. Nicola noted that her clothing was disheveled, her face flushed. "Did you do as I asked? Did you take the lord some wine, then stay and listen?"

The girl nodded.

"What happened? Did they catch you eavesdropping and reprimand you?"

Gillian shook her head.

"What is it, then?"

She seemed to gather her thoughts. Licking her lips, she said, "They talked about a place called Mordeaux. About FitzSaer, the castellan, about how he was going to go there and see to the castle defenses."

Nicola felt her breath catch. "Why?" She grasped the girl's arm. "Why is FitzSaer going to Mordeaux?"

"I don't know." Gillian shook her head, eyes wild. "I don't know."

Nicola stared at her. She believed the girl. What she didn't understand was why she appeared so unnerved. "Has someone been bothering you?" she asked. "One of the men? You know I don't tolerate anyone molesting my serving maids." She thought of the knights who had come to Valmar with Fawkes. Hardened warriors, mercenaries. Such men lived by rape and pillage. "Tell me. I promise I will protect you."

"No one. No one has hurt me." Again the girl shook her head.

Nicola released her arm. Was she too terrified to speak out? Nicola could understand that. There had been times when she was Mortimer's prisoner that she'd felt utterly alone, helpless. "If you change your mind, come to me," she told the girl. "I promise I will help."

Nicola left the kitchen, her body rigid with distress. Why was Fawkes sending FitzSaer to Mordeaux? If he expected the castle to be attacked, he would go himself. If he simply intended to secure his authority there, he would send one of his own men.

And FitzSaer—God help her—of all the knights at Valmar, he was the one she disliked the most. She knew he blamed her for what she had done to Mortimer, as if, because she was a woman, she was supposed to endure whatever humiliation and cruelty was meted out to her, and never think of retaliating.

And now that heartless bastard was to go to Mordeaux, where Simon was. It made her exceedingly uneasy.

She crossed the bailey, trying to think of a plan. When was FitzSaer going? Was there any way she could warn Gilbert and Hilary? But how was she to leave Valmar without Fawkes noticing? Since he distrusted her so much, he would think the worst, believing she went to Mordeaux to plot against him.

She would have to wait for some distraction, an opportunity to slip away undetected. If only it would come soon. She needed to see Simon, to reassure herself that he was well. Until she saw his darling cherub face and cuddled him in her arms, she would scarce be able to think of anything else.

She lifted up her skirts and started toward the gate. It was a hot, sunny day, the sky vividly blue with only a few streaks of white clouds. There was not a hint of breeze in the castle yard, and it reeked with the odors of people and livestock. Nicola felt the unbearable urge to be outside the castle, to breathe fresh air and gaze out at the rolling landscape, a variegated pattern of golden grainfields, pale green pasture-land and dark green woods.

Near the gate, the way was crowded. Hostlers and stable men unloaded carts of baskets of leeks, turnips and peas from the village. A traveling merchant, garbed in a long scarlet robe banded with green braid, had brought in two oil-cloth-covered wains. Tonight after the even meal, he would likely try to sell her something, silks and Flemish wool, or perhaps leather goods, shoes and bridles, or even copper vessels and precious steel implements. Recognizing her, he tried to catch her eye as she passed, but she hurried on. Beneath the spiky teeth of the portcullis, across the narrow bridge— where she had to move aside for a traveling friar on his mule—then down the well-worn trackway.

At last she felt as if she had escaped the shadow of Valmar castle. She moved onto the grassy slope to the left of the trackway and halted. She dare go no farther, lest the guards in the gate tower notice her. Fawkes might well have told his men to watch her. Once again, she was a prisoner.

She breathed deeply, savoring the refreshing scent of growing things, the smell of wind and sunshine and summer blossoms. Gradually, her gnawing anxiety began to ease. There was no reason to think Simon was in danger. Hilary and Gilbert loved him like their own; they would never betray her secret.

She glanced back at the castle, thinking of Fawkes. Her hunger for him ate at her—and fed her determination. As soon as she could be more certain that Simon was safe, she must find a way to get him back in her bed.

She turned back toward the castle, thinking she'd been gone as long as she dared.

Fawkes crossed the bailey and headed toward the gatehouse. He intended to find FitzSaer and discuss how many knights he should take with him to Mordeaux.

As he neared the gate, he saw Nicola entering. She wore a simple white coif and plain bliaut, but even in such ordinary attire she stood out from the rabble in the yard like a rare flower among the barren rocks of the Jerusalem desert.

She moved quickly. He could not help wondering where she had been. He climbed the stairs to the gate tower, intending to find out. In the shade of the tower, one knight stood gazing out at the trackway, while another sat on a stool and rattled a pair of dice in his hand. The two men had taken off their helms and laid them on the wooden floor, but they still wore their mail and sword belts. Fawkes cleared his throat.

The knight on the stool saw him and leaped to his feet. "Milord." The other one turned so abruptly, he almost tripped on a bundle of arrows stacked near his feet.

"Did you see Lady Nicola come back to the castle?" Fawkes asked.

The two men hesitated, then the taller one, who had a sunburned face and bushy blond brows, said, "No, milord."

"If you did not see her come back to the castle, then you likely did not see her leave either, did you?"

The two men shared a glance, then one who had spoken earlier shook his head. "No, milord. We watch for armed men, signs of unusual activity in the valley. A lone woman would blend with the rest of the traffic in and out of the castle." He paused, then said, "Is there some reason we should watch for her?"

What should he say? Did he want it revealed that he mistrusted his wife? Too late. No matter how he answered, this conversation would be all over the castle by this even. He nodded. "I have known my wife but a day, and there are many rumors surrounding her."

"You are well to be wary," the fair-haired knight advised. "She's a shrewd, devious woman."

"She had to be, to have survived that drunken sodomite," argued the other, older man with reddish whiskers and a thin neck with a prominent Adam's apple. "I can't blame her for seeking revenge after what Mortimer did to her. He was a foul, godless man."

Even the people of Valmar were divided in their opinions of Nicola, Fawkes thought. How could he know what to think if they could not agree?

"Have you seen FitzSaer?" he asked, remembering his mission.

"Check the knights' barracks," advised the older knight.

Once again, Fawkes crossed the yard. This time he was distracted by the sight of a young page running into the keep. He recognized the boy's bright hair from the day before—Thomas, the young page who had escorted him to the bathing chamber. On a whim, Fawkes pursued the boy.

He caught up with him in the hall. The page was saying something to one of the serving women. Fawkes guessed that he might be carrying a message for Nicola. He followed the boy as he ran between the trestle tables toward the stairway. "Halt, Thomas!" he called.

The boy froze. As Fawkes approached, he saw a look of dread on his face. What did the boy think—that he was going to eat him?

"Thomas—that is your name, is it not?"

The boy nodded.

"Do you serve Lady Nicola? Were you carrying messages for her just now?"

The boy nodded again.

"How long have you served her?"

"Two years, milord."

"And what do you think of her? Is she a kind mistress?"

The boy's wariness increased tenfold. "Milady treats me more than well," he answered. Then, abruptly, his posture changed, as if he had made up his mind not to flee, but stand and fight. "I would do anything for her." He raised his small chin defiantly and squared his shoulders.

Fawkes fought the urge to laugh. As if this young cub could do anything against him. "That is very noble, Thomas," he said. "I am pleased to know that you do your duty by Lady Nicola. But I would know what inspires your impressive loyalty. Has she rewarded you especially well? Done other kindnesses for you?"

"I would rather not speak of it, milord."

Fawkes raised his brows. "I insist that you tell me. You see, I have just been married to Lady Nicola, but I don't really know her character. I must gather what information that I can about my wife. A man in my position must know who his enemies and his allies are."

"I know not what Lady Nicola thinks of you. When you arrived at Valmar, she said to treat you with utmost civility and good manners, but she would order the same for any guest."

"I'm not concerned what she thinks of me, but what you think of her. There are many rumors surrounding Lady Nicola. I need to know if they are true."

The boy hesitated, then that mutinous look returned. "Milady did thwart and confound Lord Mortimer at every turn, which I have heard is improper, that a woman must always defer to her husband, not matter what a devil he is. But I, for one, am grateful for her bold nature, for she saved my life and my brother's mortal soul."

"Tell me," Fawkes said.

The boy gave a sigh and began his tale. His brother, Will, had come to the castle three years ago. Mortimer had taken the youth to his bed, and Will, being unable to endure the shame and degradation of being Mortimer's catamite, had thrown himself from the castle battlements. Lady Nicola had convinced the priest that the boy's death was an accident, and so Will was buried in the churchyard in the village instead of being relegated to the unhallowed ground at the crossroads, where those whose souls were damned were interred.

When Thomas was sent to the castle to be a page soon after, he feared that his fate would be the same as his brother's. But Lady Nicola had protected him, telling Mortimer that if he laid a hand upon the boy, she would work a spell upon him so that his manhood would shrivel up and fall off.

Fawkes listened, amazed, to Thomas's story. Someone who did not know Mortimer might believe it to be a fanciful tale, but to Fawkes, it had the unpleasant ring of truth. He'd always heard that Mortimer favored young boys for his pleasure, and the fairer and more sweet-faced they were, the better.

As for Nicola's part, Fawkes could well imagine her wanting to protect Thomas and to offer some sort of spiritual comfort to poor young Will's family. In both instances, she would be defying Mortimer and hindering his purpose. But there was genuine kindness and concern in the acts as well. Thomas portrayed Nicola not as an embittered, vengeful woman, but a compassionate and tender-hearted one. *His* Lady Nicola would never have killed her own son for vengeance. Instead, she would have found some more clever means of ruining Mortimer's dream.

Fawkes thanked Thomas and walked away, deep in thought. He wanted very badly to think that the ugly rumors surrounding Nicola were based on half-truths and lies inspired by jealousy and resentment. But he dare not let down his guard. Nicola was hiding something, of that he was certain. Until he knew what it was, he could not trust her.

Did that mean he could not bed her? He examined the notion, turning it over and over in his mind. Her power over him was so intense, so devouring. He knew if he joined his body with hers and fulfilled his fantasies, he would never be able to judge her dispassionately.

He resumed his path to the knights' barracks. FitzSaer was not there, but Reynard was. "Come," Fawkes said to him. "Walk with me to the practice field."

"How was the wench?" Reynard winked.

"The wench—oh, Gillian. Good enough."

"But not as good as your wife, eh?"

Fawkes shrugged.

"Still don't trust Nicola, is that it?" Reynard asked.

Fawkes shook his head. "There are so many secrets and rumors surrounding her that it's hard to know what to believe. Why, today, I learned something very interesting from Thomas, the fair-haired page who dogs her heels. This story shows that she has a compassionate side, and makes me wonder if some of the uglier rumors are untrue." He told Reynard the tale.

"God's teeth, what a disgusting, depraved bastard!" Reynard exclaimed when Fawkes finished. "That he abused helpless boys is even worse than what he did to Lady Nicola!"

Fawkes nodded. "At least she was a woman grown and had some means of defending herself."

Reynard made a face. "I wonder at men like FitzSaer who remained loyal to such a fiend."

"They will say that whatever his failings, Mortimer was a man, and as his wife, Nicola was duty-bound to obey him. And think of it, when we served Mortimer at first, we were proud to have him as our liege lord. He was a valiant soldier, and for some men that is enough to recommend him. I'm sure the king saw that in him and decided to overlook his other failings."

"Yea, and the king has failings of his own." Reynard smiled ironically.

"At least Richard takes men to his bed, not children. And as far as I know, they are willing, too. That is what is so corrupt and hideous about Mortimer's actions. He destroyed a helpless child." Fawkes shook his head. "I have seen many horrible things in my life, but the image Thomas gave me, of his brother's broken body lying in the refuse-filled ditch, still disturbs me. I'm glad I killed Mortimer. I have half a mind to dig up his corpse and feed it to the castle dogs."

Reynard shook his head. "That might anger men like FitzSaer, who so far seem to have accepted your authority quite willingly."

"I suppose that's true," Fawkes agreed. "Until my position here is more secure, I cannot afford to take rash action, no matter how satisfying it might be."

"Speaking of securing your position," Reynard said. "How goes it in finding out how we would fare in a siege? Have you had a report from the cook or the steward as to the available food stores?"

Fawkes suddenly realized that he had set the kitchen staff to counting barrels of salted meat and baskets of produce, but never followed up to see what they had discovered.

"That is where I was headed," Fawkes said. "If you will find FitzSaer and decide with him how many knights are needed at Mordeaux, I will find the steward and ascertain our situation in terms of supplies."

He searched the storehouses for the steward. No one was there except one servant who was busy tallying barrels of salted fish with knots on a string. "Where is the steward?" Fawkes demanded.

"He went with Lady Nicola," the man answered.

"Went where? To the hall? To the kitchen?"

"I know not, milord."

Fawkes felt a stir of irritation. He had ordered all of the kitchen help to go and tally the supplies. Had Nicola countermanded his orders? As he headed to the kitchen, he tried to calm himself. They probably did not need to know this very day how much food was in the storehouses. After all, he did not really expect attack. He was mostly trying to keep busy and not think about Nicola.

Besides, he supposed that if they were to eat this night, some of the kitchen staff must see to the cooking. As he neared the kitchen lean-to, the smell of fresh bread wafted to his nose. How many times past had he waited outside this structure, seeking to catch the eye of one of the maids who fancied him, so he could cajole a half a loaf of the heavenly, fresh manchet bread? Now he was the lord and he could go in and demand a dozen loaves if he wished. The thought soothed his mood a bit.

He did not find the steward, Warrin, in the kitchen, although he did get a loaf. As he munched on the soft, steaming bread, he decided to search for him in the hall.

A woman setting out thick slices of cheat bread to serve as trenchers for the even meal smiled at him. "Milord, how may I serve you?"

"I'm looking for the steward. Do you know where he might be?"

"He went off with milady about a candle notch ago. I suppose they might be in the solar. That's usually where she meets with him."

A rush of jealousy immediately afflicted him, but Fawkes told himself he was being foolish. It was absurd to feel jealousy. The steward was scrawny and old enough to be Nicola's father. "Which way is the solar?" he demanded.

As a squire, he'd no reason to enter the private areas of the castle, except for Nicola's bedchamber. And since he'd taken possession of the keep, he'd not bothered to explore his property fully. The woman led him up some narrow stairs to a part of the castle he had not been to before. The servant motioned, and Fawkes started down the hall.

He reached the solar and paused in the doorway, stunned. It was the most opulent chamber he had ever seen, oozing comfort, beauty and wealth. Tall windows of greenish glass on one end of the large chamber let in sunlight and warmth. The rest of the space was draped and padded and carpeted with a variety of plush materials. Sheepskin rugs with bright braided edges covered the floor. Expensive Flemish tapestries overlaid every inch of wall space. Silk- and velvet-cushioned chairs and a carved wooden table were arranged around the hearth. Nearby, a tall iron pricket held glossy beeswax candles. A bronze brazier shaped to look like a fire-breathing dragon was pushed back against a row of chests and coffers.

Nicola sat by the window occupied with some sort of needlework. The steward stood facing her. Fawkes heard the word "seed grain" and then "peas." He cleared his throat to announce his presence.

He saw her start as she saw him, then her expression turned impassive, that mask of queenly elegance. The steward gave a nervous smile and clutched his bony hands together. "Lord de Cressy, how may I serve you?"

Fawkes started toward them, then suddenly remembered his mud-caked boots. For a moment, he considered walking defiantly across the luxurious floor coverings, leaving a muddy trail in his wake. Then reason overtook him. These were *his* carpets he would be despoiling. He bent to remove his boots, then padded across the floor.

"Milady and I were discussing the food stores," the steward said. "I estimate that we have two months worth of salted meat remaining and plenty of peas and vegetables from the new crop. But our grain supply is very low. This is always a lean time, until we get the harvest in."

"How long until harvest?" Fawkes walked to the window and peered out. The glass was wavy and flawed in places, and since the solar was built on the inside part of the ramparts, the view wasn't much. But he could see the delight of being able to allow sunlight into a room without also letting in the cold. In winter this room would be a cozy, glowing haven from the chilly gloom of the rest of the castle.

"Along the river, they have already begun, but I'm not certain when they will start with the outlying fields. Over by Wilford, they are always a week or so later."

"Wilford?" Fawkes turned. "Is it another village? Part of Mortimer's . . . my lands?"

"Aye, milord. It's smaller than Valmar, and the harvest not so rich. But their sheep clip is excellent." The steward hesitated. "You really should be discussing these things with the reeve. Osbert will know more of the amounts of produce we can expect to collect. I do know that it has been an excellent year so far."

Nicola was only a few feet away from him. As always when he was near her, his cock got hard and his wits seemed to flee. He moved away from her and began to examine the rest of the room. On a table next to a black-and-white cowhide-covered chair was a chessboard, with the ivory and onyx pieces set up for a game. Whom did she play with? he wondered.

His mind was filled with the vision of Nicola and a faceless man seated close by the game board, laughing and gazing warmly at each other. Then he looked down at the floor coverings and imagined their naked bodies entwined on the beribboned and tasseled sheepskins.

With effort, he turned back to the steward. "I will find Osbert and ask him to take me on a tour of the desmense. But I still would know more about our situation here. What about fodder for the animals? Do we have enough to feed them until normal butchering time? And is there more than the one well, in case attackers find a way to poison the main one?"

Surreptitiously, Nicola watched the two men talking, the

slight, gray-bearded steward and the sleek, well-muscled knight. Fawkes gestured, making bold movements with his long-fingered, battle-scarred hands, and a shiver of longing passed through her. She remembered the feel of those hands on her body so very well. She drew in a deep breath. Somehow she had to find a way to get him to touch her like that once more.

She feasted her eyes on his slim-hipped, long-legged body and admired the grace of his movements. He reminded her of Gimlyn, the gray-and-white tomcat who prowled the upper portions of the castle, hunting for mice. Both cat and man moved with a lithe agility that belied their exceptional size and physical power. She recalled holding Gimlyn in her lap and petting his soft fur, then let her mind wander to doing similar things with Fawkes—stroking his glossy hair, then caressing his rough, whisker-darkened jaw. Her mind was filled with the image of his impressive torso looming over her, the wide shoulders like angel's wings, the heavily muscled chest, shadowed with coarse black hair, the narrow belly. Oh, to explore his tantalizing maleness, to run her hands over firm muscles and hard, smooth skin, to follow the line of hair down . . . down to that magnificent sword of flesh. . . . To hold his shaft in her hands and feel its power and hardness.

She'd had only a bare glimpse of that sleek, massive lance of flesh the night before, but she had felt it, endured all that heated length inside her. The thought nearly made her gasp. She fought to concentrate on her task, sorting embroidery thread into various colors. Her quim began to throb and grow wetter and wetter.

She glanced up. Fawkes and the steward were walking toward the door. Warrin bowed briefly before they reached it. "Milady," he said. Fawkes also turned and looked at her. He said nothing, but his dark, intense gaze seemed to mark her, igniting a trail of fire down her body. Then Warrin said something, and he turned away to follow after the steward.

Nicola fought for composure. She had to gain control over her lust. When she was around him, she forgot to be on her guard. She seemed to melt, her wits turned to pudding.

She stood, restless with unquenched desire. Somehow she must find a means of getting him back in her bed. Just that, nothing more. She couldn't trust him or feel anything for him, but she had to have him inside her. To fill her with his big, hard, burning shaft. Either that, or she would go mad.

Nine

Nicola rose early, long before Old Emma had crawled from her pallet outside the bedchamber to complain of her old, aching bones. She put on a plain brown kirtle and covered it with a drab cloak of coarse-woven russet wool. Two years ago, when she'd first started going to the village, she had traded for the nondescript garments. Somewhere there was a peddler's wife wearing the gown of rich crimson samite that she'd offered in exchange.

She left her bedchamber and moved stealthily through the castle. Most of the inhabitants were still sleeping, but out in the yard there was some activity as groggy kitchen boys carried wood to stoke the fires and pails of water to start the day's cooking. It was still half dark, a world of gray, colorless shapes. No one took note of her, but as she neared the gate, Nicola's heartbeat quickened. The Valmar guards had never questioned her when she gave her story of being a village girl who had spent the night in the castle and was on her way home. But Fawkes's knights might be more difficult.

She adjusted the cloak more securely around her face, then called up to the gate tower. "Open the gate, please. I have an errand in the village this morning."

A man poked his head out of the tower, his features indistinct in the dim light. "What sort of errand?"

"I promised to fetch some wild garlic for the cook. He needs it for the even meal."

"Are you certain it's safe for a young wench like you to be alone in the forest? Mayhap you should have an escort. Would you like me to come with you? We could hunt for greens together." Faint guffaws sounded behind him.

Nicola's lips tightened. Lustful bastards. "I doubt that Lord de Cressy would wish to hear that one of his men had abandoned his duties for such a trifling task," she said sweetly.

She heard the man mutter something, then the winch that controlled the portcullis groaned and creaked. The huge barred gate slowly moved upward, and Nicola hurried through. At least the guards had not come down and bothered her. If they had pulled off her hood and seen her black hair, she would be lost. No woman of the village had coloring like hers. Most were Saxon fair, although a few had reddish or brown hair. That had been Mortimer's difficulty when he had sought a sire for his "heir." Determined as he was that the babe should look like her, he'd had few choices. Fawkes was likely the only man among his garrison with coloring that matched hers.

A bitter pang went through her at the thought. If only their child had bred true and inherited the dark tresses of his parents . . . but, nay, Simon was perfect as he was. She would not change his angelic beauty for anything, even if it would have greatly simplified things between her and Fawkes.

She hurried down the trackway. The world brightened little by little. Colors crept out of the darkness, grew sharper and more vivid. She paused for a second to enjoy the splendor of dawn's arrival. The mist along the river turned pink and golden, floating over the valley like some fairy magic. The sun rose as a coppery ball of fire over the blue-green countryside.

As the sky's glory began to fade, she quickened her pace. Back in the castle, she would not be missed this early, and Fawkes would be leaving soon. Although she had not gone to the hall for the even meal, one of the serving men had reported to her that Fawkes was going to Wilford today to inspect the lands he held in the east.

When she reached the village, she grew wary. People here rose earlier than the castle folk. Men who toiled in the field depended on the light, and at the first sign of it, they were already at their tasks. But the mist, which had not yet burned away, aided her. As she hurried along, she heard a babe cry. A dog bark. A rooster crow. But none of them did she see. Which meant she could not be seen, either.

She skirted the village, seeking out a thatched dwelling set back from the rest of the houses. At the doorway, she groped for the rope hanging from the eaves, and, finding it, rang the bell on the end. Glennyth the midwife was often summoned in the dark of night and she'd arranged the bell as a signal that she was needed.

The hide door was swept aside and Nicola's nostrils were immediately assaulted with an overwhelming miasma of scents. Herbs, some sweet, some merely pungent, filled the dwelling. They hung from the rafters, covered every inch of the walls and overflowed from baskets set on the dirt floor. Nicola wondered how anyone could grow used to such a smothering atmosphere of scents, but then, it was much more pleasant than the reek of dung, garbage and cooking smells that permeated most village houses. Glennyth kept no livestock, preferring to barter for the salt pork and meat she needed, so she did not have to share her dwelling with goats and cows.

Glennyth wore a thin sleeping shift and her hair was unbound and fell over her shoulders. As she bent to light a candle from the banked fire on the hearth, her dark tresses glinted with reddish lights. Straightening, she faced Nicola. "Trouble?" she asked.

"I don't know," Nicola said flatly. "My new husband is a difficult man to read. But I do think that he might come to you and ask you about Simon, or rather, the babe that supposedly died."

"If he comes, I will give him the same story we concocted for Mortimer. But tell me, why should he trouble himself over a dead babe?"

Nicola pulled off the scratchy, uncomfortable cloak and threw it down on a stool. "The truth is, I have muddled things badly."

Glennyth arched a brow. "What did you do?"

Nicola took a deep breath. "When I found out that Fawkes meant to attack Mordeaux, I warned Mortimer. Although Fawkes defeated and killed him, the outcome could have been different. Fawkes still holds a grudge that I could have cost him everything."

"By the Lady, why did you warn Mortimer? I thought his death was exactly what you sought."

"Because of Simon. I thought he might be hurt if the castle was attacked."

"But you did not tell de Cressy this?"

"Of course not!" Nicola began to pace again. "Should I tell a man who has come to seize me and my dower lands that I have a son? A hawk that discovers a cuckoo egg in his nest will thrust it out. Simon is too vulnerable. I will not risk his safety to the generosity and goodwill of any man!"

"But Simon is his son!"

"Yea, a son he will never claim, a son that looks nothing like him!"

Glennyth wrinkled her forehead in concentration. "You are likely right. Men are strange about such matters, and if Fawkes is angry at you for betraying him, now is not the time to reveal Simon's existence. But what else is wrong? I sense that you are troubled by other matters."

Nicola thought about the other reason she had come here, to ask Glennyth for a love philter. All the way to the village, she'd debated the matter in her mind. Certainly there were potions that could arouse a man beyond bearing, but how could she be sure that Fawkes would spend his lust with her?

If she dosed him and he ended up in bed with Alys, she'd probably kill both of them!

She looked at Glennyth, hesitating, then said, "All this turmoil and worry has made it difficult for me to sleep. I was wondering if you could make me a sleeping draught."

Glennyth looked dubious, but she picked up the lighted beeswax candle and started toward the door to the back part of her house, which served as her stillroom. "If you wait, I will mix something."

Nicola followed the wisewoman. She was fascinated by how Glennyth could remember everything she did. The wisewoman knew of dozens of herbs and how to mix them, plus the way they should be swallowed, applied to the skin, brewed in a decoction, or otherwise ingested.

Glennyth set down the candle and cleaned off a wooden table to begin the herb mixing process. She examined the row of pottery jars on her shelf, then selected several and brought them over to her mixing bowl. Placing a fingerful of several kinds of dried herbs into the bowl, she began to crush them with a stone pestle.

"What's in the sleeping draught?" Nicola asked.

Glennyth looked at her. "You know I do not give away my secrets, at least until the time comes for me to pass them on."

"And who will you pass them on to?" Nicola fingered one of the jars on a shelf built into the wall. The strange markings inscribed on the sides meant nothing to her, although she could read and write Latin.

"Maybe I will have a daughter someday."

"But you've vowed never to wed."

Glennyth gave a delicate snort. "It does not take a husband to get with child, nor to raise one."

Nicola thought of Simon, surrounded by women. There would come a day when he would need the influence of a man in his life. Who could she trust with such an important task, and what would she desire him to teach Simon? She wanted something else for her son than the ugliness and brutality of being a warrior. Better that he should go to the Church and become a scholar.

But then he would be cheated of his birthright. Valmar and Mordeaux had been in her family since the time of the Conqueror, and before then, through her great-great-great grandmother's line, these lands had been ruled by Nicola's distant Saxon ancestors.

As it stood now, Simon would not inherit her lands anyway. That could happen only if Fawkes accepted him as his heir. At this point, the chances of that were nonexistent. Nicola sighed again.

Glennyth gave her a canny look. "Don't fret. It will give you wrinkles. Things might yet turn out much differently than you expect. Life is like that."

"Jesu, you are a rich man, Fawkes," Reynard exulted as they rode through the humid countryside of golden cornfields bordered with strips of brilliant green pastureland. "I had no idea the demesne was so vast, your holdings so rich and fertile."

"Grain in the field is not flour in the storehouse," Fawkes reminded him. "Until the harvest is actually reaped, I cannot count on it."

"But it's not merely the thick stands of barley, millet and wheat that I'm thinking of. What about the orchards down by the river, so heavy with apples that you can almost hear the trees groaning with the weight? The hay fields that are everywhere, promising excellent forage for the herds kept over the winter? Near every family appeared to have chickens and a goat or cow, and that bunch of swine we saw rooting in the forest will make for plentiful salt pork this winter."

Fawkes did not respond, but in truth, he had also been astounded by the plenty all around them. They had ridden to Wilford and there found not only the ford across the river that the place was named for, but two mills—one for grinding grain and one for fulling cloth—an alehouse, a chapel and a cluster of neatly kept houses. The sunburned, buxom goodwives of Wilford welcomed him and his men with fresh-brewed ale and hot bread spread with creamy butter and golden honey. He noted that their children looked well-fed and healthy, and the green hills surrounding the village were dotted with dozens of creamy white sheep.

It had been a very satisfying day, he thought as he slowed his mount so the reeve on his mule behind them could catch up with them. But he had not made this journey simply to explore his property. Part of his goal was to get away from Nicola. Although he had scarce seen her—she had not even come to the even meal the night before—he was constantly reminded of her presence around the castle. He kept thinking he smelled her perfume, as if the scent of it lingered everywhere. And if he had a choice, he would never again venture into the solar, where every luxurious object, rug and wall hanging seemed to taunt him with the sensual opulence of the lady who had put it there.

Her presence disturbed him so much that he almost considered banishing her back to her tower room until he could decide how to deal with her. But he would not do that. He was not petty and cruel like Mortimer. And besides, she did play a useful role in managing the castle. He was only now realizing how many things were involved in feeding so many people and keeping the castle clean and comfortable and running efficiently. Valmar's servants were mostly skilled and reliable, but someone had to oversee them and make decisions, and Fawkes realized he did not want the responsibility.

His other option was to do as he was doing now, riding out every day, busying himself with management of the rest of the demesne, its defense and productivity. And productive it was, a most bountiful land.

He inhaled deeply, enjoying the sweet, warm scent of new-mown hay. On either side of the trackway, huge haystacks rose above the stubbled fields where crows and magpies were busy picking insects from among the gleanings. Overhead, a goshawk circled, searching for mice or voles in the newly disturbed landscape. Fawkes and his men had met the harvesters earlier, brawny, sunburned-faced men in russet tunics that reached to their knees, carrying their long curving scythes over their shoulders.

Henry de Brionne drew his destrier up on the other side of Fawkes. "Milord, do we go back through the village?"

"Aye, the village," Osbert, the reeve, echoed from behind them. "It would be pleasant to sit in Maude's ale yard and rest for a time."

Fawkes turned around to look at the thick-bodied reeve. The man's face was bright red and he was sweating profusely. Fawkes wanted to tell him that the heat of an English summer's day was pleasant compared to the hellish inferno of the Levantine coast.

"It's true, you have not been to the village yet," Reynard said. "At least not an official visit as their new lord."

Fawkes raised his brows. "If all three of you conspire against me, I guess I have no choice. Very well, we'll ride through the village."

They reached Valmar late in the day. It was still very warm, and the hamlet below the castle seemed to snooze in lazy contentment. They approached by way of the river. The smooth surface of the millpond glittered in the bright sunlight like polished steel, and as they neared the mill, a man came out to greet them. He had lank ruddy hair and whiskers, a pointed nose and currant-black eyes. "Milord," he greeted Fawkes. "I'm Ethelbert, the miller." He glanced up at the cloudless blue sky. "It's very hot, sir. You must be thirsty. Can I have my wife fetch you a drink of buttermilk?"

"Actually, we were headed to Maude's ale yard," Osbert called from his mule. Now that they were in his home territory, the reeve seemed to sit up straighter and not droop so much in the heat. "But thank you, Ethelbert, for the offer."

The miller gave the reeve a peevish look and stepped forward to stand at Fawkes's stirrup. "Are you going to hold manor court soon, milord? Lady Nicola always held it in conjunction with the Lammas celebration."

Manor court? Another responsibility he had not thought of. "I'll consider doing so." He pulled sharply on the reins to urge the destrier away from the miller. "Is that true?" he asked Osbert after they had ridden a ways. "Did my wife really hold manor court?"

The reeve nodded.

"And the people accepted her judgments?"

Osbert nodded. "Although some of Mortimer's men have been critical of her authority, Lady Nicola has always been popular with the villagers. She grew up at Mordeaux and as heiress to Valmar, the people around here have considered her their 'lady' since her mother died ten years ago. Besides, there was no one else to see to things. Mortimer was piss-eyed with wine most of the time, and he'd never troubled himself with anything happening in the village."

His wife had done it all, Fawkes thought, managing the castle, holding manor court, overseeing a vast and prosperous demesne. It unnerved him a little. His wife seemed to be a part of the very heart of Valmar and the countryside surrounding it. If she ever decided to oppose him, he would probably find it very difficult to match his will against hers.

They continued on through the village. Each thatched house was set far enough from its neighbor so there was room behind for a vegetable plot and a shed for livestock. At the first dwelling they came to, a young woman with yellow braids flapped her apron to shoo a gaggle of geese away from a flush-faced toddler playing in the dirt. She saw them and picked up the toddler. The boy shrieked and squirmed as they passed, but the woman smiled at them.

"Her husband's the smith," Osbert said. "He has his shop down by the river."

A short distance away, another, older, woman sat cross-legged in front of her hut, shelling peas. She paused and wiped her brow, then saw them approaching and hastily dumped her apron full of peas into a bowl. She stood to greet them. "Welcome, milord," she said, fussing awkwardly with the strands of dark gold hair creeping out from under her sweat-stained linen coif.

Fawkes nodded to her.

"And that's Bertha, widowed these past five years," Osbert said when they had moved out of earshot. "Her husband died from an ax wound that putrefied."

"Ax wound?" Fawkes asked.

The reeve shook his head. "Not in battle. I think he was chopping wood and the ax handle slipped and he struck himself in the foot."

Osbert droned on, reciting names of the inhabitants as they passed. The word "healer" caught Fawkes's attention. "What?" Fawkes said. "What did you say?"

"I said, in the newly thatched dwelling at the edge of the common lives Glennyth, the village healer and wisewoman."

Fawkes looked past the common where a black-and-white cow grazed. "Is she also the midwife?"

"Aye, she serves as midwife to the village and castle women."

"I would like to meet her." Fawkes turned his horse.

They found Glennyth tending the garden plot behind her house. She put down her hoe and watched them approach. "By the saints," Reynard said softly. "I expected a weathered crone."

Fawkes looked sharply at his captain. All along their journey, he had sensed Reynard evaluating the village women, but this was the first time his captain had been moved to exclaim out loud. Fawkes scrutinized the healer. Glennyth the midwife appeared to be a few years older than he was.

She had wavy chestnut hair, tanned, smooth skin and catlike hazel eyes. The simple rust-colored kirtle she wore was damp with sweat and clung to her body, revealing generous curves and strong, well-formed muscles.

He dismounted and handed his reins to Reynard. Glennyth came to greet him, although she did not bow or say anything, but simply stood a few paces away, waiting for him to speak. She had a kind of aloofness about her, the feral ease of a wild animal.

"I'm the new lord of Valmar," he began. "I understand that you serve as midwife and healer to the village folk as well as to the people of the castle."

She nodded.

He moved closer to her and lowered his voice. He had no desire for Osbert or Sir Henry to overhear this conversation. "Over two years ago, the Lady Nicola gave birth to a babe. There are those who say it was born dead. Others, that you strangled it before it could draw a breath."

She cocked a brow. "People say many things. Have you asked the child's mother what transpired?"

"I have. But I want to know what you will say."

"The child was dead at birth. The cord was wrapped around its neck. There was no injury to your wife's womb, if that is why you ask," the healer added. She raised a brow ironically. "With a lusty knight like you in her bed, I'm sure she will be carrying another babe soon."

It might sound like flattery, but Fawkes thought he heard an amused, almost mocking undertone in the healer's words. He nodded curtly to her and turned away.

"So, what did she say?" Reynard asked when they had reached the ale yard and were comfortably ensconced at a table in the shade of a huge oak. Fawkes raised his brimming pewter cup and took a swallow of the rich, yeasty ale. Nowhere else but England did they brew this beverage to such perfection. Aquitaine and Poitou might be famed for their wine, Scotland for its usquebaugh, the East for potent spirits made of fruits and spices, but when a man was thirsty, all those things paled compared with this foamy, golden drink.

"I asked her about the babe," he said. "She told me the same tale as Nicola, then jibed me about being a 'lusty knight.' I felt as if she were laughing at me, as if she knew that I did not share Nicola's bed."

"Is that possible?" Reynard asked.

"Sweet Mary, I don't know." Fawkes took another hefty swallow. "Maybe she and Nicola are friends. I suspect they are both surpassingly clever in their own ways. Jesu, I felt like I was a mouse and Glennyth a cat, batting me between her paws."

"Well, she can stalk me and play with me anytime," Reynard asserted.

"That taken with her, are you?"

Reynard shrugged. "There are women that a man knows he won't have to teach a thing. From whom he might even learn something new himself."

Fawkes thought of Nicola, of all the things he would like to teach *her,* if he dared. There were so many techniques and positions they had not explored. Although he'd been celibate while on Crusade, he'd heard plenty of tales from his fellow knights, of dancing girls and expensive whores and all the ways they could pleasure a man or be pleasured by one. Some things caught his fancy more than others and he'd spent more than a few nights in his bedroll imagining himself teaching Nicola the many exotic forms of lovemaking. Now he wondered if he would ever be able to trust her enough to bed her in even the most conventional way.

No, that was absurd. Eventually, his need would grow unbearable and he would spend a night in her bed quenching his lust every way he could think of. She was his wife, after all. He controlled her, not the other way around.

"The villagers want you to come to their Lammas celebration," Reynard said, interrupting his thoughts. "I think you should. You need to make merry and celebrate for a time. Stop being so morose and moody."

"And while I am here, I suppose I must hold manor court and assert my authority as lord. If I don't, disgruntled men like the miller will probably go to my wife and ask for her judgment." Fawkes shook his head. "Can you believe her? I thought to rescue this frail, helpless damsel, imprisoned and abused by her cruel husband. Instead, I discover that Lady Nicola does not need rescuing. That she has somehow managed to reduce Mortimer to a worthless tosspot, and, at the same time build up Valmar into a rich and profitable estate. Furthermore, except for Mortimer's men, whose main complaint is that she is female, and a few sour-minded servants who would find fault with any mistress, she appears to be well-liked and respected by almost everyone."

"These are all excellent things, are they not?"

Fawkes raised a brow. "As long as our objectives are the same, then, yea, it is excellent that I have wed such a paragon. But if she seeks to undermine me or defy me for some reason . . ." He shook his head and let his voice trail off as the familiar unease crept over him.

They stayed a while longer, until the sun sank toward the hills. By then Fawkes was more than relaxed. Between the ale and the heat, he felt almost faint as he mounted his destrier. He realized he needed to get back to the castle and eat a hearty meal. Perhaps then, with his belly full of food and ale, he would be able to sleep through the night. The last few he had tossed and turned, trying to block out all thoughts of Nicola.

They had just entered the castle bailey when he heard someone calling his name. He turned and saw a knight named Will le Lupe hurrying toward him. "Fawkes, I must speak with you."

Fawkes dismounted and handed his reins to his squire,

then waited for Will. "Your wife left the castle today," the knight announced in a breathless rush. "She was wearing servant's garb, but I know it was her. I recognized her voice. As she walked down the trackway, I said to Geoffrey beside me, 'Isn't that Lady Nicola?' and he said, 'Yea, I think it is.' She'd asked us to raise the portcullis because she had an errand in the village, gathering garlic or some such thing. But she spoke so cool and refined, I guessed at once she was not a serving girl. She came back, many hours later. Because it was so hot, she'd taken off the mantle and wore a kerchief over her hair. I saw her face and knew her immediately."

"How long was she gone, would you say?"

"Oh, a good while. She left before sunrise and came back right before the priest rang the bell for sext."

All the languor and lassitude vanished from Fawkes's body. His wife had waited until he was away from the castle, then disguised herself as a servant and sneaked out. More secrets. More mystery. "You've done well," he told the knight. "Keep up the good work."

He started across the yard, rigid with turmoil. What reason could his wife have for leaving the castle in disguise? The only answer he could think of enraged him—that she had a lover.

The thought had nagged at him since he discovered her pleasuring herself. The Church condemned onanism but most men did it anyway. But for a *woman* to satisfy herself . . . it implied a very passionate and sexual nature. Once he'd reveled in Nicola's receptivity, delighting in the fact that he'd been able to make her scream and cry out with pleasure. Now he realized the implications of her incredible responsiveness, especially considering his three-year absence from her bed. Why should a woman like that stop at pleasuring herself? Why should she not seek out a man to fulfill her needs?

It was unlikely that Mortimer would have cared if she cuckolded him, not to mention that from all accounts Nicola had so terrified and intimidated her first husband that he had no control over her. It was logical that she had taken a lover. But who? And why had he not heard rumors to that effect? She must have been very careful and discreet to be able to hide her activities from the gossiping servants of Valmar.

But he'd guessed that she was clever, oh, indeed he had. But not clever enough to outwit him. He'd continue to have her watched, to set a trap for her. He'd find out her secret, and when he did, he'd kill the bastard, then take her up to the bedchamber and fuck her endlessly—until he erased from her mind the memory of any other man who'd ever touched her!

Ten

Despite the sleeping draught, Nicola could not fall asleep. Her thin linen shift stuck to her body. She sat up and jerked it off, but found no relief. Sighing, she climbed from the bed. So restless she was, her body tense with unrelieved lust. Not only did her quim ache to be touched, but her whole being. She wanted Fawkes's arms around her. His mouth on hers. His warm, sweet breath caressing her skin. She wanted him to suckle her breasts as her babe had never had a chance to. To lave her skin with his hot wet tongue and mouth.

Shivers of desire quivered down her body, and she went to the unshuttered window and climbed on the stool below it, so she could feel the night air on her naked torso. Pushing her long hair behind her shoulders, she leaned out, hoping for a cool breeze, anything to soothe the heat that prickled her skin, the yearning that kept her nipples tight and hard and made her quim swim with moisture. She had to stop thinking about Fawkes. For now. After she saw Simon and assured herself that he was well, *then* she could focus on her plan to get her husband back in her bed.

Simon—tomorrow she would finally see him. Such a long wait it had been. Even though Fawkes left the castle nearly every day, she never knew when he would return. It had been impossible to risk the half-day's journey to Mordeaux and then back again. But tomorrow was Lammas, and she knew Fawkes had been asked to attend, as she had the past two years. As representative of the castle, he would take the first bite of the loaf made from the first bread of the harvest, and be honored with small gifts. Last year, the villagers had given her fresh-made cheeses, a finely woven basket and a platter of honey cakes layered with nuts. The smith's present was a small dagger fashioned of fine steel with a handle of twisted silver, the tanner, an unblemished calf's hide that she'd had made into a pair of silky-soft slippers. The feasting and merriment would last long into the night, and keep Fawkes away from the castle until she was able to return from Mordeaux and sneak back into the castle.

Her thoughts turned back to her son. It had been almost a month since she'd last seen him. He would know many more words by now. She would have to stop in the kitchen and get a treat to take him. He did so like sweet things. And then there was the top she'd had the carter fashion out of hickory wood. Last time she'd taken him a pig's bladder stuffed with grain. He'd loved the ball and played with it the whole time she was there.

What other sorts of toys did children play with? She'd have to ask Thomas. Being a girl, her childhood amusements had been much different—dolls, ribbons, bits of fabric. Thomas, who was only ten, would probably remember such things vividly. He reminded her of Simon in many ways, the same fair coloring and pure, comely features. It was a comfort to have him around, to think that some day her own son might live with her and run small errands for her.

She moved away from the window, feeling much better. Thoughts of Simon and the relief of seeing him on the morrow had eased her mind, if not the yearning of her body. She climbed back into bed.

At the first light of dawn, she rode out of the castle on her white palfrey. She'd coaxed Peter, the rather elderly hostler in the stables, into saddling her mount. At his age, he said, a man didn't sleep much anyway. At the gate, she'd told the guards that she needed to go into the village to help with preparations for the Lammas celebration. They'd opened the gate and waved her through.

She rode past the village, not even stopping to visit Glennyth. She would do that on the way back, if there was time. Mordeaux castle was about half a day's ride from Valmar, and Nicola judged that she should return well before dusk.

She adjusted her coif so it better kept the sun off her face, then turned her mount toward her destination. The aggravations and turmoil of Valmar seemed to fall away as she traveled. Soon, she would see the light of her life.

"Christ, Reynard, you look like a popinjay," Fawkes exclaimed when the two men met in the stables to collect their mounts to go down to the village for the day's celebration.

Reynard looked down at his tunic of bright green samite trimmed with gold braid, and grinned. "I know you despise dressing like a lord, but the fact is, most women fancy a man in fine clothing. It's like the peacocks we saw in Cyprus. The male with the showiest tail gets to mate with the most females."

"I vow, no woman is worth this torment. I loathe this tunic. It's hot as purgatory and the trim scratches my neck." Fawkes shrugged his shoulders uncomfortably. "I'd wear naught but a shirt and my old dirty gambeson if duty didn't require that I dress like a noble."

"Speaking of females, do you know where your wife is?" Reynard asked as the two men led their destriers out into the bailey.

"I'm certain she'll show up later, looking elegant and queenly and breathtakingly beautiful." He made a face.

"Then you haven't settled things between the two of you yet?" Reynard asked.

Fawkes considered telling Reynard about his suspicions

that Nicola had a lover, then decided not to. So far, he had not heard any gossip that his wife was cuckolding him; he wanted to keep it that way. "My instincts tell me that this is the best course," he told his friend. "Until I know a little more about Nicola and her motivations, I'm not going to share her bed. You've heard of Samson and Delilah? Helen of Troy? Beautiful women have been the ruin of many men."

"Well, if you lose your wits out of sheer horniness, you aren't going to be much good to anyone, either. I say, if you can't trust her, lock her away. That's what old Henry did with Eleanor. Kept her out of mischief for nigh on twelve years."

"I can hardly consign my wife to a nunnery. She's the lady of Valmar. She has a right to live here."

"Well, if that's the way it has to be, then you're stuck. But at least consider relieving a little of the itch with another woman. Maybe we can find one who looks like Lady Nicola and you can pretend."

Fawkes gave his friend a dubious look. "No one looks like Nicola."

"There *was* that one dancing girl." Reynard winked.

"Hah, you got more good of her than I did!"

"So, I did." Reynard smirked. "But that wasn't my fault, either. I wasn't mooning over a woman on the other side of Christendom."

Fawkes grunted. Sometimes, especially lately, he regretted that he hadn't bedded the Syrian. But mainly, he was glad. She would have only disappointed him.

"I couldn't help being wary of her," he said. "A woman like that, one who shows her cunny to any man who looks as if he has a few coins . . ." He shook his head. "Although, I've always wanted to know—what did you do about the ring in her pussy? Did it get in the way?"

"An added enticement, rubbing against my balls. Did you know the gold actually pierced her flesh? Stuck clean through the little nub."

"You mean the place where a woman gets her pleasure?" Fawkes asked in amazement.

Reynard nodded.

"Holy Mother, that must have hurt! It'd be like having a needle stuck through the end of your cock."

Reynard shrugged. "She didn't strike me as a woman who was overly concerned with her own pleasure. Her goal was to drive a man blind with passion so she could take every penny he possessed. But, don't take my words wrong, she was worth it. Especially as I was back then, a clumsy, callow fellow, completely lacking in knowledge of women or what pleased them. She taught me a lot, as well as giving me the most thrilling ride of my life. You know, I still have her costume."

Fawkes jerked around to gape at his friend. "You *what?*"

"You know that flimsy little bit of fabric she wore—I bought it from her."

"Why?"

Reynard shrugged. "You never know, I might someday find someone who would fit into it. It would make for some delightful love play—with the right sort of woman."

Fawkes thought of Nicola dressed in the skimpy, provocative costume. It *was* a tantalizing thought—and one that made him hard as blazes.

"I have an idea, Fawkes," Reynard interrupted his lustful musings. "Why don't you try to forget Nicola, at least for today. Pretend that it's like the old times when you and I used to go to the village. We always found a pretty maid to tumble. At least *you* did. I wasn't always so fortunate in those days. But I didn't give up. I watched other men and I learned. Now, I vow I could have a different woman in my bed every night from Lammas until Yule."

"Don't you ever tire of wenching?"

"No. Every woman is different, and there are a dozen different ways to scratch the itch."

Fawkes thought of his own bone-deep passion for Nicola. "Is that all it is to you—an itch?"

"Of a sorts." Reynard grinned.

"I hope someday you fall in love with one of them and suffer the tortures of the damned," Fawkes grumbled.

"All right," Reynard agreed. "Let's say, that just for today, we exchange personna. I'll try to fall in love and utterly lose my heart. You try to forget your perfect paragon and enjoy some mindless, meaningless fucking."

Fawkes gave his friend a dubious look. He wondered if he could forget Nicola, even for a day. It hardly seemed possible.

Fawkes sat at a table under the trees holding manor court. He tried not to yawn as Ethelbert the miller complained interminably about all the villagers who had failed to pay him the proper amount for grinding their grain. In between complaints, the man tugged at his ginger-colored beard and glanced around, his dark gaze darting here and there.

A shrewd, avaricious man, Fawkes thought absently. No doubt he cheated the villagers when he could, and their slowness in paying him in barter goods was their way of getting back at him. ". . . and Godwit promised me two hams and a dozen cabbages," the miller whined. "I refuse to grind any more of his corn unless he pays me what he owes."

Fawkes put up his hand. "It's not the season for salt pork, nor are the cabbages ripe yet. Can he not pay you in honey or eggs or some other foodstuff?"

" 'Twas ham and cabbage we agreed upon," the miller said stubbornly.

Fawkes struck the table with his fist. "This court is not the place for these petty disputes. Settle this between the two of you."

The miller gave him a sulky look and moved off. Fawkes

turned to Osbert, who sat beside him. "Did Lady Nicola really involve herself with this sort of nonsense?"

The steward nodded. "She would hear him out, then suggest some compromise, as you did."

"Jesu, she has more patience than me."

"Most women are patient," Osbert pointed out. "They are always waiting, for men to order their lives, for their babes to be born, for their husbands to come back from war." He shrugged.

"Lady Nicola does not strike me as having the placid nature you describe," Fawkes growled. It was on the tip of his tongue to ask the steward if he had seen Nicola in the village, but he restrained himself. He did not want the man to think he wasn't able to keep track of his wife.

Fawkes regarded the next petitioner. The fellow was lean as a sapling and had squinty blue eyes and a flushed face. "I've come to make a complaint, my lord. That witch Glennyth has cursed me. She's caused my manhood to shrivel up. I can barely make water, let alone swive my wife." Fawkes stared. "You've got to do something about her," the man continued. "She's an evil, meddlesome creature. I'm not the first man she's struck down, milord."

"I'm afraid that there have been complaints about her before," Osbert confided in Fawkes's ear. "Several villagers have suggested that she doesn't always use her knowledge of herbs and simples for benign purposes. There has been talk of people who've crossed her falling sick or even dying." He nodded gravely.

Fawkes motioned to the villein. "How do you know it was Glennyth who did this to you?"

"I came home one day to find her and my wife whispering together. Before she left, Glennyth gave me the evil eye. It was soon after that I discovered I could no longer . . . do what a man needs to do."

"What's the 'evil eye'?" Fawkes asked. "Did she say something to you? Chant a spell?"

"No." The man looked down at the ground and shuffled his feet. "She has a way of looking at you, as if you were a loathsome sort of bug and she was about to squish you. All I'm asking for is justice," the man insisted. "If you don't burn her, at least banish her from the village."

Fawkes realized he was going to have to say something, pronounce some judgment, or the fellow would never leave. "I'll speak to the woman Glennyth," he said.

The man nodded, but clearly looked dissatisfied. "Beware that she don't do the same thing to you, milord," he said sourly.

Other complaints and disputes followed. Most were fairly insignificant, and Fawkes had the sense that some of the villagers simply wanted to see what sort of man he was. More than once he told the individuals involved that they must find ways to work out these things themselves; he wasn't going to concern himself with every missing pig or every cow that trampled a vegetable patch.

At last, the line of petitioners ended. Fawkes rose stiffly. "I vow, that is thirsty work."

"Indeed, it is." Osbert grinned at him. "Why don't we go to Maude's ale yard. At least until it's time for the people to bring you gifts and for the corn queen to be chosen."

"Gifts? Corn queen?" Fawkes asked.

"The gifts are nothing much, merely small tokens to show that they honor you as lord. As for the corn queen, every year a maid is chosen to represent the fertility of the harvest. In the old days, in the Saxon tradition, all the men of the village would couple with her in the newly harvested field. Then they would ritually kill her, chop her body into pieces and plow it into the ground to ensure the next year's harvest. Of course, we don't do that now."

"Jesu!" Fawkes exclaimed. "Those old Saxons were savages!"

"Not really," Osbert said defensively. "It was all done with reverence, and it was considered an honor for the maid chosen."

Fawkes realized suddenly that Osbert was at least half Saxon, as were most of the people of Valmar. He'd best watch his tongue.

They entered the ale yard. Fawkes took a seat on the bench beside Reynard, and watched as Maude the alewife poured him a foaming tankard. "Are there any rituals involving the corn queen these days?" he asked after taking a hearty swallow.

"Indeed there are." Reynard spoke out before Osbert could respond. "The maid is decked in flowers and necklaces of braided wheat grass. Then she is given to the lord of the castle for his pleasure." A sly grin curled Reynard's mouth.

Fawkes set the tankard down with a thud and turned to Osbert. "He's jesting, isn't he?"

"No, milord." Osbert solemnly shook his head. "Although they have not observed the tradition for several years, the people wish to revive it."

"But why?" Fawkes asked. "This year's harvest seems bountiful enough. Why do they think it's necessary to bring back what is obviously an old pagan rite?"

"You're not a man who makes his living from the earth, milord." He gestured with broad, blunt-fingered hands. "Nature is fickle. One year the harvest is bountiful; the next, it fails. It does not hurt to remember the old ways, to propitiate the old gods."

"When will this . . . ceremony take place?"

"Oh, later in the day." Osbert gave a careless wave. "There is plenty of time for you to eat and drink your fill."

Fawkes exchanged a glance with Reynard, then took another swallow of ale. By the Cross, this was all he needed, to be forced to take another virgin to bed, and to once again have no choice in the matter! He well remembered what had happened the last time he was in these circumstances.

A quick tumble, he'd thought, an easy means of winning

the goodwill of his employer. Hah! That one incident, lasting less than two candle hours, had been his downfall. He'd fallen in love with Nicola, and exchanged his carefree, cheerful life for this hellish existence. But how was he to refuse this time? He didn't want to offend anyone.

And where *was* Nicola? Taking another deep draft, he glanced around. The village women, after fussing over the food table, had retired beneath one of the oaks with their sewing and spinning, to gossip and relax. The men congregated in another area to drink their ale and discuss the weather and the crops, subjects of endless fascination to men who toiled in the earth. The village children were occupied in exuberant play. The older ones had devised a game using a stuffed pig's bladder and sticks. One group batted the bladder toward the other group, which then sought to bat it back out of their "territory."

The older youths had gone down to the river to swim, and predictably enough, the maids had followed to watch them. Fawkes could imagine the young bucks showing off for their giggling, wide-eyed audience, entertaining them with fancy dives and daring acts, then making them shriek and run by splashing water at them. He well remembered those carefree days. No more, he thought resentfully. Now his life consisted of responsibility and duty, and a bewitching wife who was fast driving him to lunacy.

He looked around for Reynard and saw him beneath a tree, talking to Glennyth. She faced Reynard boldly, with a provocative expression on her face that said that this was no maid to be cozened, but a grown woman who knew exactly what she wanted and was determined to get it. Fawkes wondered if, for once, Reynard had not gotten in over his head. He certainly hoped so.

His thoughts had turned to Nicola again when a woman came and asked him if he would judge the handiwork competition among the women of the village. Lady Nicola had judged it the last two years, she said, but since she was not there, they wished for him to do it. He was led over to a table on which were arranged a dizzying array of braided belts, embroidery, colorful pieces of woven fabrics and other sorts of needle and weaving work. As he examined the things, all he could think of was Nicola. Where was she?

He chose those pieces that appeared the most pleasing to the eye. To his dismay, the women who had made the things immediately insisted that he accept them as gifts. He called for Osbert to gather up the gifts, then started to walk off, intending to find Reynard and ask him what he made of Nicola's absence. Edith, the smith's wife, stopped him. "Milord," she said sweetly, "the food is ready. We would like you to be the first to dine upon our humble fare."

He was led to a table groaning with food. There were pickled eggs, fresh cheeses, griddle cakes seasoned with herbs and lampreys cooked in butter, dumplings in gravy, meat pasties, honey cakes with hazelnuts, spiced pasties, apple and blackberry tarts. As the women who had cooked all this bounty watched, he filled a wooden platter with food.

He tried to sample almost everything, lest he offend any of the women who prepared it, but not particularly caring for sweets, he ignored the tarts, and was told he must have a blackberry one as it was traditional fare for Lammas. Another woman suggested a sort of seedcake. All the women giggled, and Edith, blushing, told him that the poppy and caraway seed topping was supposed to be an aphrodisiac.

Fawkes considered that he might as well eat the thing. He would need all the help he could get for the coming ritual. Finally, he stepped back from the table. "Please," he told them, "if you have any mercy, you will not force me to take any more. If I do, I will look and feel like the stuffed pig's bladder that the children are kicking about." The women laughed gaily.

He went back to the table beneath the oak and ate what he could. It was all delicious, better than the food of some of the banquets he had attended when with the king. Then, insisting that the ale had gotten to him, he made his way off to the midden heap behind the ale yard to relieve himself. All he could think about was Nicola. Had she really stayed behind at the castle? He could hardly imagine that. More likely, she'd seized upon his absence as an opportunity to meet with her lover.

At the thought, he started back to the ale yard, thinking that the villagers be damned, he was going back to find her. Then he saw the miller and the smith coming toward him and knew he was trapped. "Milord, it's time," the smith said, grinning. "You and the corn queen will eat the first loaf and then go off alone together."

"Don't look so sour," the miller added. "You've not seen the corn queen yet. She's a ripe, juicy piece. I, myself, would give my right ball for the chance to swive her."

She was a beauty, Fawkes had to agree when the girl was brought to him. Hair the pale hue of fresh butter, cornflower-blue eyes, bright cheeks and lips. She was arrayed in masses of flowers, with a chaplet of woven wheat encircling her head like a crown. But for all her fresh, blushing beauty, she did not move him.

He took his place beside her near the center of the common, and as the villagers and a few of his knights gathered around, he broke the steaming-hot loaf and took a bite, then offered some to the girl. It was maislin bread, dark, rich and chewy, very unlike the refined wheat bread eaten at the castle. As he ate, the people cheered, then they stepped forward to take their own shares of bread. As men, women, children and knights crowded the common, the girl took his hand. "Come," she said.

Eleven

The corn queen led him to one of the finer houses near the river. He followed unwillingly, trying to think what he could tell her, how he could gracefully refuse to bed her. They entered the dwelling. Inside, the hard-packed floor had been swept clean, the walls whitewashed, all the foodstuffs and cooking things arranged neatly near the hearth. There was a plank table, a bench and two stools in the main room. As he glanced around the dim interior, thinking he should find a lamp or candle, she took his hand and tried to pull him toward the ladder that led to the loft.

"Wait," he said. She was obviously nervous. Her hand felt clammy and cold in his, and he could see the rapid pulse in her throat. "We must talk first."

She shook her head. "They expect this." She pulled on his hand again. When he resisted, she cried out, "Please! Let us finish the thing!"

Her words flung him back into the past, back to another virgin who waited for him to deflower her, another woman who urged him to hurry, that the thing might be finished quickly. But that woman had spoken like a queen ordering a servant. This woman sounded hysterical.

He removed her clutching fingers from his hand. "What's your name? Tell me."

"Alesia, my name's Alesia," she gasped. "Oh, please. Come to bed! Do it now!"

"Nay, I will not." He grasped her shoulder and shook her gently. "I don't want to do this either. I'm a Christian; I don't believe in these old pagan ways. Besides, I don't want to get a bastard on you."

All at once, she began to weep. At first, he could not tell if it was relief or disappointment, then she began to babble. He was so kind, she said, to spare her. She had a sweetheart already and she feared he would not feel the same way about her, knowing that another man had had her. Besides, she sobbed, she was not a maid anyway. Johnny had taken her down by the river and he had done it to her. It had hurt, but he promised it would get better. Was that true? she asked him. Would it feel better next time?

Fawkes stared down at this lovely woman-girl, her tear-filled eyes wide and rapt as she waited for his reassurance, and almost groaned aloud. He felt like the most cynical, hardened man in creation. He wanted to tell her that her Johnny was probably a crude, stupid lout who didn't deserve her. That he would never give her any pleasure, but grunt and groan and sweat over her and get her with a babe every year until her looks were ruined. And then, once she was not so fair, he would leer after that year's corn queen and say crude things like the miller had.

Instead, he said, "Yea, it will get better."

She gave a little sigh and hugged him. He gently pushed her away. "Now, go throw your crown and your garlands upstairs on one of the pallets. I'll find a way out the back for you, and after a while I will go out the front and make a show of adjusting my clothing and grinning like a man well-satisfied."

She hugged him again, then climbed the ladder with the agile grace of a child. Fawkes stood in the empty room and caught his breath. He was aroused. Who would not be with that exquisite young woman pressing close? But he did not regret his decision. That his own life had turned out sourly did not mean he had to crush the youthful hopes of others. Let them find out for themselves how unsatisfying love really was.

"Oh, Simon, you've grown so much!" Nicola felt tears prick her eyelids as she held out her arms. So quickly the time was passing. Her baby was almost not a baby anymore.

As always, Simon hugged her back, his bright blue eyes round and curious.

"Do you remember me?" she asked.

He nodded. "You bring sweets."

Harsh pain shafted through her. That she must buy her son's love with confections. "That's true, my darling. I bring you sweets. This time I have brought you some blackberry tarts. Do you like tarts?"

Simon nodded. She bent down and offered him the basket the Valmar cook had prepared. He took out a pastry and with concentration, began to eat it. Nicola looked up and met the gaze of Hilary, wife of Gilbert de Vescy, the castellan of Mordeaux. Hilary was a few years older than Nicola and had soft blue eyes, reddish-blonde hair and a mild manner. "He's growing so fast," Nicola choked out.

"That he is," Hilary said with a smile. "He talks more and more every day. Quite a chatterbox he's become."

Simon finished cramming the tart into his mouth and swallowed. He turned to Hilary. "Mama? Joanie like tarts." He nodded wisely.

"Of course, love, go fetch her," Hilary responded. "Hurry now."

As Simon rushed from the solar, little legs churning, Nicola let out a sob.

"I'm sorry," Hilary whispered. "He began calling me 'Mama' a while ago, and I had not the heart to correct him."

Nicola nodded. "I . . . I wouldn't want him to feel different . . . to think he does not have a mother." Her heart was breaking. She knew this day would come. If only things were different. If only she did not have to hide the truth from everyone, even her son.

"I do love him like my own." Hilary's fine-boned face suffused with tenderness. "And he is as much an angel as he looks. Most children of his age are willful and selfish, fighting over toys and such. But he is, as you see, ever generous and sunny-natured. I wish my own Joanie was half so easy to manage. I vow, she is a little tyrant. And with Simon a year younger, he gets the worst of it. I have to keep an eye on them, to see she does not bully him too much." Hilary paused in her cheerful rambling and looked at Nicola. "Now that Mortimer is dead, can't you finally tell the truth about Simon?"

Nicola stiffened in misery. If only she had not made an enemy of her husband. She shook her head. "Nothing has changed. I must still keep his identity a secret."

"What sort of man is Lord de Cressy?" Hilary's normally soft voice rose. "Is he as spiteful and cruel as Mortimer, that you must hide your son away from him?"

"My lord husband hated Mortimer even more than I did. Once he sees Simon, he will think that he is Mortimer's son. Given his hatred for the man, he might well hold a grudge against the boy."

"Is there no way you can convince him otherwise? Surely de Cressy has heard rumors of Mortimer's . . . affliction. If you explain the situation, tell him that Simon was sired by a young squire sent to your bed by Mortimer, surely then de Cressy will relent." Hilary gazed at her hopefully.

"Things are not so amicable between myself and my husband. I cannot risk that he might decide to use Simon as a means of punishing me."

"Punishing you? Punishing you for what?"

Nicola shook her head. She did not want to go into the matter once again. What was done was done. "It's a complicated matter," she said. "Suffice to say that my husband does not trust me."

Simon came scampering back into the room, followed by a little girl with blonde braids and a stubborn set to her small jaw. The two children proceeded to the basket of tarts and gleefully began stuffing themselves, purple berry juice running down their small faces and smearing their chubby fingers.

"But look at him," Hilary murmured wistfully. "Who could behold that angelic countenance and wish him ill? I don't understand, milady."

Nor do I, Nicola thought. It had all turned out so differently than she'd anticipated. Who was to guess that the unknown squire that Mortimer had sent to her bed would turn her whole life upside down? And now, over three years later, he was still wreaking havoc on her peace of mind.

Alesia finally left the house, after kissing Fawkes twice and telling him that she would never forget his kindness. He deemed it prudent to wait there a while longer. When he finally ventured out, expecting catcalls and rude jests, he found that most of the villagers were too busy to even notice him. The storm he had anticipated earlier was well on its way. The sky had become a dark mass of roiling clouds and the once languid air felt damp and unsettled. Sudden gusts tore at the villagers' clothes as they sought to put away the food and the tables and benches.

From his experience in past years, Fawkes knew that the celebration should not be over yet. There would be more drinking and merriment, and as it grew dark, a bonfire would be lit and people would dance and carouse around it late into the night. That is, if the thunderstorm did not ruin things.

Either way, he was finished with the Lammas festivities. He was going back to the castle and find Nicola. Her absence in the village had turned his suspicions into raging, jealous anger that was eating him away. All he could think of was her and a lover sating themselves on the plush carpets of that magnificent solar.

As the first raindrops splattered cold against his face, he tried to find his knights. It seemed they had all vanished. He finally spied Henry de Brionne hurrying away from the area where they'd picketed their horses. He had a wineskin in one hand and his gambeson was hanging open.

"Henry!" he shouted against the fierce wind. "I'm going back to the castle."

"What the devil for?" Henry shouted back. "The storm's almost here. Why don't you find a warm, sheltered place and stay cozy until it passes." He raised the wineskin and winked. "That's what I'm doing."

Fawkes shook his head. "I want to get back. Do you know where Reynard is?"

Henry jerked his head toward the healer's cottage. "What do you think?" He leered.

Fawkes swore. By now, Reynard and the wisewoman were well involved in a bout of "mindless, meaningless fucking."

He started back toward the horses. The rain started to come down in earnest, soaking his heavy tunic. He saw one of the squires, Robert, also searching out supplies from one of the saddle packs. "Milord," Robert said, "I was just getting some things for Engelard."

"Where is he?" Fawkes asked.

"The shed behind the tanner's." The youth grinned. "With all three of the tanner's daughters."

Fawkes had half a mind to drag the knight out of the shed and order Engelard to accompany him back to the castle. Then the squire, who had started off, turned, and as an afterthought added, "By the way, Engelard said to tell you—he saw Lady Nicola ride out of the castle this morning at first light. He said you'd want to know."

Fawkes stood stunned for a moment, then strode after the squire. He pulled Robert around with a jerk. "Get Engelard!" he gritted out. "Get him now."

Fawkes stood in the rain, his mind churning with shock and fury. She'd ridden out, but hadn't come to the village. Where was she? Who was she with? His hand went to his sword belt and found it wasn't there; he'd left his gear with his horse, thinking he would not need weapons at a peaceful village gathering.

He made his way to his destrier and dug out his sword belt and sword and put them on. Engelard came running toward him, his clothing in considerable disarray. "Yea, milord. What is it?"

"Lady Nicola," Fawkes said. "You saw her leave the castle?"

Engelard nodded. "At the time, I assumed she was going to the village. It didn't dawn on me until we were here a while that she wasn't around, and by then . . ." his voice trailed off uneasily.

"By then you were too busy flirting with the tanner's daughters—all three of them!" Fawkes's voice rose in a bellow of rage.

"I'm sorry, milord," Engelard said. "But you didn't tell us to watch Lady Nicola. I didn't know that you suspected that she would . . ." Again, the knight looked uneasy. Fawkes guessed what he was thinking, that Fawkes wanted his wife watched because he feared she was cuckolding him. It was beyond awkward; it was humiliating.

Fawkes struggled to sound calm, to act as if he were simply concerned for Nicola's welfare. "Well, I'm telling you now, I don't want my wife riding out alone. It isn't safe. Who knows what could happen to her? She might have been set upon by brigands, anything."

"I thought she was going to the village," Engelard argued. "I knew here she would be safe enough."

Fawkes thought about what he would do if he found Nicola with another man. The way he felt—it was beyond murder. "I'm going to look for her." He started for his horse.

"Milord?" Engelard called. "Do you want me to come?"

If he found her with another man, he certainly didn't want the whole world to witness his moment of utter debasement and outrage. "No!" he growled. Engelard hurried away, obviously eager to be out of the rain and away from Fawkes and his difficulties.

Fawkes went to his destrier, Scimitar. He'd said he was going to look for Nicola, but where? Should he beat the bushes down by the river? Search the forest? If she had met a lover in those places, they would have taken shelter by now.

He could invade every house in the village, sword drawn, looking for his wife. What a fool he would look like then. Besides, for all he knew, the two lovers had returned to the castle long ago.

There was a flash of lightning, then the low rumble of thunder. The destrier nickered uneasily. The other horses also seemed restless. Fawkes glanced up at the slate-gray sky and the advancing darkness in the west. This storm was no little squall, to pass by quickly. It would be foolish to try to ride to the castle in this. His tunic was already soaked. Grabbing his saddle pack, he raced toward the nearest dwelling.

As he neared it, he realized with dismay that it was the healer's cottage. He rushed past the door and to the small shed behind the dwelling. After yanking the rain-swollen door open, he pushed inside.

The shed was dark and close and humid, but unoccupied by either man or beast. He gradually felt his way around and found bundles of spinning wool piled on a small table and a waist-high heap of straw, probably for use as bedding. He put down the saddle pack, then stripped off the sodden tunic and began to dry himself with the hay.

Outside, the storm worsened. He could hear the low rumble of thunder and the shriek of the wind. He thought of the horses, wishing he had managed to get them to shelter. Guilt gnawed at him. Scimitar, in particular, hated storms.

He swore, realizing he had no choice but to go out again.

Then he thought of Reynard, snug and comfortable in the healer's bed, and decided if he had to suffer, then his captain should also.

He would get his gambeson from his saddle pack, have some wine to warm his blood, then fetch Reynard. They should be able to get the horses to the cover of the oaks that sheltered the ale yard.

Nicola shivered in her light summer mantle as the rain-drops pelted down. She dearly wished she had worn her squirrel-lined cloak. But the sky had been clear and blue when she set off that morn. Even when she left Mordeaux, it had not appeared threatening. Or perhaps she had simply been too caught up in her grief at leaving Simon to notice the weather.

She was trapped now. Although there were a few cottars' dwellings between Mordeaux and Valmar, she knew if she stopped at one to wait out the storm, she would not arrive at the castle until after dark. And if she reached Valmar after the gate was closed, Fawkes might guess that she had been gone all day.

She rode on, bending low over the horse's withers, feeling the rain seep through the mantle and chill her skin. Not much farther now. She could see the village in the distance, a blur of gray buildings huddled beneath the stormy sky, which seemed to glow with an odd, sickly light. A jagged bolt of lightning flashed, then a crash of thunder boomed out. The mare shied. Nicola clung to the saddle pommel. The castle was too far; she'd never make it. Glennyth's. If she could reach her cottage, she could wait out the storm there.

With her last measure of strength, she dug her heels into the mare's sides, urging her on. The wind whipped the mantle off her head and tore at her hair. At last she neared the thatched dwelling. She slid down off the rained-slicked horse and, grasping the reins, staggered to the storage shed behind the house. If she could get the mare inside, she would not be spooked by the storm and run off. When it cleared, she would be able to remount and ride to the castle.

She fought the heavy door, struggling to pull it open in the wind. Behind her, the mare whinnied. "Easy girl," she called, "we're almost there."

At last the door gave. It swung outward, nearly knocking Nicola over. She started to pull the horse into the shed, but a figure blocked the doorway. She froze in shock at the sight of her husband. His black hair was plastered to his head and his chest and upper body were bare. He stared at her, his dark eyes wild in the strange light. "You," he rasped.

She wanted to run, to get back on the mare and ride off as fast as possible, but he grabbed her by the arm. The wet reins slipped out of her hand and she careened into the shed, landing in a pile of straw. He pulled the door shut behind them and everything disappeared into darkness.

She could hear him breathing. Harsh, almost labored. If she had not just seen him, she would have thought him ill. But it was not breathlessness that made him sound like a man with a lung wound, but powerful emotion. She had the panicked thought that he was going to kill her. Had he found out her errand to Mordeaux? Did he think she was plotting against him?

He approached. Two, three footsteps muffled in the straw. She felt him near, then he reached down and found her cloak. Grabbing a handful of wet wool, he dragged her upward. She'd barely found her feet, then his arms went around her and his mouth ground into hers.

She struggled for breath, then tilted her head so she could breathe through her nose. His mouth felt hot against her chilled skin, and she could taste the warm sweetness of his breath, tinted faintly with wine. Her fingers grasped his bare shoulders, feeling the smooth heat of his skin. She was aware of his scent blending with the odors of wool, hay and damp that filled the shed.

His kiss devoured, ravaged. Her lips parted, wanting more, his tongue, the liquid fire of his mouth. He gave her his tongue briefly, a lush, satisfying taste of fulfillment, then he lifted his head. Holding her pinned against him with one arm, he fumbled with the brooch fastening her cloak. Nicola absorbed the heat of his body, feeling the life course through him. She was breathless with excitement and anticipation. *Please,* she thought to herself, *love me, fill me, make me yours.*

His breathing still sounded harsh, his movements jerky and uncontrolled. She wanted to help him with her clothing, but she was afraid. This man was past reason or restraint, half animal, all male. She had no idea what he would do to her, only the wild hope that he would finally love her as he once had.

He finally got the cloak unfastened and flung it away from her. Then he grabbed her again, pressing her hard against his body. She could feel his jutting erection against her belly, straining against his braies. She began to shiver with desire.

He touched her neck with warm fingers, then pushed the wet strands of her hair away from her jaw and neck. His lips made a shimmering foray of the sensitive skin there, then lightly teased at her earlobe. Her knees wobbled and she fell against him. He clutched her buttocks with both hands, lifting her so the juncture of her thighs met the swollen heat of his shaft. A piercing ache shocked through her, and she moaned aloud.

Only a moment did he let her feel the promise of his maleness, then he released her. He clawed at the neck of her gown, but the tightly woven linen thwarted him. Again he kissed her. Hard, searching, demanding. His lips said "yield, surrender." Moaning, she forgot that she had meant to seduce him, to use his lust to meet her needs. She was past reason or control, aware only of warm skin and blind hunger.

He drew away. She heard him fumbling with his own clothing. He barely had time to undo the drawstring and thrust his braies down, then he grabbed her again. This time, he pulled at her skirts, working them upward.

Her whole body was on fire. She could hardly stand it. She helped him get her skirts up and tear off her loincloth. Hard fingers met soft, wet flesh. She dissolved, gasping with near unbearable yearning, trembling with need. With both hands between her thighs, fingers braced on her bottom, he lifted her. She grabbed his shoulders and held on.

He put her down on some sort of table. She could feel cool, damp wood against her skin. The smell of wool was strong and there was a soft bulk behind her. With one hand he rucked her skirts up farther. His other hand played, fingers splayed against her wet center, one callused fingertip probing the entrance of her slippery sheath. Then, with a suddenness that robbed her of breath, he removed his hand and shoved his shaft into her with one violent thrust.

Nothing could have prepared her for this. Not the determined probing of her own yearning fingers nor the memories of their coupling. Closest was the straining pressure of childbirth. Unbearable fullness, hot and alive flesh wrenching hers apart.

He seemed twice the size she remembered. And all that burning fullness stretching her was attached to a man. A man with sleek, strong muscles and strong, solid hips. She was impaled, helpless, vulnerable beyond imagining. Closing her eyes, she took deep, even breaths.

Still, he didn't move. He was panting, his hands beneath her clutching desperately, his fingers slick with sweat. "God," he breathed.

They seemed locked together, frozen. The pressure was intolerable. She wriggled, trying to ease it. He groaned, his voice husky and deep. The sound seemed to echo through her. She moved again, seeking to force her thighs farther apart, to assuage the throbbing, almost tearing ache. He grasped her hips more tightly, as if to hold her still.

She tilted her head up, moved her hands from his shoulders to his face. Slowly, gently, she stroked him. His hair was still damp, but it seemed to dry against her fingers. She could feel the prickle of his whiskers growing in from when he'd shaved that morning. His mouth felt smooth and soft.

He endured her exploration as if he were made of stone. She continued because it helped distract her from the fierce sensations assaulting her lower body, and because she had wanted to do this forever, to touch him the way he had once touched her. Like a blind man, exploring every contour and texture of her body.

His shoulders were hard and wide. His chest, silky smooth at his neck, then rough with sprinkles of coarse hair against her palms and fingertips. Beneath the skin, she felt his thick chest muscles tighten. She trailed her hands down to where his chest hair faded to a thin line. His skin seemed to shudder beneath her fingertips. His breathing quickened. Down to his navel, the hard, taut strength of his belly. Down to where they were joined.

She felt where the thick cylinder of flesh met her own body. Some of the discomfort had begun to abate as her body yielded. Her quim grew wetter still, swimming with dewy moisture. She could smell herself, smell her arousal. Lighter, softer, less piquant than his sexual musk.

Her nipples were taut points, tender, almost painful. There seemed to be a sort of fine thread that connected her body from mouth to nipples to groin, like a web, where a slight vibration in one place sent ripples of sensation to the other parts. She touched herself again, feeling the slippery opening of her sheath stretched around him. Deep inside, her womb convulsed, throbbing. Her nipples grew harder still. Her mouth watered with expectation.

He groaned once more. She encircled the root of his shaft with her fingers. All at once, he began to move. Her quim seemed to tighten around him. He struggled to free himself, then he plunged in again, his hands gripping her buttocks, spreading her, opening her for his assault.

She arched her back and thrust her hips forward, enduring the tempest of sensation. Ripples inside her became waves, great roaring waves of pleasure. Yearning finally satisfied. Ecstasy.

The table shook. The shed shook. The world shook. She clutched at him, seeking his solid strength in the storm of sensation. He thrust into her with one last wild lunge, then his body stiffened. He gave a cry like the bellow of a stag, then went still.

She expected him to release her, his softening shaft to slip out of her. But he did not move. She wondered if something was wrong. This was like no coupling she'd ever heard of. So frenzied and violent. And now, what would he do to her now?

Twelve

Was he still alive? Fawkes wondered. Or had he died and gone to heaven? Nicola's silky body was next to his. His whole being was relaxed and deeply satisfied. If there was a paradise, how could it be better than this?

But there were prickling reminders of the corporeal world. The realization that he was still wearing his boots and hose, and that his damp braies were bunched around his ankles. That the woman whose lush bottom he gripped was squirming slightly as if uncomfortable. The tickle of cold moisture against his groin.

He shifted his body and his cock slipped out and dangled loose, itchy with drying moisture. Gradually his mind began to function again. He heard the rain on the roof and remembered taking shelter in the shed. He also remembered his conversation with Engelard, his anger and jealousy, his determination to find Nicola. Most of all, he remembered the shock of seeing her in the doorway. Her oval face stark white against the sleek blackness of her wet hair and the vivid crimson of her cloak; her small form and fine features; those unforgettable eyes, as gray and pearlescent as the stormy sky.

He had not planned for this. Some madness had come over him, and nothing had mattered but that he should possess her. He felt as if he were under some sort of spell, as if nothing was quite real in this place. The past, the future, neither seemed important. There was only the two of them.

At the thought, desire again built inside him. He wanted to see her, to behold the remarkable beauty that had obsessed his dreams.

He drew up his braies and fastened them, then fumbled his way to his saddle pack and searched for his flintstone and the cloth bundle of pitch-dipped rushes he always carried. The rushlight almost caught, then sputtered out. He swore and tried again. A small glow in the darkness. He looked around for a place to put the light. Somewhere so it would not fall into the straw and incinerate them both. He finally found a small knothole in the wall and secured the rushlight. He lit another and stuck it in the dirt floor.

She was still sitting on the table, although she had pulled her skirts down. Her braids were half undone, her eyes dazed. He walked over to her, wanting her naked, wanting to see it all.

He began with her hair, starting at her temples, raking his fingers through the tangled strands, dragging out the braids and the ribbons that secured them. She sat utterly still as he smoothed her hair so it lay like a dark cloak around her shoulders.

He played with one strand, rubbing it between his fingers. Desire tingled through him. How many times had he dreamed of how her hair would feel against his skin? A cool, soft river flowing over his chest. Slippery coils stroking his body. A web of silk entangling their nakedness. Unbearable, tickling rapture as the long strands brushed against his cock.

He suppressed a moan and looked at her face. She sat like a statue. Frozen. Waiting. He did not care what she thought, what she wanted. His gaze moved over her hungrily. Her damned clothing. He wanted it off her, every stitch! He wanted to see her. Her bliaut was fastened with lacing under her arms. He began to undo it.

He wanted her again, she could sense it. Even that wild, raw ride wasn't enough for him. His insatiability thrilled her.

They might not have more than this, this intense, breathless interlude before her secret came between them once again.

She let him unlace her bliaut, sitting passive and still. She wanted him to do whatever he wished, for him to have his way as he once had, bending her body to his will, making her desire things she could never have imagined desiring. As soon as the laces were loosened, he thrust his fingers into the openings and found her breasts. He stroked his thumbs over her nipples. They tightened, hardening into aching peaks. She closed her eyes and parted her lips.

No, Fawkes thought as he caressed the liquid magic of her breasts. He'd changed his mind. He did not want to wait, to take it slow and gentle the second time. He wanted her again. Now.

Releasing her breasts, he tore at her skirts, dragging them upward. He found her wet, slippery cunny. There was so much moisture. A flood. A mingling of his spilled seed and the wetness of her desire. He fondled her, feeling how open and ready she was. She jerked at his touch, as if she could scarcely bear his caresses. His cock rose in painful anticipation.

He wanted to look at her, to spread her legs wide and explore the swollen, dripping folds of her sweet, delicious quim. But his body couldn't wait. Years of denial had bred a tidal wave of need. He moved his hands to her buttocks, squeezing. She was still slender, her hips relatively narrow. Hard to imagine that she had borne a babe. The thought threatened to shatter his mood. He forced it away, breathing hard. Nay, he would not think of those things now.

He dragged her off the table and set her down shakily on her feet. Then he undid his braies and freed his cock. She tried to touch him. He pushed her hand away, then thrust her against the table. He grabbed one of the bundles of wool and spread it out, making a sort of cushion on the table. She watched him, her pupils dark and huge. He took her by the shoulders and turned her around, so her back was to him.

He heard her gasp of surprise, but he set his jaw. Pressing close, he rucked up her skirts, then lifted her so she was sprawled across the wool-covered table.

She was not certain what he was doing now, and it frightened her a little. Now that some of their passion was spent, she'd expected love play, the slower, more sensual pleasuring he hadn't bothered with before. But as his hand stroked between her buttocks, finding the damp slit and spreading it with his fingers, she decided that this way was rather intriguing.

Fawkes ran one hand over the smooth half-moons of her bottom, while with the other he teased the wet jewel between them. He knew he must arouse her intensely to take her this way and not hurt her. When she was dripping with wetness, he slid a finger inside her. He heard her pant and waited, then pushed another finger deep. She moaned, her body shivering. He thought of filling her with another one, then decided to tease her cleft instead. With his thumb he sought the little nub and rubbed very gently, provoking the reaction he'd hoped for. She spread her legs wider, squirming and gasping. His fingers were drowning in slick heat. A little more, he thought, and she would let him do anything.

Nicola heard herself whimper. He was torturing her. His fingers inside her did not ease her need, only inflamed it. And the way he played with her. Jesu, had he no mercy!

But then the torturing touch went away, and she found that even more unbearable. When he withdrew his fingers from her quim, she wanted to weep. She tried to turn to look at him, when she felt his shaft—hard and thick, pressing against her bereft, aching slit. She squirmed, wanting it, needing it.

Gritting his teeth, he sought to be gentle, to ease his way in. He could tell from her frantic breathing that she was intensely aroused, but he was not sure it was enough. Then his own desire took over and he decided that he did not care if she was ready. He wanted, needed, to be inside her. So deep that she could not escape him.

He pushed in an inch, then another, and another. He felt intense tightness, but there was more for her to take. Slowly, he eased deeper. As the full length of his cock breached her, she screamed.

He froze, wondering if it was a scream of pleasure or pain. He was half mad with the pressure himself. Her tight sheath squeezed him like a fist. But she was wet, so very wet. He could feel her melting around him, her body yielding. Leaning over her, he again brought his right hand around to touch her clit. She moaned and wriggled. His cock slid in even deeper.

He touched her gently, barely brushing the delicate nub of flesh at the apex of her cleft. She shrieked and bucked against him. Her movements nearly undid him. He went still, struggling for control. When he had found it, he began to move. A slow, even rhythm. Stretching her, making her feel the length of him. But careful. He was aware of how small she was beneath him, how fragile. Her delicate woman's sheath strained, distended, filled to bursting with the heated length of him. Yet, she had borne his babe. She could take him.

Closing her eyes, she fought for breath. He was so big, enormous, stroking in and out. The tip of his shaft touched her womb. With each stroke, the walls of her quim convulsed, pulling him deeper. She was impaled, spread wide. Her outer lips forced open, stretched, stinging with sensation. The strain was so intense she thought she would faint. Rippling waves of pleasure built inside her, spreading outward. Shattering, mindless.

From the way her breath came in shuddery gasps, he could tell she was near her peak. He moved his fingers up to touch one of her breasts, feeling the hard nipple. Her moans turned to small, frantic cries. In his other hand, he cupped her cleft in his palm, helping her. She tightened convulsively around him and screamed like a wild vixen. He nearly went over the edge himself, but held on for another few divine, magical heartbeats. Then he exploded, feeling his hot seed spurt into her, filling her, making her his.

She closed her eyes and breathed through her mouth, striving to return to earth. She was sprawled across the table with Fawkes on top of her. The warm wool under her was sticky against her skin. Her legs dangled from the table and her naked bottom was pressed against his groin. She could feel him softening inside her, his once rock-hard shaft melting into the puddle of hot liquid they had made together. Her body felt sore, but exquisitely, deliciously satisfied.

She'd experienced everything she had yearned for the past years. All those nights of frustration, her body aching with need. Sometimes the craving had been so intense, so miserable, she'd sobbed with the unfairness of it all, that he should awaken her so expertly, then leave her to pine for him.

But finally, he had given her what she wished. He had ignited her body with desire, then appeased it with his big, burning shaft. He had filled, stretched her, completed her. Her intimate parts still throbbed, and tiny pricks of pleasure quivered through her womb.

With a groan, he pulled himself off her. She slid down off the table. Her legs were so wobbly, she could hardly stand. Moisture dribbled down her thighs. With shaking fingers, she pushed down her sweaty, wrinkled skirts. She turned around and braced her body against the table, wanting to look at him, to see this man who had done this to her, had taken her to such magnificent heights.

He didn't glance at her as he adjusted his clothing, then he staggered over to the pile of straw and collapsed upon it. Leaning back, he closed his eyes. Nicola watched him, thinking how beautiful he was. His hair hung damp and loose around his face, framing his well-made masculine features. There was a softness in his countenance she'd never seen before. Or perhaps she had, all those years ago. Relaxation muted the sternness of his jaw. His mouth looked soft and sensual. For once, his fierce hawk eyes did not hunt her.

His body entranced her, as well. The sleek shoulders, the intriguing contours of his chest—rounded muscles, dark nipples, black curling hair. The flat plane of his belly with the tantalizing arrow line of hair leading downward. Down to that miraculous piece of masculine flesh.

Now his shaft was no more than a soft bulge in his braies. But the sleeping beast could wake at any time and grow huge and hard and formidable. She had felt its power and size, rending her, filling her, conquering her. A weapon against her. And the sweetest fulfillment of her desire. The missing part of her, as if her sheath had been made exactly to fit his hard, slick dagger.

She looked up and saw that Fawkes had opened his eyes. Her heartbeat quickened. Had he seen where she was looking? Did he guess that she was thinking about his shaft? Embarrassed, she said, "Do you have a cloth?"

He regarded her a moment, then rose and fetched her a piece of clean linen. He held it out, his eyes challenging. She realized he was waiting for her to clean herself and that he was going to watch her. He sat down again.

Once more, she felt breathless with expectation. There was something so intimate in doing this in front of him. Shakily, she pulled her skirts up. Let him look at her. Let him see the rivers of wetness he had put inside her.

It soaked the cloth. Not all of it was from him. Never had she dreamed that her own body could make so much creamy, slippery moisture. It was as if she had melted, dissolving like a candle held over a flame. Or rather, the hard "candle" of his shaft had turned her to molten liquid.

As she wiped it away, more wetness seemed to flow from her. The rough rasp of the cloth was arousing her, making her tender, well-used quim tingle and ache.

She looked up and saw the expression on his face, satisfied, almost gloating. He was thinking of what he had done to her, how he had held her open and wide with his hand and put himself into her as deep as possible. She remembered the feeling of the tip of his shaft thrusting against her womb, the aching, swollen sensation, the deep, shuddering rhythms inside her. Her sheath like a mouth sucking at him, drawing him in, swallowing him.

He could not be aroused again, Fawkes thought. It was not possible. Less than a candle hour had passed and he'd already experienced two earth-shattering climaxes. More than enough for any man.

But, looking at her, his body was not convinced. Her boldness tantalized him anew. The way she had lifted her skirts up so that he could see it all, the neat black triangle of her maidenhair, the rounded curve of her hips, the pale, slim thighs. The way she cleaned herself, her legs slightly apart, moving the cloth delicately over her crotch. Thorough, yet careful, as if she were sore there. How could she not be, after what he had done to her?

He could imagine the folds of her cunny, swollen, slightly red, like the bruised petals of a flower. And that thought led him to another—could she take him again? The expression on her face told him, yea, she could. She was readying herself for him, wiping away the slick dew of their coupling so that they could begin again.

But he was in no hurry. The urgency had left him. This time, it could be slow. He would begin by kissing her. Then he would strip off all her clothes, as he'd meant to the last time—

A sound outside made him stiffen and glance at the door.

"I don't care whose horse it is, get it out of my garden!" A woman's angry shriek. The softer, near inaudible voice of a man answering.

He had been held in a spell of enchantment. With those few words the spell broke and he remembered where he was. Nicola's horse. She had been trying to lead the beast into the shed when he had dragged her in.

He knew a moment of bitter resentment. How dare his responsibilities intrude, just when he had begun to realize his dream? But the world out there was real, while this one . . .

He glanced at Nicola, feeling vaguely uneasy. He didn't know what this last hour had meant. A kind of madness had overtaken him, and he had not cared about anything but his potent, furious desire, that white-hot lust born of three years of waiting. Now he felt uncomfortable, wondering what she thought of him, if she'd really liked what he had done to her.

The voices outside intruded again. He told himself they would come looking for him, that he had no choice but to leave her. Then he got to his feet and began to search the shed for his tunic. When he found it, he threw it aside, realizing it was too wet to wear. Instead, he dug in his saddle pack until he discovered an old linen shirt. He shrugged into it, grabbed his sword belt.

A reflexive action. He wouldn't need a weapon to chase a horse. For a second, he looked down at the scabbard, then remembered why he'd gotten it out in the first place. He still didn't know where his wife had been all day.

He glanced at her. She had arranged her skirts, tidied her hair, sought to make herself look like a lady again. As she shook out her mantle, smoothing the bloodred fabric, he realized he wanted to watch her forever, to slip back into the world of sex and sensation that had consumed him. But he pushed the yearning aside. "I must go," he said, then went to the door and pushed it open.

Nicola's hands trembled as she put on her mantle. She felt as if she had woken from some wild, fantastic dream. Glancing at the table, she thought of herself bent over it, her bare bottom lifted, thighs spread wide. It seemed shocking to her now, but she could not deny how badly she'd wanted it, how she'd reveled in the raw, primitive way he took her.

She took a deep breath. Nor could she deny that she wanted to do it again.

* * *

Outside, Fawkes blinked in the sudden brightness. The storm was over, the sky was beginning to clear. The world was transformed to jewel-like green, glistening with wetness. He went around to the other side of the shed and saw the white palfrey grazing in a garden a few houses away. A village woman and a knight were trying to grab the horse's trailing reins, but every time they got near, the animal shied away. Fawkes ran to help.

The garden was a slippery morass of mud. While the mare maneuvered easily, the three of them struggled to find sure footing. Fawkes almost fell down twice, thinking that if he did slip and land in that black ooze, he was going to kill the horse.

Finally, between the three of them, they were able to corner the beast. Fawkes grabbed the reins on one side, while the knight got hold of the horse's bridle on the other. As he muttered soothing words to the mare, Fawkes saw that the knight helping him was Engelard.

"Isn't this Lady Nicola's horse?" Engelard asked. "Did you ever find her?"

Fawkes nodded to both questions. He wanted to explain, so Engelard would forget his suspicions that Fawkes was being cuckolded, but there was no way to do it without sounding impossibly crude. "Yea, I've found my wife and I've been fucking her the past candlehour," simply wouldn't do. Engelard would have to think what he liked.

Fawkes led the horse over near the shed. He wondered how much the animal had eaten while running free. Probably enough cabbage and other succulent vegetables to give it terrible colic. "Stupid beast," he told the mare. "If you suffer from a bellyache and bloat, it's no more than you deserve."

Then he considered that his own situation was not much different. While the storm raged, he had indulged himself and given in to the erotic madness Nicola aroused in him.

As he wondered whether he was also going to pay for his rashness, Nicola came out of the shed. She looked delectable, her formidable beauty heightened by her flushed glow, the unmistakable look of a woman well-tumbled. He wanted to smooth her hair away from her face and hold her in his arms. But she seemed distant as always. "I found your horse," he said. "Can you ride?"

She nodded. He moved near, leading the palfrey. "I'll help you up."

The horse nickered at Nicola and suddenly became docile. Fawkes dared to let go of the reins so he could grasp Nicola by the waist and lift her up. The lightness and fragility of her body in his arms aroused a pang of guilt. Had he used her too hard? She was such a fine-boned, delicate woman. And he had ridden her like a stallion.

He settled her on the mare and handed her the reins, then looked up at her face. Was she sore? Another arrow of guilt afflicted him. He wanted to take her down from her mount and carry her in his arms all the way to the castle.

But before he could act, he heard someone calling his name. Grimacing at another interruption, he said, "I'll see you at the castle. Godspeed." He slapped the horse on the rump, then watched her ride away. A vision. The graceful white horse, the woman in her crimson mantle, her long hair, black as onyx, streaming over her shoulders. A fantasy from his dreams.

The storm was over, the world returned to normal. His body felt replete, deliciously satiated. But he still did not know where his wife had been since early that morn, or who she had been with. He still did not know if he could trust her.

He forced himself to concentrate on mundane matters. He must gather his horses and his men and return to the castle.

Turning on his heel, he strode to the shed to fetch his saddle pack, then went around to the cottage door. Seeing the bell on the rope, he grabbed it and rang it loudly. When there was no response, he shouted through the wooden door, "Reynard, you lustful prick, get out here."

He waited a while, shifting his weight from one foot to another. As he was about to go inside and drag Reynard out, the door opened. He moved aside to let Reynard by. The woman, Glennyth, also came out. They were both decently dressed, and their calm, relaxed manners suggested that they had sated themselves some time ago and were simply lingering in the afterglow of their pleasure.

As Fawkes watched, Reynard bowed low over the wise-woman's hand and kissed her capable tanned fingers. She smiled faintly, looking amused and indulgent. "Mistress Glennyth," Reynard said, "I bid you good day. It has been a pleasure."

She nodded, her face smug with a felinelike contentment.

Reynard released her hand and the two men left. "She seems an odd sort for you," Fawkes remarked.

"A delightful change from giggling maids and frowsy kitchen wenches. You know I've always fancied experienced women."

"And is she?" Fawkes jerked his head in the direction of Glennyth's cottage.

Reynard smiled. "Deliciously so. She has her own sort of magic, more subtle than an eastern dancing girl, but potent nonetheless." Reynard gave a satisfied sigh.

Fawkes thought of his own recent liaison with Nicola. There had been more than a little magic in it. Dark, dangerous magic.

"What of you?" Reynard asked. "Did you find the corn maid to your liking?"

"What? Oh . . . the corn maid. She started babbling about her sweetheart and how he'd done her down by the river. After that, I didn't have the heart for it."

"You know if the crops fail next year, it'll be your fault."

Fawkes faced Reynard's grinning countenance. "If the fertility of their fields depends on the potency of the man who rules them, it seems to me the people of Valmar should have starved years ago. You know Mortimer didn't plow the belly of any corn maid in his time."

"Maybe he had some other man do it for him," Reynard jibed. "Speaking of which, did you ever find Lady Nicola?"

They'd reached the horses, which amazingly, had not broken free of their hobbles and run off. Fawkes went to Scimitar and busied himself with tying his saddle pack onto the destrier. Reynard followed him. "Well?"

Fawkes turned, thinking of exactly how he had found Nicola, wet and wild-eyed from the storm. Of dragging her into the shed and what he had done to her there. He took a breath and said, "Yea, I found her."

Thirteen

When she got back to the castle, Nicola decided that the first thing she needed was a bath. She was sweaty and sore, and besides, if Fawkes came to her bed this night, she wanted to be clean for him. He still had not pleasured her with his mouth, and she longed for that, had been obsessing about it ever since he left Valmar over three years ago. If she could entice him into the act, she wanted her quim to be fragrant and sweet, to taste good to him.

She had some squires drag a wooden bathing tub up to her bedchamber and fill it with hot, almost scalding water. Old Emma brought towels and a bowl of soap. Tossing a handful of herbs into the tub, the servant asked, "Do ye want me to bathe ye?"

Nicola shook her head. She wanted to be alone, to savor her memories of the afternoon.

When Old Emma had left, she sank down into the steaming water, sighing as the blissful heat soothed her. The muscles in her thighs were tense and sore from riding all day as well as her other exertions. And her quim. As she touched herself she thought she still felt puffy and swollen there. And vaguely aroused. As her fingers explored the soft folds, thinking of them stretched around Fawkes's thick shaft, she knew that if he came to her bed wanting more, she would be more than a match for him. Perhaps he could be a bit gentler this time, but she certainly would not deny him.

She sighed and leaned back in the tub, lightly stroking her breasts. He had barely touched them. Nor had he kissed her except at the very beginning. The fact was, she wanted it all, every sort of pleasuring he could offer her. She was greedy, insatiable for his loving.

Shaking herself from her reverie, she stood to soap her body, then rinsed herself in the tub. She climbed out and dried herself, then went to the coffer and searched among the jars and vials stored there until she found the container of lavender oil. She poured some into her hand and began to smooth it over her body. Over her breasts. Under her arms. Down her belly. Along the inside of her thighs.

Then she took out the smaller flask of rose oil, remembering how Glennyth had grumbled about how many blooms it took to make this small jar. She'd had to ask for help from a village woman, Glennyth said. The woman had picked the roses at the height of their lushness and then crushed the mass of petals for the wisewoman to distill.

Nicola stroked the rich essence behind her ears, on the pulse point in her throat, in the cleft between her breasts. Then she poured more into her hand and carefully rubbed it on her quim, making certain every fold and nook of her private parts—even deep in the crack of her bottom—was well annointed. She knew that rose oil, unlike lavender, tasted sweet and was even sometimes used in cooking. Let him think her delicious, a banquet for his tongue and mouth.

She donned her shift and robe and called for Old Emma to have the squires dump the used water down the garderobe and take the tub away. When they had gone, she removed her shift and lay down on the bed. She wanted him to find her naked, as he had when he interrupted her soon after that brief unsatisfying coupling on their wedding night. She intended for him to know she was ready and willing, eager for everything he could do to her.

* * *

"Are you coming in?" Reynard asked as he and Fawkes reached the knights' barracks. They'd finally made it back to the castle and gotten the horses to the stables. "You could share a jack of wine with me," Reynard suggested. "Perhaps join in the dicing."

Fawkes shook his head. "I think I'll just go to bed."

"With your wife?"

Fawkes didn't answer. A knight named Rob of Mulin walked by and punched Reynard in the arm. "What are you doing here? Shouldn't you be out wenching?"

"Nay," Reynard retorted. "Believe it or not, I'm going to sleep alone tonight."

"Surely you jest!" Rob clutched his chest in mock amazement. "Can it really be that you've satisfied your ferocious lust?"

Reynard shrugged.

Henry de Brionne, leaning out the doorway, interjected, "The young fox has at last been bitten by the love bug. And right glad of it, I am. Now there may actually be some wenches left for the rest of us!"

Henry and Rob erupted with guffaws. Shaking his head, Fawkes left them.

He took his time walking to the keep, thinking of Nicola. He glanced up at the tower where her bedchamber was, the "lady's tower" the servants called it. What was she doing? Was she asleep yet? She should be tired. He was. All the strenuous and exhilarating activities of the day had left him with a pleasant sort of fatigue.

He entered the hall and wavered a moment. The stairways that led to the bedchamber where he slept and the lady's tower were on opposite sides of the cavernous room. Which should he choose?

He thought again of their wild coupling. It had been total gratification for his body, but his mind was far from content. Where had she come from when she jerked open the door to the shed, her mare in tow? Engelard said she had left the castle early that morning, yet he had not seen her until hours later. It was still possible that she had a lover, that she'd actually been with the man before she came to the shed. No, it was impossible that she could have responded so passionately to him if she'd been fucking some other man all afternoon. No woman was that lustful.

More likely, she'd not had a chance to meet the man that day. Perhaps something had altered her plans. The storm? He sighed as he started toward the stairs to his bedchamber. The puzzle of his wife remained unsolved. He thought of the conversation he'd had with Reynard on the way back to the castle.

"I'd like to help you understand your wife," his friend had said. "But I know no more about Nicola than you do. I hear more gossip, yea, but it's simply that—gossip. I don't know if it's motivated by envy or resentment, or if it's based on the truth."

"What gossip do you hear?" Fawkes had asked.

"That she's a cold-hearted bitch who poisoned her husband so she could run Valmar the way she wished and exert an unnatural interest in men's affairs. And that she's a kind and generous lady who suffered grievously at the hands of Mortimer." Reynard shrugged. "Two very different tales. Take your pick as to which one is the truth."

Somehow he had to find out more about his wife, Fawkes thought as he made his way down the hall to his sleeping quarters. Whatever else she was, his wife was a lusty and eager bed partner. Maybe, just maybe, he could use her sexual need as a means of breaking through the cool façade she used as a barrier between them.

On their wedding night, he'd left her aching and unsatisfied. Then, later, he'd caught her in the act of pleasuring herself, trying to relieve the lust he'd so deliberately aroused. What if, instead of obeying her cold command to leave, he'd stayed and offered to give her what she wished, but only if she truthfully answered all the questions troubling him? Would it have been possible to *seduce* the truth from her?

He did not know, but it was yet worth trying the technique. He had nothing to lose. Even if he could not break through her wary reserve, he would enjoy this method of trying. Already he was planning what he would do to her, how to fulfill his own fantasies and at the same time cajole the truth from his closemouthed, mysterious wife.

Nicola lay in bed, alert to every faint noise around her. She could not help listening for the sound of footsteps on the stairs leading to the tower. Bold, rhythmic footsteps that would signal the approach of her husband.

Through the open window drifted the noises of the castle. A dog barked in the yard. The sentries on the ramparts spoke to each other in faint, indistinct voices. The bell in the chapel rang, signaling compline, time for the last prayers of the day. Old Emma snored on her pallet in the hallway. But there were no footsteps. Only a faint scratching at the door.

Sighing, Nicola rose and let Gimlyn in. The big tomcat rubbed against her ankles, purring loudly. "He's not coming," Nicola whispered to the cat. She sighed again and tried to banish her disappointment. "I'm a fool," she told Gimlyn. "Why should he come to my bed tonight? He's already satisfied himself."

She climbed back into the bed. Gimlyn settled himself beside her, kneading the linen sheet with sharp, ruthless claws.

Nicola was near the weaving shed the next morning, making sure all the newly shorn fleeces were being properly washed, when Fawkes's squire, Will, found her. "Lord Fawkes sent me to find you," he announced. "Said that you were to put on a loose, comfortable gown and meet him in the bailey. He wants to go out riding with you today."

Will bowed faintly, then hurried off. Nicola stared after him in surprise. Riding?

She walked toward the hall, puzzling over Fawkes's request. The mention of a "loose, comfortable gown" intrigued her. Did that mean he wished her to wear something easy to remove, that he was tired of fumbling with the laces on her more elaborate bliauts?

The idea that there was some sort of sexual innuendo in his words made her quicken her pace. She was pleased she had bathed the night before, although she might take a moment to wash her quim and rub herself with more rose oil. And she decided she would not wear a shift under her gown, nor a loincloth. In her fullest, loosest kirtle, the one she wore when pregnant with Simon, there would be enough fabric in the skirt to protect her crotch from chafing in the saddle.

If Fawkes had different intentions in taking her out riding, he need never know how little she was wearing. And if he *was* taking her off alone for more of the mindless coupling they had indulged in yesterday, he would know as soon as he embraced her that she was ready and eager for more.

She rushed through changing and washing, then hurried down to the bailey.

He was waiting for her with her palfrey, Buttermilk. Fawkes's eyes gave nothing away as he examined her clothing, then he nodded, apparently in satisfaction, and held out his hand to help her into the saddle. It seemed his hands lingered on her waist longer than necessary as she mounted. Nicola's breathing quickened.

As he climbed onto his own horse, she saw that he had chosen to ride a sleek brown courser rather his warhorse. She noted also that he wore only a plain russet tunic and dark green braies. He had no armor and carried no weapons other than a dagger in his belt. But although he was attired simply, he still maintained a commanding appearance. With his tall, broad-shouldered, well-muscled physique, he exuded menace and power.

At the thought, Nicola felt a little shiver of apprehension. What if she were wrong about his intentions, and he was really taking her out into the woods to punish her for betraying him to Mortimer? He might want to make certain no one interfered, to carry out his chastisement of her in private. As she urged her horse through the gate after his, her sense of anticipation ebbed. She was so poor at reading him, and his usual hawklike, brooding gaze and fierce soldier's mien did not exactly inspire trust.

Or, she thought as he led the way down the trackway, turning east toward the forest rather than the village, his plan this day might be very mundane and innocent. She knew that he had dragged Osbert the reeve all over the countryside this past sennight, insisting on examining every field and manor under his control. Maybe he wanted something similar of her. To discuss crops or flocks or furlongs and hayfields.

But if so, why was he riding into the forest? It seemed obvious that he wanted to be alone with her, although the reason why was still a mystery.

He led her along a winding, narrow game trail. Tall oaks formed a canopy above them, and the air was still, moist and heavy, the sense of lassitude broken only by the calls of birds in the treetops and the scuffle of small animals in the brush. The lush, bright green of high summer was now edged with hints of gold and silver, the first real signs of autumn only a month or so away.

It made her feel a vague sense of loss, of time passing. She realized suddenly that Simon was almost three years old, and wondered if she would be able to get away to Mordeaux to celebrate his birthday. A pang went through her as she thought of the precious moments of his childhood that she had already missed. Then Fawkes pulled the courser to a halt, and her awareness returned to the present. He dismounted and motioned to her. "Wait here," he said, then led his horse into the trees.

Wait? What else would she do? She had no idea where she was. She'd been too caught up in her thoughts to take notice, and besides, this sort of dense wildwood always made her get turned around and confused.

She waited, listening to the trill of birdsong and the buzz of tiny insects. Could he mean to leave her here to perish, to be devoured by wild beasts or simply to starve? As a child, growing up near a similar forest by Mordeaux, she'd heard tales of people getting lost in the woods and never being seen again.

An absurd notion. He needed her to enforce his claim to Valmar. It was the only thing that had kept Mortimer from killing her; she could only think that it must also be some sort of deterrent for Fawkes.

And then, suddenly, he was back, and the expectant, hungry look on his face told her that her first reading of his plans was the most likely one.

He approached her wordlessly, then reached up to help her off the horse. As he did so, he drew her close. The reins slipped nervelessly from her fingers as she felt him gather up her skirts, reach beneath them and stroke her buttocks. A vague embarrassment stung her. She had wanted him to know she was eager for him, but still, she felt wanton.

"Mmmm," he muttered. He gripped her bottom with both hands, kneading. Then he moved his hands, trailing one long finger down either side of the crack between. When he reached the juncture of her thighs, he applied a gentle pressure, squeezing the lips of her quim together but not touching them. "I want you wet," he whispered. "Before I even touch you there, your cunny will be dripping."

The sound of his words, his teasing manipulation of her already throbbing quim, almost made her swoon.

Then, as suddenly as he had gripped her, he released her. Her skirts fell into place as he stepped away. He started for the palfrey, grabbing the reins before the animal could jerk away. After tying up the horse, he turned back to her.

"Come." He motioned with his head toward a pathway through the trees.

She followed him through the dense foliage to a place where it opened up into a bright meadow. The vivid hues of red poppies, purple harebells, yellow loose-strife and goldenrod, white daisies and maywood glinted in the sunlight, and the scents of honeysuckle, bedstraw and meadowsweet perfumed the air. In the center of the space, a large woven blanket had been spread out over the flowers. Nearby was Fawkes's saddle pack.

Fawkes turned toward her. He placed his hands on her hips, then grabbed her full skirts and jerked them over her head. Except for her gartered stockings and shoes, she was naked. His gaze raked her. "I've wanted to do this since that day long ago when I explored your body in the dark. Since then, my dream has been to see you properly. Not by candlelight, nor faint daylight coming through a window, but like this, so every facet of your beauty is revealed to me." He stepped nearer, dark eyes gleaming. "I want every part of you, all of it exposed. I vow, I will see the dew of your love juices glisten on your cunny before I lick it off."

Her lower body seemed to dissolve. She took a deep breath.

He nodded toward the meadow. "After you, milady."

It was clear he wanted to watch her, to observe her naked backside. She took a step, then another, acutely aware of his eyes on her. By the saints, this man made her hot for him!

She reached the blanket and sank down, trying to arrange her legs so she did not appear too lewd and eager. Her whole body felt hot and prickly. Her nipples were engorged, almost painfully hard.

He moved quickly to join her on the blanket. Only an arm's length separated them. Kneeling, he shrugged his tunic over his head. Assaulted with the sight of that much tanned hard skin and curling dark hair, she swallowed hard. As much as he wanted to observe her nakedness, she desired the same of him. But he did not remove the rest of his clothing, but instead, sat back, his dark gaze skimming over her body. "Why don't you take off your stockings and shoes," he suggested.

She slipped off her shoes easily, but in this position, there was no demure way to remove her garters and hose. She did the best she could, well aware that she was flashing him bold glimpses of her quim. He watched her intently, and the fever inside her built. Now, at last he would take her in his arms and ease her need.

But he remained sitting, his dark gaze impassive. "I wanted to explain yesterday," he said. "Why I took you roughly, the way a stallion takes a mare. I was overcome. You see, I have thought of . . ." he paused and his mouth twitched, ". . . of making love to you every night for over three years."

He had wanted to call it something else, she knew. He was trying to be tactful and refined. But was not what they had done yesterday more "fucking" than "lovemaking?" That was part of the magic of it, the raw, insatiable, primitive need they had both felt.

He reached out and took one of her braids in his hand. Stripping off the ribbon fastening it, he began to unravel the plait. She remembered him doing the same thing the first time he came to her. "There are many men who think I am a fool or some sort of madman," he continued, "but the truth is, I did not touch another woman during those years I was away from you."

It took a while for his words to sink in, and then she could scarce believe it. A randy, potent man like him? Forgo release for years? It did not seem possible. Maybe he meant he had taken no *gentlewomen* to bed, only whores and servants.

He went on, "While on campaign it was not that difficult. The whores and washerwomen were so well-used, a man

would have to be truly desperate to go to them. But when
we reached the eastern lands, there were indeed tempta-
tions." A muscle twitched in his jaw, and his gaze seemed
faraway. She wondered what he was seeing in his mind, who,
or what, had tempted him.

Then, without speaking, he moved around behind her, so
that her back was against his chest, her bottom cradled between his thighs. He spoke softly, his mouth next to her ear.
"The only woman who ever made me think seriously of for-
getting my vow looked very much like you. Small, graceful
and finely made. Her hair was dark and straight like yours,
but did not appear so fine and silky. Her face was nothing
compared to yours, of course, but the way she offered herself
to me . . ." He lowered his voice, until it was a rumble in
her ear. "Shall I tell you? Do you want to know what an
utterly shameless whore does to tempt a man?"

She took a deep breath. "Yea," she whispered, "I want to
know." And she did. She was fascinated. What was the secret
to enticing this proud, virile man? Once she knew, would
she be able to lure him to her bed anytime she wished?

He moved his hand down to stroke her breast. "It was in
a room full of men—knights, squires and retainers. There
was a table along the center of the room, and the Syrian
danced there. She wore little bells tied around her ankles,
and someone hidden in the shadows played a drum. Her costume was scandalous. It covered her from neck to ankles,
and yet revealed near everything. The fabric was so sheer
you could see her nipples and the shape of her buttocks."

Nicola licked her lips, thinking of dancing for a room full
of men, letting them look at her the way Fawkes looked at
her.

He moved his hand to her other breast and flicked his
finger across her nipple. "She danced from one end of the
table to the other, then moved back the other way and stopped
in front of me. She put her hands on her groin and peeled
away the piece of fabric covering her there." He paused.

"Underneath she was shaved, the lips of her cunny bare and hairless. And at the top of her cleft was a gold ring."

Nicola felt spellbound. She could see the woman flaunting herself to Fawkes, blatantly, crudely, offering him that which he'd vowed not to take.

He took a breath and trailed his hand down Nicola's belly, letting his fingers come to rest in the dark coils of her maidenhair. The darting quivers inside her grew more intense. "I found out afterward that some of the knights had paid her to show herself to me. They thought they could make me forsake my vow."

He fondled the dark hair beneath his fingers. Nicola longed to change position, to give him better access, but she also wanted to hear his tale, and feared he would never tell her the rest of it if she distracted him. "What did you do?" she whispered.

His stroking grew more intense. Nicola moved her hips fractionally. He was almost touching the little nub at the very top of her cleft. She fought the almost unbearable urge to tilt up her hips and open her legs.

"I got up and left," he said. "As provocative and exotic as she was, I knew that she would show herself the same to any man who paid her. And I also knew that she would not smell like you, or"—he paused as he found the nub, then pressed his mouth against her hair—"taste like you."

Surrendering, she moved her thighs apart. She could resist no longer. Let him know she wanted him to fondle her, to do the things that he'd promised.

"You always smell so good," he said, "as sweet this meadow. And your cunny, when I tasted it, was pure, luscious . . . paradise."

She closed her eyes and moaned. "Please," she murmured. "Taste me now. Put your mouth on me. Lick me."

"I will. I will." His voice caressed her ear, the vibrations of it tangling and entwining with the heated quivers fanning through her body. "But first, I will do other things. I promise, this time I will take it slow. I will not leave an inch of you untouched."

She groaned again, as if she could not wait. Fawkes knew a surge of triumph. The cool, disdainful lady of Valmar lay limp and helpless in his arms, trembling with sexual hunger.

With his free hand he pushed her hair aside and kissed her neck. His other hand played between her thighs, rubbing her clit, petting and stroking the soft outer lips of her quim. She squirmed, clearly wanting more, wanting him to touch the hot, wet inner lips. He could feel them beneath his hand, burning, swollen, as she writhed with need. How sublime to put his mouth on them, cool them with his breath, spread them so her sheath was revealed, pink and slippery.

He took a deep breath, fearing his own control would not last. Her bottom was pressed against his cock, and he was hard to bursting. He released her and sat back. "Turn toward me," he said.

She did so. Her face was flushed. Her eyes wild and dilated.

"Lie back," he said. "Spread your legs for me."

Her color deepened as she obeyed him. Her breathing grew more rapid, and he could see the pulse throbbing in her neck. His gaze traveled slowly down her body. The hard, wine-pink nipples thrusting up from the white mounds of her breasts. The flat, narrow belly. The black moss of her maidenhair. The rosy bloom of her cunny, vivid between her slim, graceful thighs. Magnificent. Did he have the strength for this, a long, slow seduction?

He took a breath and moved to sit between her thighs. Leaning over her, he fondled a nipple. "Your breasts are fuller than I remember," he said. "The nipples darker. I wonder if they taste the same?" He cupped her breast in his palm, making the nipple thrust out even more, then dipped his head to take it in his mouth. Fierce enjoyment swept through him. He licked lightly at first, then used his teeth, grazing her, then sucked deep and hard.

She was making little wordless moaning noises. Writhing. He gave her other breast the same thorough attention, then straightened. Moisture shone on her nipples, their dark pink hue echoed in the roseate velvet of her cunny.

He shifted slightly to ease his burgeoning erection, then put his hand on her belly, feeling the smooth skin. "Your skin is so fair and creamy," he said. "And so soft. I like to look at the contrast between our bodies. You're so smooth and delicate, while I'm tanned and hard and hairy."

He took both hands and followed the curve of her hips down to her thighs, then up again, feeling the sleek, delicious curve. "Your hips are wider than I remember, as well. From bearing a babe, no doubt." He took a breath. "It pleases me." He smiled down at her lasciviously. "More to hold on to when I thrust into you." He looked up at her face and saw her eyes widen with expectation.

He squeezed her buttocks, raising her hips slightly. At the motion, she arched her back, offering her cunny. He paused, fighting for control. The urge to press his lips to her there was almost unbearable. Finally, he released her bottom and brought his hand to her mound, splaying her with his fingers, touching her lightly. "Your quim is different, too. Stretched from bearing a babe. That pleases me, as well. Now you can take me better. I could never have done what I did to you yesterday three years ago."

"Please!" she gasped, sounding frantic. "Don't make me suffer anymore. Touch me! Fill me! Take me!"

He almost took pity on her, but then he remembered his plan. He took his hand from her mound and pulled down his braies. She moaned and leaned back, eyes closed, obviously expecting that he would enter her. "Nay," he said. "I have not tasted you yet. Nor have I decided how I will love you."

He put his hand on her mound again, trying to ease her. His fingers milked slippery wetness from her as he said, "There are so many positions for a man and a woman to find pleasure in. Do you want to learn about them?"

Her eyes opened, as if she were curious despite her need. She nodded.

He bent over her and blew on her cunny. She gasped.

"There is the way we did it the first time. The woman on her back, legs spread. She can also close her legs to hold the man tightly, or raise them up so he can thrust deep. Or bend her knees and open herself to him that way." He kissed her, caressing her delicate folds with the merest pressure from his lips until she shuddered.

He raised his head and continued. "There are the two ways we did it yesterday, with the woman sitting, legs spread and the man standing, or with her bent over something while he enters from behind. Or, the woman can get on her hands and knees while he is behind her, or lie down flat on her stomach, or lie flat and spread her legs."

He nibbled lightly, then sucked her whole swollen cunny lips into his mouth, suckling the moisture from them, hot and salty. She gasped and moaned and clutched violently at the blanket.

He drew away, thinking he would tell her every position he knew, so she could choose. "The woman can sit on the man while he lies down. Or they can both sit while she wraps her legs around his waist. Or he can lie down and she can sit backward on him."

He laved her with his tongue, licking the wetness from the outer lips, then the inner ones, then the oozing slit between. "Or they can stand," he said, raising his head, "while he braces her against something and thrusts into her. Or she can wrap her legs around him as he holds her up."

He paused, thinking. There were more ways, he knew, but he doubted that she would fault him for not mentioning them. Then he thought of another intriguing position, although it was not really fucking. "These are all ways they can join and mate," he said. "But if it is simply a matter of pleasuring each other, there are many other things they can do, ways to arrange two bodies so that they both gain satisfaction." He licked upward along her cleft, then sucked her engorged clit into his mouth. She screamed. He waited until she stopped bucking with her hips, then released the tender nub.

He wondered if she was still listening to him or if she was too caught up in the intensity of what he was doing to her to care. "If a woman wishes to pleasure a man while he does the same to her, then they can lie head to feet so she can take him in her mouth while he sucks her sex."

She went still at this, as if stunned. He wondered if she would ever do such a thing with him. It was one of his fiercest longings, but not for this day. All this love play and crude erotic talk had taken his control to the edge. If she were to take him into her mouth now, he would explode. He did not think she was ready for that. For that matter, if he were to manage to last at all, he must enter her soon.

"Tell me," he said, looking at her face. "Which position do you desire to try?"

Fourteen

Nicola shook her head, unable to answer. She was in a frenzy of arousal, so overwrought with the urgent craving to have Fawkes enter her or satisfy her in some other way that she could not think. "Whatever . . . you . . . wish . . ." she finally gasped out.

"Whatever I wish," he repeated. He stretched out over her although their bodies did not touch. "A tantalizing thought." He kissed her mouth. "Perhaps for now we should not try any of the exotic ways."

She kissed him back, mentally begging him to release her from her torment. She had done everything she knew to coax him to mount her. "Please," she whispered. "Fuck me any way you wish."

She heard him suck in his breath and knew her crudity surprised him. She did not care. That was how she wanted it. Uncontrolled, passionate, like the wild, unholy mating they had engaged in the day before.

He hesitated, as if he wanted to draw things out further. Then his shaft was against her, pressing deep.

Despite her arousal, he had to push hard to penetrate her. And then he was in. Glorious, dazzling heat. Soothing the ache, stretching flesh that had been too long tense and engorged.

"Lift your legs," he murmured, and she did so, feeling how this brought his shaft even deeper inside her. He moved, thrusting, and she felt the jolt of his balls, teasing against her bottom. The sensation was exquisite. He plunged into her, hard. His balls slapped against her, and she grasped his hips, struggling for something indefinable.

His rhythm inside her quickened. She raised her legs higher. Spread them wider, greedy for every delicious stroke of his shaft. In and out. Searing friction. The cadence of his thick lance striking her womb.

Her body wrenched with the force of her climax, and she dug her nails into his back, moaning.

He felt her peak and allowed himself his own blessed release, pouring his seed into her, his body twitching out of control. She seemed to melt beneath him. As she lowered her legs, he slid out of her, then lay sprawled on top of her, enjoying the cushion of her woman's body, the scent of their sex mingled with her rarified fragrance. She squirmed slightly and he knew she was uncomfortable. He rolled off of her, covering his eyes against the bright sunlight.

Well, so much for his plan to bring her to the edge and then ask her the questions he wanted answers to. When she'd told him to *fuck her any way he wished,* that had undone him. It was so raw, so unlike the cool, elegant lady he thought he had wed. Her words had aroused him so much his body seemed out of his command. But now he was in control again. He hoped.

He opened his eyes and turned to look at her. She was sitting up. Her glossy ebony hair tangled loose over her shoulders, half covering her breasts. Her lips were red and swollen. She was so beautiful. Bewitching. Perhaps that was the reason more than a few men called her "witch." There would be no better time than this to ask her the things he must know if he was to sleep sound tonight.

He reached up to toy with her hair. She turned and smiled at him. "Was it better today than yesterday?" he asked.

She gave a shiver, her gray eyes alight. "I would not want to say. Are not heaven and paradise the same?"

Sweet praise. It made him want to preen like a strutting cock. Still, he would not be put off. "But yesterday was in a crude shed, and we were both half soaked and ravaged by the storm." He paused a heartbeat. "Tell me, where were you coming from when you sought shelter there?"

Her eyes changed, narrowing almost imperceptibly. "I . . . I was coming back from an errand in the forest."

He took a strand of her hair, playing with it idly. "What sort of errand?"

He saw her breath catch. Knew that she wanted to pull away from him. Perhaps flee. He counted the heartbeats until she answered. "An errand for Glennyth, the healer."

"You do errands for the village women?" He raised his brows. "I know that Glennyth is a high-and-mighty sort of wench, but you are her lady."

She flushed. "The errand was really for me. The herbs I was gathering were for my benefit." She took a breath. "I went to Glennyth for a sleeping potion, and she did not have the things she needed to make it. She claimed she did not have time to fetch them, that she was busy with something else and that if I wished her to make the sleeping draught, I must find the herbs myself."

"And it took all day?" He released the strand of hair he was fondling and sat back, the better to watch her face.

She gave him a quick, furtive look, then said, "I got lost. I've ever been poor at directions, especially in the woods. I got turned around and could not remember which way I had come. Then the storm came and it was even harder to find the path."

"But you did," he pointed out. "You arrived at the shed in the midst of the storm."

She nodded. "I thought to get Buttermilk to shelter. Then I was going to seek shelter for myself in Glennyth's croft."

"But instead, you found me."

She nodded again.

He was struck by the absolute certainty that she was lying.

Her tale seemed preposterous. "You told the man at the gate that morning that you were going to help with the Lammas celebration," he pointed out.

"I was. I didn't think my errand would take so long. I thought Glennyth would make me the potion and I would be on my way."

"Why did you take your horse? It's only a little ways to the village. Why didn't you walk?"

She looked at him rather defiantly. "Why do you and your men take horses when you go to the village?"

"That's different. We're knights." It didn't matter, he thought angrily. She was lying. Trying to cover up her true motive—which was that she had ridden into the forest intending to meet someone. The familiar jealousy surged through him.

She rose from the blanket, still naked, utterly delectable. "Is there a stream or spring nearby?" she asked.

He wanted to tell her to clean herself in front of him as she had the day before. But he also wanted her to leave so he could think clearly. It was impossible to do so when she was around, looking so distractingly erotic. "Yea, there is a little runlet near where we left your horse. To the right, down the ravine."

She bent down and put her stockings and shoes back on. He watched her. Then she turned and walked gracefully into the woods. He decided that he was going to have her again this day, scheming liar or no.

Nicola squatted down and splashed the cool water of the stream over her crotch, easing the sticky soreness. She stood up, dripping, and stared unseeingly into the trees. Did she dare go back there? He'd trapped her.

The story that she'd gone into the woods to gather herbs was a pathetically lame one. But she'd been unable to think of anything better. His question had caught her completely

Take **4 FREE** Books!

We created our convenient Home Subscription Service so you'll be sure to have the hottest new romances delivered each month right to your doorstep — usually before they are available in book stores. Just to show you how convenient Zebra Home Subscription Service is, we would like to send you 4 Kensington Choice Historical Romances as a FREE gift. You receive a gift worth up to $23.96 — absolutely FREE. You only pay for shipping and handling. There's no obligation to buy anything - ever!

Save Up To 30% On Home Delivery!

Accept your FREE gift and each month we'll deliver 4 brand new titles as soon as they are published. They'll be yours to examine FREE for 10 days. Then if you decide to keep the books, you'll pay the preferred subscriber's price. That's all 4 books for a savings of up to 30% off the cover price! Just add the cost of shipping and handling. Remember, you are under no obligation to buy any of these books at any time! If you are not delighted with them, simply return them and owe nothing. But if you enjoy Kensington Choice Historical Romances as much as we think you will, pay the special preferred subscriber rate and save over $7.00 off the bookstore price!

We have 4 FREE BOOKS for you as your introduction to
KENSINGTON CHOICE!

To get your FREE BOOKS, worth up to $23.96, mail the card below or call TOLL-FREE 1-800-770-1963
Visit our website at www.kensingtonbooks.com.

Take 4 Kensington Choice Historical Romances FREE!

YES! Please send me my 4 FREE KENSINGTON CHOICE HISTORICAL ROMANCES (without obligation to purchase other books). I only pay for shipping and handling. Unless you hear from me after I receive my 4 FREE BOOKS, you may send me 4 new novels - as soon as they are published - to preview each month FREE for 10 days. If I am not satisfied, I may return them and owe nothing. Otherwise, I will pay the money-saving preferred subscriber's price plus shipping and handling. That's a savings of over $7.00 each month. I may return any shipment within 10 days and owe nothing, and I may cancel any time I wish. In any case the 4 FREE books will be mine to keep.

Name _____

Address _____ Apt No _____

City _____ State _____ Zip _____

Telephone ( ) _____

Signature _____

(If under 18, parent or guardian must sign)

KN072A

4 FREE
Kensington
Choice
Historical
Romances
are waiting
for you to
claim them!

(worth up
to $23.96)

See details
inside....

||..||..||....||...||.|.|..|.|..|.||..|.|..|..||..|

KENSINGTON CHOICE
Zebra Home Subscription Service, Inc.
P.O. Box 5214
Clifton NJ 07015-5214

off guard. The way he'd pleasured her had made her think that things were going to be all right between them. But she was wrong. For all she knew, he'd planned on doing this. Taking her here, arousing her until she was witless, then ensnaring her with his casual question.

She should have expected he would ask her sometime, and been prepared with some plausible excuse. It was stupid of her not to have thought about it. But he'd distracted her so. Since their coupling in the shed, all she'd been able to think about was how good it felt and how she could get him to do it again. She'd forgotten how she must always be wary, always think about protecting Simon. She'd given in to her selfish desires and now her son might be in danger. He would not let the matter go, she was certain of it. He would keep asking questions. A shiver of fear afflicted her. What had she done?

She bent down again, giving her quim another few splashes. Damn her traitorous body! It made her too vulnerable. Maybe now that he'd satisfied her most urgent desires, she'd be able to maintain better control. Even if she let him bed her again, she had to make certain that she did not once more slide into that mindless pit of sexual need.

She straightened and walked back to find Buttermilk. Her kirtle was lying somewhere nearby. It would afford her some sort of protection against his avid, hungry gaze.

She'd put on her gown again. It was the first thing he noticed when she came back to the meadow. It made him angry. Was she trying to hide her body from him as she hid her deceit? Well, he would have it off of her soon enough. He was not finished with his wife this day.

She came and sat down on the blanket. He'd laid out the food he'd brought, although his appetite was gone. She picked up one of the apricots and took a delicate bite. He couldn't tell for certain, but he thought her hand shook as she ate. "How did you find this place?" she asked.

"I discovered it years ago. When I was squire at Valmar. I used to bring serving girls and wenches here." He wondered if she was jealous. If she was disappointed that she wasn't the first woman he'd tumbled in this meadow. "I was quite popular with the maids. For a time, I thought that's why Mortimer had chosen me to fuck you."

She flinched at the word when he used it. Maybe it was different when they weren't engaged in the throes of passion. It did sound cold and crude that way, reminding her how Mortimer had used her, treating her like a broodmare.

"Of course," he added, "I now know that my 'way with women' had nothing to do with it. I finally figured it out on the way to London." He pointed to his hair. "My coloring. Mortimer thought I looked enough like you that no one would question the babe's parentage." He gave a snort. "As if anyone who knew his taste in bed partners would believe he might be able to father a child.

"Of course," he continued, "there were so many times in the last few years that I agonized and worried that somehow he had found the means to rape you. I imagined you pregnant, not with my offspring, but his. And I wondered, if I came back and found you'd had a fair-haired, blue-eyed babe, what I'd do, if I'd ever be able stand the sight of Mortimer's whelp."

She rose abruptly. Her face looked stricken. Was it the mention of the babe that distressed her? Did she mourn it, or feel guilty that she'd killed it?

"You asked me about the babe before," she said. "I swear it died at birth. I used its limp body to taunt Mortimer, but that was only because I could not help myself." She turned her gaze on him, bitter and harsh. "Why do you keep bringing up this matter? Have I not endured enough?"

He felt sorry for her, but he also saw in her vulnerability and agitation a weakness, a means to pry the truth from her.

"There are those who say that you poisoned Mortimer, put a spell on him, cursed him with some foul malady. You cannot blame me for wanting to know a little about the woman who shares my bed. If you plotted against your first husband, what is to say that you won't do the same to me?"

"You are not Mortimer. You've given me no reason to despise you." Her words were cold, impersonal. They did not reassure him.

He said, very softly, "And should I ever give you reason to despise me, then you would deal with me the same way you did Mortimer?"

She took an agitated breath. "I don't believe you would ever be so cruel and vicious. You cannot imagine what he was like. For near a year, he kept me prisoner. Sometimes I lashed out, taunting and defying him. But always I had held something back, knowing that if I went too far, the beast in him would gain mastery over the man and he would kill me."

"But you did get the better of him eventually," he said. "Everyone says so, and I saw myself when I did battle with him, that he was not the same man."

She took another deep breath. "After the babe was born dead, I decided I did not care if he killed me. I not only taunted him, but threatened him. I told him that he would never have what he wished of me. That I hated him and prayed for his death. And then I told him that I had put a curse on him, that from that day on, he would not be able to become aroused, that his shaft would grow diseased and useless."

She gave a faint, slightly hysterical laugh. "I don't know what came over me. There was no force behind my words. But, strangely, he acted as if he believed me. A look of fear came into his eyes, and he left me, failing to bother to lock the door.

"I knew that I had discovered his weakness, his secret dread, and that somehow I could make use of it. I had my servant fetch Glennyth, and I asked her if she knew of some drug or potion that would make a man impotent. She said she did, and she gave me some. I dosed Mortimer's wine that night."

She shook her head. "Astoundingly, it worked. He came to my chamber and swore and raged at me, but I could tell that he was terrified. I played upon his fear, telling him that never again would he be able to indulge his unnatural taste for boys or find any sort of sexual satisfaction. I thought that the potion had caused his affliction, and I dreaded the day when the effects wore off and he regained his confidence. But even though I stopped dosing him soon after that, he remained fearful and wary. Never again did he lay a hand upon me. He stopped locking me in my chamber. Everything changed.

"His men noticed, especially FitzSaer. They accused me of witchcraft, or somehow poisoning my husband. But they could find no proof of any treachery. In fact, I had stopped doing anything at all. There was no need. Once I planted the seed in Mortimer's mind, it took root and grew, like a weed taking over an untended garden. His wits were naturally fearful and weak; it did not take much to push him into madness."

When she glanced at him, as if to see if he believed her, he found that he did. "I still remember when Mortimer came to your bedchamber after we'd made love and taunted you for being a slut when he was the one who had sent me to bed you." He shook his head. "I have thought since then that he was not right in his mind. It would seem that all you did was push him deeper into derangement."

"That is what I think. When I threatened him with what he dreaded most, it pushed him beyond reason." She hesitated, then said, "Do you blame me for what I did?"

"Nay, I can't blame you. You did what was necessary to survive." Fawkes picked up the wineskin and took a swallow. He did not blame her, and yet, he did not trust her, either.

She sat down again and picked at the roast capon and

cheese that he had brought. He watched her, thinking how remote and self-contained she looked. Hard to imagine that only a short while ago she had offered herself to him, begged him to take her. He liked her much better that way, open and unguarded and vulnerable. He put the wineskin down. "You're not eating much," he said.

"I'm not very hungry," she answered.

"I am. I'm insatiable." Her gaze flew to his face, and he knew she guessed exactly what he meant, that he was speaking of his sexual appetite rather than his desire for food. Would she try to act coy and demure?

She watched him with a kind of breathless alertness—like a doe that sees a wildcat ready to spring. Her obvious uneasiness reminded him that she had lied. It reminded him that he still had no idea where she was the day before. The thought made his cock, which was already rising, grow even harder. He wanted to possess her, control her, make her so irrefutably his that she would never dare betray him. He might never know the truth of where she was the day before, or if she had a lover. But he could make certain that from this moment on, she was incapable of even thinking about another man. He would fuck her until she surrendered, until she was his slave. "Take off your gown," he said.

The way he was looking at her made her want to flee into the forest. A short while ago, the naked hunger on his face had excited her. But her desire had fled when he said he would never be able to accept a child that looked like Mortimer. She had to think of her son, rather than her own base urges.

Yet, she could not deny him. It would only make him more suspicious and angry. She could sense an edge of menace in his voice when he told her to undress. She must make haste to obey him.

Jerking the kirtle over her head, she fought the urge to hold it over her crotch. She felt so exposed and vulnerable. She hoped he would not make her spread her legs for him again. But at the thought, a faint heat built inside her. Her body did not care that Fawkes might be a dangerous, ruthless man. Indeed, her body seemed drawn to that aspect of him.

"I've decided," he said.

She regarded him suspiciously, wondering what he had decided. Was he finally going to punish her?

"I want you on your hands and knees."

She swallowed. Her quim tingled in anticipation of how deep and hard he would be able to thrust his cock when she was in that position. But she didn't want to feel like that, her insides mushy and aching with surrender. She wanted to be cold and unmoved, to lie passively while he took his pleasure.

He began to undress. This time he took off everything. Last time he had only pulled down his braies, and she'd felt as if his keeping the rest of his body covered was a sort of tease, as if he knew he withheld something she desired. Now, having him bare himself completely seemed a kind of threat. She could see how aroused he was. His shaft jutted upward, huge and purplish. His balls dangled below, big and full. The memory of them slapping against her bottom made her whole groin tingle.

He nodded to the blanket, indicating he wished for her to position herself there. "Don't worry," he said. "I won't hurt you. I'll take plenty of time to ready you."

She should be relieved that he was not going to hurt her, she thought as she got down on her hands and knees. But she was not. What he was going to do to seemed worse. He was going to make her helpless with need.

He pushed her legs apart and spread her buttocks with his fingers. She took a shaky breath. His fingers stroked her quim lightly, teasingly. She felt her body responding, the aching heat that meant she was growing wet. He said, "You seem dry and tight." His touch was unrelenting, tormenting. But then she felt the wetness of his mouth against her naked, exposed slit and shuddered. She was powerless now.

She had not thought he would do this when she was in

this position. Thinking of her buttocks in the air, her legs spread so he could view everything, made her feel wanton, and incredibly, desperately, aroused. His lips played upon her skillfully. Stretching her, licking her, tantalizing her. Then he brought his fingers to her cleft, and she thought the twin torments would drive her mad. It felt as if she were gushing with moisture, but still he laved her with his tongue and caressed her with his lips. Still he played with the excruciatingly tender nub in her cleft.

She was moaning wordlessly now. Her whole body trembling. He had no doubts that she was ready, but he indulged himself a while longer. This was the only way he knew how to rule this proud, distant woman. He felt her body stiffen, and knew a rush of satisfaction. He had made her peak. Her sweet, hot love juice filled his mouth. He drew away for a moment, wondering how many times he could make her climax.

She gave a ravaged moan and he took pity on her. Though he thought he could make her beg him, he did not want to wait for that satisfaction. He was too impatient to fill her and thrust into her, over and over.

She felt the head of his shaft rub against her quim, softly parting her. He pushed in slowly, as he had the day before. But this time he did not seem to be doing it in order to spare her, but to increase her need. Inch by slow inch, he gave her his shaft. Big and burning, wrenching her open. Her quim convulsed, tightening and thobbing uncontrollably. She could feel her climax approaching and he wasn't even inside her all the way. He went still as she trembled and stiffened, the waves of her release racking her whole body. Then he began to thrust inside her.

She felt as if she would faint. The waves of sensation gripped her and would not let go. One after another, violent spasms made her quim contract and shudder, her womb pulse with sharp pangs of rapture.

He drove into her roughly, rapidly. A long keening cry

filled her ears and she was barely aware that it came from her mouth. He finally gave a yell and went still inside her. She could feel his shaft quivering, spilling hot seed deep inside her.

He waited until every spurt of liquid had filled her, then withdrew. He lay down on the blanket next to her. She collapsed beside him, dizzy and dazed.

It took a while to return to the reality of the flower-strewn meadow and the warmth of the sun upon her face. And the man beside her. Forever now she would be torn in two. Her heart belonged to her son. Her body to Fawkes de Cressy.

Fifteen

She was silent on the journey back to the castle, and several times Fawkes resisted the urge to turn around and look at her. What would be the purpose? If she had not given up her secrets in the last few hours, it did not seem likely she would do so except under torture. The thought appalled him. He could no more damage that exquisite body than he could batter his own flesh. If nothing else, he owed her something for the pleasure she had given him.

And, dear God, what pleasure it was. Mind-numbing, transcendent ecstasy. He was a lusty man, but he had never known lovemaking could be like that. As if their bodies were made exactly to fit, so that her cunny was the perfect size and shape to afford his cock maximum stimulation and delight. Her body was the most erotic, arousing vision there could be in the world. Everything about her beguiled him. Her scent and taste. The feel of her skin. By the saints, if he thought about it any more, he would get aroused again!

But nothing was perfect in this world. The woman who fulfilled his dreams had one fatal flaw. He couldn't trust her. Not with his life, and certainly not with his heart.

It was late afternoon when they rode into the castle yard. As he expected, as soon as he'd helped her dismount, Nicola excused herself, telling him that she must see to preparations for the evening meal.

Fawkes handed their mounts over to a hostler, then called

after the man to tell him to empty the saddle pack on the courser and give whatever food was left to the most deserving squires in the stables. Then he paused for a moment, trying to decide what to do with the rest of the day. He really wanted to go up to his bedchamber, lie down and close his eyes and relive the magic he had just experienced. But that seemed too hopelessly indulgent. He might be the lord of the castle, but he had a responsibility to set a good example and not lie about like a slugabed.

Instead, he decided to visit the knights' barracks, thinking he should make certain that all his men had made it back from the village the day before. As he started toward the barracks, he heard someone call his name. He turned and saw Engelard hurrying toward him.

"I saw you come in the gate with Lady Nicola," the knight said. "Maybe you've patched things up by now, but I did want you to know that I've figured out where she was yesterday."

Fawkes could almost hear his heart thudding with expectation. At last, he would learn at least one of her secrets.

"She went to Mordeaux."

Fawkes felt his mouth fall open in amazement.

Engelard nodded solemnly. "You know who told me? Sir Stephen. He's one of the knights you sent with FitzSaer. He came this morning with a message for you from FitzSaer that it's time to pay the masons. He wanted to know if you wished to pay them out of Mordeaux's funds or Valmar's since Valmar is the richer demesne and he will need the Mordeaux monies to pay the garrison this winter. You can ask Sir Stephen about the message if you want. He's in the hall."

"And Sir Stephen said that Nicola was at Mordeaux yesterday?"

Engelard nodded. "He would recognize her, since he was one of Mortimer's men."

Fawkes felt as if he'd been struck by a lance. Mordeaux?

What the hell was she doing there? And why had she made up such an elaborate, stupid lie rather than tell him the truth?

He went to the hall where Sir Stephen confirmed the story. He'd seen Lady Nicola arrive about midmorning. When he'd mentioned it to one of the Mordeaux knights, the man told him that Nicola frequently visited Mordeaux, at least every month or so.

With every word he heard, Fawkes felt his anger and turmoil deepen. There was no reason for Nicola to go to Mordeaux that frequently. *Unless she has a lover there.*

Nearly choking with jealousy and rage, he went searching for her. He wanted to kill every servant and page who told him blankly that they had no idea where she was. He finally learned that she was in the solar and climbed the stairs to the upper portion of the castle with slow deliberation.

Old Emma was with her. The stout serving woman was winding up some wool. She paused when she saw him, the roll of thread frozen in her hands. "Milady," she said in a strained voice.

Nicola, who was sitting on the window seat examining a piece of fabric in her lap, looked up. For the briefest moment, he saw fear in her eyes. Then the cool mask descended.

"Leave us," he said curtly to the servant.

Old Emma began to gather up the tangled skein of thread. Fawkes's jaw clenched as the servant fussed over putting it away in the sewing basket. Was she deliberately dawdling, trying to give Nicola time to think up more lies? "Get out!" he shouted.

The servant hurried out, moving faster than he would have thought possible, given her girth.

Fawkes paced to the far side of the room, afraid of what he would do if he got too close to Nicola. "You told me that yesterday you went gathering herbs in the woods." His voice came out in a bitter hiss. "But I have just been told that you were seen at Mordeaux Castle."

He saw the blood drain from her face, and he took a step toward her, trying to intimidate her.

She stared at the sewing in her lap. "It's true," she said. "I did go to Mordeaux."

"Why? What was your purpose in making such a journey?"

She licked her lips. "I am friends with the castellan's wife, that is, her husband was castellan before you sent Adam there. I went to visit her."

"If your errand was so innocent, why did you lie to me? Why make up a foolish tale about gathering herbs in the woods?"

Her head snapped up and her eyes flashed with anger. "After years of being mistrusted and gossiped about and called a witch behind my back, I have learned to lie about everything!"

"*I* have not mistreated you nor called you names," he answered coldly. "There was no reason to lie to *me!*"

"I did not think you would like it—my riding out alone!"

"You are right there. Indeed, I have half a mind to lock you away as Mortimer did." He glared at her, wondering if she might possibly be telling the truth. She'd probably had to learn to be deceitful and cunning in order to survive. It would be difficult for her to trust any man, even him. "Tell me, what is this woman's name, the one you went to visit?" he asked.

"Her name is Hilary, wife of Gilbert de Vescy."

He nodded. "Perhaps I will go to Mordeaux tomorrow," he said. "It's past time that I visited there anyway."

He watched her, gauging her reaction. She nodded stiffly, but otherwise her face was a blank, beautiful mask.

Nicola paced to the window. What was she going to do? There had to be some way to prepare Hilary for Fawkes's questioning. But how?

Fawkes had said he would go tomorrow. That gave her time. She could send a message to Hilary, alerting her to Fawkes's arrival and his purpose in coming. But who to send? It had to be someone she trusted, someone who would not reveal her to Fawkes. She sighed heavily. There was no one at Valmar like that. Except Old Emma, and she would never make it to Mordeaux, not in a day, certainly!

Nicola racked her brain. The message would have to be cryptic, mentioning Fawkes's arrival and not expressing her fears for Simon. She could send one of the squires, and tell him she wanted to make certain Mordeaux was prepared for Fawkes's arrival so he could be greeted properly. That was it. Since Adam was unwed, Hilary still served as chatelaine of the castle. It would be reasonable to send her a message explaining that Lady Nicola knew her husband was journeying there on the morrow and wanted to make certain the castle was prepared to entertain him with a sumptuous banquet.

The squire would not think anything odd in the message, but Hilary would. Given that Nicola had told Hilary of the strain between her and Fawkes, Hilary should guess that something was afoot. Not a perfect plan, but better than nothing.

Nicola started for the door. She would find the squire named William and set things in motion.

Fawkes stepped out of the recess in the hall where he had hidden and started after his wife. He followed her to the lower levels of the castle and out into the yard. She looked around, then hurried toward the armory.

He went to the gate tower and climbed the stairs. The knights on duty nodded to him. He spoke to them briefly, then went to the side of the tower that overlooked the yard.

He did not have long to wait. In a few moments, a squire walked briskly through the gate, not even pausing to look up at the guard. He continued across the bridge, then turned east, the direction of Mordeaux Castle.

Fawkes bit down hard. It looked like Nicola was sending a message to someone at Mordeaux.

He hurried down the tower stairs and through the gate. Although the youth walked quickly, it did not take Fawkes long to catch up with him. "You there, halt!" he shouted when the squire came in sight.

The squire turned. Fawkes recognized him as young William. A plain-faced, rather gawky fellow, just the sort to be overawed by a beautiful woman, to be willing to do anything to win her favor.

Fawkes approached, scowling. William looked like a frightened coney being chased down by a wolf, but, to his credit, he did not run. "Milord?" The young man gazed at him, brown eyes wide and alarmed.

"Where are you going?"

"Milord, I . . . I am carrying a message for your wife. I have not neglected my other duties, I swear it!"

"What sort of message? Who is it to?" Fawkes resisted the urge to grab the squire and shake the truth out of him.

"I . . . I . . . I'm supposed to tell Lady Hilary that you will arrive tomorrow. To make certain that the castle is ready for your visit."

"Ready? Ready in what way?"

"Why, to offer you a fine meal. Lady Nicola said in order to be able to prepare a banquet befitting you, the steward at Mordeaux must have warning so that they can either butcher a steer or send out a hunting party."

Fawkes released his breath in a sigh of frustration. He might have known. Nicola was cleverer than to send the message directly to her lover. And the way she'd worded it—as if she were a dutiful, considerate wife, anticipating her husband's needs.

Fawkes took a step back. The youth was visibly trembling. Poor bastard. It was not his fault that Nicola had ensnared him in her plot. At William's age, he would have behaved the same. "I'm sorry to frighten you," he said. "The fact is,

I've changed my mind about going, so there is no need for you to relay the message."

No, he would not go tomorrow. When he decided to visit Mordeaux, he would do it unexpectedly, so Nicola would not have time to send a message.

He nodded to the squire, dismissing him. The youth started off, then turned around once to glance at him. Fawkes wondered what the fellow made of his anger, his strange behavior. Was the whole castle whispering that Lord de Cressy did not trust his wife, that he obviously suspected her of cuckolding him?

He returned to the castle and started for the stairs to the ramparts, then changed his mind and entered the interior of the castle. On a whim, he made his way up to the solar. Nicola was there, sewing. He observed her a moment, and saw that it was a child's garment she worked on, which surprised him. She put it down quickly when she heard him enter.

"I intercepted your messenger," he said. "Since I have decided not to go to Mordeaux tomorrow, there is no point in sending word of my arrival. I would hate for them to prepare a banquet in my honor and have it go to waste." His voice dripped sarcasm.

He saw the flash of fear in her eyes, then she said, "Does this mean you accept my explanation for my visit there?"

"Of course. Why should you not visit your friend?" He moved near, so close that he could see her hands trembling slightly. "But next time, it would be well if you informed someone of your destination, or better yet, took an escort. There could be brigands or wolfsheads lurking in the woods and a lone woman is an easy target."

"Of course, milord," she breathed.

He stood there a while longer, trying to make her as uncomfortable as possible. From now on, he would have her watched every minute. If she did anything suspicious, he would confine her to the tower. A crude idea came to him, that the way he would make certain she did not escape was to take all her clothing away from her. Then she would be naked and accessible whenever he wanted her.

He reached out and grasped her by the hands. Her sewing fell to the floor as he raised her to her feet. He bent his head and kissed her, slanting his mouth hard upon hers, then, giving in to temptation, reached down to stroke her buttocks through the fabric of her gown. He lifted her, pressing her groin against his, and filled her mouth with his tongue. A brief kiss, but long enough to leave her gasping when he released her. "Don't lie to me anymore, Nicola," he said. "I am not Mortimer. I am not so cruel as he was, nor am I as much of a fool."

Nicola released the pent-up breath she'd been holding and stared after the retreating figure of her husband. She bent to pick up the shirt she had been sewing for Simon and experienced a wave of queasiness. Fawkes was getting too close to the truth, far too close. What if he started to put the pieces together—the baby that supposedly died at birth, her regular visits to Mordeaux? She shuddered.

Fawkes steadied the lance in his hand and pressed his thighs into his mount, urging the destrier forward. He focused on the red X painted on the shield of the quintain, tensing, counting the seconds. *Thunk!* The heavy lance struck the shield and the counterweight swung around, missing him by a hairbreadth. Cheers sounded around him, and Fawkes suppressed a smile and turned his horse to give it another go.

"Fawkes!" a familiar voice called. "Quit showing off and come over here."

Fawkes trotted his lathered destrier around the practice area to cool off the animal, then rode to where the watching knights and squires were gathered. He pulled Scimitar to a halt and dismounted. Handing the reins to his squire, he walked toward Reynard.

"You're a cruel bastard." His captain shook his head as Fawkes approached. "You know what's going to happen. One after another, every squire here is going to have to try to duplicate your feat, and most of them will end up unhorsed and lying disgracefully in the dirt. We'd better go into the castle right now and have one of the women start boiling up some self-heal and boneset to make poultices and salves for their injuries."

Fawkes shrugged, but could not altogether suppress his smile. "No one's ever died at quintain practice. It'll be good for them."

"Yea, but you shouldn't have made it look so easy. If you'd missed once, or at least let the counterweight graze you a bit, they'd have a better idea of what they're in for."

"This way they'll be prepared for the surprises of battle. Or the treacheries of women, for that matter."

"Still brooding about her visit to Mordeaux, are you?" Reynard asked.

Fawkes nodded grimly.

"Maybe you could coax it out of her."

"Tried that."

"Threaten her?"

"That's just made things worse. Now, she's so wary of me, I think she'd lie about what we were having for the evening meal if I asked her." Fawkes grimaced. Everything was falling apart. He hadn't touched his wife for two days, afraid that if he took her to bed, his anger and frustration would overwhelm him and he'd hurt her.

"Mmm," Reynard said thoughtfully. "That's one of the things I like about Glennyth—that we can talk so easily."

"I don't want to hear it," Fawkes answered sharply. "And what did you want me for, anyway? Were you simply trying to save Valmar's garrison from some bruises and broken bones, or did you have some purpose in interrupting me."

"Oh, I near forgot. I did fetch you for a reason. A group of musicians and mummers is passing by, returning from the fair in Shrewsbury. They wanted to know if the lord of the castle would be interested in a night's entertainment."

"So, that was the commotion I saw on the bridge earlier." Fawkes shrugged. "I hardly feel in the mood for merriment, but the servants and knights usually delight in that sort of thing. I won't deny them for my sake."

Reynard nodded. "I thought you would relent. In fact, I took the liberty of sending young Thomas to tell Lady Nicola that you'd given permission for them to perform and to suggest that she have the cook plan for an extra few mouths at the meal."

"Wise of you to send Thomas," Fawke said. "Perhaps since he's her darling, Nicola won't freeze him in his tracks with that icy stare of hers."

Thomas came rushing into Nicola's solar, his face flushed with excitement. "I'm supposed to tell you that a group of mummers and musicians on their way from the fair at Shrewsbury are to entertain us tonight!"

"Mummers and musicians," she repeated. Nicola's body went cold. How many caravans of entertainers traveled to the Shrewsbury fair? Could this be the same troupe that passed by earlier in the summer?

"What do their wagons look like?" she asked with trepidation "Are they the same ones that stopped around St. John's Day?"

Thomas nodded enthusiastically.

"Did you see the jongleur who was with them last time? The one with dark curly hair?"

"Nay, but I barely had a look at their wagons before Sir Reynard sent me to find you."

Please, God, she thought. *Let him not be with them. Or,*

*better yet, let him be bringing the news that Prince John has
no interest in a minor castle like Valmar.*

"What do you want me to do?" Thomas asked. "Go to
the kitchen and tell them we have visitors?"

Nicola nodded "I will be there soon."

Thomas ran off. Nicola took a deep breath, fighting for
control. She would go downstairs and see to the meal and
pretend nothing was amiss. And with luck, nothing was.

The performers had arranged their wains and other pos-
sessions on the far side of the castle in a makeshift camp.
The musicians were tuning their instruments, while the acrobats, garbed in their loose costumes, stretched and prac-
ticed their routines. A crowd had formed to watch, and
Fawkes, vaguely curious, joined them for a time. He was
about to continue on when a flash of brightness near one of
the wains caught his eye. There was a man standing there,
and the gold braid on his crimson tunic gleamed in the sunlight. The man was talking to someone, someone hidden in
the shadows, a woman. A strange sense of warning came
over Fawkes and he moved so he could see more clearly. His
insides went cold as he made out the woman's small, delicate
form and dark hair.

He took a deep breath. It was perfectly reasonable for
Nicola to speak to the entertainers, well within her responsibilities as chatelaine to discuss things like payment, timing
of their performance and a half dozen other practical con-
siderations. He was being foolish. Nicola would surely not
plan a liaison with a man she'd only just met.

Unless the troupe of entertainers had been here before.

Fawkes grabbed the nearest person he saw and demanded,
"These entertainers, have they been to Valmar previously?"

The woman, after getting over her surprise at being ac-
costed by the lord of the castle, nodded vigorously. "Aye,
milord. They were here soon after sowing time."

"You're certain it's the same ones?"

"Oh, aye. I remember the tumblers, I do. And that man there, talking to Lady Nicola"—she pointed—"that's Alan de Romy, a famed jongleur. Once sang for Eleanor of Aquitaine herself." Fawkes observed the jongleur through narrowed eyes. The singer wore his glossy black hair in long curls and his clothing was gaudy and bright. Hardly the sort of man he'd imagine appealing to Nicola. But then, how well did he really know her?

At last, Nicola moved away from the jongleur. She started in Fawkes's direction, looking distracted. When she spied him, her eyes widened and she hesitated. For a heartbeat, he saw guilt and fear on her face, then the serene mask descended. She approached him. "I was discussing payment with the entertainers," she said. "They wanted more than earlier this summer, and I told their leader that we would have to see the performance first."

Despite her cool, casual voice, he observed the rapid throb of her pulse in her neck. It was exactly as it had been when he'd asked where she was the day of the storm. Her words might be plausible, but he knew them for lies. Although he was raging inside, he said calmly, "You've done your duty. Now come and sit beside me in the hall." He grasped her arm, giving her no choice but to obey him.

Nicola let her husband escort her into the hall, her mind racing along frantically. Never should she have begun this dangerous intriguing. But a few months ago things had been so much different. She was desperate to be free of Mortimer, and so she had asked the jongleur, Alan de Romy, to carry a message to Prince John telling him that Valmar was ripe for the taking. The price for Valmar's submission was that she should have some choice in her next husband and that Mordeaux Castle should not be taken by force.

She had heard nothing over the past months, and she had decided that either Prince John had never received her message or, if he had, he had been too busy with his own problems to consider the future of Valmar. But just moments ago she had learned from Alan that he had indeed carried her message to the prince, and that John was very interested in Valmar. The saints help her, but what if her plotting brought an enemy army against them?

The thought made her stomach twist, and she glanced at Fawkes, wondering how she would tell him what she had done.

The hall bustled with servants carrying pitchers and jugs. At the plank tables, villeins and tradesmen and their families, knights and other castle workers all conversed eagerly, their sunburned faces growing more flushed as they imbibed the ale and ate heartily. Everyone—from the youngest page to an ancient toothless widow who had been brought from the village in a wheelbarrow—seemed to be in a fine mood. But Fawkes's state of mind could hardly be more agitated. Once again, he had caught his wife in a lie, and although he did not yet know what it meant, his suspicions enraged him.

He wanted to drag her off alone and threaten her that if she did not tell him what she really had been speaking of with the jongleur, he was going to beat her senseless. She sat beside him, rigid and pale, as if she guessed how angry he was. He could scarcely eat, and he was half relieved when a servant came and told him that the performers were ready.

He nodded grimly. "Tell the men to clear the tables away so there is a space for them to perform."

Nicola watched as the hall was readied for the performers. She would wait until the entertainment began, she decided, then tell Fawkes she had to use the garderobe. He surely could not refuse her that. All she needed was a moment to tell Alan that he must carry another message to Prince John, this time warning him that Valmar was now in the hands of a formidable crusader knight who would defend it valiantly.

She took a deep breath. Surely Prince John could under-

stand the difference between taking a castle defended by a
fierce, experienced warrior and one defended by a half-witted
drunkard. If only she could head off an attack before Fawkes
learned of her scheming. She could not tell him about this,
not now, when he was already convinced that she was a devious, meddling liar.

The sounds of tambor, cryth and viol filled the hall, and
the acrobats paraded out, dressed in their costumes of bright
rose and saffron. The two women wore short snug tunics on
their upper bodies while a sort of braies gathered at the waist
and ankles covered their legs. A short filmy skirt preserved
a bit of their modesty, although as they twirled in graceful
cartwheels and flipped head over heels, the lithe, graceful
shape of their legs and hips was clearly visible. They both
had dark hair and eyes and swarthy skin and looked as if
they might be sisters. Their long hair was restrained in a
single tight braid that whipped around wildly as they performed. Soon a man joined them, also dark and dusky-
skinned. He was not much bigger than the women, but his
superb muscles bulged beneath his snug costume, which was
dyed the brilliant shades of scarlet and apricot.

The man walked halfway across the hall on his hands, then
executed a series of flips that flung his body miraculously
high into the air. Gasps and exclamations erupted from the
crowd, and Nicola turned her head to observe her husband.
His expression had not softened, although he did appear to
be watching the performance.

She turned her attention back to the tumblers. The man
joined hands with the two women and the three of them
began to perform flips and cartwheels in unison. The acrobats paused and bowed. Another man appeared, donned in
vivid green and saffron. As the two men balanced the women
on their shoulders, Nicola cast another glance at Fawkes.
When should she excuse herself? Now, or wait a few moments longer? Having seen the players previously, she knew
that next the mummers would perform a raucous, silly skit

portraying a man and a woman taking a pig to market. As the husband and wife fought, near beating each other black and blue, the "pig" would escape and end up sitting on the lap of the one of the prettiest maids in the hall. Nicola had never understood the hilarity of watching people strike each other and shout insults, but she knew by the end of the performance most of those gathered in the hall would be so overcome with mirth, they would be wiping tears from their eyes. If Fawkes was like most of his fellow knights, he might be amused enough by the skit that he would take less note of her absence.

When the acrobats began their finale—forming a tower with their bodies—Nicola stood and mouthed the word "garderobe." Fawkes frowned at her, but made no move to stop her departure.

"You hedge-witted varlet!" the woman screeched. "With the money from the pig, we must buy a new cauldron. My old one has so many holes you could use it for a fishing weir!"

The man thrust his shoulders back and his chin forward, glaring at the woman. "We'll buy a plow!" he bellowed. He took a swipe at her, nearly knocking her off the table that served as their "stage." "Take that, you sow-faced, swag-bellied old wench!"

Behind the two, the "pig," who was really a man in a tan costume, complete with real pig's ears and a curly tail, waggled his rear end and farted loudly.

Loud guffaws of laughter sounded. Fawkes hardly noticed. He was aware of little except the fact his wife was no longer seated next to him. She'd been gone long enough, he thought as he got to his feet. Long enough that he might have a chance to catch her in her latest deception. Maybe she really had needed to relieve herself, but he doubted it very much.

* * *

"You must carry a message to John," Nicola insisted. "He must know that circumstances have changed at Valmar."

Alan de Romy spoke without glancing at her. "Nothing has changed. Valmar is in the hands of one of Richard's supporters."

"But instead of the drunken, worthless Mortimer, whoever John sends will be facing a seasoned knight who will defend Valmar most valiantly. It will not be an easy conquest, but a long, protracted siege!"

"Too late," the jongleur responded. "Things are already set in motion. It will not be the prince who actually leads the attack, but some baron who has other properties in this area and seeks to enlarge his power. I am to report to you that Mordeaux will be taken first, then Valmar."

"Mordeaux! In my message to the prince, I said Mordeaux must not be attacked!" Nicola drew her breath on a gasp. "They cannot take Mordeaux first! They cannot!"

Alan de Romy shrugged. "Of a certes, they can. Having asked for John's aid, you cannot be so choosy about how he goes about giving it. Obviously, he has decided that Mordeaux is the weaker fortress and should be taken first to create a base for the assault on Valmar."

Oh, sweet Jesu, what have I done! Nicola took another panicked breath. In her attempt to rid herself of Mortimer, she had inadvertently endangered Simon. And Fawkes—what would he do when he found out that Mordeaux and Valmar were in danger and she was to blame for it?

She clutched at Alan's arm. "You have to carry a message to the prince! You have to help me halt this disaster!"

He shook his head, his eyes regretful. "Lady, if I could aid you—" Abruptly, his expression turned to one of wariness. "I will be happy to sing the song that you request, Lady Nicola." He bowed stiffly and moved away.

Nicola gazed at the jongleur in puzzlement, then a strong hand clamped onto her shoulder. She turned and looked into the furious onyx eyes of her husband.

Sixteen

The rage on her husband's face filled Nicola with fear. He had seen her with the jongleur; he knew she was plotting something. She could not think what to say, how to explain. She had no opportunity to try, for Fawkes grasped her arm in a ruthless grip, and muttered through clenched teeth, "You're coming with me. I warn you, if you resist, I'll shame you in front of the whole hall."

She allowed him to guide her rapidly toward the stairway in the corner of the hall. This stairway led to her tower room, and the memory of being beaten and abused there by Mortimer intensified her dread. They were only a little ways up the winding stairs when Fawkes paused and thrust her against the wall. The rough stone rasped against her back. "How many times, Nicola?" he demanded. "How many times did he fuck you? Were you planning to meet him again tonight? Were you planning to cuckold me?"

Nicola blinked in surprise, then suddenly recognized his fury for what it was—jealousy. He did not think she was intriguing with the jongleur but arranging a tryst. "No," she whispered. "No."

Fawkes's fingers dug into her arm. She could feel the raw power of his grip; he could crush her bones without even trying. "You were touching him!" he ground out. "I saw you. You traitorous, lying slut!"

She shook her head, thinking frantically how to respond.

She could not let him believe that she and Alan were lovers. But how could she explain without revealing her ill-advised plot to deliver Valmar into Prince John's hands?

"Now I know why you were so eager for it. Some other man has aroused your needs and taught you how to get your pleasure." Fawkes was trembling, his voice taut. "Tell me, is his cock as big as mine? Does he lick your cunny as well as I do? Has he taught you things that I have not?"

Nicola shook her head again. She was mute with panic. What should she do? Faced with his senseless rage, it did not seem that anything she could say would possibly satisfy him.

She gasped as she felt him lifting her skirts with his free hand. He found her loincloth and tore it off her. "Are you wet already? Does your cunny go all slick for him like it does for me? Do you spread your legs as wide?" His fingers probed her roughly, opening her. He slid one inside. Deep. Despite her fear, Nicola felt her quim clench around him. Her body knew this man's touch so well. "Is that why you could take me from the back, because some other man had stretched your pussy and made it want as much hard cock as it can take?"

"Nay," she whispered. "No other man has ever touched me. No one. I swear it."

"Lying, treacherous bitch!" His voice hissed through his teeth.

She began to tremble. What if he did not believe her? What if he decided to kill her?

"Don't move," he whispered. He released her, leaving her pressed against the wall of the stairwell, her skirts falling back into place. She waited, panting with dread as he fumbled with his own clothing. He freed his cock, then jerked her skirts upward. His other hand found her quim, and his fingers spread her thighs. With his other arm, he lifted her up, bracing her body against the wall. He used his hand to position himself, then shoved into her, driving hard with his hips.

Nicola groaned at the pressure. The weight of her body thrust her down upon him. She was impaled. He used his free hand to touch her where they were joined. "Did he do this to you?" He ground out the words between gritted teeth. "Did he fuck you hard and fast against a wall?" As he said the words he began to thrust into her, his powerful hips ramming his cock deep.

She whimpered. It did not quite hurt, but lingered on the edge of pleasure-pain. He changed position, grasping her buttocks with both hands as he pressed her against the wall and lunged into her with deep, violent thrusts. She clung to his shoulders, searching for some stability as the world heaved around her. The maelstrom raged as he pounded into her. Her quim throbbed and burned. Her body shuddered with mindless, intense sensation. With a final savage thrust, he groaned in release, then went still.

She waited breathlessly, feeling limp and weak. He slid out of her and released her so she slid down the wall. Her legs nearly gave out, but she braced herself to keep from collapsing. Dampness trickled down her thighs. She closed her eyes, thinking that perhaps now that his jealous lust was spent, he would leave her.

But a few heartbeats later, he grasped her arm again. "Come," he said. "We're not finished yet."

He started to push her up the stairs ahead of him. She took the steps slowly, legs quivering. When they reached the tower room, he opened the door and pushed her into the bedchamber. As she looked around, a sense of suffocating dread came over her. She remembered Mortimer beating her in this room, remembered him striking her and knocking her to the floor.

Fawkes fetched a cresset torch from the stairwell and lit the night candle, then placed the torch in a bracket on the wall. As light filled the room, she saw his face, flushed and grim. "I know you want more," he said. "You're insatiable when it comes to having a hard cock inside you. But I am merely a man, and it will take a while for me to become aroused again. In the meantime, you will entertain me. You will tell me what you did with this jongleur, this Alan de Romy. You will tell me everything he did to you."

"He did nothing," she breathed. "Nothing. I hardly know the man. I have scarce said a dozen words to him in my life."

"I did not ask what endearments he spoke to you, but what he did to your body."

She shook her head. "Nothing." How could she convince him? Why was he so obsessed with the idea that she had a lover?

His eyes narrowed. "So many times you have lied to me, Nicola. Why should I ever believe what you say?"

She shook her head again. It was hopeless. He saw her deceit and misunderstood it.

He stared at her, then grabbed her by the arm and pulled her against him. He put his hands upon the sides of her head, his fingers twining in her hair. His face was still an angry mask. "You are so beautiful," he said. "How can someone so lovely be such a lying, scheming bitch?"

She gazed at him, paralyzed. He glared at her for long moments, then slowly began to stroke his hands along her face, his touch changing from taut, barely controlled violence to breathtaking gentleness. "But you are mine," he said. "And I will get my pleasure of you this night."

He stepped back, his eyes narrowing speculatively. "I know a means of speeding my arousal so I can fuck you again." He motioned toward the bed. "I want you to take off your clothes and lie down facing me. Then I want you to pleasure yourself as you were doing on our wedding night." He smiled faintly and his nostrils flared. "I've often thought of that night. How I should not have left but stayed and watched. And learned. When I am fucking you, I am too caught up in my own pleasure to observe you properly. I

want to know what your cunny looks like as you climax. I
want to observe the expression on your face as you reach
your peak. And I want to see how you satisfy yourself so I
can learn exactly what pleases you. How you like your
breasts caressed. Your clit touched. How many fingers you
put inside yourself to pretend it is a thick, hard cock."

She licked her lips. Her body seemed to go from terrified
to aroused in seconds.

He nodded toward the bed. "Show me. Perhaps if you
convince me that I am the man you desire, the *only man,* I
will not lock you away as Mortimer did."

Lock her away? She did not think he would do such a
cruel thing, but she could not be sure. He was incredibly
jealous and possessive. If he locked her up, she would never
be able to visit Simon. Besides, what he wanted was not so
awful. When he'd burst in on her that night when she was
touching herself, she'd been embarrassed, but that did not
mean she'd wanted him to leave. She thought of the Syrian
dancing girl showing herself to him. There was a kind of
power in enticing a man. Perhaps if she could arouse him
enough, she would not feel as if she was at his mercy. "I
need your help undressing," she said.

He came and undid her laces. As soon as they were loose,
she pushed him away. She wanted him to see her clearly as
she removed her clothing. Slowly, she drew off her bliaut,
then lifted the bottom of her shift and pulled it up inch by
inch, gradually letting him see her legs, her crotch, then her
belly and breasts. Slipping the shift over her head, she let it
fall. She stood still for a moment, letting him look at her.
Her nipples were hard, thrusting out.

She removed her filmy veil and began to undo her braids,
remembering he had once smoothed out the plaits, his fingers gentle, almost reverent, as he slid them through her hair.
When her hair was loose, she shook it out, then combed
through it with her fingers. It fell in a dark curtain over her

shoulders. She pushed it back, wanting to make certain he saw her body clearly.

She sat on the stool by the bed and began to remove her shoes and stockings. This time she did not try to be ladylike, but very deliberately raised her foot to the stool so that her quim was exposed. Slowly, she removed her shoe, then her garter, then rolled down the silk stocking. She placed her foot on the floor, then wriggled her bottom against the cushioned stool and arched her back to thrust her breasts out.

Glancing at him, she saw that he was watching her intently. His heated gaze increased her own arousal, which was intensifying by the moment. There was a thrill in having him watch her, in his knowing that she was deliberately provoking him.

She removed her other shoe and stocking in the same manner, then went to the bed. Sitting down on the edge of the bed, she leaned back, spreading her legs wide. The air felt cool against her wet quim, still full of his seed. She was almost too wet, she decided. But she would not wipe it away, she had a better notion.

She dipped her fingers in the moisture and brought it to her mouth. She rubbed it over her lips, then licked them. It tasted faintly sweet, yet salty. She gave him a bold, mocking look, then touched herself again. This time she took a fingerful of the creamy liquid and rubbed it on each of her nipples. As the moisture started to dry, it made the sensitive skin tingle.

She was still very wet. Closing her eyes, she rubbed her fingers over the slippery folds of her quim. She was vaguely sore from the rough way he had thrust into her, her mound slightly swollen. It made her deliciously sensitive. She fondled the outer lips, rubbing them, then stretching them gently between her fingers.

She opened her eyes and looked at him. "Are you hard yet?" she asked tauntingly.

"Perhaps. But not hard enough for you. With a horny

wench like you, it takes a rock-hard cock to fill you properly." He nodded to her. "Continue. I want to see you reach your peak. I want to see what your cunny looks like when you come."

She was not certain she could do what he asked. It was difficult for her to satisfy herself, especially now that she knew he could do it so much better. She climbed onto the bed and spread her legs wide, making certain he saw all he wanted. She began to stroke her breasts, trying to remember how he touched them. He was wrong if he thought he could learn anything from her. He knew her body better than she did, and his touch was infinitely more arousing than her own.

"Tell me what you are thinking," he said.

"I'm thinking about you, about how your big, callused hands feel against my skin."

"Touch your cunny and tell me how it feels."

She moved her hand down and began to stroke. "I'm imagining that it is your mouth kissing me there, remembering the way you suck on me, then lick each fold." She slid a finger a little ways inside "I'm thinking about when you put your tongue in me, just enough to tease me, to make me ache and quiver." She pushed the finger deeper. "About when you ease you cock in little by little, until I can scarce bear it."

It was working. Somehow, between describing each detail and knowing that he was watching her, her body had begun to respond. She could feel new wetness and the tight, squeezing ache of need. It almost hurt, demanding to be soothed, demanding the succor of his big, hard cock. He was right. She was like that, hungry, insatiable, in thrall to that mysterious, rigid rod of flesh between his legs.

She eased the finger in deeper, trying not to think about what a poor substitute it was for what he could offer her.

"Touch your clit," he said. "The little nub buried in the top of your cleft. It's the seat of a woman's pleasure."

"Is that what you would do?"

"Yea. If I wanted to make you peak quickly, I would rub it lightly and rapidly."

She closed her eyes and concentrated, arching her hips. Little flickers of sensation fanned out, building. She strained and moaned. A faint ripple stirred inside her, nothing like the roaring waves she felt with him, but a kind of release.

She opened her eyes, panting.

"That's nothing compared to what I can make you feel," he said. "Is it?"

She shook her head. "Are you hard yet?" she asked.

"Almost." He began to remove his clothing.

What a lie that was, he thought. He was as rigid as a slab of ice. But he was not ready to enter her. Then, all too soon, the feel of her tightness, her incredibly responsive body would make him climax and it would be over. He wanted their loving to last the night.

His anger was fading. Part of it was her beauty, weakening him as it always did. But part of it was that now his violent fury was spent, he'd begun to doubt his own accusations. How could she possibly think she could manage to get away long enough to make love with another man? To plan a tryst when her husband was right there, watching her—it seemed an act of incredible foolishness. And Nicola was no fool. No, she was cunning and clever and unpredictable, always.

Besides, if she were to pick a lover, surely she could do better than that foppish bastard of a jongleur. Maybe she had let Alan de Romy bed her in the past, before she knew a *real man* was coming to claim her. But he could not hate her for that, even if the thought of it enraged him.

Yet, she was a maddening, deceptive woman, and he wanted to make certain she knew that he controlled her body, if not her mind. He wanted her to never forget this night, to have the pure sexual ecstasy he'd make her feel be branded upon her soul forever. He wanted to make her come and come, until she was breathless and limp and faint with exhaustion.

She was looking at his groin, very boldly, very obviously. She wanted him to know what she wanted. Yea, he thought, perhaps he could bear to tease her that way for a little while.

He began to undress, pulling off his tunic and linen shirt, then sitting down on the stool to remove his boots, his hose and cross garters. He had not felt quite at ease in either the shed or the forest. His soldier's training made him feel that he must always be ready to jump up and defend himself, even in the midst of lovemaking. But now he was in a private bedchamber, in a well-defended castle. It seemed safe to be totally naked. Clearly, that was what she wanted. Her gaze was avid, hungry. "Do you like what you see?" he asked.

She nodded, licking her lips. He thought of the position he'd told her about, "head to tail" so that they could both pleasure each other with their mouths. But he doubted if he could last that way. The feel of her mouth on him would be too unbearably arousing.

He approached the bed. She reached out and grasped him. He winced at the white-hot surge of pleasure that whipped through his cock. She started to play with the tip, tender, innocently exploring. He gasped. Nay, this was not what he wanted. He wanted to make her come, not himself! He pushed her hand away.

It was unfair! Nicola thought angrily. Never would he let her touch him, to learn the secrets of that magic rod of flesh he called his "cock." As soon as she started to caress him, to experience the delicious sensation of iron hardness beneath velvet skin, he drew away.

She regarded him resentfully. He met her gaze with a hooded, threatening look. "I will let you enjoy my cock, but it will be the way I wish it."

He climbed on the bed and arranged the pillows beneath his head so his shoulders were slightly raised. His cock thrust almost straight upward, fascinating her. "Now, straddle me," he said.

She realized that he wanted to try the position where the

man lay down and the woman mounted him. The idea filled
her with tingling expectation. How gratifying to be on top
for once. She moved over him.

"Wider," he said, staring at her quim. "You'll never be
able to take me unless you spread your thighs and open yourself for me."

She took a shaky breath, aching and ready once again.
She opened her legs more, showing him everything. "Now,"
he said, "hold my cock in one hand and spread your cunny
lips with the other."

She closed her fingers around rigid heat, then touched
herself, spreading the wet, soft folds. Carefully, she placed
the blunt, thick arrow tip of his cock against her quim. He
thrust his hips upward, impaling her.

He grasped her buttocks and pulled her down. Hard. She
gasped. Searing pressure. Too much of him. Too deep. "Relax," he said. It sounded as if he were gritting his teeth. He
reached to touch her where she was stretched around him.
"Don't fight it. Think how much you want it. How much
you enjoy my big cock inside you, filling you, rubbing, stroking."

She took a deep breath, panting. The tension built inside
her. She could not relax. She felt as if she were going to
burst. He reached up to touch her breasts. "What I like about
this position, is that I can watch you. I can see your lovely
face, see your breasts with their swollen, rosy nipples." He
fondled one of them, and she felt an answering echo of pleasure deep inside her. He caressed her nipple, then flicked his
finger over it. Then he put both of his big hands on her
breasts and kneaded. Shimmering fire erupted inside her.
She shifted her hips restlessly.

"That's it. Find how you like it best inside you. Find the
position where my cock touches the deepest, most sensitive
part of you." He moved his hands from her breasts to her
buttocks. He spread her that way, forcing her pelvis down
upon his. His fingers teased in the tight crack of her bottom,

then played with her quim from behind. She writhed with agonized craving, searching for something, something . . . He thrust his hips upward suddenly, giving her what she sought. She moaned, feeling her body squeezing tight around him, the convulsive waves of her climax rippling through her.

He felt her peak and gritted his teeth, staying as still as possible. Her cunny grabbed him, compressing tightly, pulling him deeper, as if her pulsing womb was trying to suck the seed from him. But he would not give in yet. He wanted to make her helpless with satiation first.

When she began to relax, he lifted her off of him. She opened pleasure-slitted eyes and stared at him. "Nay, I have not come yet," he said. "I want to do more things to you first."

Although it seemed impossible, with the waves of her release still washing through her, his words aroused her. She was panting and weak, and yet, her body wanted more. She truly was insatiable. And he was reveling in it, she could see. Finally, she knew what he meant to do to her, drive her mad with sexual pleasure, kill her with ecstasy.

He shifted positions on the bed, so he was sitting to the side. "Lie down," he said. "Face down."

Slowly, still trembling, she obeyed him.

"Now, lift your bottom into the air. Nay, leave your face and arms on the bed. Then, spread your legs. Wider."

This was the most wanton, lewd position he had yet devised, worse than being on her hands and knees. Her bottom was in the air, displaying everything for his pleasure. She did not know what to expect—the warm wetness of his mouth, the hard pressure of his cock, the teasing caress of his fingers. She waited in expectation, her quim clenching, ever ready for the next delight he could offer.

Hard fingers, slightly rough. He squeezed the lips of her quim together, and her insides reacted with another pang. Each time he pleasured her, it seemed to grow more and more intense. As he slid a finger inside her, then two, she climaxed again. He waited, fingers buried deep, while she arched her back and went rigid, the blood pounding in her head.

Heartbeats passed. His fingers were still inside her. The ache built again. She could feel the moisture dripping out of her. He slid his fingers out slowly. She immediately felt bereft and wanting. His breath caressed her, then he tongued her gently. She writhed, barely able to endure it. "Mmmm," he said. "I can taste you, your come, so hot and sweet. How much can I make flow from you?"

"Please," she whispered.

"Please, what?"

"I don't know," she gasped. "I don't know what I want. To rest perhaps. I feel as if I will faint."

"But I have not made you peak this way yet, with my mouth."

She shuddered, groaning. But her quim did not care how weary and trembling she was. It responded as eagerly as ever as he mouthed her. His hands gripped the place where her thighs joined her body and his fingers played along the front of her cleft, spreading, stroking, easing near her clit, then tormenting it with light, quick strokes. So much stimulation. Every sensitive part of her aroused and provoked. His mouth against her quim, both hands squeezing her buttocks, fondling the crack between, one finger brushing her clit. Her insides wrenched as the tension built. And then it came, the crest of a wave of rapture, drowning her. She could not breathe, could not think, could only tense and strain and scream.

She finally came to awareness again and collapsed on the bed. He ran his hand down her back, soothing, then patted her buttocks. She groaned. "I have not found my release yet," he said. He leaned over her, smoothed her hair away from her face and kissed her neck. "You don't have to do anything. Just lie there. You're so wet you'll barely feel me enter you." Once more he spread her thighs. Her body was limp and unresisting. As he'd said, her cunny was so slippery he slipped in easily.

He sighed in satisfaction. She fit him so well now. After so many climaxes, her sheath was so slick and pliable she could take all of him with the first penetration. He began to move, enjoying the slight tightness, but also the comfortable ease with which he slipped in and out. He moved rapidly. No need to worry about hurting her, making her ready. She was perfect. Divine, exquisite cunny. The best in Christendom, he thought.

His pleasure built. He drove in hard and fast, uncaring whether she was responding or not. Her body was passive, accepting, offering the fuck of his dreams. He came, groaning. His body buckled as the currents of ecstasy pulsed through him, along his cock into her womb.

He rested a moment, then pulled out with another groan. Rolling over onto his back, he closed his eyes and waited for his heartbeat to slow. Now he could sleep. The thought came to him that he had never slept with Nicola. He reached out and pulled her close. *Mmmm*. To hold her close, to know the comfort of her soft, silky woman's body.

She felt him relax against her. For now at least, she was grateful that he slept. She could not have endured much more. He had fucked her near unconscious. His hand pressed against her breast, but not in a lustful way. She sighed, giving in to deep contentment herself. There were still so many troubles between them, so many secrets and lies. But for this brief time, she would not worry about them. She would enjoy this moment of perfect bliss.

He woke abruptly. The woman in his arms shifted and sighed. Nicola. He had often dreamed of this, of lying next to her in the aftermath of their pleasure. The torch was extinguished; the night candle was near guttered out, but there was still faint light to see her by. He sat up to look at her, the flow of her long hair over her body, the curve of her hip, her fine, elegant features. Mysterious, beguiling Nicola. When would he ever know her mind, discover the answers to the puzzling secrets haunting her beautiful gray eyes? If she did not have a lover, what was she keeping from him? This night had been miraculous, but he wanted more from his wife than just the delight her splendid body could offer. He wanted her heart. He would not give her his until he knew he could trust her.

He puzzled over the matter, trying to put the pieces together. Mordeaux, he thought. Maybe it was the key. Maybe if he went there, he would find some clue to the mystery of his wife.

He lay back down. A few more hours of sleep, then he would ride to Mordeaux and see what he could find there.

Seventeen

When Nicola awoke, sunlight was streaming into the room through the unshuttered window, and there was no sign of Fawkes. She felt uneasy, wondering where he was. Had he gone to talk to Alan? To threaten him? She very much feared that the jongleur would reveal her secret. In a panic, she rushed to the door and called for Old Emma. Even when the servant did not sleep on a pallet outside the room, she usually waited near in the morning for Nicola to rise so she could help her dress and do her hair.

The old woman came waddling in. "Ah," she said, regarding Nicola's nakedness. "It's just as I had hoped. Ye and Lord Fawkes are finally getting some good of each other."

"Help me dress," Nicola demanded, ignoring the servant's words. "Hurry now. There's no time to waste!"

"Why must we hurry? What sort of trouble are ye in now?"

"I must speak to the jongleur before Fawkes does." Nicola took an exasperated breath. "I can't explain now. Suffice to say that Alan de Romy has knowledge that Fawkes can't learn about."

Old Emma shook her head. "The entertainers are gone. Left this morning at first light. Milord did not rise early enough to catch them, nor did he ride out after them, so ye can rest easy on that account. Now he's busy getting ready to ride out to Mordeaux."

"Mordeaux?" Nicola felt her heart skip a beat. In a panic, she pulled away from Old Emma, who was trying to fasten the lacing on her gown. "Oh, dear God, no, he can't go there. What if someone tells him about Simon?"

"Relax now. No one at Mordeaux knows about Simon except Hilary and Gilbert, and they'd not betray ye, I don't believe it."

"But what if he learns about my visits there? What if he puts the pieces together? He already knows I gave birth to a baby boy."

"A babe that everyone thinks was born dead," Old Emma soothed. "Why should he go looking for a child he does not think exists?"

Nicola took a deep breath. Perhaps Old Emma was right. There was no reason for Fawkes to discover Simon. But still, she could take no chances. "I must get ready quickly anyway," she said. "I intend to go with Fawkes when he rides out."

"Mmph," the servant snorted. "If Lord Fawkes wants ye to go with him, ye will. And if he don't, ye won't."

"I'll convince him," Nicola said tightly. "Somehow."

"I want to go to Mordeaux with you." She'd found Fawkes in the stables and voiced her demand in a cool, confident voice. "My friend Hilary is expecting another child and I want to take her a special herb mixture from Glennyth, something to settle her stomach. I promised her that I would bring her some."

He regarded her thoughtfully. "You look a bit disheveled this morning. I did not know you usually wore you hair loose outside of the bedchamber."

Nicola flushed. She had not taken time to have Old Emma braid it. She'd not thought he'd notice.

"You look . . . beguiling. But I'd rather not have my men enjoy your beauty—which you should save for me alone. "

His eyes narrowed. "Tell me, why did you not mention Lady Hilary's condition before this? It might better have explained your last visit there."

"I didn't think of it." He was trying to fluster her, but she would not let him. One way or another, she would go with him. "Please," she said. "It would relieve my mind to see Hilary and talk to her."

"Yea," he said thoughtfully. "You may go."

"First, I must go to Glennyth's croft in the village and pick up the medicine for Hilary. Will you also give me leave for that errand?"

"Since the village is on the way, why don't we meet you at the healer's croft and travel from there?"

She nodded. "Meet me there in one candle hour."

"What was that all about?" Reynard asked, coming to stand beside Fawkes.

"I don't know. Perhaps you can entice the truth from Glennyth after we leave for Mordeaux."

"Huh," Reynard answered. "As if she would tell me anything. But I will have a pleasant time trying to coax it from her anyway."

"By the Lady!" Glennyth exclaimed. "Your troubles seem endless. No sooner do we solve one difficulty than another arises." She paused in examining packets of herbs, then looked at Nicola thoughtfully. "The crux of all your problems is Simon. If you would only tell Fawkes the truth about his son, none of this plotting would be necessary."

Nicola shook her head. She only had a few moments alone with Glennyth. She did not want to spend it arguing. "I have told you, I cannot do that. My husband is a man of intense passions, in every way. I fear that his capacity to hate is every bit as great as his capacity to love. I will not risk Simon's safety to my husband's uncertain temper."

"And so, once again, you scheme and intrigue, hoping

that your plotting will have the result you desire. And never does that happen. Always something goes awry and you are forced to contrive something else to extricate yourself from disaster."

"Are you saying that I should not have hidden Simon away?" Nicola demanded. "That I should have endured Mortimer's domination and cruelty with meek acceptance?"

"Nay, but Fawkes is a different man than Mortimer was. There is reason to hope that he might come to care for Simon and accept him. Reynard has told me a bit about him, and he does not sound like a man who would harm a child, regardless of his feelings for the father, or who he supposes the father to be."

"Perhaps Reynard does not know Fawkes as well as he thinks. My husband told me how much he dreaded the thought that I might have borne Mortimer's child. And the look on his face when he spoke of the matter was not pleasant! I must protect Simon at all costs."

"And cost you, it may," Glennyth grumbled. "It is one thing to meddle in matters of the heart, the women's world of love and lovemaking. But when you interfere in the man's realm of power and war, pride and honor, you put yourself at grave risk. It is a cruel, brutal world, driven by rules and beliefs that profit no one. For ambition and pride, men will do anything, even destroy that which they love."

"The very reason I must keep Simon a secret," Nicola said coldly. "Now, will you help me, or not?"

She seemed very distant and secretive even now, Fawkes thought warily. They had ridden almost all the way to Mordeaux and Nicola had scarce said anything. Even when they stopped beside a stream to refresh themselves with a drink, she had remained brooding. It gnawed at him, her eagerness to join him on this journey, her visit to the healer's croft. But at least she was with him now, where he could see her and watch the expressions on her face. He would observe her carefully. Maybe she would slip up and reveal something.

Mordeaux Castle. Fawkes watched the weathered keep come into view. It seemed smaller than it had a month ago when he had first arrived, ready to claim it for his own. Compared to Valmar, it *was* small. It had been built some years before Valmar and had a simpler, less strategic layout. He could see that FitzSaer had made some improvements. The ditch had been cleaned out and the curtain wall repaired on one side. But still, compared to Valmar, the castle seemed worrisomely vulnerable. Apparently, the keep had only one well, and a shallow one at that. In the event of a siege, Mordeaux would not be able to hold out long.

The castle gate was open and there was brisk traffic to and from the village. They entered the keep and were greeted by Adam FitzSaer. "Milord." He bowed to Fawkes, then glanced at Nicola. Dutifully, he bowed to her, then turned his attention to his lord. "I expected you would visit to see how things are progressing. Come, have some refreshment in the hall, then I will show you what has been accomplished."

"Refreshment is not necessary. We stopped to drink only a short while ago." Fawkes nodded to Nicola. "My wife has come to see Lady Hilary. Apparently she is with child. My wife promised to bring her a tonic to ease her unsettled stomach."

"I didn't know Lady Hilary was expecting," FitzSaer said.

Nicola did not respond, her queenly disdain implying that a mere man could not be trusted with women's matters. One of the squires helped Nicola from her horse. "I will be in Lady Hilary's solar if you need me," she told Fawkes.

He waved her away. Fawkes turned to FitzSaer. "Tell me. Who among the Mordeaux knights do you trust? Who has been here long enough to tell something about my wife's relationship with the former castellan's wife?"

* * *

"You're certain he's getting better?" Nicola leaned over the bed and stroked her son's soft curls as he slept.

"It's merely a slight summer ague," Hilary assured her. "He really is much improved, although his nose is stuffy and he naps more than usual. But when he's awake, he's as alert and cheerful as always. Joanie had the same thing and she is completely recovered."

"Oh, my poor baby." Nicola sighed. "You were sick and I was not here to comfort you." An aching pain tore through her. The thought that Simon might fall ill and die distressed her so much she could scarce breathe. "If ever he gets something like this again—anything, even the slightest cold or colic—I want you to send word to me."

"Of course, milady. But what will I have the messenger say? Are you going to tell your husband about Simon? Is that why you are here?"

"Nay, he must not know about him." Nicola shook her head emphatically. "If anything happens, send a message saying that one of your children has fallen ill and that you need me. My husband accepts that we are friends, that I would want to help you in time of crisis."

"Of course, milady. Whatever you wish." Hilary's voice was brittle. Nicola gave her a sharp look. "You think I am making a mistake in not telling him, don't you?"

"Yea, I do. He is bound to find out someday, and then I fear it will go ill with you for keeping such a secret from him."

"Why is he 'bound to find out someday'?" Nicola demanded. "No one at Mordeaux knows about Simon except you and your husband." She left the bed and approached Hilary. "Have you let something slip? Does FitzSaer guess that Simon is not your son?"

"Of course not! FitzSaer pays little attention to me or my family. Indeed, he lets me continue to supervise the servants and order the castle household as I see fit!"

Nicola took a deep breath. She should not take out her

worry and distress on poor Hilary. She needed her, not only to protect Simon but to help with the new strategy she had devised. "I'm sorry," she said soothingly. "I know you have done your best for Simon, and I thank you from the bottom of my heart. I appreciate your loyalty and I am afraid that I . . . I must call upon it once again."

Taking a deep breath, Nicola told Hilary about sending the message to Prince John in early summer, and the answering message the jongleur had brought. Then she told her about her plan to have Mordeaux surrender before it could be attacked.

"Jesu, lady, what you suggest is a kind of treason!" breathed Hilary, her tawny freckles stark against her milky skin. "If de Cressy discovers what we have done, he is likely to dismiss my husband, if he does not kill him instead!"

"If Fawkes discovers the plot, I will take all the blame. I will tell him that I *ordered* you and Gilbert to do this thing, and you had no choice but to obey."

"For me, that might serve, but not for my husband. What man would accept that another man would feel that he must obey a woman rather than his lord?"

"I promise you, all will be well with you and Gilbert. And you must see that this is not only for Simon's protection, but the protection of your children as well. If Mordeaux is besieged, everyone inside the castle will be in danger. Are you willing to risk that Joanie and young Gilbert might starve or go thirsty?"

"If Mordeaux is besieged, then de Cressy will come with reinforcements. He will defend the castle, I have no doubt."

"Does the idea of a pitched battle outside the walls of Mordeaux make you feel more secure? I do not think whoever John sends will easily allow this property to slip through his fingers. Nay, there will be bloodshed and suffering aplenty."

Hilary went to a stool near the small glazed window in the solar and sank down. "What a coil. I see your reasoning.

If we surrender the castle, no one will suffer. But then Fawkes and his men will come to reclaim Mordeaux and there will be fighting anyway."

Nicola shook her head. "Once they feel Mordeaux is secure, the attacking army will turn their attention to Valmar. The main battle will take place there."

"And then?"

"I have no doubt my husband will prevail. And once he has defeated the enemy army, it will be easy to convince those who hold Mordeaux to surrender it. The prince's army will leave, and you and your family, and Simon, will be safe." Even as she reassured Hilary, Nicola wondered if all of this would indeed come to pass. Was it not possible that the siege of Valmar would be long and costly? And what if, heaven forfend, Fawkes were defeated?

Nay, she would not think such things. All that mattered was that Mordeaux surrendered quickly, so that the main thrust of the fighting would be away from her son.

"I have the drug here." She patted the leather pouch she had brought to the solar. "All you have to do is put a small measure into a wineskin and take it to the men guarding the gate. If you can find a means to drug FitzSaer, all the better. The main thing is that your son must carry a message to the enemy commander, telling him to wait until night and then circle around so that they can enter the castle by the postern gate, which your husband will make certain is open and unguarded. Once the enemy is inside, the garrison will see that there is no point in resisting and surrender the castle."

"But my husband's sworn duty is to guard Mordeaux against enemies. How can I ask him to betray his oath?"

"What of his responsibility to his own family? Would he dare put you and the children at risk?"

Hilary bit her lower lip, looking agonized. Nicola pitied her, knowing what it was like to be trapped between two choices, neither of them comfortable nor pleasant. But she had no doubt that Hilary would choose as she had, doing what she had to do for the sake of her children. She also had no doubt that Hilary would be able to sway her husband. Gilbert de Vescy was a good man, but a weak one. That was probably why Fawkes had sent FitzSaer to serve as castellan.

"There is another thing," she added. "I have told Fawkes that you are with child, as a means of explaining why I am bringing you the pouch of herbs. He has told FitzSaer, which means the whole castle will soon hear the tale."

"And what do I tell everyone when my belly fails to swell?"

"Miscarriages are common. After the castle has surrendered, you could take to your bed, saying the stress of everything has made you ill. Then Gilbert can announce soon after that you lost the babe. It is reasonable enough under the circumstances." Nicola looked at her friend, so frail and harassed-looking. When life battered Hilary, she bowed and surrendered. She would never have survived being married to someone like Mortimer.

"I'm sorry to ask another boon of you," she said, "when you have already done so much for me. But think of it this way—you are doing this for Simon and your own children. If the castle is besieged, your son is of an age to fight. I cannot think that you are ready for that."

"Oh, Holy Mother, no!" Hilary cried. "Gilbert is but fifteen." She took a ravaged breath. "I could not bear to lose him. I could not."

"Exactly how I feel," Nicola said with a sigh. "I will do anything to protect Simon. Anything."

"You've done well," Fawkes said. "But the lack of a secondary well still worries me." He paced to the edge of the curtain wall and looked down. "In the event of a siege . . ." He let his voice trail off.

"Do you expect one?" FitzSaer asked. "Not to be overbold, but I don't really understand why you worry so much about Mordeaux's defense. As far as I know, the castle has not been attacked outright since the days of the conflict between Maude and Stephen."

Fawkes gazed out at the rich lands around the keep, gradually edging from green to gold as autumn approached. "Maybe I've spent so many years of my life at war that I see enemies over every hill and swell in the landscape." He shook his head. "But there is an uneasy feeling inside me that will not go away. Besides, it hurts nothing to be prepared."

FitzSaer nodded. "I'll not argue with you there, milord. I have no complaint against your orders. I merely wished to know if I should be more on my guard than I already am."

Fawkes turned and smiled at the castellan, trying to shake off his apprehensive mood. "You've done well, FitzSaer. I know that if nothing else, I can trust you to hold Mordeaux until I can arrive with reinforcements."

They sat in Mordeaux's hall, enjoying a repast of roast duckling, pickled eggs, stewed borage and blancmange with plum sauce for dessert. Nicola sat beside him, with FitzSaer on her right. To Fawkes's left sat Lady Hilary, and next to her, her husband, Gilbert de Vescy, the former castellan. Fawkes watched Lady Hilary carefully. She did seem pale and ill at ease; maybe she really was with child. He'd found out very little so far. All he'd been able to learn from the garrison knights was that Nicola visited Mordeaux regularly, spending her time in Lady Hilary's solar. She had been coming for over two years, ever since she'd been able to intimidate Mortimer into letting her leave Valmar.

He also watched Nicola. She appeared poised and reserved, as always. But he was intrigued to see that every so often, someone would come up to the high table to speak to her. Serving women, older knights, craftsmen, even skullery girls sought her out to say a few words, to say that it was good to see her back at Mordeaux and to reminisce about when she was a little girl growing up there. At Valmar, his wife was honored and respected. Here at Mordeaux, she was *loved*. The people's obvious affection for his wife made him uneasy. If they had to choose whom they would be loyal to, he did not think it would be him.

When Nicola rose, murmuring that she was off to see someone's new baby sleeping in a cradle near the hearth, Fawkes mentioned to Lady Hilary the fondness with which his lady wife was regarded.

"She grew up here," Lady Hilary said. "It's natural that we consider her one of us." A fiery blush suddenly lit her pale complexion. "That is to say, milord . . . not that we don't think the same of you, but . . ."

"You can be forthright with me, madam," Fawkes assured her. "I understand that I am a stranger here, an object of suspicion and wariness. How could it be otherwise, especially after what you endured at the hands of Mortimer? But I promise you, I intend to be a fair and dutiful lord and protect Mordeaux from all enemies."

Lady Hilary gave him a look of distress. Fawkes felt a tingle of warning flash down his spine. She rose abruptly. "I'm suddenly not feeling well," she said. "It must be something I ate."

She hurried across the hall.

Fawkes turned toward Gilbert de Vescy. "When is the babe due?"

"Sometime next spring, I suppose."

Fawkes pursed his lips thoughtfully. Why did the man not know for certain when his own child would be born?

Nicola glanced nervously at the tall canopied bed in the bedchamber adjoining the solar. It was traditional to offer the best bedchamber to the overlord of the castle when he came to visit, but Nicola dearly wished that Gilbert and Hilary could have found some excuse not to give up their room in this circumstance. She did not want to sleep with Fawkes, not here, with Simon only a short distance away in the solar. It seemed a betrayal of her son to share a bed with a man who might well be his enemy. At Valmar, it did not bothered her so much. But here, with her son so close, the potential danger Fawkes represented to her beloved Simon agonized her.

She especially did not want to engage in heated, uninhibited lovemaking with Fawkes this night. But how was she to explain her wishes without making him suspicious? He was suspicious enough already. He'd watched her like a bird of prey all evening, and said something to poor Hilary that made her flee the hall like a frightened coney.

Nicola sighed. She'd have to think of something, some excuse.

Fawkes took his leave of FitzSaer and climbed the stairs to the living quarters of the de Vescy family. Nicola should be waiting for him, and he was very much looking forward to being alone with her. His eagerness for her body never seemed to wane. He was also reassured that he had found no sign that she was plotting against him or engaged in any sort of treacherous behavior. Maybe it was simply her nature to be secretive and circumspect. Maybe those years with Mortimer had scarred her so badly, she'd learned to habitually lie about her actions. Over time, if he treated her with kindness and affection, she might begin to trust him and tell him the truth.

He walked through the solar, where Lady Hilary was sewing. She rose quickly and curtsied, then pointed to a doorway. "In there is the room where you will sleep."

"Are you feeling better?" he asked.

"Yea, milord."

As he crossed the room, he saw two young children sleeping on a pallet. He stopped and looked down at them. One child had reddish braids, while the other, a boy, had bright golden curls. "Yours?" he asked.

"Yea," she said. "The girl is called Joanie, the boy, Simon." She approached the pallet and pulled the covers up over them.

Fawkes felt a pang. They were near the age his own son would be if he hadn't died. He shook off the thought, then turned and went into the room that Hilary had indicated. Nicola was already in bed when he entered. He undressed and slid in beside her. She did not move, and he wondered if she was asleep. He reached out for her, pulling her close. She was wearing a shift, which surprised him. After all they had shared, it seemed absurd that she felt the need to wear anything to bed.

He started to pull up the shift, anticipating the delicious feel of her cool, smooth skin. She pulled away from him. "Nay, Fawkes, not tonight. I ate something that made my belly ail."

He went still, his hand still clutching the thin linen of her shift. There seemed to be a virtual epidemic of stomach problems in this place, although he had found nothing wrong with the food. The cynical thought made him want to ignore Nicola's plea, but then he decided that if she did not want him, he would not force her. Never before had she refused him, or even acted unwilling. Either she really was ill, or something here at Mordeaux had made her withdraw from him. What could it be? What was the piece of the puzzle that he was missing? He turned on his back, contemplating the matter as he stared into the darkness.

Nicola listened, waiting for his breathing to deepen and slow so she would know he was asleep. Only then would she be able to relax and sleep herself. She shifted, trying to ease the ache of desire in her traitorous, wanton quim.

That part of her did not care if her bed partner was her enemy. To the senseless, thoughtless core of her, this man represented succor and comfort and endless delight.

Eighteen

Fawkes was in the practice yard, watching two squires face off with blunted swords, when he saw Reynard hurrying toward him, accompanied by a familiar-looking youth with reddish-gold hair and pale gray eyes. "This is Gilbert FitzGilbert of Mordeaux," Reynard said in a taut voice. "He says the castle has been taken."

Fawkes's mind reeled. He had been at Mordeaux only a few days before. Although he worried about a siege, the castle had seemed sound and impregnable otherwise. "How?" he rasped.

Reynard looked at the youth beside him. "Maybe young Gilbert should tell you himself."

After swiping his brow, the youth began his tale. The day before, an army had appeared outside Mordeaux's gates. The castle garrison had made preparations to defend the castle, but during the night, someone—a spy or cohort of the enemy apparently—had opened the postern gate, and by morning, Mordeaux was full of enemy knights. Reginald FitzRandolph was the leader of the conquering army, and he said he was claiming the castle in the name of Prince John.

"What happened to FitzSaer?" Fawkes demanded. "Where was he when all this was taking place?"

"The spy in the castle drugged many of the garrison knights, including FitzSaer," Gilbert answered. "By the time he woke in the morning, it was too late to defend the castle. The enemy was already inside."

"And where is FitzSaer now?" Fawkes could scarcely keep the fury from his voice. All his preparations had been for naught. No one could plan for that sort of treachery from within.

"FitzRandolph and his men put him in the oubliette."

"And how did you get away?" Fawkes asked. "How did you manage to escape so you could come and tell me this?"

"There was a lot of confusion in the bailey. I managed to slip away."

Warning prickled down Fawkes's spine. A disciplined and experienced commander would never let a messenger "slip away" so they could ride to warn of his approach. Either FitzRandolph was a fool, or he wanted Fawkes to know he had taken Mordeaux.

Fawkes glanced at Reynard, then said, "You've done well in coming to warn us, Gilbert. No doubt you are hungry and thirsty after your ride here." He motioned to one of the squires. "Alexander will escort you to the castle and show you where to wash, then take you to the kitchens to get something to eat. I'll meet you in the hall shortly. I'm certain I'll have more questions."

Fawkes gave Alexander his instructions, then the two young men started for the castle. As soon as they were out of earshot, Reynard said, "This all seems very strange, Fawkes. How could one man bring down a castle? He would have had to drug all the guards, then somehow open the postern gate and keep watch until enough of the enemy were inside to seize control." He shook his head. "If you ask me, it sounds like several people were involved. Maybe the former castellan and his knights. And even some of the servants."

"That's an interesting thought," Fawkes said. "Especially since the former castellan is Gilbert de Vescy, and that young man"—he jerked his head to indicate the youthful messenger striding off behind a Valmar squire—"is his son."

Reynard frowned. "Then it cannot be de Vescy. For if it was, why would he have his son come and tell us what has come to pass?"

"Indeed." Fawkes said. "Unless his message is meant to warn someone inside Valmar." He looked toward the castle as he said this, and a sick feeling built inside his stomach. Had de Vescy's son come to tell Nicola that her scheme had worked? But why would Nicola want Mordeaux to fall into enemy hands? Unless she was in league with FitzRandolph. Was he her lover, the man she had hoped would take control of Valmar and rescue her from Mortimer, instead of him?

"What's wrong?" Reynard said. "Why do you look like that, as if you had been struck a blow?"

Fawkes shook his head. He didn't want to talk about his terrible suspicions with anyone. *Please, God, let it not be true,* he prayed silently. To Reynard, he said, "Go to the castle and tell everyone what has taken place. Have them begin preparing for attack. We need bundles of arrows and other weaponry brought out. Barrels of pitch to use in setting fire to ladders and scaffoldings if they try to scale the walls. Have the women fill all the water butts they can find and gather clean, washed fleeces to use in putting out fire. Put the cook and steward on notice to reduce rations and keep a close guard on the keys to the storerooms. And send someone to the village to warn them there."

Reynard nodded. "And where will you be?"

Fawkes clenched his jaw. "I will be with my wife, trying to discover where her loyalties lie."

Nicola hurried toward the solar, her heart pounding in her chest. She well knew why Fawkes had sent Thomas to find her and ask her to meet him in the solar. Her husband was going to ask her what she knew about Mordeaux falling into enemy hands.

When she first heard the news that Mordeaux was taken, she'd panicked and considered fleeing the castle before the gates were closed. But reason told her that running away would only confirm her guilt in Fawkes's eyes, and she still had a faint hope that she might be able protect her son and yet not utterly destroy things between her and her husband. If things proceeded according to her plans, the invading army would eventually be defeated by Fawkes and he would reclaim Mordeaux. Once Simon was safe, she would turn her attentions to winning back her husband's trust. But to have any hope of that, she must now pretend to know nothing about Mordeaux's capitulation.

When she reached the doorway and saw him pacing across the solar, her resolve wavered. Could she manage this, another lie? So far, she had not been very convincing. She suspected that every day since they left Mordeaux, his doubts had grown, rather than decreased. Silently, she cursed herself for deciding to tell him that her courses had come. She'd wanted to avoid his lovemaking, since it aggravated her sense of guilt and made her feel like a traitorous, unfeeling slut who could allow a man to pleasure her one moment, then aid his enemies the next. But now she regretted spurning his attentions. Not only had she lost her last chance to experience the miraculous pleasure he could give her, but she suspected her sexual reticence had lessened her hold on him and made him view her more in cold, suspicious terms. *Too late now,* she thought sinkingly.

She entered the solar. He heard her approach and turned to face her.

Fawkes probed his wife's elegant countenance, searching for cracks in the queenly mask. Was there not hint of guilt in her eyes, a certain tension in her stance, as if she were prepared to flee at any moment? "Have you heard the news about Mordeaux?" he asked.

She nodded.

"Do you not think it strange that the castle was taken so easily?"

"I know little about defending a castle, milord."

Milord? Why was she suddenly acting as if they were strangers? It angered him. He took a step toward her, waiting to see if she flinched. He thought he discerned a subtle tensing of her muscles. "So, you know nothing about this?" he said. "Nothing at all?"

"You examined the defenses just days ago." Her voice was faintly accusing. "I thought you were satisfied that the castle was secure."

"No castle is secure against treachery."

"Mordeaux was taken by treachery?" She looked surprised, either that or she was feigning surprise.

"That is what Gilbert FitzGilbert says. He says that someone drugged the guards, then opened the postern gate for the enemy." She said nothing. He continued, "FitzSaer was one of those drugged, but I have not heard where Gilbert de Vescy was when the castle was taken." Still she did not respond. "The man who took Mordeaux is called Reginald FitzRandolph. Do you know him?"

She seemed to think a moment, then nodded. "I have met him, some years ago. He is the son of a man who was one of my father's allies during Henry's reign. But I cannot tell you much about his character. He was barely a man when I met him."

The truth, or another lie?

He let the silence draw out between them, then said, "I'm surprised you have not asked about your friend Hilary, to make certain she is well."

He saw a look of alarm in her eyes. "I had heard that there was no bloodshed."

"Who told you that?"

"One of the women. She said she had heard it from the guards at the gate." She took a step toward him. "Was she wrong? Has something happened to Hilary or her family? Have you spoken to Gilbert to find out if everyone is all right?"

Her anxiety seemed genuine. He thought he had caught her in a lapse when she failed to ask about her friend. But maybe she had in fact assumed from what she heard that everyone inside Mordeaux was safe. Should he reassure her, or leave her to worry? "Yea, I spoke to Gilbert, and little as he was able to tell me, he did say that everyone is well. The castle was taken peacefully."

She released her breath in a sigh. He stood staring at her, burning with frustration. Was there no way to learn how much she knew? He had tried everything he knew to pry the truth out of her. Verbal traps, seduction, intimidation. Nothing seemed to work.

"May I go?" she asked. "Someone needs to oversee the women in doing their part to defend Valmar."

"Of course," he said coldly. He didn't want to look at her any longer. He was afraid he would end up shaking her senseless. Either that, or fucking her senseless as a means of releasing the terrible tension inside him. He doubted that would be wise. Sex with Nicola always ended up softening him toward her. And at this moment, he needed to stay wary and angry and acutely on guard.

Nicola hurried past the hall and out a side entrance of the keep. Guessing that after making his report and eating Gilbert would seek out the company of other young men, she decided to search for him in the stables.

As soon as she entered, she saw him talking animatedly to some squires Fawkes had set to polishing mail in preparation for the coming conflict. "Gilbert," she called.

He looked at her, then approached and bowed. "Milady." She took his arm and led him past the other squires, who gawked at them with wide-eyed curiosity. When they reached a back portion of the stables where bundles of new-mown hay lined the walls, she demanded, "Tell me truly, how fares your mother and the little ones?"

"FitzRandolph's knights have not bothered them, if that is why you worry. But my mother is distraught anyway."

"Why? Does she think Fawkes will punish your father for his part in Mordeaux's fall?"

Gilbert shook his head. "I believe she is too worried about Simon's cough to think beyond that."

"Simon is sick?" Nicola gasped. "But when we visited, I thought he was much better!"

Gilbert shrugged. "I don't know what happened, only that instead of getting well as Joanie did, Simon got sick again."

"Holy Mother!" Nicola cried. "Has your mother had the healer to look at him?"

"The old midwife, Aldyth, died last spring, and there is no one else. My mother has dosed him with several things, I know."

Stark terror struck Nicola. After all her struggle to protect him, to think that Simon might die of a summer ague. Her mind raced. She had to go to him. And she had to take Glennyth with her. The healer would know what to do. Somehow she would help him.

"Lady, are you well?"

She dragged herself back to awareness and saw Gilbert staring at her. Since he had no idea that Simon was her son, he must think her reaction rather extreme. "I'm sorry to frighten you," she said, "but we had a sickness like that here at Valmar some time ago and several children died of it. I can't help thinking of your poor mother, how terrified she must be."

"I suppose she is," Gilbert said. "But she is always fussing over the little ones. It might not really be that serious."

"Are you going back there?" she asked.

"To Mordeaux?" He shook his head. "Lord Fawkes said I must stay here for now. Besides, if FitzRandolph besieges

Valmar, I want to fight." Gilbert's gray eyes glowed with excitement.

"Have you considered that FitzRandolph might press some of the Mordeaux knights into service for him? You could well end up fighting your friends, or even your own father."

"Jesu! I had not thought of that! Do you really think that might happen?"

"I don't know, but it is certainly possible. War is nothing to be eager for," she said harshly.

She turned and started to walk away. Halfway out of the stables, she began to run.

"Ye're going to Mordeaux? Are ye mad?" Old Emma cried. "If ye flee to the enemy's camp, yer husband will never forgive ye!"

Nicola paused in stuffing clothing into a saddle pack. "And if anything happens to Simon and I'm not there, I'll never forgive myself." Cold dread made her hands shake. She could hardly think what to bring. There was every likelihood that she would never return to Valmar. As Old Emma said, if she fled to Mordeaux, Fawkes would assume that she was in league with his enemies and want nothing more to do with her.

Tears stung her eyes. She wiped them away with her hand. There was no time for self-pity. She must get away while Fawkes was busy preparing the castle for attack.

"What if I carried a message to Glennyth?" Old Emma suggested. "She could go to Mordeaux to care for Simon. Ye need not make the journey yerself."

"You don't understand," Nicola said. "Simon is my son. The heart of my heart. I have to be there with him. I *have* to go."

"I think ye are making another foolish mistake." The maidservant shook her head and clucked under her breath.

"Fawkes will never forgive ye. He may have a *tendre* for ye that goes far beyond what most men feel for their wives, but he is still a knight, a warrior. If he thinks ye have aided his enemies, *ye* will become his enemy."

Old Emma's words sickened Nicola, but she struggled to shake off the awful feeling. Things between her and Fawkes were doomed from the beginning. In truth, she should be grateful for the few hours of rapture they had shared. Although for a time she had forgotten, the fact was that life was harsh and cruel. She'd been a fool to think she might know happiness with Fawkes.

She'd made up her mind. She would go to Mordeaux and somehow find a way to cure Simon. Then she would take him away and go off in the woods to live. Glennyth would help her. If no one knew who she was or where she was, they could not hurt her or her son. It was the only way to keep Simon safe.

"I'm ready," she said. A strange feeling came over her as she looked at Old Emma. The maidservant had been with her since she was a small girl, scolding and fussing the whole time. But at the thought that she would never see her again, Nicola was filled with a sense of aching loss. Impulsively, she hugged the plump, toothless old crone.

"There now," Old Emma sobbed, "it's not like we're saying good-bye forever. Ye'll soon be back again at Valmar, I know it."

Nicola said nothing. And then she was out the bedchamber door, and all her energies focused on getting out of the castle and through the gate before Fawkes was alerted.

Glennyth met her at the door of the cottage, then wordlessly stepped aside to let her enter.

"I need your help," Nicola said, still out of breath from the rush of getting there as quickly as possible. "Simon is ill. We have to go to him. I don't know exactly what the sickness is, but I believe he has a cough and maybe a fever. You must take whatever you think you will need."

Glennyth raised a dark brow. "As I understand it, Mordeaux is in the hands of your husband's enemy. How do you propose to explain your presence there? Everyone will think you have betrayed him."

Nicola exhaled in exasperation and began to pace. "I know all that, but it changes nothing. Simon's my son! He needs me! I must go to him no matter the cost to myself! Now, please hurry and find the things you must take and let us go. I have brought a horse for you."

Glennyth motioned that Nicola should follow her to the stillroom. "How did you manage to get away without anyone noticing?" She lit a lamp, then began to select jars and packets of herbs from the cluttered shelves.

"When Henry de Brionne questioned me at the gate, I told him that Fawkes had sent me into the village to get you, so that you would be available to deal with battle wounds and such." Nicola fidgeted in the tiny space. She longed to urge Glennyth to hurry but realized that she should not distract the wisewoman while she was concentrating on selecting what herbs and medicines to take.

"And he believed you?" Glennyth asked.

"Yea, why should he not? I don't think Fawkes has told any of his men of his suspicions of me, except maybe Reynard."

"Reynard." Glennyth's mouth quirked. "You realize that if I go with you, Fawkes will also see me as his enemy. Reynard may be forced to choose between being loyal to him or to me."

Nicola regarded Glennyth with surprise. "Are you telling me that Reynard is more than a casual dalliance?"

"I am carrying his babe."

"But . . . I . . ." Nicola paused, confused. Then she said, "I know you, and if you bear his child, it will be because you want to."

Glennyth continued with her task. "That is true."

"And so you have decided to bear Reynard's child? Why?" Despite her anxiety and haste, Nicola could not help being curious. Glennyth had always been so contemptuous and cold when it came to men. "Why did you choose him?"

"He is loyal and good-hearted." She turned to look at Nicola, her eyes a misty, ethereal green. "And there is the matter that I have looked into the scrying bowl and seen our daughter."

A chill ran down Nicola's spine. The villagers gossiped that Glennyth could see the future, but she had thought it was simply that their ignorance and fear caused them to see the healer as having magical powers. What if Glennyth really was a witch woman? "Have you ever tried to see my future?" she asked breathlessly. "Or Simon's? Or Fawkes's?"

Glennyth dumped another jar into her healing bag. "I'm ready," she said. "We can talk as we ride."

Glennyth gathered some clothing and food, then Nicola helped her carry the things out to the horses. After securing their supplies to the saddles and mounting, they set out, riding through the woods behind Glennyth's house rather than through the village. It was only when they were some distance from Valmar and out in open country where they could ride side by side that Nicola finally said, "If you have seen something regarding my future, please tell me."

"For the most part, I think it is better that people do not know what is to come."

"Is it so terrible then, that I could not bear it?" Nicola felt her heart begin to pound. What if Glennyth told her that Simon was going to die? How would she go on?

Glennyth looked thoughtful. "Yea, I have seen things in the scrying bowl regarding you and those you love."

"Tell me," Nicola whispered.

"Everything was indistinct and confused. I saw you weeping, and I sensed pain and despair surrounding you." Nicola's heart sank. "But I cannot tell if I was seeing your past or your

future," Glennyth continued. "One thing I am certain of"—
the healer's gaze caught and held hers—"there is much danger
ahead of you. Even now, as we ride toward Mordeaux, I can
feel it. By going to help your son, you risk your own life."

Nicola shook her head. "My life means nothing without
him. Tell me." She paused, her chest tight. "Have you seen
anything of Simon's future?"

"Children are difficult," Glennyth said, frowning. "Their
futures are often unformed and uncertain, their destinies
complicated by the decisions of others."

"And yet, you say you have seen your and Reynard's
daughter. How can you know what she looks like if she is
not yet even born? What if you were to die? Then she would
never be."

Glennyth smiled. "The fact that I have seen her reassures
me that I will not die, at least not until after next spring."

"How can you know her future and not know Simon's?
How can you be certain your child will live yet be unable to
reassure me regarding mine?"

"Maybe it is because I am carrying her in my belly at this
moment."

Nicola remembered what that was like, to have Simon
inside her, safe and secure. Her precious, precious Simon.
"What of Fawkes?" she asked. "Have you seen anything of
his future?"

"The sense of death and danger surrounding him is even
stronger than it is for you. But again, I do not know if it
represents the past or the future."

Death. Danger. When Fawkes left Valmar three years ago,
she'd been convinced that Mortimer intended to kill him.
Somehow, he had survived. But for what purpose? So he
could come back to Valmar and be betrayed by the woman
he loved? A deep sense of guilt assailed her.

She shook off the mood. At this moment, Simon was the
one who needed her. "We will have to leave our horses behind before we enter Mordeaux," she said. "We will pretend

to be villeins' wives, come to the castle with herbs to sell to Lady Hilary."

"And after we see Simon and treat him for his sickness, what will you do?" Glennyth asked.

"I am going to take him into the woods where he will be safe." Nicola felt a twinge of doubt. Would Glennyth agree to go along with her plan, especially now that the wise-woman was carrying her own babe?

Glennyth gave her a doubtful look. "You intend to give up your status as a lady and live in the wildwood?"

"It's the only way I can be with Simon and keep him safe."

"What will you do for food? How will you keep warm when winter comes?"

"We'll find some sort of shelter. And I have money. I brought a whole cache of silver pennies in my pack, as well as some pieces of jewelry."

"Think you that silver or jewels will buy you food this winter? Who will you purchase it from? Wolfsheads and bandits?"

"I have no choice!" Nicola exclaimed. "If I want to be with my son, I must endure whatever I have to!"

"Let us not worry about that yet. For now, I think we must concern ourselves with getting into Mordeaux and tending to Simon."

The healer's practical words made Nicola's stomach twist. If Simon did not survive this sickness, then there was no future to worry about.

They left their horses at a cottar's hut in the woods outside Mordeaux. After changing into rough homespun kirtles and linen headdresses, they started out for the castle. As they approached the bridge, Nicola saw a green-and-yellow banner flying from the gatehouse. The impact of what she had done suddenly struck her. Mordeaux was in enemy hands—and she was to blame.

Nineteen

As he climbed the stairs to the ramparts to see what else needed to be done, Fawkes met Henry de Brionne on the stairs. "All's ready up here," the knight reported. "How do we fare in the way of supplies?"

"With our current food stores and the two wells, we ought to be able to hold out for some months," Fawkes said.

Henry nodded. "It's surprising that the enemy waited until this late in the summer to attack. Once the weather turns cool, we'll have the advantage. They'll be out in the elements and forced to live off the land."

"Ah, but with Mordeaux as a base, they're actually in an excellent position to carry on a prolonged siege. FitzRandolph will be able to resupply and reinforce his army from there."

Henry grimaced. "God's blood! I had not thought of that!"

"It appears that this campaign has been planned for some time, perhaps since word went out that I killed Mortimer and took over Mordeaux and Valmar."

"That's what is odd," Henry said, "that John waited until you were in control to make his move. Mortimer would have made a much easier target, but John did nothing these past years while Valmar was ripe for the picking." Henry shrugged. "And Mortimer was the king's man as much as you are."

"It's possible this attack is not merely a move to seize control of property, but a strike against me," Fawkes said.

"But why? Have you enemies that wish to bring you down?"

Was his wife his enemy? Fawkes's body went cold at the thought. "I don't know who is behind this attack, other than John. Whoever our enemy is, whoever his allies, he will not have an easy time of it if he tries to take Valmar."

"Fawkes! Fawkes! Are you up there?"

Fawkes hurried to the rampart stairs and saw Reynard coming up. "Fawkes!" he panted. "FitzSaer is here, but he will tell us nothing until you come."

Fawkes exchanged a glance with Henry, then started down after Reynard. "How did he get free?" he asked his captain.

"One of the Valmar knights helped him escape the oubliette," Reynard called over his shoulder. "Another got him past the guards at the gate. He said he thinks that FitzRandolph didn't really care if he escaped. That the man is surpassingly arrogant and believes taking Valmar will be easy. I'd say the bastard's in for a nasty surprise." Reynard turned and flashed him a grin.

Fawkes nodded grimly.

Adam FitzSaer sat at one of the trestle tables in the hall. His face was unshaved and his clothing dirty and disheveled. But when he saw Fawkes, he rose straight and proud. "Milord," he said. "I'm sorry to report that I have failed in my duty to protect Mordeaux. But I vow, they would not have taken the castle except by treachery."

Fawkes nodded. "I know. Gilbert FitzGilbert has given us the tale."

"FitzGilbert!" Adam's eyes flashed and he spat in the rushes. "His father was part of the deceit, if not the actual leader."

"How do you know?" Reynard asked. "Have you proof?"

"Proof? I think the fact that all the servants were part of the castle's capitulation is a kind of proof. They were the ones who drugged me and my men. Someone must have given them the order. Who could it be but Gilbert de Vescy, the man they served for the past years?"

"If that's true, then why did young FitzGilbert come to tell us what happened?" Reynard asked. "It does not seem reasonable that he would ride here to announce Mordeaux's fall if his father was guilty of betraying the castle."

"Ah, but that is because the main traitor is here at Valmar." Adam's mouth twisted. "Begging your pardon, milord, but I believe de Vescy and all the rest of them were carrying out your lady wife's orders when they offered Mordeaux into FitzRandolph's hands."

Fawkes took a deep, ravaged breath. It was true. He'd been hoping against hope that he was wrong. Now his worst fears were realized.

"Why would she do such a thing?" Reynard asked.

Adam shrugged. "I don't know. Maybe she favors John's cause. Mortimer was the king's man. What better way to thwart a man she hated than to conspire with his enemies?"

"But Fawkes is also the king's man," Reynard argued. "Why would she betray her husband and aid his enemies . . . unless . . ." He frowned. "Do you think she had some prior arrangement with FitzRandolph, some agreement for him to come and take over Mordeaux and Valmar, and rescue her from Mortimer?"

"If she had such an agreement," Fawkes said softly, "then she has had over a month to tell me of it."

"Are you saying that she has not changed her plans? That she wants FitzRandolph to defeat *you?* But why?" Abruptly, Reynard's blue eyes widened. "Unless . . . unless they were lovers and she has not changed her loyalties despite wedding you."

Fawkes clenched his jaw so tight, it hurt. It was bad

enough to face Nicola's treachery, but to hear it spoken aloud was near unbearable.

FitzSaer and Reynard both looked at him, then Reynard said, "We really don't know any of this for certain, Fawkes. It's possible de Vescy acted on his own."

FitzSaer shook his head. "Do you really think that a man like de Vescy could hatch this plot by himself? Have you seen how his wife orders him about? He has no more backbone than a hunk of gristle."

"All the better for FitzRandolph or some other man of John's to manipulate him," Reynard argued.

"What of the servants?" Adam's expression grew even grimmer. "Think you that they have such loyalty to de Vescy that they would risk their necks for his sake? Nay, the order must have come from Lady Nicola. Only she has such influence over them. She grew up at Mordeaux, and the people there see her as some sort of queen or goddess!"

Reynard seemed to have no answer for this. He flashed Fawkes a look of pity.

Too bad he had not died in the Holy Land, Fawkes thought bitterly. To come back here and marry Nicola and then find out she loved another man was crueler than any death he could imagine. He said woodenly, "I guess it's time to confront my wife, to lay the facts on the table and make her admit the truth." He started toward the stairwell, wondering if he would find her in the solar or some other area of the castle.

"I'll come with you," Reynard called.

When they reached Mordeaux's gate, Nicola pulled her coif around her face and whispered to Glennyth that she should speak for them.

"Who goes there?" demanded a knight that Nicola had never seen before. "What is your business in the castle?"

"We are herbalists," Glennyth answered. "We wish to see

Lady Hilary. She has purchased our healing remedies in the past."

"Hilary de Vescy is no longer the chatelaine of the keep," the guard said. "All goods and services are purchased now by Lord FitzRandolph's steward."

"Oh? And does Lord FitzRandolph have a healer among his forces? What if one of you falls ill or is injured?" Glennyth's voice turned warm and purring. "If you were hurt, which would you rather be tended by—a brutish army leech or a skilled wisewoman?"

"Skilled? In what manner?" the guard asked huskily.

"My touch is deft and sure, and I am very experienced." Although she could not see Glennyth's face clearly, Nicola could well imagine the healer's seductive expression.

"I'm certain you are," the guard responded. "Mayhap you could come up to the gatehouse and look at this old wound on my thigh."

"Oh," Glennyth said silkily. "Is Lord FitzRandolph so sure of his hold on Mordeaux that he will not mind if you leave your post for a time?"

The guard swore.

Glennyth said, "But mayhap later, after I have seen Lady Hilary and you are no longer on guard duty, we'll chance to meet in the hall."

"We might at that," the guard said as he waved them through.

"I didn't know you could play the trollop," Nicola said dryly as they hurried toward the keep.

Glennyth gave a delicate snort. "It's not so difficult. Most men keep their wits in their braies."

They reached the castle and climbed the outer stairs to the entrance to the hall. As they entered, an older maidservant stopped them. "Who are you? What is it that you seek?"

Glennyth stepped forward. "We wish to see Lady Hilary regarding purchasing our wares." She held out her basket, fragrant with the scent of dried herbs.

The maidservant regarded the basket with interest, then shook her head. "Lady Hilary no longer barters with peddlers and goodwives. Lord FitzRandolph's steward does all the castle business. I can take you to him if you wish."

"Do you really think a man knows anything about healing remedies and decoctions?" Glennyth asked.

The maidservant started to answer, then Nicola stepped forward and pulled her coif away from her face. "It's me, Emma. I have to see Hilary."

Emma turned ashen. "Milady," she squeaked. "What are you doing here?" She glanced frantically around the hall. "You can't let FitzRandolph or his men see you!"

"Then escort us up to the solar, and quickly," Nicola ordered.

The maidservant nodded and led them through the hall. Outside the solar she paused, distraught. "What is it, lady? Why are you here? We did exactly as you asked, but now we worry that FitzRandolph means to turn us out to starve. He says we are all traitors and that once he has taken Valmar, he will bring his own people here to serve him!"

"I'm sorry that he has frightened you," Nicola said. "But rest assured that I will do everything I can to make certain that he does not rule Mordeaux for long."

"I don't understand any of this," Emma said. "Why did you want us to surrender to FitzRandolph?"

Nicola touched the maidservant's arm. "I can't explain at this moment, but I promise you that all will be well."

Emma smiled at her and curtsied. "It's always good to see you, milady. God keep you safe."

After the servant left them, Glennyth said, "You should be careful what you promise."

Nicola sighed. "Jesu, what a wretched mess this all is. Bad enough that I'm torn between Simon and Fawkes, but now I must somehow protect the people of Mordeaux as well."

"With power comes responsibility," Glennyth said soberly. "It has ever been so."

They entered the solar. Hilary, who was sewing, jumped to her feet in surprise. "Nicola! What do you here?" She looked anxiously toward the door.

"I will explain soon, but for now, where is Simon?" Nicola asked. "How does he fare?"

"Simon? Oh, he is better. Much better. Come. I'll take you to him." Hilary led them into the adjoining bedchamber. On a pallet near the hearth, Simon slept peacefully, his thumb in his mouth. "He has not had a fever since last even and his cough is near gone," Hilary said.

Nicola bent over the sleeping child. Never had he looked more like a cherub sent from heaven. His skin was flushed from sleep, and his hair curled in golden tendrils around his plump baby face. She felt a rush of love so intense, it was like a knife in her chest. "Oh, Simon," she whispered. She put out her hand and stroked his gilded curls. They were damp, and she moved her hand to feel his forehead. Warm but not hot. She touched his cheek, soft as swan's down. His eyelashes, dark gold crescents against his cheek, fluttered. He opened his eyes. "Mama?"

"Yea, it is me," Nicola soothed. "I have come for you."

For a moment, his deep blue eyes regarded her with dazed sleepiness. Then, abruptly, his gaze cleared. "Mama?" he said again, this time in puzzlement. He sat up and looked around for Hilary.

Nicola felt her heart breaking. Hilary was the only mother he had ever known. How could she take him away from the family who had loved and protected him all his short life?

Reassured at seeing Hilary and knowing where she was, Simon turned to Nicola and held out his arms. She hugged him tightly, fiercely. When he wriggled, she released him. "Did you bring sweets, Auntie?"

Nicola sighed, tears stinging her eyes. "Yea, I did." She dug in her pocket for one of the cinnamon-and-honey cakes she had brought, thinking that they might help to keep Simon quiet as they sneaked out of the castle. As he ate it, she said to Hilary, "I've decided to take Simon away. Once I've found a safe place for him, I will return and try to sort out things with FitzRandolph."

Hilary gaped at her. "But . . . milady . . . what about your husband?"

Merely thinking of Fawkes made her want to weep. Nicola shook her head.

"What's going to happen to *us?*" Hilary twisted her hands together. "FitzRandolph says we are all traitors and that he means to replace us with his own loyal servants once he has taken Valmar."

"He will not take Valmar," Nicola assured her. "Fawkes will never let that happen."

"But if Fawkes prevails, we are still in trouble, lady. He will also think we are traitors. And he might do worse than turn us out of the castle. He might decide to hang—" Hilary gave a gasp, unable to finish.

Abruptly, Nicola realized the danger she had brought upon her friends. When she'd asked them to allow FitzRandolph to take the castle without a struggle, she'd had in her mind that Fawkes would defeat FitzRandolph at Valmar and then reclaim Mordeaux. But she had not really considered how Fawkes might perceive Gilbert and the others who had carried out her scheme. Somehow she would have to make him understand that they had done it for her. That they were not being disloyal but obeying her orders.

But what good would it do for her to argue their cause if Fawkes hated her? And how would she ever dare face him after what she had done? He would think that she had used and manipulated him, and never cared for him. He would hate the sight of her.

Nicola glanced at Hilary and then at Simon. Despite her own dread, she had to be strong. "I will not let Fawkes harm any of your family," she said. "I promise you."

Hilary heaved a sigh, then came and tearfully embraced Nicola. "Oh, I thank you, lady. I knew we could depend on you."

Glennyth had gone to examine Simon. Now she looked up at Nicola and frowned. The message in her hazel eyes was clear. *Do not promise what you have not the power to bring about.*

Nicola sent her an equally firm unspoken message. *I have no choice. It serves us ill for her to be panicked and fearful.*

Nicola gently released Hilary. She was on the verge of asking her to gather up Simon's things when there was the loud sound of boots on the stairs. Nicola turned to the door, expecting to see Gilbert de Vescy, Hilary's husband. Instead, a well-dressed nobleman with curling brown hair and black eyes stood on the threshold. Behind him were two knights with weapons drawn.

The young man smiled. "Lady Nicola. Well met. By coming here on your own, you have saved me a great deal of trouble."

Vaguely, Nicola remembered those dark eyes. The face they belonged to was much younger back then. Uncertain. Awed to be in the presence of Nicola of Mordeaux, a rich heiress a year or two older than he was.

"Lord FitzRandolph, well met." She nodded regally, although her heart pounded with fear. "I have come to Mordeaux to visit my friends, Gilbert and Hilary de Vescy."

"It does not matter why you have come. Only that you have saved me the trouble of rescuing you from that low-born usurper, de Cressy."

"Fawkes de Cressy is the king's man and my legal husband. I hardly see how you can call him a usurper," Nicola answered coolly.

A look of uncertainty crossed FitzRandolph's face. "I was told that you petitioned Prince John to rescue you and your property."

"That was when I was wed to Walter Mortimer, a foul,

worthless tosspot and a sodomite. I have no complaint against my current husband. He is a valiant and admirable knight who serves Valmar well."

FitzRandolph looked nonplussed. But he quickly recovered himself and said, "It does not matter if you favor your second husband over the first. He is still Richard's man, and Richard rots in Germany as we speak. I have been given an opportunity to enlarge my properties and I intend to make use of it."

"Whatever you think," Nicola said. "Now, if you will excuse me, having finished my visit with Lady Hilary, my companion and I will be on our way."

She started toward the doorway, hoping that she could intimidate FitzRandolph and his men into moving aside. FitzRandolph did not budge. "My apologies, Lady Nicola, but I cannot allow you to leave Mordeaux."

"I don't see what use I am to you."

"Don't you?" Dark eyes bored into hers. "You are the heiress of Valmar and Mordeaux. Even if I take these properties by strength of arms, I can be certain of my claim only if I am your husband."

Nicola willed herself not to panic, to breathe slowly and evenly. "But I am already wed. And you, I believe, were betrothed some time ago. By now the woman has surely come of age."

"Oh, I have a wife. But since she is my cousin as well, I doubt that I will have any trouble having the marriage annulled on the basis of consanguinity. With John's help, of course." FitzRandolph smiled at her. A cunning smile.

Fear settled on her chest like a crushing weight. Once again, she was caught in the treacherous scheme of an ambitious man. While FitzRandolph might not be as repulsive or vicious as Mortimer, he would still use her for his own ends. Men were all alike, she thought bitterly—greedy, power-mad fools. Except Fawkes. He had desired her for herself, rather than using her as a pawn. She thought of their wedding banquet and the ring he had given her. Despite his lusty treatment of her, there was a tenderness in Fawkes that few men possessed. Pain lanced through her at the thought of what she had lost.

"You look troubled, Lady Nicola. I have heard stories of Walter Mortimer's loathsome behavior, and I assure you I would never deal with you in so base a manner. To demonstrate my consideration, I will leave you now and allow you time alone with your companions." He started to leave, then turned and spoke again. His voice remained silky and cultured, a courtier's voice, but there was no mistaking the determination underlying his words. "For all my regard of your feelings, Lady Nicola, I must insist that you do not leave this portion of the castle."

When FitzRandolph had left, Nicola went to Simon, who sat on the floor playing with some wooden toys. She wanted desperately to hug him, to draw strength from his sweet, precious warmth. But she did not want him to sense her distress.

"Someone must have told him you are here," Glennyth said. "Mayhap the maidservant, Emma."

Nicola shook her head. "It was not Emma. As we passed the gate, I saw one of FitzSaer's men. I thought he would not recognize me, dressed as I was, but he must have."

"What will you do?" Hilary asked.

"I'm not as trapped as he thinks," Nicola answered. "I grew up here, and I know ways out of the castle that no one else does."

"You're going to flee? But where will you go? And what will happen to us?" Hilary's voice rose in distress.

Nicola sighed. "Although I can escape, there's no way I can take Simon with me." She looked at Hilary. "And besides, I owe you and your family and so many others here at Mordeaux a great debt. I would not leave you to FitzRandolph's wrath." She turned her gaze to Glennyth. "But you, if you can, you must leave Mordeaux and return to Valmar."

"Oh, I have no doubt that I can find my way out of this place," Glennyth said. "The question is, what do I do then? Do I tell Fawkes that you are being held prisoner at Mordeaux?"

Nicola shook her head bitterly. "If he believes I am FitzRandolph's prisoner, he will think 'good riddance.' "

"Perhaps not," said Glennyth. "His passion for you is so great that he might well try to rescue you despite the danger."

Nicola considered the possibility. Fawkes *was* drawn to her with a kind of unholy intensity. And there was always the chance that he would try to rescue her simply because he knew that losing her might mean losing Valmar. She did not want him to attack Mordeaux. Not only would it endanger Simon, but it would also put Fawkes at a disadvantage. Better that he should fight FitzRandolph at Valmar and be the besieged rather than the besieger.

"You will say nothing," she said. "If Reynard questions you, tell him that you do not know where I have gone."

"You're certain?" Glennyth said. "Mayhap it is time to tell your husband the truth."

Nicola paced across the solar. So many lives depended on her decision. She looked at Simon playing on the floor. Although his safety was still her first concern, she had a responsibility to Hilary and the other people at Mordeaux who had shown her such loyalty. And then there was Fawkes. FitzRandolph intended not only to defeat her husband, but kill him. The thought made her feel sick.

Proud, passionate Fawkes. He had endured so much for her sake already. If he learned he had a son at Mordeaux, but nothing else about him, that knowledge might goad him into taking risks that he would not otherwise take. She shook her head. "Learning the truth now would only confuse him, and he needs to keep his wits about him, to think clearly and coolly. Better that he should think I have betrayed him and hate me for it. At least his anger may help him defeat FitzRandolph."

Glennyth cocked a brow. "Whatever you wish, lady. But remember, someday the truth will come out, and then there will be a reckoning."

Nicola felt a chill at the wisewoman's words, but she shook it off. By the time Fawkes knew the truth, she would be gone. As soon as FitzRandolph and his knights left to attack Valmar, she would take Simon and seek sanctuary in the forest. She would leave Fawkes a message explaining why she had betrayed him and begging him not to deal harshly with the people of Mordeaux. She did not think he was cruel or vengeful. He would blame her for everything. Gilbert and Hilary and the others would be safe. Simon would be safe as well and he would be *hers*. She knew he would miss Hilary, but he was such a dear, trusting child, she did not think he would fret long.

She went to where he was playing and crouched down beside him. He held up a small wooden figure. "This is a knight," he said. "Gilbert carved it."

"Yea, it is, lovey," she whispered.

"The knight is going to fight a war." Simon nodded gravely.

Nicola looked at the intricately carved toy. *Fawkes,* was all she could think of. *Oh, Fawkes, please take care. Even if I can't have you, I want you to be safe.*

"Gone! What do you mean she's gone?"

Reynard shook his head. "Henry saw her go through the gate hours ago. He thought she was on an errand for you in the village. I just now went to Glennyth's cottage and there was no sign of either of them—except for two sets of hoofprints leading into the woods."

As Reynard grimly made this report, the ache in Fawkes's gut grew deeper. He stared unseeingly off the ramparts. She'd gone to meet her lover. The cold knife inside him twisted.

"I knew there were secrets Glennyth kept from me," Reynard said in a troubled voice. "Things regarding Nicola especially. But I still don't think she would betray me."

"Why should your situation be any different from mine?" Fawkes asked scathingly.

Reynard did not respond. Fawkes continued to gaze out at the countryside, where the stubbled fields and pastures were rapidly turning brown in the last hot days of summer. He struggled to hold on to hope, to the belief that there was some benign explanation for everything, for Mordeaux's surrender, for Nicola's flight. But the twisting pain in his gut told him that there wasn't, that he had been the worst kind of fool, and the last three years of his life were a bitter jest.

Twenty

It was almost dawn. Wearily, Fawkes observed the faint brightening of the sky off the eastern ramparts of the castle. His eyes felt gritty and raw, and his body ached with fatigue, but he knew if he went down to one of the bedchambers, sleep would elude him. As soon as he closed his eyes, intense, heated images of Nicola would fill his mind, accompanied by searing pain. How could she leave him? How could she turn her back on what they had shared?

He wanted to go to Glennyth's cottage, rouse her from her bed and demand answers. That had been the final blow, when Reynard came back to the castle and told him that Glennyth had returned, but refused to say where Nicola was. The wisewoman insisted that Nicola cared for him. In leaving, she had only done what she felt she had to do.

What did that mean? That she cared for him, but she cared for another man more? The horrible thought gnawed at him, like a festering wound eating away his soul. How long had she plotted this, that FitzRandolph would rescue her from Mortimer, claim Valmar and make her his wife? Was that the reason she had betrayed him to Mortimer, that she did not want *him* to rescue her but another man?

She must have thought that Mortimer would kill him, or at least defeat him, and then she could proceed with her plans to marry FitzRandolph. But it had not turned out that way, and she'd had to scramble to adjust. Conniving, lying witch that she was, she had pretended to accept him as her husband. But even as she shared her body with him, reveled in the pleasure he could give her, she was still plotting with FitzRandolph. Her visits to Mordeaux suddenly made sense. FitzRandolph had a spy there, or perhaps all the servants and garrison had already given their loyalty to FitzRandolph. It was only a matter of time until her unsuspecting husband was lulled him into complacency, then FitzRandolph would strike.

Fawkes leaned against the crenel, wanting to vomit. There was nothing in his stomach. He waited for the waves of nausea to pass.

"Milord, should you not move back? You make too clear a target for an archer and you do not have your helm on."

Fawkes raised his head and stared at the young knight standing beside him. It took Fawkes some time to recognize Aubrey of Malmsbury from the shape of the man's mouth and jaw beneath his helm and the details of his armor.

With a sluggish movement, Fawkes stepped back from the arrow slit. "I didn't realize how light it was getting."

"Do you expect them to attack soon? Is that why you have stayed up here all night?"

The eagerness in the young knight's voice grated on Fawkes's nerves. Did the puling fool not realize that siege warfare was less than glorious? In fact, it usually meant tedious, miserable months of constant vigilance with little chance for combat.

"I don't know when FitzRandolph will attack," Fawkes answered. "But my guess is that it will be soon." There was no reason for FitzRandolph to delay now that he had Mordeaux *and* Nicola in his possession. Teeth clenched, Fawkes regarded Aubrey. How much did his men know of Nicola's defection? Did they see him as a hapless wretch who had been betrayed by an evil woman? Or a weak, pathetic dolt who had been done in by his idealistic dreams of love?

As if to answer his unspoken question, Aubrey said, "I'm

sorry to hear about Lady Nicola leaving. I guess after what she endured as Mortimer's wife, she was incapable of being loyal to any man." He shrugged. "Woman are weak, malleable creatures anyway."

Weak? Malleable? Was that what Nicola was? Or was she a cold-hearted, cruel she-devil?

"But even if Lady Nicola is gone, Valmar is still worth fighting for," Aubrey continued. "I would give near anything to possess my own manor some day, let alone a splendid keep like this one. You are a fortunate man, milord. And everyone says you are favored with the greatest luck in battle. I'm proud to serve you, Fawkes de Cressy."

Aubrey's words heartened Fawkes. And his wistful words about owning land reminded him that no matter what happened with Nicola, he must fight to hold Valmar and keep that much of his dream intact. "Thank you for your loyalty, Aubrey," he said. "I vow that I won't disappoint you. The only way I will relinquish Valmar or Mordeaux is if our lawful king, Richard the Lionhearted, strips me of the properties, or if I am dead."

"Do you think Richard will ever be freed?" Aubrey asked. "And if he is, will he—"

"A little early to be discussing politics, isn't it?" Reynard interrupted as he joined them. Following behind him were two knights come to relieve Aubrey and the other guard.

"It helps pass the time," Fawkes said sourly. He could not help nursing a kind of resentment toward his friend. It did not seem fair. Why had *he* been the one to fall in love with a treacherous, cold-hearted bitch?

Aubrey turned to Reynard. "Captain, do you think Richard will ever come back? And if he does, will he have a kingdom left to claim? If John gains control of more and more castles, he might eventually have enough power to wrest England away from Richard."

Reynard gave a snort of contempt. "Mark my words, once Richard is freed, all John's followers will abandon him. What

John is gambling on is that Richard will never be freed or that he will somehow 'accidentally' die in prison."

"And how can you be certain that won't happen?" one of the other knights asked.

"Because of Eleanor," Reynard said. "Even as we speak, the queen mother is traveling around England raising money to liberate her son. Fawkes and I saw Eleanor in Messina before we sailed for the Holy Lands. Having personally observed her energy and determination, her astounding vigor, I don't doubt that she will succeed in freeing Richard. This is a woman who refused to allow twelve years in captivity to break her spirit, who journeyed halfway across the continent to arrange Richard's marriage, who once went on a crusade herself." Reynard shook his head. "Eleanor has a will of iron, and she is not about to let anything happen to her favorite son and England's annointed king."

Fawkes shifted restlessly. At this moment, he did not really want to hear Eleanor's praises sung. In her own way, she was as disloyal and deceitful as Nicola. Henry had locked her away primarily because she was plotting against him with their sons.

"I hope you're right about Richard," Aubrey said. "I've heard that he is the perfect parfit knight, noble and heroic in every respect."

"Oh, Richard has his faults, he does," Reynard responded. "He has a fiery temper, much like his father did, and he can be the very devil himself if he thinks he has been crossed. I think killing two thousand Saracen prisoners because Saladin delayed too long in paying their ransom shows just how ruthless he can be."

The memory made Fawkes's belly clutch. He started to say something to turn the direction of the conversation to less gruesome matters, but before he could speak, a flash of movement along the valley arrested his attention. He pointed. "They've come."

He gave orders for Aubrey and the other knights to wake

the castle and get the archers up on the ramparts, then he and Reynard joined Henry de Brionne in the cover of the watchtower to observe the enemy's advance.

The army crawled along, a mass of men and horses. Under the overcast morning sky their mail appeared dull gray, and their banners hung limply in the muggy air. A good-sized army, Fawkes thought, but not overwhelming. And meanwhile, they were well-prepared, snug and secure inside a solid fortress. "We'll see just how badly this FitzRandolph bastard wants Valmar," he said grimly. The other men nodded in agreement.

Fawkes could make out FitzRandolph's device at the head of the force, some sort of white figure on a field of blue and green. He squinted, staring at the plain white banner above the other rider. "It's the flag of truce," he said in surprise. "FitzRandolph must want to parley."

"If he really wanted to negotiate, he could have sent a message," Henry pointed out. "Why march here with a full army if he does not mean to attack?"

"Mayhap he thinks when we see his force, we will meekly surrender as Mordeaux did." Fawkes's jaw tightened at the memory of Mordeaux's easy capitulation and Nicola's part in it.

"Or it could be a trap," Reynard said.

When the army reached a place just outside of arrow range, the squire carrying the white banner and the knight next to him broke away from the main force and rode toward the bridge. "Fawkes de Cressy, I am Reginald FitzRandolph, and I would like speak with you," the knight called loudly.

Fawkes slammed on the helm he was carrying. "Have someone bring my horse!" he shouted down from the tower.

"Fawkes, are you certain you should parley with him?" Reynard said. "I'll tell you frankly, I don't trust this FitzRandolph."

"What do you think he's going to do?"

"I don't know. But I have an uneasy feeling about this,

and Glennyth has told me that whenever I get that unsettled, churning sense in my gut, I should heed the warning."

Fawkes grunted. He had felt that way for days now, and so far, all his worst fears had come true. If FitzRandolph planned some sort of treachery, he might as well face it now.

"At least take someone, an escort," Reynard said as he scrambled down the tower after Fawkes. "I would be happy to accompany you."

"Nay." Fawkes turned around so abruptly, Reynard almost ran into him. "If anything happens to me, then you must defend Valmar." *But for what?* The thought flashed through Fawkes's mind that if he were dead and FitzRandolph defeated, control of Valmar and Mordeaux would revert back to the king. He had no heir to leave it to.

He thought once more of the little mounded grave by the chapel. Nicola had killed his son, he was certain of it now. The bitter grief assaulted him anew, and he had to close his eyes and breath deeply to steady himself. There was only one reason to live, one purpose to fighting for Valmar, and that was to make certain that Nicola's cruel scheme was ruined. He could not let her win, could not let her make of his life a worthless jest.

He mounted Scimitar, then motioned to the two knights near the gate to also mount their horses and accompany him.

The portcullis creaked loudly as it was raised. He rode across the bridge, acutely aware of the stillness of the air around him, the almost eerie quiet. No sheep on the common lands bleated, no hawks circled the valley, calling out to their mates, no sparrows chattered in the thornbushes growing at the edge of the moat. It was as if the world were holding its breath.

His mind traveled back to that fateful day not three months ago when he had regarded Mordeaux Castle in the distance and contemplated how close he was to realizing his dream. Pain shafted through him at the thought, but this time it honed his determination rather than demoralized him. He would salvage something from this quagmire of deceit and faithlessness. He was the king's man, a knight and a crusader. For the honor of his name alone, he would fight.

Fawkes approached the enemy envoy, and his gaze took in the details of his nemesis. Beneath his helm, FitzRandolph's mouth looked soft, his chin weak. His green-and-blue surcoat was of the finest samite, bearing no marks of battle or previous use. A young man and an untested one, Fawkes thought. Was this what Nicola wanted? An elegant, almost pretty courtier?

He thought of how he must look, dark stubble on his chin, his expression grim and harsh, his helm dented and worn, with no fine surcoat over his battered, much mended mail. Had she detested him because she saw him as a crude, ill-mannered lout? A base, coarse soldier like her first husband?

A dark, rank taste filled his mouth. He could not change what he was. And she had liked him well enough in bed. Hadn't she?

"De Cressy." FitzRandolph jerked his head up in a gesture of recognition. Fawkes did not respond.

"I'm told that some months ago, you challenged Walter Mortimer for the right to hold Mordeaux." A faint smile curved FitzRandolph's lips, a hint of gloating. "Now, I would issue the same challenge to you for the honor of Valmar castle."

He wanted to accept, to fight FitzRandolph sword to sword and send this sweet-faced infant straight to hell. But he could not help remembering Reynard's warning. "I think not," he said. "If you want Valmar, you'll have to take it, your army against mine."

FitzRandolph did not like this. His red, full lips tightened. Then he said, "You know, your wife is at Mordeaux. She abandoned you without a backward glance. I guess she prefers a man of her own rank to a base hireling who rose to power by becoming a favorite of the king's. What did you do to win the honor of Mordeaux, de Cressy? Let Richard fuck you up the ass?"

A red froth rose up before Fawkes, blinding him. He wanted to seize FitzRandolph by the throat and snap his slender woman's neck in two. But he remembered himself in time. FitzRandolph was simply engaging in the common battle strategy—taunting his enemy to make him lose control. FitzRandolph wanted him to become so enraged that he would attack him. Then FitzRandolph's men could move in and kill Fawkes, claiming he had broken the terms of parley.

Fawkes forced himself to smile coldly and return the insults in kind. "That would be Mortimer you were thinking of. And is there not mayhap a hint of jealousy in your words? A comely, foppish fellow like you is more fit to warm the king's bed than I."

FitzRandolph's mouth quirked. "What wit you show, de Cressy. Mayhap I was mistaken and you have learned court manners after all. Still, you failed to charm Lady Nicola. After sharing your bed, for what—near three months, is it?— she deserted you as soon as she glimpsed another opportunity on the horizon. Tsk, tsk."

It was like salt rubbed in a gaping wound. He had given Nicola his heart and she had thrown it to the ground and stomped upon it. But he would not let his enemy see his weakness. "You may possess the heiress of Valmar," he said, "but you will never possess the property itself." He turned his horse and started to ride away.

The pain and hatred was like a raging fever in his blood, pounding in his ears, blinding him, sickening him. Then, despite his turmoil, some instinct suddenly made the skin on his neck prickle. *I don't trust this FitzRandolph,* Reynard had said. Fawkes turned in the saddle. Even as he did so, he heard a strange whistling sound, then a violent impact knocked him from his horse. As he struck the ground, a fiery pain burst in his shoulder. Dimly, he heard the shouts. "Treachery! Treachery! De Cressy's been hit!"

FitzRandolph shouted back, "I've done nothing! The bolt came from the woods, not my archers! Look! Do you see any of my men carrying a crossbow?"

"Bastard," someone muttered. Fawkes felt himself being picked up and carried. Before he knew it, Reynard was there, shouting into his ear, "Fawkes, Fawkes, can you hear me? Give the order and we'll attack. We'll chase down FitzRandolph's army and kill them, every one!"

Fawkes tried to talk. His tongue felt too big for his mouth. "Nay . . . do not. . . . It's what they want . . . they'll . . . slaughter . . . you." Fear gripped him, making him struggle even harder against the rising darkness. Even if he died, he did not want to lose Valmar.

Nicola paced across the bedchamber and back again. "Surely someone will send word." She paused and took an exasperated breath. "If anything happens, we'll know, won't we?"

"You must calm yourself," Hilary pleaded, although she looked less than composed herself. "If you don't, you're going to wake the children. They've been fussy all morning and they need to rest. Your pacing does not help a bit!"

Nicola nodded and forced herself to take a seat on a stool by the window. She felt as if she were losing her wits. The waiting seemed unbearable, endless.

"Mayhap you could sew," Hilary suggested. She was working on a small tunic for Joanie. Her needle moved in and out, making neat, tiny stitches.

Nicola gave a strangled laugh. "If I tried, I'd likely stitch my fingers into the garment. Right now I'm so frightened I can scarcely get my hands to function."

"Gil says it could be days and days or even months before this business is settled. You cannot pace and worry every moment."

Nicola sighed. What she *should* do was gather up Simon

and his things and try to sneak out of the castle while FitzRandolph was away. But somehow she could not bring herself to leave until she knew how Fawkes had fared. She could not shake the feeling that something horrible was going to happen.

"He's inside a well-fortified castle," she murmured to herself. "Well prepared for the attack and with every advantage. He's a fierce fighter and experienced in siege warfare. There's no reason to think he will not prevail." She sighed again, then stood, unable to remain still any longer.

Hilary frowned at her, so Nicola moved closer to the window. There was a muffled cry. Nicola whirled and started toward the bed where the two children were sleeping. Simon had sat up and was sobbing. Nicola gathered him into her arms. "Hush, lovey, it's all right." She rapidly felt his forehead. It seemed cool, if slightly sweaty from sleep. "What could be wrong?" she asked Hilary, feeling helpless and frustrated. She was his mother. She should *know* what was wrong.

"A bad dream, mayhap," Hilary suggested. "He has them sometimes. Or it could be that he senses your distress."

"But he was asleep," Nicola protested. "How could he know?"

"Little ones sense the mood of those around them. They understand so much more than most people realize."

"Poor baby," Nicola whispered. She met Hilary's gaze. "How can I comfort him?"

"Keep doing what you're doing. Hold him. Speak softly and soothingly."

There was nothing in the world she wanted to do more, Nicola thought. To snuggle Simon's small precious body close.

He nestled against her. His eyes drifted closed and his breathing deepened. Nicola felt tears prick her eyelids. Sometimes she loved him so much it hurt. She smoothed a damp curl away from his face and wondered again why he had cried out. Did he somehow know his father was in danger? Preposterous. He did not even know his father existed.

She looked down at Simon. Amazing to think that Fawkes and she had created this beautiful child. She saw nothing in him of herself, and only a little of Fawkes. There was a resemblance to his father in the shape of his eyebrows, and his substantial size made her think that he would someday be tall and well-made like his father. Would he also grow up to be a knight? She did not want that for him, but if he was ever to claim his birthright, he would have no choice. The familiar gnawing fear afflicted her. "Please, God, keep him safe," she whispered. "And Fawkes, as well."

"There's news!" As the serving girl dashed into the room, Nicola remembered enduring a similar moment when Old Emma had come to her chamber to tell her the outcome of conflict between Mortimer and Fawkes. That time all had been well, but this time . . .

"De Cressy was shot by an assassin and is sore wounded," the girl announced in a singsong voice. "His men dragged him into the castle, but it's not certain if he yet lives. FitzRandolph and his men have begun besieging Valmar, but it is said that de Cressy's men fight like demons. Their archers have picked off a half-dozen men so far."

Sore wounded . . . not certain if he yet lives. Nicola's mind could barely function beyond those horrifying words. She staggered to the stool by the window as her legs collapsed beneath her. For a moment she sat, numb and unseeing, then the tears began to course down her cheeks.

From a distance, she heard Hilary questioning the serving girl. "An assassin? What does that mean?"

"The crossbow bolt that struck Fawkes came from a shot fired by someone in the woods, not from one of FitzRandolph's men. FitzRandolph says he is not responsible if Fawkes dies."

Bitterness engulfed Nicola. FitzRandolph had obviously hired someone to kill Fawkes. The cowardly bastard was afraid that he could not beat Fawkes in fair combat, so he had sent a murderer after him! Fawkes might die, or even be dead already, and it was her fault. She had set this deadly plot in motion, then failed to warn him of what she had done. It must look as if she had been scheming with FitzRandolph all along. . . .

A new wave of sick pain assaulted her. If Fawkes died, she deserved to die, as well. She had ruined him, repaid the love he gave her with lies and betrayal.

"Auntie?"

Nicola felt small fingers clutch her arm. She looked up, wiping at her tears. Simon looked at her, blue eyes wide and troubled. *Dear God, I've killed your father!* Nicola thought.

"Don't cry, Auntie." Simon patted her arm. "Please."

He was right. Tears solved nothing. Fawkes might still be alive. She must go to him and explain . . . make him understand . . .

She hugged Simon fiercely. "Don't fret, little one," she whispered. "I won't let him die, I promise."

She released Simon and stood. "I'm leaving," she told Hilary. "I must go to Fawkes."

"But how?" Hilary asked. "FitzRandolph has posted a guard on the stairs and more at the gate. You'll never be allowed to leave."

"I know Mordeaux Castle better than anyone. I will find a way. There are several privy holes that are no longer used. I'll climb down one of them and escape through it, under the wall."

"You're mad!" Hilary gasped. "You'll fall and be killed. Or else you'll end up in the moat and drown in that stinking morass!"

"If I fail and die, it's likely no more than I deserve," Nicola said. After days of anxious waiting, it was a relief to have a clear plan, a sense of purpose. And in truth, if Fawkes died, there was a part of her that would want to die as well.

Poor Simon, she thought. *What if he ends up without either of us?* But he would have Hilary and Gilbert. He thought they were his parents, anyway. With them, he would be safe and secure and loved. It was the best she could give him. At this moment, she must put Fawkes before her son. He needed her.

The serving girl was still in the room. Nicola went to her and said, "Go down and find the page William for me. I want to speak to him."

The servant curtsied and hurried off.

"I'm going to have William sneak a horse out of the castle for me," Nicola said. "He'll relish the challenge, and he's young enough that if he's caught, they won't punish him too harshly."

"You're determined to do this, aren't you?" Hilary said.

Nicola nodded. "I owe this to Fawkes, to at least let him know that I was not part of FitzRandolph's scheme." She approached Hilary. "If anything happens to me, I want you to know how much I appreciate what you've done for Simon. Just keep loving him and caring for him as you have been." She paused, realizing that she'd made another decision. She went to the coffer in the corner and withdrew her crimson mantle. Grasping the hem, she began to rip apart the layers of fabric.

"What are you doing?" Hilary cried.

"If FitzRandolph prevails, you'll have take Simon away from here. I'm going to give you the means to do that."

From between the layers of the garment, Nicola began to pull out gold coins. When she had all of them, she wrapped them in a piece of the tattered hem and brought them to Hilary. "There should be enough here for you to provide for your family until Gilbert can find a position at another castle. You must raise Simon elsewhere, so he will be safe. Then, when he is older, he can decide if he wants to reclaim his birthright. As soon as he is old enough, I want you to tell him who his parents are."

Hilary gaped at her. "But . . . but who will believe him? What proof will he have that he is the heir? As you have said, he looks nothing like either you or Fawkes."

"I have thought of that. Soon after Simon was born, I had a servant take a missive to the prior at Malvern. In it, I swear to the facts of Simon's birth and name him as my heir. I asked the prior to reveal this information only upon my death. With that paper and Glennyth's corroboration of what happened at his birth, Simon should have enough to force a claim."

"What if you reach Valmar only to find that Fawkes is . . . deceased. You know FitzRandolph will force you to marry him."

Nicola shook her head. "I'll not marry another man against my will. I'll either escape or die trying."

"Oh, lady," Hilary began to weep. She came and embraced Nicola. "What will happen to us? How will we go on?"

"You will do as I have told you." Nicola hugged Hilary tenderly. "You will take Simon away from here and raise him with love and gentleness. And I pray someday he will forgive me for all the mistakes I've made." A sob rose in her own throat as she felt Simon against her leg. The dear babe was trying to hug both her and Hilary at the same time, to comfort them.

She released Hilary and bent to pick up Simon. "It's all right," she whispered. "I promise nothing will happen to your . . . mother." She kissed Simon, then handed him to Hilary. "Now, I must ready myself for my journey. I can hardly climb down a privy hole in this gown!"

Twenty-one

Nicola gripped the rope and tried not to breath in too deeply. Although it hadn't been used as a privy in years, there was still a lingering stench in the narrow shaft. She struggled to find purchase with her feet on the slick stone walls as she slowly made her way down the rope. Sweating with the effort, she tried not to think about what might await her beyond the small patch of light glimmering beneath her.

Not that much farther, she told herself. Then all she had to do was find the horse William had left for her and ride to Valmar.

Dear God, don't let me be too late! The thought of Fawkes lying wounded and perhaps near death gave her new strength. She had to see him, to tell him that she loved him, that she would never have plotted his murder. For some reason, she had the feeling that if he knew she had not betrayed him, he would live. "Oh, please!" she cried aloud. "I'm coming, I'm coming!"

She was at the end of the shaft. Now all she had to do was let go and fall to the ground. If only she could tell what she was going to land in. She could see green beneath her, but could not tell if it was grass or water. Taking a deep breath, she bent her knees and let go.

She landed in marshy, muddy goo. Although she grimaced at the sound of the muck sucking at her slippers, the smelly morass had cushioned her fall and kept her from being injured. The drop down from the shaft was much farther than she had thought.

She left her slippers and slogged barefoot through the mire, trying not to think about what disgusting stuff she might be wading through. As soon as she found a stream, she was going to wash thoroughly!

The reeds grew tall, blocking her from view. She moved along slowly, searching for the pile of stones she knew should be there. That is, if only someone had not moved them away, or used them to repair the curtain wall. She found the pile by nearly falling over it. Taking a deep breath, she leaned down and began to push aside the largest stone. It was massively heavy, and Nicola remembered that the one time she had used the passageway, over ten years ago, it had taken her and two pages pushing with all their might to dislodge the stone.

At last the stone slid aside and a narrow passageway into the ground was revealed. Another worry struck Nicola. She'd been a small child when last she used this secret way out of the castle. What if she got stuck?

She reassured herself that the passageway had been made so the lord of the castle and his family could escape in case of attack. It must be large enough for a man to pass through, let alone a woman.

Taking another deep breath, she let herself down into the space. With her body halfway in, balancing on the narrow stairs, she fumbled in the bag of supplies tied to her body. She'd never be able to endure it if she did not have some light to see where she was going. She struck the flintstone and lit a rushlight. Then, after replacing the flintstone in her pack, she started downward.

Rats, spiders and other unknown horrors all weighed upon her mind with every step. The passageway smelled ancient and evil, like rotting things. She fought down the dread that made her skin crawl. She was doing this for Fawkes. It was the only chance she had to go to him.

The air grew thicker, denser and more foul-smelling. Nicola began to wonder about the opening on the other end. What if it was blocked? What if she was trapped? "Stop it!" she whispered fiercely. "If it becomes your grave, so be it. You must at least try."

Abruptly, the passageway ended in a small chamber, so small that she had to crouch down to fit into it. Nicola held the rushlight up toward the ceiling of the chamber, searching for a sign of an opening. She tried to remember how they had got out last time. One of the pages had used a stick to probe the stones until he found a loose one. But she didn't have a stick.

Grimacing, she reached up and felt the ceiling with her free hand. All the stones seemed solid. Her panic returned. So close. She could not be but a few feet from fresh air and freedom. She closed her eyes, trying again to remember. It seemed as if the opening was toward the back, at the far edge of the chamber.

She reached upward and again explored the stones, shuddering as some sort of insect crawled over her hand. Suddenly, she felt loose earth sifting down into the chamber. She pushed at the rock near where the dirt seemed to be coming from. More earth poured into the chamber, coating her face and extinguishing her light. She coughed, then swore. Without the rushlight she could not make her way back. She had to find a way out now. Dropping the extinguished light, she reached upward with both hands and clawed and pushed with all her strength.

The rock gave way, showering her with dirt. She swiped at her face, and when she could see again, gave a sigh of relief to see a small patch of daylight above her. Now that she knew the way out, she set to frantically shoving the rocks aside. At last, she cleared a large enough opening to wriggle free. She pushed her head and shoulders through and thrust herself out.

A few feet away, a sheep regarded her with placid disinterest. The passageway apparently led to the common grazing area outside the castle embankment. She was safely out of the castle, but also in clear sight of anyone watching from the ramparts. After climbing the rest of the way out of the passageway, she got to her feet and ran for the forest.

It seemed to take forever to reach the safety of the trees. There, she stopped and doubled over, panting. She could only hope that she hadn't been seen. Only hope the page had been able to get the horse out of the castle and the mount was still waiting for her.

She rubbed at her sweaty face and grimaced at the streaks of dirt on her hand. What a mess she was! She looked down at her filthy feet and gown, her scratched, broken-nailed hands. As anxious as she was to reach Valmar, she simply had to bathe before she entered the castle. No one would believe it was she, otherwise. Lady Nicola—the well-groomed, refined gentlewoman—now looked and smelled as disgusting as the gong farmer who mucked out the castle privy holes.

She searched in her supply bag for the spare pair of shoes she had brought, then, after putting them on, set out through the woods.

Fawkes was vaguely aware of being carried to the upper part of the castle and placed on a bed. Women hovered around him, speaking in low, urgent voices. They undressed him and made him drink some bitter stuff. He tried to see through the mist that surrounded him, to overcome the terrible pain that pressed down on his chest, muddling his thoughts. *Nicola—where is she?*

Then he remembered. He wanted to shout and scream, but all he had the strength to do was moan. He could hear the sound from far away, hear the women murmuring, hear the fear and anxiety in their voices. They thought he was going to die. And at this moment, he wanted to.

* * *

He was awoken from peaceful oblivion by excruciating pain. They were tearing open his shoulder and thrusting hot daggers into it. Strong arms held him down. He could not escape the torment. He tried to scream, but his mouth was too dry. His stomach roiled and the darkness loomed. He pitched into it, praying for relief from the agony. It ebbed, but did not leave him. He felt a cup pressed against his lips, and he drank greedily. He was so thirsty, so . . .

Emptiness. Endless quiet. He floated in the dark, wanting to stay there, away from the pain, away from the terrible battle that he did not have the strength to fight. He was so weary, so very weary.

Thank God she was almost there, Nicola thought as she urged the nag through the underbrush. She could not go much farther. The muscles in her arms and legs trembled with fatigue. The climb down the privy hole and the journey through the underground passageway had taken more out of her than she realized. She never would have been able to walk this far. The old mare—slow and stubborn though she might be—truly was heaven sent.

And then there was the matter of getting past FitzRandolph's forces. She'd thought for certain she'd be seen, but then a mist had conveniently drifted across the end of the valley where they were camped, and she'd been able to reach the forest undetected.

Nearing the edge of the woods, Nicola glimpsed Glennyth's cottage. She would stop there to rest and have something to eat. Although the wisewoman would probably be at the castle tending Fawkes, this would be a safe place for Nicola to recover her strength. As anxious as she was to see him, she realized she would do him little good if she fainted from exhaustion before she could even speak to him.

She dismounted near the shed behind the cottage and teth-
ered the mare. She started toward the cottage, wincing with
each step. At the entrance of the cottage she swept the hide
door aside, then froze as she saw Glennyth sitting near the
hearth, her concentration focused on a bowl she held between
her hands. All around the room, candles glowed, bathing the
dwelling in a rich golden light.

Nicola's first thought was that Fawkes was dead. She
closed her eyes and felt the dirt floor loom up beneath her.

When she opened her eyes, Glennyth was bending over
her, a wry expression on her face. "You look as if you've
been to hell and back," she said. "Indeed, I've seen soldiers
after a battle who looked better, certainly they were cleaner
and smelled fresher."

"I tried to wash in a stream," Nicola whispered. What did
it matter if she stank if Fawkes was dead? Tears stung her
eyes as grief struck her anew.

"Well, it did not work. I will heat water for a bath. But I
think you should drink some wine before you bathe. You
look as if you might swoon again at any moment."

"I don't want wine," Nicola moaned. "I don't want a bath.
I want to die!"

"By the Lady, that's no way to talk! While Fawkes yet
lives, there is hope!"

Nicola struggled to sit up. "He's alive? Why aren't you
with him? Does that mean that the injury was not that
grave?"

"Oh, it's grave enough—a crossbow bolt through the
shoulder. I'm certain they had a devil of a time cutting it
out."

Nicola felt as if she would faint again. But she fought off
the nausea and asked, "Who cut it out? And why aren't you
with him, tending him? You should be at his bedside at this
moment!"

Glennyth's eyes turned a stormy green. "They will not let
me near him. They would rather that he die than be tended

by a 'witch woman.' " Her mouth twisted into a bitter grimace.

Nicola got to her feet, fury suddenly giving her strength. "What about Reynard? He can insist that you be allowed to help Fawkes!"

Glennyth shook her head. "Reynard has no say in the matter. Adam FitzSaer has taken command of Valmar."

"Adam! But he has no right!"

"He claims that he has every right. That when Fawkes made him castellan of Mordeaux, he became his second in command."

"But Reynard should protest! *He's* Fawkes's captain, not FitzSaer!"

"Mayhap he would if he were not sitting in Valmar's oubliette at this moment."

Nicola felt a cold chill travel down her body. FitzSaer, who hated her, now controlled Valmar Castle. He would never let her see Fawkes.

"Come," Glennyth urged. "Sit down before you faint again." She led Nicola to a stool by the table and poured her a cup of wine. "Drink. If you don't regain your strength, you won't be able to help Fawkes."

"How can I help him?" She was on the edge of despair. To have come so far and to have struggled so hard, only to come to this.

"You can help him by not giving up!" Glennyth exhorted. "You must have faith, you must believe he will live."

"Unless FitzSaer does not want him to . . . unless *he* is in league with FitzRandolph." A new wave of hopelessness struck her.

Glennyth shook her head. "FitzSaer is not Fawkes's enemy. He means to be loyal, to protect his lord. But losing Mordeaux was a bitter thing for him. He no longer trusts anyone, especially anyone who was loyal to you. He insists that you and I were both part of the plot to murder Fawkes. When Reynard argued otherwise, FitzSaer had him thrown into the oubliette. He says that because Reynard is my lover, he cannot be trusted, either."

"How do you know all this?"

"Old Emma came and told me."

"Old Emma? She walked all this way to give you the news?" Nicola felt a rush a tenderness for the elderly serving woman. For all her complaining, when the need was urgent, she had done her best.

"Yea, she did. She wanted me to go and find you and convince you to come back to Valmar. Although many of the servants, and likely a good share of the garrison, don't believe FitzSaer's lies, they can't act against his orders."

"But what can I do?" She felt defeated. FitzSaer controlled Valmar; he had made her the enemy.

"Somehow you must get inside the castle and rally those servants and knights who are still loyal to you. Convince them to ignore FitzSaer and let me come and tend Fawkes."

"But how will I do this?" Nicola asked. She was exhausted in body and spirit, discouraged and heartsick. "And what if I am too late? What if Fawkes . . . if he . . ."

"He's not dead," Glennyth said. "No doubt they have muddled things and allowed his wound to become poisoned." She gave a sniff of disgust. "But he yet lives. I have seen him in the scrying bowl."

Nicola glanced at the bowl sitting on the floor near the hearth; it had a murky, shiny surface, like oil. "Was that what you were doing when I came here?"

Glennyth nodded. "I was also able to see your escape from Mordeaux and aid you when I could. Why do you think the mist came at exactly the moment when you needed it to hide you from FitzRandolph's army?"

"You sent the mist?" Nicola shivered. Glennyth was truly a sorceress. It frightened her, but also relieved her. With Glennyth's magic, perhaps there was hope she might be able to sneak into Valmar and see Fawkes.

As if guessing her thoughts, Glennyth said, "I can't aid

you in getting into the castle. You'll have to find a way to do that on your own. And I can't heal Fawkes from a distance. Somehow you must get FitzSaer out of the way so I can bring my healing medicines to treat him."

Nicola shook her head. "So many things could go wrong. If I fail . . ."

"You must not think about that. Now, drink the rest of the wine; it contains a tonic that will hearten and strengthen you. Then we will bathe you and find something clean for you to wear."

Sometimes the best course is the most brazen one. No one will expect the lady of Valmar to walk boldly up to the gate and demand entrance.

Nicola walked steadily through the village, shaking her head as she recalled Glennyth's words. The plan seemed mad, utterly witless, but she had not been able to think of a better one. She didn't know any secret ways into Valmar, and with FitzRandolph's army camped outside the ditch, there was virtually no traffic in or out of the castle. She could not pretend to be a farmer's wife come with produce, or any other sort of ruse she had used in the past. Glennyth had promised that the mist would be enough to get past FitzRandolph's men. Then it was mostly a matter of who guarded the gate. Would it be someone who was loyal to her, or to FitzSaer?

Nicola glanced around. So far Glennyth's scheme seemed to be working. She'd seen two people in the village, old Widow Aldyth and Edgar, one of the villeins, but neither of them seemed to notice her. Aldyth continued to sweep the old floor rushes out of her house, the besom moving in slow, rhythmic strokes. Edgar didn't even glance her way, but continued on toward the forest, likely planning to cut withies or gather firewood from the looks of the ax over his shoulder.

It was as if they thought her a wraith or a phantom, and decided it was better not to acknowledge such things.

Nicola walked steadily toward the castle. The mist was rising—the dragon's breath, Glennyth had called it. Nicola glanced down at the ground, carefully following the muddy, much-used trackway. She dare not lose her way and accidentally stumble into the enemy army. Through the mist, sounding eerily near, she could hear noises from their camp—voices, the ring of hammers as men repaired mail and constructed equipment to use in the siege, the restless sounds of the horses at their pickets.

Glennyth said FitzRandolph had not attempted any attack on Valmar. Nicola wondered if he was waiting for Fawkes to die. He might think that deprived of their leader, the Valmar garrison would surrender easily. At the thought, she quickened her pace.

She sensed from the slope of the trackway that she neared the castle, and at last she glimpsed the bridge across the moat. Thank the saints that it was down. She had only to get the guards to raise the portcullis.

She paused on the bridge and stared up at the curtain wall. The mist was thinning and she could see the gatehouse clearly. Should she call out or otherwise seek to gain the guards' attention? But what if it was one of FitzSaer's men who first noticed her? A helmeted head peered through one of the crenels. She threw back the hood of the mantle Glennyth had lent her and held her breath. They would surely recognize her. Either they would let her in or they would raise the hue and cry.

She heard voices, not loud, not shouts of warning. Standing as tall and proud as she could, she called out, "It's your lady. Let me in."

She heard more talking, then the grinding rasp of the portcullis being raised. When it reached above her head, she walked through. The guards released the stop and the gate crashed down behind her with a thunderous clatter. For better or worse, she was inside Valmar.

She started across the bailey, wondering if it was really going to be this easy. She heard footsteps behind her and turned.

"Lady?" Henry de Brionne dragged off his helmet and stared at her. "What are doing here? Where have you been?" He took a step closer. "God's blood, it really is you. For a moment, we thought"—he gave a nervous laugh—"we thought you were a ghost."

Nicola moved near him, and spoke in a low, urgent voice. "Take me to Fawkes."

"Of course," Henry fell in step beside her. "I'll warn you though, FitzSaer will not like it. He's blaming you for everything."

Nicola glanced around nervously as they walked toward the keep. At any moment, she expected FitzSaer to appear and order her thrown into the oubliette. "Whatever you have heard regarding my betrayal, it isn't true," she told Henry. "FitzRandolph imprisoned me. I knew nothing of his plot to murder Fawkes."

"By the rood, murder is the thing to name it!" Henry struck his palm with his fist. "The crossbow is an evil weapon if ever there was one. Rips clear through the best mail and is accurate from a great distance if the archer be skilled." He gave a snort of disgust. "FitzRandolph claims it was an assassin, but who else besides him wants Fawkes dead? Scheming, yellow-hearted bastard doesn't have the guts to face Fawkes in battle, so he arranges for him to be shot during a parley. I vow, if Fawkes dies and FitzRandolph takes Valmar, I'll never serve him. I'd rather lie down in the grass with a poisonous adder!"

Nicola scarcely heard him. At the words "if Fawkes dies," she began to run.

Suddenly, from behind her, she heard shouts. "Stop her! Stop that woman!"

When she was halfway up the ramp at the back entrance of the keep where the food was brought into the hall, strong arms grabbed her from behind. She was whirled around and met the startled gaze of Engelard. "Milady," he breathed. He released her and stepped back. "I didn't know it was you."

"Don't let her get away!" someone shouted. "She's come to finish off de Cressy!"

Nicola considered fleeing while she had the chance. But the odds were that before she reached the upper chambers of the castle, she would be captured by someone who was more in awe of FitzSaer than of her. Besides, she was sick of hearing his lies.

She turned around, and, staring down into the bailey, gave Adam FitzSaer a look of utter contempt. "I have not come to kill my husband, but to see that he is properly tended to. If you cared for his life at all, you would have the healer Glennyth at his bedside at this moment. If he dies, it will be on your conscience, not mine!"

"She lies!" FitzSaer shouted. He looked around at the crowd gathering in the bailey. Scullery boys and serving girls from the kitchen, pages and chambermaids, weavers and craftsmen. He pointed at Nicola. "She plotted to betray her husband to his enemies, then joined with them in scheming to have him murdered. No matter that she is the heiress of Valmar, you cannot let her treachery go unpunished." He gestured to the knights gathered around. "Seize her. Put her in the oubliette with Reynard."

The knights moved toward Nicola, and she suddenly realized that those people who were loyal to her had no weapons. They could not defend her against armed knights. She turned to Engelard, who still stood on the ramp. "Please. Help me."

His dark eyes were anguished. "Lady, I . . ."

How could she convince him? What could she say to make him believe her? "I love my husband," she said fervently. "I would willingly die for him. But that is not what he needs now. What he needs is a healer. Even if FitzSaer imprisons me, promise me that you will fetch Glennyth from the village. Only she can save Fawkes's life."

Engelard nodded jerkily. "Yea, milady. I will do as you ask."

"Hold her there," FitzSaer called. "Do not let her flee."

Engelard did not seize her, but neither did he move aside. Nicola watched FitzSaer approach. She tried frantically to think of a plan.

But before FitzSaer could reach the ramp, Weyland, the armorer, stepped in his path. Agelwulf, the burly Saxon cook, joined Weyland, then, suddenly, there were a dozen people blocking FitzSaer's way.

Nicola saw FitzSaer's jaw tighten in fury. He glanced up at her, and his expression changed again. Nicola turned to look up the ramp and saw more servants—women and young pages—coming out of the castle, looking wary but determined.

FitzSaer made a frustrated movement. "What are you doing? What does it matter if she is your lady? She is deceitful, treacherous! Because of her, Valmar Castle may be taken!"

No one moved. Nicola could feel the knights flanking FitzSaer grow more and more uneasy. They might have the weapons, but they did not want to be ordered to break through the mass of people surrounding her.

"Have you no sense?" FitzSaer raged hoarsely. "She already destroyed one husband, now she seeks to destroy another! How can you seek to defend such a monster, a wicked she-devil!"

"She is our lady!" Weyland answered in a booming voice. "She has always seen to our welfare, made certain that the food stores went to feed us instead of being sold for coin. She has nursed our children when they were sick, and sat in judgment on our disputes. *She* is *Valmar,* not Fawkes de Cressy or Walter Mortimer." He raised the pike he was hold-

ing in a threatening gesture. "And, God as my witness, I will
not stand here and listen to you slander her! Let her go to
de Cressy if she wishes it. And if you are so concerned for
Valmar's safety, go back to your watch at the gate and leave
Lady Nicola in peace!"

Jesu, she had not known they cared so much for her! All
these years she had felt alone and helpless, never knowing
that she was surrounded by such brave, faithful folk. It
brought tears to her eyes to think of the risk they took for
her sake.

Beside her, she heard Engelard exhale in relief. "He's defeated now," the knight murmured. "FitzSaer cannot stand
against such eloquence. Come, lady, let me escort you to the
bedchamber where Fawkes lies."

"Nay, I do not need an escort. Hurry now, do as I bid,
ride out to the village and fetch Glennyth."

"But FitzRandolph—"

"His men will not meddle with a lone man. It serves no
purpose. And on the way back, Glennyth can weave a spell
of enchantment to keep you safe."

"She's a witch, then, in truth?" Engelard suddenly looked
pale.

Nicola nodded. "I only pray to God that she knows
enough magic to save Fawkes."

Twenty-two

As soon as FitzSaer moved off, back to the gate tower, Nicola called out to the servants gathered, "Where is Fawkes? Where is milord?"

"They put him in the bedchamber he usually sleeps in, milady," Bertha, one of the serving women answered.

Nicola hurried into the castle. At the far end of the hall was the stairway leading to the upper portions of the castle. She raced up the stairs and nearly ran into Old Emma coming down. "Thank heavens ye've come!" Old Emma cried. Her face crumpled with anxiety. "Fawkes is sore fevered."

Nicola grasped the servant's shoulder. "Go and find Henry de Brionne and have him fetch Reynard from the oubliette. Tell him that I need him."

"But FitzSaer—he'll not allow it!"

"Yea, he will. Now, please, do as I tell you." Nicola rushed past Old Emma, her heart in her throat. Many more men died from wound fever than from the wounds themselves. She could not help thinking of her father's miserable death. At the end he had stank like a rotting carcass.

Outside the bedchamber, she paused for a steadying breath. Glennyth would come soon. She would know what to do. Somehow she would save Fawkes.

The chamber smelled of sickness and fear. The shutters were closed tight, the room stifling hot. In the dim light from two candles, Nicola could see two women standing near the bed. One of them turned at her approach, and she recognized Gillian.

"Oh, milady," Gillian gasped. "Nothing we have tried has worked. We washed him down with cool water, but still he burns."

Wordlessly, Nicola moved toward the bed and pushed aside the curtains. Fawkes lay on his back, stiff and still. Except for the feverish flush on his cheeks, he might have been a carved marble effigy. He was naked except for a strip of linen across his groin, and Nicola could not help thinking how beautiful his body was. He had lost some flesh, but his leanness only made his muscularity more obvious. In the breadth and size of him and the graceful lines of his strong, powerful limbs, she saw the fierce, formidable warrior, the consummate swordsman and knight.

A knight who had been struck down not in battle but by treachery. Treachery that she had brought upon him. Guilt stabbed into her.

She touched his face, feeling the dry heat of his fever, the rough stubble on his jaw. A thousand memories flooded her senses as she stroked his cracked lips. What pleasure he had given her with that mouth. "Oh, Fawkes," she whispered.

She fought for strength, then reached out and lifted the bandage. Every inch of his shoulder seemed to be bruised and swollen, and angry red lines showed where they had cut him open to remove the crossbow bolt and then sewn him back together again. She could feel the heat of him even from a distance and smell a sickly odor that she recognized as putrefying flesh. She closed her eyes. She'd thought that once she was near him, could touch him and tell him how much she loved him, that she could somehow heal him. But now she saw how ill he was and despair weighed down upon her.

She replaced the bandage and moved away from the bed, unable to bear to look at him any longer. She wanted to weep, to pour out her guilt and pain. But she felt too empty, too drained, too numb with hopelessness.

"Milady, you must sit down," the other woman, Anna, urged. "Can I get you anything? A cup of wine? Something to eat?"

Mutely, Nicola shook her head. She would never eat again. She wanted to die. If Fawkes was gone from the world—and because of her own stupid scheming—then there was nothing to live for.

The women moved a stool near the bed and Nicola sat down. She took Fawkes's limp hand in hers and brought it to her face. At the feel of his callused fingers against her cheek the memories washed over her, excruciating, as bitter as verjuice. She had not known what she had. She should have cherished every moment, every kiss, every caress. Instead, she had been consumed with worry for Simon.

Why could she not have trusted Fawkes? Found some way to tell him about Simon and yet not risked her son's life? There must have been a way. Instead, she had betrayed her husband and left him to his enemies. She should have known that FitzRandolph was not to be trusted. He had said he meant to kill Fawkes.

The guilt and regret was almost unbearable. Fawkes was going to die and it was her fault. And the worst of it was that he would never know how she felt about him. She pressed his palm to her mouth, almost physically ill with remorse. Why had she never told him what he meant to her? How many times in the afterglow of their lovemaking had she thought the words, but never allowed them to pass her lips? *I love you. I adore you. You are my very soul.* "Oh, my darling," she whispered, "I am such a wretched fool."

"Not as much as these sorry wenches!" Glennyth's tart voice startled Nicola from her miserable contemplations. The healer marched across the room and threw open the shutters. "What are you trying to do, suffocate him!" she demanded of the serving women. "He needs fresh air and light to aid his healing."

"Nay!" Anna protested. "You'll let in foul humors! If he's exposed to the air, he'll sicken even more."

"Hmmph," Glennyth said. "How many wounded men have *you* treated? And how many have died thanks to your inept attentions?" She didn't wait for an answer. "If you wish to make yourself useful, you can fetch me some things from the kitchen."

Anna made an outraged sound and left. Gillian approached Glennyth. "I'll do whatever you ask. Some years ago, you aided my mother when she was in travail with my brother. Although he was too big to fit through the birth passage and my mother died, you were able to save Bertram. He's now a big strapping fellow and a great help to my father."

"I remember your mother, poor soul," Glennyth said. "Now, what I need is a bucket of hot bran and boiled onions—steaming hot. Also some wine—it doesn't matter if it's sour or poor quality. And some moldy bread, lots of it. Can you do that?"

Gillian nodded. "If I tell Agelwulf that it's for the lord, he'll give me whatever I wish."

"I also need some strong men to hold him down."

"I can see to that." Reynard entered the room. He nodded to Nicola, then gave Glennyth a brief, warm smile. She acknowledged it with a lift of her brows, then motioned for him to go fetch the men.

"What are you going to do?" Nicola asked as Reynard left. She was utterly puzzled by Glennyth's requests. Did the healer intend to use the bran and wine to make some sort of offering to her pagan gods?

"The wound should never have been stitched up. Now poison is growing inside. I'll have to cut it open again and wash out what corruption I can, then pack it with bran to draw out the rest. Then, when the wound is clean, I will stitch it up again and cover it with moldy bread. There is something in the mold that aids in healing."

"Will he . . ." Nicola took a sharp breath. "Will he live?"

"He is strong and young. He has a chance."

"What can I do?" Nicola asked.

"You can't stay here, certainly. This is an ugly, gruesome thing that I am about to do, and I don't want to be bothered by you fainting or weeping."

"But how can I leave him?" Nicola asked. "What if something happens and I'm not here?"

"Nothing will happen. He will survive the treatment, although he may cry out as if he is being tortured. I will give him as much poppy draught as I can, but he will still feel pain."

Nicola shuddered. Poor Fawkes. He had suffered so much already. She went to the bed and kissed him on the lips. "I love you," she whispered. "I will make everything up to you, I promise."

She left the bedchamber. At the bottom of the stairway, she met Reynard. Behind him were Henry and Niles. "Lady," Reynard nodded, his eyes cold. "Once again you leave him."

"It's not what you think!" Nicola protested. "Glennyth made me go. She thinks it better that I don't watch what she is about to do. But promise me that you will fetch me as soon as she is finished."

"Why do you even pretend to care?" Reynard asked bitterly. "Why are you even here? Do you wish to sit by his bedside and gloat?" She had never seen Reynard look like this. His blue eyes burned with suspicion and hatred.

"Sweet Mary, surely you don't think I meant for this to happen!" she cried. "I promise you, I didn't betray Fawkes! I have spent the last few days as FitzRandolph's prisoner. I finally escaped by climbing down a privy hole. I knew nothing of his plot to murder Fawkes. If I had, I would have found some way to warn my husband, I swear it!"

"But why did you leave? Why did you go to Mordeaux when you knew FitzRandolph was there?"

"I had no choice." She hesitated. For so long, she had kept her secret. It was not easy to say the words. "You see . . . my son is at Mordeaux. I was afraid for him."

"Your son?" Reynard's eyes bulged with surprise.

"Yea, my son. And Fawkes's son, as well, although I fear he will not believe it. Simon has been raised in secret at Mordeaux all these years." She sighed heavily, relieved to have the burden lifted. "Near everything I have done that has caused Fawkes pain is because of Simon."

"But the babe you bore died," Henry protested. "That's what everyone said. That's what drove Mortimer mad— knowing that you kill . . ." He broke off.

"That I killed his heir?" Nicola said. "Is that what the men have said about me? I guess I can understand that you might think such a thing. After all, I didn't care if Mortimer thought I had something to do with the babe's death. For him to think that made my triumph all the sweeter." She shook her head. "But the dead babe he saw was not mine. It belonged to one of the village families. It was born dead and its mother died soon after. Glennyth took *my* babe to Hilary de Vescy at Mordeaux. She has been raising Simon ever since."

"And you say it is Fawkes's child?" Reynard gripped her arm and his eyes glowed with fierce warning. "If that is true, why did you not tell him as soon as we arrived at Valmar? Why all these months of deceit?"

"Because"—Nicola looked at Reynard, then at Henry and Niles—"Simon does not favor Fawkes. Nor me, either. He is fair-haired and blue eyed . . ."

"Like Mortimer," Reynard finished.

Nicola nodded.

Reynard released her. "Even if it is Mortimer's child, you should have told Fawkes. He would have raised the boy as his heir. For you, he would have done anything."

"And how was I to know that?" Nicola asked. "Fawkes hated Mortimer. I feared he would hate Simon for looking like him, even if he is *not*"—she emphasized the word—*"not* Mortimer's son."

"Maybe I can understand your fear in the beginning," Reynard said, "but now—surely after living with Fawkes for months, sharing his bed, you should know that he would never hurt a child."

Nicola met Reynard's righteous anger with her own. "He told me once that if I had borne a child by Mortimer, he did not know what he would do. I didn't know for certain that Simon would be safe! Even if Fawkes did not raise a hand against him, that does not mean he would not send him away and strip him of his birthright! He is the rightful heir to Valmar and Mordeaux!"

"And how did you think he could ever claim his inheritance if you never told anyone who he was?"

They were shouting now. Nicola began an angry retort, then she saw Gillian behind Reynard, carrying a basket. "There is no point to any of this if Fawkes dies," she said. "Move aside and let them bring the things for Glennyth."

Reynard quickly did so, and Gillian and two knaves carrying buckets of steaming bran hurried up the stairs. "You'd better go, as well," Nicola said. "Glennyth will need you."

Reynard shot her a hostile look. "If Fawkes dies, I will hold you to blame. Though you may have meant him no malice, it was *your* lies that brought him to this sorry state!"

Reynard and the other men hurried after the servants, and Nicola took a deep, steadying breath. She could not deny Reynard's words. If Fawkes died, she *was* to blame.

She started out of the castle, wondering where she could go so she would not hear Fawkes's moans and cries of pain. Rather she would thrust a knife in own her breast than hear her love scream out in agony.

In the bailey, several servants stopped her to express their concern for Fawkes, and their loyalty to her. She thanked them warmly, trying not to break down. Thomas's protestation of devotion finally undid her. She began to weep. The startled youth patted her arm. "Don't cry, milady, I'm certain all will be well. Glennyth is the best healer I've ever heard of. And milord is strong and fit. He'll pull through this, I know it."

Nicola nodded through her tears, trying to believe him. "Thank you, Thomas," she whispered. She rushed off, afraid to be waylaid yet again.

She made her way to the garden, remembering all the times she had gone to the one at Mordeaux when she was a little girl. It was her refuge, especially when she was in trouble, which was often enough. As she took a seat among the rose bower, where profuse yellow and pink blossoms filled the air with their spicy, soothing scent, she shook her head grimly. What had happened to the free-spirited girl she had once been? Ever since she wed Mortimer, her whole existence had become a struggle for survival, first for herself, then for her child. There had been little happiness in her life, and what pleasure she had experienced was nearly all at the hands of Fawkes. Now it appeared that those few hours when they made love might be all the joy she was to have.

She picked a lush, full yellow bloom, but it fell apart in her hand, the petals drifting down to the ground around her feet. Life was so fleeting, so fragile. All anyone could do is try to savor whatever joy they were given. She crushed the remaining petals in her fingers, inhaling their delicate sweetness. "I promise, Fawkes," she said aloud, "if you live, I will make it up to you. I will be the wife you have dreamed of, and I will trust you and love you with all my heart."

Tears coursed down her cheeks, and the fierce knot in her stomach grew tighter. After a time, she stood up and went to the herb portion of the garden, where she discovered Gimlyn, hunting. He came up to her and rubbed against her legs. "It's no use," she told him. "My heart belongs to another, and only his warm, tender smile will ease my pain."

She gave a sob, then turned at the sound of footsteps. Thomas stood there, looking embarrassed. "Glennyth says it is time for you to come and help her."

"Of course," Nicola said, surprised to be summoned so soon. "What does she want me to do?"

"She says only you can give him the will to live. She wants you to call his spirit back from the other side."

Nicola felt a cold tremor pass down her spine, and looking at Thomas, she guessed that he was also uneasy with Glennyth's words.

She followed Thomas back to the castle. Entering the bedchamber, her nose was assaulted by a nauseating mixture of odors. "The wound was more tainted than I thought," Glennyth said grimly. "I only hope that the poison has not gotten into his blood."

"What . . . what does that mean?" Nicola asked, fearing the answer.

"Once the poison spreads in his body, it is much harder to cure. Then it is up to him. His own strength and will to live is all that can save him."

Nicola approached the bed. Fawkes looked dead already, his skin blanched white. A mass of cooked bran and onions covered his shoulder, thankfully blocking her view of his wound. "What should I do?" she whispered.

"Take his hand, touch his face, speak to him. Tell him that you love him. Ask him, nay, demand that he come back to you!"

Nicola raised a startled gaze to meet Glennyth's.

"He didn't even stir when I opened the wound," the healer said. "That means that he has already gone to the world of shadows and spirits."

"He's dead?" Nicola felt frantically for Fawkes's pulse.

"Nay, not dead," Glennyth reassured her. "He still breathes. A part of him remains with us. He can hear you. Feel you near him. That is why what you do can make a difference whether he lives or passes on to the other side."

Nicola's stomach clutched with dread. Glennyth said that it was up to her, that only she could call him back. But what if he no longer cared for her? What if he hated her?

"Push the doubts from your mind," Glennyth said, as if knowing her thoughts. "Concentrate. Send him your strength, your love. Give him a reason to live. Don't think of yourself, of how you have failed him. Think of how much you love him. Of the joy you have known together." Glennyth nodded toward the bed, then left the room.

Nicola let the memories wash over her. . . .

How tender he had been that first time. So gentle and caring. So determined to make it good for her and give her pleasure. How many women ever knew such ecstasy the first time with a man? Or ever? "Oh, Fawkes," she whispered. "You were the best, most magical lover a woman could have."

She leaned over him and, with trembling hands, began to caress him. The soft, wavy hair, like the feathers of a sleek black bird. The fine, proud contours of his face. As she felt the roughness of his whiskered jaw and then the warm, soft shape of his mouth, a sigh swept through her. He had worked sorcery with that mouth. Joined to hers, sweet and tender, rough and demanding. Against her body—sublime.

She bent down and kissed him, wetting his dry lips with her tongue. His skin was dry and hot, but she pretended to herself that it was passion that heated his body, rather than sickness. She stroked his strong, magnificent neck, then her eyes shied away from the mess of the wound. She gazed instead on the enticing planes of his chest on the other side. The soft mat of curly black hair. The piquant dark point of his exposed nipple. She touched it delicately, trying to make it tighten with arousal.

Sighing, she moved her fingers lower, moved aside the strip of linen covering Fawkes, then traced the line of dark hair down his flat, hard belly. What a stirring, lovely body he had. So strong and well-made. So very, very male.

Her gaze sought his cock, now soft and unprepossessing, hanging down limply from the thatch of dark hair. Hard to imagine that gentle-looking appendage swelling into the great, purplish, upthrust thing she remembered. A sigh of pleasure escaped her at the memories. What he did to her— filling her, tantalizing her, gratifying her with hard, delicious heat. She cast a glance at the door, then dared to move her hand lower, to touch the silky, loose flesh. She encircled him easily with her fingers, wondering if he would ever rise and grow hard for her again.

At the thought, tears filled her eyes. She worshiped his body, its beauty and graceful form, the wonderful things it could do to her. What if it was too late, and all that dazzling maleness doomed to decay to dust?

Desperate, she began to stroke him. Blinded by tears, she caressed him, trying to make her fingers convey all the love and tenderness she felt. "Don't leave me," she whispered. "There are so many things we have not tried, so much we have not shared. Live for me Fawkes. I will give you plea- sure. I will fulfill your fondest dreams."

He was in a place of shadows, writhing, threatening, op- pressive. Enemies lurked in the dark mist surrounding him, unseen and terrifying. He thought it must be hell, yet it was not what he expected hell to be like. There was no torture, no flames, no pain. Only a weight upon his chest and the tormenting shadows. He wanted so badly to see their faces, to know who pursued and taunted him. Unless he could see them, he could not fight.

And he knew he must fight them, knew with some fierce instinct that it was his duty to defeat them, that the survival of his very soul depended upon it. But he could not see them, could not move. And he had no weapon. He was helpless.

And then, out of the dark mist, one of the shadows touched him. He could feel its fingers clutching his groin. And still he could not move. He gritted his teeth, thinking that they would dismember him, rip his manhood from his body. But the fingers were gentle, caressing. He could not understand it.

The phantom hand provoked and aroused him. He could feel himself rising. Maybe, this was the torture, he thought. Maybe in hell, the damned were aroused by demons and then left to suffer. No satisfaction, no release. Only teasing, provocative fingers.

A female demon. He could sense from the way the shadow touched him. Only a woman would be so deft, so careful, so skillful. He imagined a demon with Nicola's face—even in hell he could not forget her. He would lie like this forever, tortured by his hopeless love, wanting her even in death.

His arousal intensified. He could feel his shaft swelling, throbbing, pulsing with blood. But he could not move, could not satisfy the hunger building inside him. It was agony, and yet, it was not.

He was rising. As unbelievable as it seemed, his cock was growing hard, filling with hot blood, filling her hand. Nicola stared at the plum-colored tube of flesh her fingers encircled. This part of him was alive, healthy and strong, defying the affliction of his body. And so intriguing, so enticing.

She fondled him, playing with the silky tip, brushing her fingers across the eye-like opening until a drop of milky moisture appeared. She glanced once at the door, then bent over him. Her fingers still surrounded his flesh, experiencing pulsing, rigid heat. She brought her mouth to the tip and licked up the dewy drop. His love juice. A teardrop from the blind eye of his manhood. And she would make it weep with pleasure.

It tasted faintly sweet, while his skin was salty and piquant. She explored with her tongue, delighting in the texture of his flesh. Liquid and solid at once, the lush tip filled her mouth like a perfectly ripe fruit, whole and delicious. She sucked him deeper, until the velvety tip caressed the recesses of her mouth. Her mouth watered with delight, and she closed her eyes and suckled him. The sensitive skin of her lips felt hot and aroused, stretched by his fullness. The pressure of the thick head against her throat made her shiver.

She began to move in a pulsing, erotic rhythm. Her inner core seemed to throb and quiver in time with the thrust of his hard flesh deep in her mouth, and her body remembered his slick length probing deep in another orifice. But she could not take all of him this way. He was too big. And she found it more pleasurable to savor the length of him, to glide her mouth up and down, lingering long on the succulent, swollen tip. She used her teeth, gently caressing, feeling the rest of him swell and throb in her fingers, where she held him near the base of his shaft. Now her tongue played, licking, swirling, exploring texture, shape and taste. She licked the long length of him as if he were a honeycomb filled with sweetness, then fluttered her tongue against the opening where another pearl of moisture had formed, then back to teeth, applying the faintest pressure to the most sensitive part of him.

He was going to burst, so intense was his need. His aching flesh was swallowed by sweet, hot paradise. Inflamed by gentle, insistent pressure. Tortured by the delicious pull of teasing lips, then the cool torment of being licked and then nibbled by the firm, grazing pressure of teeth used with exquisite care. This was a demon, a being who knew his every secret desire, his every longing. She was using his lust, priming it, igniting his need to a white-hot fury, tempting him into hell. He thought of Nicola, of her beautiful body, naked, legs sprawled wide, waiting to take him. With supreme effort, he struggled to move, to reach for her . . .

She felt his whole body tense, heard his gasp, felt the pulsing waves move through his cock, spilling his seed in her mouth. Tears of joy burned her eyes as she swallowed down his essence. He was alive. His body had responded to her.

She released him, feeling drained and dazed. The taste of him was in her mouth, faintly sweet. Despite his grave injury, she had been able to reach him, to remake the connection between them, the bond of sex and desire that joined them so intensely. But although he might respond to her pleasuring, that did not mean he did not hate her. She still had to explain to him, to make him understand about Simon.

His eyes were closed, his breathing deep. She wondered if he slept, or if he had slipped back into the realm of shadows. In a panic, she reached out to touch his face. She sighed with relief as he opened his eyes, then a knock at the door startled her. Sweet heaven, she could not let them see her like this! Smoothing her clothing, she called out, "Come in."

Glennyth entered. She took one look at Nicola and the man on the bed, then her mouth quirked. "Well, I see that my scheme has succeeded. I thought perhaps you would know the means to bring your husband back to life."

Nicola flushed hotly, wondering how Glennyth could know.

"And what sort of life has she brought me back to?" Fawkes spoke from the bed, his voice dry and harsh.

Glennyth went to him and began to rearrange the blankets. "Whatever sort of life you will make it. You have a wife who loves you, and a son you can be proud of, and a fine castle to rule. I would think that would be enough to content most men."

"A son?"

Glennyth looked at Nicola. "You have not told him?"

Nicola let out her breath. "We have not spoken since he . . . since I . . ." She blushed again, thinking about what she had done, the uninhibited act she had indulged in, alone with her husband, enticed by his beautiful, stirring body.

"Hmm," Glennyth said. "First things first. But now it is time to tell him the tale of Simon."

Nicola nodded and approached the bed. There were so many things she wanted to say, but it was so hard. She knew how to pleasure him, how to delight his body, but what she did not know was how to convince him that she cared, to explain all the terrible things she had done.

She took a deep breath. "Yea, you have a son. He doesn't look like you, but I swear he was born of our first coupling. Sometimes, in the shape of his jaw, the way he moves, I see a little of you." She took another frantic breath. She had to make him believe her, she had to. Tears started in her eyes. "I know it's hard to imagine all of this. I cannot blame you for doubting me, when I withheld the truth from you for so long." The fear that he would never believe her, never forgive her, welled up and choked her. She struggled to hold back a sob. "I'm sorry I didn't trust you, that I didn't tell you about Simon long before this. I'm so sorry."

The child didn't look like him. What a surprise, Fawkes thought. She was lying again, trying to pass off some other man's child as his so he would excuse her scheming, her lies that had nearly cost him his life.

She began talking again, her voice intent, urgent. He tried not to listen, knowing that she was trying to beguile him once again, to make him care. "From the first time, when you came to claim Mordeaux and I warned Mortimer, I was doing it for Simon. I was afraid he would be hurt if Mordeaux was attacked. I never thought Mortimer would ride out with his whole army. I thought he'd simply send a message to Mordeaux, or maybe a few knights. I thought, that way, Hilary might have time to get Simon safely away."

He heard her sniffle and wipe her nose, then she continued. "She's done such a wonderful job of caring for him. Raised him if as if he were her own. Indeed, sometimes I think she actually favors him over Joanie, her own daughter. It's because Simon's so sweet-natured and adorable. None of this would have happened if he had dark hair and eyes, but still I can't regret his angelic looks. His hair's a little darker now, but it was almost flaxen when he was born, and his eyes so blue I knew they wouldn't change." She sighed. "My darling son. All the years I have lost." She sighed again.

A memory stirred in Fawkes's mind. Walking through the solar at Mordeaux and seeing two young children sleeping, a girl with reddish braids and a fair-haired boy. At the time, he thought the boy looked much different than the rest of the de Vescy family. But what made Nicola think she could possibly convince him to claim that little flaxen-haired toddler as his son? Was she mad? Or did she just think him an utter fool?

"Glennyth," he called. "Come here."

The healer approached the bed. "This is a thing between you and Nicola. I don't wish to interfere."

"No, you must answer my questions," Fawkes said. He motioned with his good arm for her to move closer. "When I asked you two months ago if Nicola's babe was born dead, you said it was true. Now she gives me this foolish tale that the babe is alive and despite looking nothing like me, is my son. Why should I believe her?"

"Because it's the truth. I was there when the babe was born. I, myself, took the infant to Mordeaux. Upon my honor as a midwife and healer, I vow this."

"But you can't be certain the child is mine, can you?" he challenged. "You were not there for the begetting. You don't know that Mortimer did not rape her after he sent me away. Or send another man to bed her."

"Nay, I cannot vouch for that, but I believe Nicola."

Fawkes gave a snort of disgust. Nicola might have convinced Glennyth, but she had not convinced him. To him, it sounded like more lies, a ridiculous tale she'd made up to explain her treachery. Suddenly he was weary unto death. He turned away and closed his eyes. When he felt Glennyth press a cup against his lips, he willingly took a swallow. He wanted oblivion, a chance to heal and to forget.

"Should you give him that?" Nicola asked anxiously as

she saw Glennyth giving Fawkes the sleeping draught. "If he goes to sleep, can we be certain he will awaken later?"

"You brought him back once from death. I believe you can do it again."

Nicola gave a ravaged sigh. Yea, she had brought him back to life, but there was no assurance she would not lose him anyway.

Twenty-three

Reynard entered the bedchamber and glared at Nicola, as if he wished to lay hands on her and throw her out the door.

Gripping Fawkes's hand tightly, Nicola glanced to Glennyth for help.

"That is no way to treat your lady," Glennyth said. "Especially since it is her presence that secures your gravely ill friend to this world. Although Fawkes is better, he could still die. He needs to know Nicola is there, so he will fight harder to live."

"Huh," Reynard said. "Maybe her presence here does inspire him to live, so that someday he can make her suffer as she has made him suffer."

"Silence your bitter words!" Glennyth ordered. "This is between the two of them!"

"So, did he believe your story that you did it all for *his* son?" Reynard's gaze rested on Nicola, hostile and harsh.

"That is enough!" Glennyth's hazel eyes flashed with fury, and Nicola thought that if Reynard was able to face the healer down when she looked like that, he was much braver than she. "Hold your tongue," Glennyth said. "Your opinion is neither wanted nor needed."

Reynard moved back from the bed, but Nicola could tell by the set of his jaw that he was still very angry. She repressed a sigh. Would all of Fawkes's knights hate her forever? Would no one ever believe her about Simon? She glanced down at Fawkes. If *he* came to believe her, that was all that mattered. Nay, if he *lived,* that was all that mattered. She would not ask for more.

She leaned forward to touch his brow. It was still hot. "He's fevered," she told Glennyth.

"That means his body is fighting the poison. I have given him something to ease his fever, but he will still have one for a few days."

"But he is better?" Nicola asked, then held her breath.

"Yea, he is better. As I have said, he is young and strong. And now that you have given him something to live for, he should fight very hard to remain in this world."

"Something to live for. . . ." Nicola shook her head sadly. "I doubt that. He despises me. And he does not believe me about Simon. He thinks I am offering him more lies, more excuses."

Glennyth approached the bed. "I've been thinking. Maybe we should send for Simon, bring him here so Fawkes can see him. It might be easier for him to accept a living, breathing child."

"But then he will see that Simon does not look like him. He will be more convinced than ever that I am lying."

"You cannot be sure of that," Glennyth. "It is at least worth a try."

"But what about FitzRandolph?" Nicola gestured toward the window to indicate the enemy army camping nearly in the castle's shadow. "How will we get Simon safely here?"

"FitzRandolph does not know he is your son, let alone Fawkes's," Glennyth said. "And FitzRandolph does not guess that in giving up Mordeaux, Gilbert de Vescy was acting on your orders, rather than betraying the castle to him. De Vescy should be able leave Mordeaux and take Simon when he does. Then, once he arrives here, he only has to get Simon to my cottage in the village. I will meet him there and bring Simon to the castle."

"What if something goes wrong?" Nicola breathed. "What if FitzRandolph's troops stop Gilbert?"

"Then he tells them that the boy is sick and he has journeyed here to see me, since there is no healer at Mordeaux. I don't think they would do anything to a sick child, no matter if they are suspicious of Gilbert."

"But, who will go to Mordeaux to tell Gilbert of our plan?" Nicola asked.

Reynard, who had been listening, said, "Why couldn't Gilbert FitzGilbert carry the message? He's known to FitzRandolph's men, and he could make up some story about wanting to go to Mordeaux to see how his mother fares. A young squire like him is unlikely to be harassed. For that matter, why could not FitzGilbert bring Simon here? They are thought to be brothers; it would be reasonable for his mother to have him take his sick sibling to the healer."

"So, you agree with Glennyth's plan?" Nicola asked in surprise.

Reynard shrugged. "It can't hurt to bring the boy here. I'd like to see him for myself." He shot Nicola another hostile look.

Glennyth raised her brows questioningly, "Do *you* agree, Nicola? Will you for once put aside your fears for Simon and think of Fawkes?"

"Yea, I will," Nicola answered.

"I will go and speak to young Gilbert," Reynard said. "Once Simon is safely here, I intend to lead an attack on FitzRandolph's army. They seem to have made little progress in building siege machinery. I don't think they truly intend to wage war on Valmar. I think they are waiting for Fawkes to die. FitzRandolph assumes we will then surrender willingly."

"Stupid, arrogant man," Nicola said. "He does not realize that Fawkes might have troops that are loyal to him and who would want vengeance for his death."

Reynard nodded. "Stupid and arrogant—FitzRandolph is

both those things, as well as a poor strategist and commander. That's why I want to surprise him by attacking. I think that if we go on the offensive, he will run. Then it is only a matter of regaining Mordeaux."

Nicola nodded thoughtfully. "Why couldn't Mordeaux be regained the same way it was lost—by deceit and betrayal? The servants could drug FitzRandolph's men the same way they drugged FitzSaer and his small force. Then, once the enemy knights are unconscious, simply drag them out of the castle. Voilà. Mordeaux is again in the hands of knights who are loyal to Fawkes."

"Jesu, you're skilled at this sort of plotting," Reynard said. "No wonder you deceived Fawkes so easily, and so often."

Nicola turned back to the man on the bed, feeling a pang of intense guilt. So many lies and betrayals. Would he ever forgive her?

"I'll go now," Reynard said, "and set things in motion. If Gilbert can return with Simon by midday tomorrow, we'll plan the attack for after sunset. FitzRandolph will never expect a night assault. He's too inexperienced. And no matter how seasoned the mercenaries that Prince John has given him, they'll not willingly risk their necks for a man who turns out to be a puling coward."

More dreams. Dark and sinister, full of shadows and pain. He was back in the passageway beneath the walls of Acre. He could barely see by the light of the smoking torches, barely breathe the rank, stale air. The passageway turned and twisted, and he had the sense that he had lost his way, that he would never escape. His heart pounded in his chest and sweat broke out on his skin. He came to a place where the passageway divided. The ceiling of the chamber rumbled above him, showering him with stones. He knew with certainty that if he took the wrong way he would be lost in the bowels of the earth forever.

And then he saw her. In the dim light her fair skin seemed to glow; her dark hair swirled wildly around her face. She beckoned to him, her gray eyes sad and tender. She was carrying something. A baby. She cradled it against her body, using her other hand to beckon once again. He felt frozen with terror. This was hell, this place of darkness and suffocation. If he made the wrong choice, he would be trapped here for eternity.

Her mouth moved, but there was no sound. "I love you," her lips said. Then her image began to fade. Not much time. He had to decide. He reached for her . . . and fell into nothingness.

He woke with a gasp. It was night, and a candle burned on the coffer by the bed. He could hear someone in the room, breathing slowly and evenly. Nicola. She haunted him in life and in his dreams. He thought of the feel of her mouth upon him. Of all the other memories. Then he reminded himself of what she had done, betraying him. He sighed heavily, watching the shadow of the candle waver. He was so tired and weak, too tired to make her go away. He sighed again and closed his eyes.

Nicola stood up and stretched, trying to ease her cramped muscles. She'd slept for a time on a pallet on the floor by Fawkes's bed, but the night had hardly been restful. She'd kept waking up and listening to make certain her husband still breathed. Early in the morning, giving up the quest for sleep, she'd dragged the pallet aside and sat down on the stool to resume her watch over her husband. Then at sunrise, Glennyth had come, and after removing the disgusting bran poultice, stitched up Fawkes's wound and covered it with moldy bread. She said by nightfall they should know if the wound was healing. If his fever spiked and his shoulder began to swell, then the treatment had failed and the wound was filling with poison once again.

Nicola went to the window and stared out, trying to fight the tears that threatened. The sun was barely up, the sky still pink and golden and glorious. By the time the glowing orb traveled across the sky, she would know if she was doomed to grief and despair, or if, by some miracle, there was hope that her life might be worth living. *If* Fawkes began to heal. . . . *If* Simon arrived safely at Valmar. . . . All her happiness depended upon those things.

After treating Fawkes, Glennyth had gone to the village to wait for Gilbert and Simon. Reynard was gone to prepare Valmar's forces for the attack on FitzRandolph. She would be alone with Fawkes all this long, agonizing day.

She went back to the bed and sat on the stool, then reached to take his right hand in hers. Thank the saints that the wound was in his left shoulder. Glennyth had said that even after it healed, there would be some residual stiffness, but at least this way it would not affect the use of his sword arm.

Not that she ever wanted him to fight a battle or be exposed to danger ever again. Yet, she knew that being a warrior was important to him. Part of what he was, of his sense of himself as a man. For his sake, she was glad that he could recover and lead an army someday if he had to.

Tonight, Reynard would lead his army for him. Every man of the Valmar garrison was eager to pounce upon FitzRandolph and his men and make dog meat of them. She had little fear for Valmar's knights. FitzRandolph had chosen a coward's path. She guessed that his men knew it and would abandon him in a rout.

Fawkes stirred slightly, and she reached to stroke his face, to soothe him. Glennyth had been forced to drug him again for the stitching, but by now the medicine was wearing off. She said Nicola could give him more poppy draught if he really needed it, but it was better if he could do without and remain aware. There were dangers in leaving someone in the world of shadows too long.

Nicola shuddered. Had Fawkes really been on the brink

of death, the very threshold of heaven? Or had he been in the other place, the one that Glennyth spoke of—the Otherside? She did not want to know, only that he had come back to her, and she had been given another chance. "Oh, Fawkes," she whispered. "I will make it up to you. I will love you with all my heart. I will."

He groaned and his eyelids fluttered.

She leaned over and kissed his dry lips. The bitter taste of poppy was still on his breath, but she did not care. He was so precious to her.

Abruptly, he jerked awake. "Nicola?" His voice was hoarse, faint. He opened his eyes. They were still fever-glazed, the pupils huge and dark. But she wanted to weep with joy just to have him look at her. But then his expression abruptly turned cold. "Why are you here? To take pleasure in my suffering?"

She started to move away from the bed, feeling the pain twist inside her. Then she stopped and faced him resolutely. "I love you, Fawkes. When I learned that you were badly injured and near death, I had to come to you. I climbed down an old privy hole and crawled through a dark, dank tunnel to escape Mordeaux so I could come to you. All I could think of was that you might die without knowing how I felt."

"It's too late," he said. "Once I would have done anything to hear your words of love. But I have suffered so much, endured so many lies. I no longer believe anything you tell me."

She turned away, her heart breaking.

"Where's Simon?" Nicola asked when Glennyth entered the room later in the day.

"He fell asleep on the way to the castle. Reynard is carrying him up." Glennyth went to the bed and began to examine Fawkes.

"How is he?"

"Much improved."

Nicola let out her breath in a sigh. Glennyth looked at her. "You should be relieved, yet you appear utterly desolate."

"He's not going to forgive me. In trying to save my son, I've lost the man I love."

"Give him time."

Nicola shook her head. "He hates me. He says he cannot trust me."

"He's ill and in pain. When he heals, he will remember what he felt for you."

Reynard appeared in the doorway, a sleeping Simon in his arms. Nicola went to get her son. "My sweet little darling," she murmured.

"Not so little," Reynard said. "He felt pretty heavy by the time I reached the top of the stairs."

"He promises to be a tall, robust man, like his sire," Glennyth said.

"Mortimer was also a large man," Reynard noted.

"You still don't believe he's Fawkes's child, do you?" Nicola shifted Simon's weight, then carried him to the stool and sat down with him on her lap.

"Nay. And neither will Fawkes, once he sees him."

Nicola looked down at the sleeping child and sighed.

Fawkes woke up to the sensation of someone in bed with him. He reached out, expecting to feel Nicola's lithe, silky form and was startled to encounter a small body curled next to him, nestled against his side like a puppy. The room was dark, and he had no strength to sit up anyway, so he had to content himself with examining his bed partner by touch. He felt silky curls, a round face with cheeks as soft as swan's down, a sturdy child's body, slightly sweaty in sleep. His son? Nicola said so, but how could he believe her. Maybe she no longer knew the truth herself.

Fawkes thought of the little grave by the chapel where

some hapless villager's child was buried. But this boy had lived, this child of Nicola's body, if not his. Weren't all children precious, to be cherished and loved?

But what if the boy was Mortimer's son? There'd been a time when the thought of raising his enemy's offspring filled him with revulsion. But having the actual child lying next to him, so close and trusting, made him realize that he could not so easily transfer his hatred to an innocent babe. The boy's small body felt robust and healthy. He would make a valiant, skillful knight—if he were properly trained.

But he was getting ahead of himself. First, Reynard must defeat FitzRandolph and they must get Mordeaux back. Damn! He hated lying there, helpless, while his men went to battle. He was fairly sure of the outcome. FitzRandolph had shown himself to be a fool and a coward, and such men seldom had success in war. Groaning, Fawkes shifted his throbbing body. If they could ever capture FitzRandolph, he'd like to put a crossbow bolt through *his* shoulder!

Nicola must have closed the shutters, it was so dark. That meant any sound of the victorious army returning to the castle could not easily be heard. He strained his ears. All he could hear was the faint sound of Nicola's breathing and the noisier tones of Simon next to him. He listened a while longer, then the pain and fatigue got the better of him, and he gave in and slept.

"Milady, wake up!"

Nicola sat up, disoriented. What was she doing on the floor?

Old Emma grasped her shoulder. "Glennyth said I should fetch ye."

Nicola rose groggily, then froze at the sight of Fawkes and Simon sleeping side by side.

"Looks as if ye've finally got yer wish," Old Emma said. "Yer son and yer husband, together and safe."

"This does not mean Fawkes will accept Simon," Nicola said. "After all, he allows *me* to sleep in this room, even though he despises me."

"Does he, now?" Old Emma raised a brow skeptically. "Once he mends, we'll see if yer husband can resist ye. I would not wager on it myself."

The servant's words started an idea in Nicola's mind. That Fawkes hated her did not mean that he was no longer desired her. After all, she had brought him back from unconsciousness with sexual pleasuring.

"I'm pleased to tell ye that FitzRandolph is defeated," Old Emma said.

"And what of Valmar's army? Have they returned safely?"

"Aye, for the most part. A few men wounded. Glennyth is seeing to them. But they drove off FitzRandolph's troops. Turned tail and ran for their lives, they did. Left half their gear behind. Sir Reynard harried them all the way to Mordeaux. They got a nasty surprise there when nobody would open the castle gates for them. Quite a clever scheme that, milady, to have Mordeaux pretend to surrender, then turn on FitzRandolph's when he needed refuge."

"You know that's not what happened. That I was only trying to protect Simon when I had them give up the castle."

"Aye, I know, but they'll be saying ye planned it all, that it was just a ruse to humiliate FitzRandolph. He got away, I fear. Reynard wanted to capture him and at least ransom his worthless arse, if not make him suffer a little, but the yellow-livered slime abandoned his men and took off through the woods near Mordeaux. Not like to find him there. But then, mayhap something will eat him, or some bandits get ahold of him. We can hope." Old Emma grinned toothlessly, contemplating their enemy's fate.

"I guess I'm ready. Unless you think I should change my bliaut."

"Nah, nah, ye look fine. All ye have to do is go down and hear Reynard's report and reassure everyone that Lord

Fawkes is mending. They've already broken out the wine and ale, so they're busy at that, and not caring what ye look like."

Nicola glanced toward the bed. "I hate to leave, even for a time. I spent so much of the last few months worrying that I'd lose one or both of them."

"It's yer duty as the lady of Valmar to welcome home the men who fought for ye. I'll stay here with Fawkes and Simon. Grew into a fine-looking little tadpole, he did. Though he don't look a thing like his sire."

"Jesu, do you think I don't know that!" Nicola said in exasperation. "I'm going now. Keep watch over them and I'll be back as soon as I can."

"Where are you going?" Nicola demanded. She was just about to enter the bedchamber when she met Fawkes going out, flanked on either side by Reynard and Henry.

"I'm going down to the practice field to watch the men," Fawkes said, glowering. "I vow, if I have to stay up here in that stuffy room another candle hour, I'll go mad."

"But your shoulder—"

"Is mending. Even Glennyth agrees there is no harm in my walking around. It's my shoulder that's hurt, not my legs!"

Nicola shook her head in exasperation as she let them pass. Men! Glennyth said they made the worst possible patients, and she could see now that it was true.

She entered the bedchamber. Glennyth was busy with something by the window. Gillian, who was stripping the linens off the bed, bobbed a curtsy. "Milady," she murmured.

Glennyth looked up from her task. "I heard you in the hall," she said. "There is no harm in Fawkes getting up and about. His wound is mending well. And besides, if he keeps too quiet, his shoulder will stiffen up and it will be even harder for him to regain the use of it. If he can tolerate the pain, he will actually heal faster if he remains active."

"He's still in pain?" Nicola exclaimed. "But I thought you said you had stopped giving him poppy juice."

"I have," Glennyth said. "But that does not mean the wound will not continue to trouble him. An injury like that takes a long time to heal."

"I feel so bad that he should suffer so much."

"Why? You did not shoot the crossbow bolt."

"But I sent the message the ended up bringing FitzRandolph here."

"That was before you knew Fawkes was even alive, let alone that he would come and claim Valmar and Mordeaux."

"Still. I lied to him many times."

"To protect your son."

Nicola nodded.

"And how are things between Fawkes and Simon?"

"I don't know. He treats Simon with fondness—which is better than I had hoped. But I fear he still does not believe that Simon is his son."

"Mayhap over time . . ."

Nicola nodded, then approached Glennyth. The healer's basket was full of the jars and bags of herbs she had brought to treat Fawkes. "You're going back to your cottage, aren't you?"

"I have neglected my garden long enough. And there are others in the village who need me."

"Reynard has gone every day to tend your garden."

Glennyth raised her brows. "Such as he is able. He does not know basil from parsley, nor deadly nightshade from his own rear end. Besides, I would like to be back in my own home where I can have some privacy." She made a face. "Here in the castle there are too many people. Every time I turn around there is some maidservant or page asking foolish questions about how I managed to heal Fawkes."

Nicola smiled. "I didn't know it was such a trial for you,

staying here with Fawkes. I thank you for making the sacrifice. I will always be grateful for what you've done, all of it."

Glennyth shrugged. "This is my calling. And Fawkes is lord of these lands, and a fair and generous one at that. If he had died, everything would have been thrown into turmoil. Many people would have suffered."

"Jesu," Nicola said. "To think I almost lost him for the second time."

"But you did not. You can thank the Goddess for that."

Twenty-four

Nicola crossed the bailey yard, drawing her crimson mantle around herself against the chill. At the gate, she called up, "I'm going into the village to see Glennyth. She has a healing medicine I need for Fawkes."

Henry poked his head over the gate tower. "Take care, milady, the trackway is muddy and treacherous. Are you certain you don't want to ride or take an escort?"

She shook her head. The walk would give her time to think, to perfect her plan.

The wind whipped at her hair as she left the castle yard, and as Henry had said, she had to step carefully to avoid the mud. The autumn rains had begun. She looked out at the valley. The forest and open fields were a spill of copper, gold and bronze, tarnished with the faint silver of the morning mist. Nearly two months had passed since FitzRandolph was defeated, and winter was fast on its way.

She continued down the trackway. The villagers who were working outside near their crofts came out and greeted her.

"Good day, milady. How is de Cressy?"

"Aye, tell us how milord fares?"

Nicola shook her head ruefully. "I think he would heal faster if he did not push himself so hard. He went out into the practice yard yesterday and went a few bouts with one of the squires, just to get used to holding a shield again." She recalled Fawkes coming to the castle later, his face white with pain. She'd hoped he'd learned that lesson for a time. "Today he is going to try riding, which should not tire him quite as much."

The villagers nodded, obviously pleased. "He's young and strong," one of the men said. "It won't take him long to get back to his old self."

Nicola nodded. She hoped that was true. She couldn't bear to wait much longer to set her plan in motion.

She nodded farewell to the villagers, then continued on to Glennyth's. When she rang the bell, the healer came to greet her at the door. Glennyth stepped aside so she could enter. "Is everything well at the castle?"

Nicola nodded. "And how is it with you?"

"I'm rather tired some days, but Reynard comes and helps me."

"What does he think of the fact that you're going to bear his babe?"

"He's delighted, of course." A faint smile quirked Glennyth's mouth. "He thinks it's going to be a boy."

Nicola smiled in response. Poor Reynard. "Well, I'm certain he will be a good father. He's warmed right up to Simon, takes him all over the castle with him, even out into the practice yard." She felt her smile fade as she took off her mantle. "I'm not certain I'm pleased with that. He's only three years old, after all. There is plenty of time for him to learn about fighting and weaponry."

"It's in the blood," Glennyth said. "No doubt he'll be a knight as his father was." She started toward the hearth. "How does Fawkes act with him?"

Nicola followed Glennyth, watching the healer use a metal hook to pull a pot of steaming liquid off the fire. "He treats him kindly enough. Indeed, I wish he treated me with the same amount of warmth."

"He's still angry and cold with you?"

Nicola nodded. "I think I understand though. He has such a stubborn, single-minded temperament. Once he makes up his mind about something, it's not easy to change it. The same hard-headed determination that enabled him to survive for three years and never lose sight of his goal of returning to Valmar and saving me, now makes him just as obstinate and stiff-necked when it comes to forgiving me. But I have a plan to change all that."

"Have some of this tonic," Glennyth handed Nicola an earthenware cup. "Then take a seat by the fire and tell me what you intend to do."

Glennyth listened without speaking, although her eyebrows shot up once or twice and her mouth quirked frequently. "I am very impressed with your boldness. But then, you did always have a cunning mind."

Nicola grimaced. "Yea, and I've thought many times that my propensity for plotting and scheming has cost me dearly. But I don't know what else to do, how else to act. Tell me truthfully, what do you think of my plan? Do you think I will succeed?"

"Whatever anger Fawkes feels for you, I would wager his desire is stronger. I doubt very much that he will be able to resist you."

"I will need your help," Nicola said. She licked her lips nervously. "And Reynard's. Do you think he will aid me?"

Glennyth shrugged. "He's already softening toward you. It's not his nature to be angry and vindictive, and once I pointed out that is was natural for a woman to think of her child's welfare above all else, he understood your actions better. He sees things in a different light now that I am carrying his babe."

Nicola breathed a sigh of relief. "We can't do it without him, although I don't want him to know the details. The other question is—when? I can hardly bear to wait much longer, but I want him to be healthy enough to . . ."

"Take advantage of the situation?" Glennyth asked.

Nicola nodded.

"He's healing well. I would not think it would be many more days. Long enough for us to arrange the other aspects."

"Thank you so much for helping me," Nicola said. "I'm so grateful to you for all you have done. Because of you, my son is safe. And now, if my plan succeeds, I will finally have my husband's . . . affections back, as well."

"It's all part of the pattern," Glennyth said. "You and Fawkes are meant to be together."

"I hope so," Nicola said, swallowing her nervousness. *I am very impressed with your boldness,* Glennyth had said of her plan. Well, never had she done things by half measures. No point starting now.

"No, no, Thomas," Fawkes shouted. "Not like that! You have to hold your sword level and be ready to thrust with it!" He sat back in the chair they had carried out to the practice field for him and suppressed a groan of frustration. He hated this, hated being on the sidelines. His fingers itched to hold a weapon, to rush out on the practice field and show young whelps like Thomas exactly how it was done. But Glennyth had warned him severely not to overdo, and Reynard had also been adamant that he should not tire himself. Odd for his captain to be so solicitous. Being around Glennyth all the time must be rubbing off on him.

A twinge of bitterness went through him. Reynard had a woman he adored and a babe on the way, while he had . . . Nay, he would not think about her. It was hard enough to live in the same household with his traitorous wife. He wanted to send her away, lock her up in a priory somewhere as Henry had done to Eleanor. But he could not. The people here adored her and would never give her up. He would have to endure this hell.

He turned his attention back to the practice field, then, out of the corner of his eye, saw Reynard approaching. He was carrying Simon, and the boy was squirming to get down.

"Here now, tadpole," Reynard said. "If you aren't going to behave, I'll take you back to the women."

Simon grew instantly still. Reynard grinned as he set his charge down next to Fawkes. "The boy has discovered that there is a whole wide world outside Lady de Vescy's solar. Horses, weapons, knights—he's fascinated by it all."

"I'm not certain that the practice yard is the place for him," Fawkes said. "If anything happens to her darling son, Nicola will have your hide."

"I thought the boy could sit next to you. If he sees you sitting quietly and watching, he might follow suit."

"That's right," Fawkes snarled. "Remind me that I am as helpless as a squalling infant. A fine friend you are."

Reynard shrugged and started off. "I just do what Glennyth tells me to do," he said over his shoulder.

Fawkes looked at the child sitting on the ground beside his chair. The boy smiled at him. "Reynard says I will learn to be a knight here." He pointed to the practice field.

"Yea, that is so," Fawkes said. He felt strangely tongue-tied with this toddler. Could the boy truly be his son? He searched the round, cherub face, looking for some hint of de Cressy blood. But that was not fair, he told himself. How many men resembled the child they were at three years?

But at least Simon was a likely lad. Even if he was Mortimer's get, he had all the makings of a soldier.

Thomas came rushing up. "Did you see that?" he demanded. "I had Gilbert down in the dirt, and he's near a head taller than me!"

"Good job, Thomas. You've done well this day. Although you must learn to hold your sword properly. Think of it as if it were part of your own arm." Fawkes stood and gestured, slashing the air.

"Like this?" Both Fawkes and Thomas looked down to see Simon waving a nonexistent sword, blue eyes wide and intent.

"Would you like to hold mine?" Thomas gripped the

wooden blade and held his weapon out to Simon. The child grasped the hilt in both hands, then strained to hold it out straight. Although it was merely a wooden practice sword and shorter than a grown man's weapon, it was a bit much for a three-year-old. Fawkes and Thomas laughed as they watched Simon single-mindedly focus on holding the weapon. His little arms quivered with the strain, and his face was a mask of seriousness. For a brief moment, Fawkes found himself reminded of someone. Had not his brother Rolf, who was a smith, looked just the same when he was fashioning a weapon on his forge?

"Too big," Simon said ruefully as he finally gave up and let it touch the ground.

"Aye, it is," Thomas agreed. "But I'll bet Weland could be persuaded to make you a smaller one, of iron, even." He glanced at Fawkes. "Since you are Valmar's heir, you must have a sword."

Fawkes said nothing. He did not know what he thought of this child who might or might not be his, but he did not begrudge the boy his rightful heritage. After all, the way things were between him and Nicola, it was unlikely they would conceive another child. That was the thing that filled him with bitterness.

"Let's quit this for today," Reynard said. "I need a bath, and it would not hurt you to soak in a hot tub either."

Leaving Simon with Thomas, they walked back to the castle, talking about the beginning squire's progress. "I'll bet Nicola was none too pleased with you when you told her it was time to train Thomas as a squire," Reynard said. "It will not be easy for her to find a page as devoted as that one."

Fawkes grunted. "She did not say what she thought."

"The two of you are still estranged then?"

"You could say that. Every time I look at her, I think of her deceit, and it fills my throat with bitter gall."

"There are those who would say she was justified in what

she did. A mother must think of her child's welfare before
her own."

Fawkes shook his head. "If only she'd trusted me. She
should not have thought I would hurt an innocent child."

"She was used to Mortimer, crazed, violent bastard that
he was. With a first husband like that, you cannot blame her
for being reluctant to trust you."

"Are these your own thoughts, or is this Glennyth speaking?" Fawkes asked cuttingly.

Reynard shrugged. "There's nothing wrong with allowing
a woman to persuade you to her viewpoint. In fact, I've discovered there are many benefits to it."

Fawkes snorted. Reynard could do what he liked, but *he*
was finished being manipulated by women!

They went to the bathing chamber. Fawkes was surprised
to see that everything was ready for them. Steam rose from
the large bathing tub, and the scent of fragrant herbs floated
to his nose. He looked at Reynard suspiciously. "This looks
like Nicola's doing."

Reynard shrugged. "I told her that I wanted to have a real
bath because I was going to Glennyth's this evening. I guess
she desires me to be pleasant-smelling for her friend."

Fawkes grimaced. The exotic, subtle scent aroused too
many memories. He started toward the door.

"Don't be a fool," Reynard called. "A nice long soak will
do wonders for your sore muscles and injured shoulder. You
did tell me that your legs were still stiff from riding yesterday."

Fawkes looked at the tub. Why should he let something
she had done keep him from doing what *he* wanted? He'd
told himself he would not become obsessed with avoiding
her as he once had been obsessed with being near her. "You
first," he told Reynard.

"I'll agree to that if it means you will lie back and soak

when it's your turn. I've even brought some wine. Between that and the heat, your shoulder should loosen up nicely."

Fawkes nodded. It did sound pleasant.

Reynard stripped off his clothing and got in. He hurriedly soaped himself and dunked down to rinse himself. In seconds, he was out.

"That wasn't much of a bath," Fawkes said.

Reynard grinned. "Unlike you, I don't want to get all relaxed and sleepy. I have a lady waiting for me."

Fawkes scowled.

"All yours," Reynard said, motioning with his head toward the tub as he rubbed himself down with a towel. "Get in and I'll pour you some wine."

"And then, I suppose you intend to abandon me."

Reynard winked. "I'll send one of the serving girls to look in on you and see if you need anything."

Fawkes felt his scowl deepen. He didn't want any damned servant girl fussing over him. Although he supposed eventually he'd have to find some sort of sexual release.

He undressed and climbed into the still steaming water. It was a huge tub. Big enough for two, he thought, then cursed himself. He'd have to think of something else, some mundane distraction, or he'd never be able to relax.

He took the cup of wine Reynard handed him and took a sip. "It tastes funny," he told his friend.

"Glennyth added something, I think. Some tonic or healing potion."

Fawkes nodded. If only Glennyth could give him some drug or elixir that would banish all thoughts of Nicola from his mind. That was the only thing that would truly aid him. While the injury to his shoulder was mending well, there seemed to be a gaping wound inside him that would not heal.

He drank some more of the wine, then lay back. The hot water lapped around his injured shoulder, soothing it. The tense muscles in his legs began to relax. He sighed heavily. The wine was working, making him sleepy. He'd better wash while he could still move, he decided. He dunked his head to wet his hair, then stood up unsteadily to soap himself. He rinsed thoroughly, then lay back against the rim of the tub and closed his eyes. A delicious lassitude swept over him.

When he woke, he was no longer in a bathing tub, but in a pitch-black room, lying on a bed. He jerked to awareness, then felt his heart jump into his throat as he realized that his hands were bound behind his back. Trying to sit up, he discovered that the bonds that secured his wrists were attached to the wall. He could sit up, but he could not get off the bed.

Fury replaced his panic. How dare anyone truss him up and hold him prisoner!

He struggled briefly, enough to be certain that the bonds were secure, then went still, panting. It was then that he realized someone was in the room with him. He felt a prickle of fear. What had happened? He'd fallen asleep in the bathing chamber of his own castle. How could an enemy manage to take him prisoner? What did they want with him?

Slowly, his sleep-muddled senses gradually returned to normal and he knew. Nicola. There was that familiar scent of her in the room. He wanted to cease breathing, to block out the beguiling odor and all the memories it aroused. Damn her! How could she do this to him? How dare she have him held again his will! A vague sense of unease mingled with his anger. Maybe she had decided to be rid of him after all. Maybe she'd had him kidnapped and brought to this place to be left to die. But she could not have done that without Reynard's help, and his friend would never conspire against him. No, there must be some other purpose to this.

He tried again to free himself. His ire built with each failed attempt. The strips of fabric binding his wrists were not overly tight, but they were very secure. Abruptly, he sensed movement in the room. He went still, waiting.

There was a flicker of light. Someone was lighting candles

around the room. Little by little, their flames illuminated the familiar aspects of his bedchamber. But he still could not see her, merely a dark shape floating here and there among the flickering shadows. He wanted to shout at her to free him, but he was not positive it was Nicola. There was a strange, dreamlike quality to everything around him. The drug in the wine was befuddling his wits, yet also heightening his senses.

The room was bright, but still he could not see his captor clearly. It must be her, he thought. The dark form approached, pausing a few feet away, and he was suddenly aware of his nakedness. The realization made his cock throb, then grow hard. He didn't want to be aroused, but he could not control his body. The thought of her looking at him filled him with all the aching need of two months of celibacy—since she'd taken him in her mouth when he was first injured. As that intense, feverish memory filled his mind, he grew harder still.

He clenched his jaw in fury. He didn't want to give her the satisfaction of knowing that he felt anything for her, even if it was only blind, animal lust. She was his enemy. If only his treacherous body could understand that.

She approached him and let the hood of the cloak slip back so he could see her face. He was reminded of exactly how potent a weapon her beauty could be. The knife edge of her clear, perfect features. The piercing authority of her exquisite eyes. The potent, overwhelming affect of her delicate, rosy lips. She rendered him stunned, bowed, overcome.

She perused his nakedness. He felt her gaze like a rush of hot air moving over his skin, singeing him, burning him, making the blood boil and bubble in his veins. It filled his cock with hot, hard need, and it rose proudly, eagerly. For a long moment, she stared, until his whole body seemed glazed with fever, his heart pumping like a bellows in his chest, his breathing harsh and fast. His anger at her effect on him seemed to fuel his arousal. He had never been harder, rigid with raw sexual hunger.

He looked at her face. The pupils of her eyes were huge and black. Her lips parted slightly. Her nostrils flared with intense emotion. She was remembering what he had done to her, his mastery of her pleasure. He wanted to taunt her, to remind her that he'd once held her in thrall, made her helpless and weak with wanting. But he knew that he was now the one who could not control his desire. His cock thrust higher and harder. His skin felt near to bursting.

She took a sharp breath and threw off the mantle. The vision that met his gaze struck him like a blow. She was wearing the flimsy costume of the Syrian dancing girl, her slim, beautiful body temptingly, teasingly arrayed in the near-transparent garment. As his mind struggled to fathom how she had come by the costume, his body was assaulted with the potent image of dark nipples, creamy curves, the shadow of maidenhair—all of it was visible and yet coyly overlaid by the gossamer fabric. Her fine, silky hair, braided at the temples to keep it out of her face, flowed down over her body, enhancing the sense of mystery, of things hidden and yet revealed.

If possible, his arousal grew even more intense. This was what he had dreamed of, the merging of his most potent fantasies. All the exotic, sultry promise of the dancing girl combined with Nicola's untouchable, queenly allure. She was an Eastern goddess, the essence of sex and desire. Despite his anger and resentment, he wanted to fall to his knees and worship her.

Her expression changed, becoming feral and provocative. She began to sway sinuously. He stared, entranced. The Syrian girl had moved with cool, calculating intent—her whole purpose a blatant plan to fire a man's blood, to tease and cajole and take as much money from him as possible. Nicola's dance was more self-contained and mysterious.

Her eyes were closed, as if she were lost in the sensations

sweeping over her as she danced, and her mouth curved into
a vague smile. She seemed to be celebrating the delight of
her own sinews and muscles stretching and contracting, the
sensuous rubbing of the sheer fabric against her skin, the
quickening pace of her own arousal. He could sense it even
as he watched. The soft bouncing of her breasts as she moved
was making her nipples tight and hard, the swaying rhythm
of her hips teasing the flesh between her thighs until she was
wet and throbbing.

She was aware of him, aware of his eyes on her, devouring.
She knew her power over him, could sense that his breathing
had begun to come in time with her movements, that the
very blood pulsing through his veins, filling and stretching
his cock in exquisite, near unbearable engorgement, was
moving to the same taunting rhythm with which she swayed
her hips.

She held him poised on the edge of the precipice. He felt
sweat break out on his body. His muscles drew tight. His
skin trembled with excitement. His shaft reared and thrust
out like a maddened stallion raging against its fetters.

She turned, affording him a view of her pert, rounded
buttocks, covered only by the sheer fabric. The cleavage between them reminded him of her sweet, hot chasm, and as
she swayed, her hair swung back and forth, revealing, con-
cealing, tantalizing him with the perfect, graceful lines of
her body. Curves and softness, elegant skin and smooth,
sleek flesh.

His breathing came rapid and harsh, and he was not certain
he could bear much more. Then she moved nearer, and he
realized why he was bound. She meant to torture him.

She whirled close and he felt the light sting of her hair as
it whipped across his chest. The stir of air from her wake
brushed against the tip of his cock, inflaming him all the
more. But he could not reach out and stop her, could not
halt her wild dance. His hands were bound and he was
trapped against the bed. He was her prisoner.

She moved closer, still swaying and writhing. He could see the pulse of blood in her slim neck, observe the rise and fall of her chest. Her breasts jiggled, taunting him with the memory of their soft, liquid warmth. Her skin was flushed, glistening. Her face, intent and rapt. Her perfume filled the air, sexual musk and heated, roused woman.

She paused in her dance and threw her head back, then shook it so her hair fell back over her shoulders. Then she gave him a look, sensual and taunting, keen as a battle cry, and slowly began to remove pieces of the garment she wore.

I'm not doing this, Nicola thought. *I'm not standing in front of Fawkes, blatantly flaunting my body.* But she was. Obviously, there had been something in the wine Glennyth gave her to drink. Something to relax her, the wisewoman said. But, oh, it had done so much more. Arousing her, heating her blood, making her skin tingle with wanting. All her nervousness and embarrassment had vanished. She had wondered how she could possibly dance without music, but when the time came, when the cloak was off and she stood before Fawkes in the outrageous garment of an Eastern dancing girl, music had suddenly filled her head. A primitive ancient rhythm, the soft, pat-pat of drums, the sinuous melody of a shepherd's pipe. Music from the hills, from some memory she had not known she had.

The music drove her, told her what to do, made her body move of its own accord. She was aware of every inch of her body, but especially the hard, tight tingle of her nipples, the fierce, spreading heat between her thighs. Her breasts felt full and heavy, as if they needed to be suckled. Her quim ached to be filled. Yet the rest of her felt exhilarated and weightless, powerful. Her dance was a celebration. Of her womanhood. Of the pure potent magic of being alive and young.

And the man watching . . . her proud, beautiful lover. He sat straight and fearless, despite his bound hands. The candlelight caressed the pure, sculpted lines of his face, played over his muscular torso and lean belly, and cast his jutting erection into bold relief. She could not stop looking at that fascinating part of him, that ruddy, pulsing spear projecting from his body. A weapon, and yet she did not fear it. Instead, she longed to touch it, fondle it, explore the contrast between velvety skin and firm, implacable flesh.

But it was not time yet. She had not finished her dance, her performance. *Think of yourself as a mummer in a play,* Glennyth had told her. *Transform yourself into the thing he desires most, the epitome of his longings. Offer him yourself, show him what you will give him. Make him want you with excruciating desire.*

Tentatively, her fingers unhooked the piece of fabric covering her other breast and peeled it away. She felt as if she had thrown off a heavy garment, although the fabric was actually as light and sheer as a spider's web. Her breasts were bare to his gaze, and they had never felt so heavy, so full and hot. Her nipples tightened until they hurt. The merest breath of air seemed to rasp against her skin. She reached to touch herself, cupping her breasts, making them thrust out even more, the nipples engorged and swollen.

She saw his mouth move, knew how badly he wanted to close his lips over those dark, aching tips. Heaven it would be, to feel herself drawn into the hot wetness of his mouth, to feel his lips work upon her, inflaming and soothing.

But there was more to offer him. More to tease him with. She turned around and pulled her hair forward so nothing blocked his view. Then she touched her buttocks, tracing their shape, letting him imagine how they would feel in his hands, warm and smooth and firm. She curved her fingers beneath them and spread the cheeks slightly, making him remember where the crease between them led, the back entrance of her womanly passageway.

How could he not think of thrusting his shaft there, feeling the softness of her bottom close around him, pulling him in, urging him deeper? The very thought seemed to make a wave of wetness surge from her already damp, swollen quim.

She turned again and took a deep breath. And now—if this did not enrapture him and make him forget he hated her, then nothing would. Her fingers sought the fastening that secured the transparent fabric over her crotch. She unhooked it on one side, then the other. With another discreet movement it fell away, like a butterfly's wing wafting to the ground. She could feel his eyes riveted to her body.

He could not believe what he saw. Nicola stood before him, her crotch completely bare. A little ring of gold glinted among the enticing pink folds of her cunny—which had been shaved to better reveal every detail of her sex. He was dazzled, stunned. It was the image of his dreams, only better. Nicola's delicious quim, but even more silky-smooth and naked. The hard bright glitter of gold highlighting her clit, teasing him with the thought of the contrast between cool metal and wet, heated flesh. He wanted to suck the ring into his mouth, along with the little nub of her pleasure.

She brought her hands to her groin. With her fingers, she spread the lips of her cunny, then thrust her hips forward, displaying herself.

She heard his breathing quicken. His face looked as if he were being tortured, his eyes mere slits of hunger, his nostrils flared. His agonized arousal pleased her. Never had she felt such power. It was like taming a wild beast. Coaxing a stallion to docility. The man before her was her helpless captive. Even if she removed his bonds, he would remain under her control.

She slid her fingers downward to touch herself. As she stroked the wet slipperiness, she knew he was feeling every caress as an almost tangible sensation. She watched him intently, knowing that he remembered exactly how she felt there. Silky, loose flesh. Moist heat. She dared to probe the inner slit, overflowing with warm liquid. Let him think of that river of womanly heat washing over his own fingers, bathing him in the essence of her desire.

She took a deep, shaky breath. As delightful as it was to tease and tempt him like this, her own need was growing unbearable. A piercing ache assailed her, and she felt that if she did not ease it she would go mad. She moved nearer to him, feeling his heat radiating over her, smelling his scent, a mixture of the herbs from his bath and his own potent maleness. His breath wafted against her face, warm and pro-vocative. She leaned down and put her hands on his face, then pressed her mouth to his.

Their bodies did not touch, only their mouths. Lips found lips, tongues mated. She squirmed, tormented by the craving inside her. Her hair brushed against his cock, and he groaned aloud, sending shuddering vibrations flowing down her body. She tangled her fingers in his thick silky hair, trying to hold his mouth against hers, to deepen the kiss, but he jerked away. He arched his neck, regarding her with glittering dark eyes. "If you want me to soothe your need, to fill you deep and hard, you'll have to untie me." A satisfied smile curved his lips.

She leaned away, breathing hard. She did not want to free him. She was enjoying this exhilarating sense of control. "Nay," she said. "I will not."

She pushed him and he fell back, sprawling on the bed. He half sat up, resting on his bound hands, and glared at her. His cock jutted upward, like a fiery obelisk. She moved to stand between his legs. If he truly wanted to, he could easily move away from her, but as she reached out to touch that quivering lance of flesh between his legs, she did not think that he would.

Twenty-five

She placed her hand on his cock and curled her hand around him, pale, narrow fingers against thick, blood-dark flesh. Starting at the arrow-shaped tip, she stroked downward. He quivered and throbbed in her hand like a living thing, and her breath caught, thinking of this huge pulsing thing inside her.

She glanced up and met his gaze. Fierce and wild, he stared at her. But there was also a helplessness there, as if when she touched him like this, she touched his soul. She caressed him, watching his face. His eyes were like burning coals, his features contorted, as if the pleasure was so intense, it pained him.

She moved her fingers in a slow rhythm, from soft tip to hard, thick base. He moaned. His eyes clenched shut and his whole body went rigid. The muscles in his broad neck stood out like ropes.

Her fingers sought the softly furred, pendulous flesh below. The pride of his manhood, his balls were big and firm, like some ripe succulent fruit. She fondled them, sensing the way his breathing quickened, the control with which he held himself. So intriguing his body was, bluntly and rawly sexual, so different than her own, with its hidden, subtle mysteries.

He could not hide his arousal, his flagrant need. In touching him like this, she exerted such tantalizing control over him. She could feel his violent passion, barely leashed. Power, scarcely contained, like a rushing torrent held back by a dam. At any moment, the dam would burst.

She realized that she wanted the flood to wash over her, to inundate her. His thick, hard cock inside her, his furious, fiery lust overwhelming her. She released her grip upon his shaft and leaned over him. He looked so strained, intent. She touched his jaw, faintly roughened with a day's growth of whiskers, then pressed her lips to his. A hungry, desperate kiss. It brought tears to her eyes.

When she drew back, he was looking at her breasts. She saw that he was in agony to touch them, suckle them. Her nipples tightened at the thought. But that would mean untying him and letting her power slip away.

Instead, she leaned her torso close to his face and stroked herself. Her fingers glided over the curves of her own body, feeling the softness of her flesh, then plying the hard, engorged nipples, making then swell and turn an even deeper, darker color. His mouth worked and his pupils grew huge, his whole face a beautiful mask of desire.

She kissed him again, caressing his eager mouth with her own. Then, slowly, carefully, she straddled him, and brought her crotch against his upthrust shaft. He groaned loudly, and she feared for a moment he would lose control and peak even before he was inside her. Balancing herself, she sought his cock with her right hand and tried to guide it into her sheath. The silky tip touched her, inflaming her own need to boiling point. She wriggled her hips and brought them down, seeking the hot, sweet comfort of impalement. At the same time, he thrust his hips upward. She screamed as firm, unyielding flesh stretched her, filled her and thrust deep.

It was as if he had reached the very core of her, and beyond. She panted hard, struggling to endure the cataclysmic sensations assailing her. She feared to lose consciousness, as if the intensity of what she felt had wrenched her from the mundane realm and thrown her into the fantastic, mindless world of dreams. Pleasure-pain, it made her grit her teeth as she moved against him, trying to accommodate the relentless pressure. *Oh, dear God, she had missed this, missed the feel of him inside her!*

Her movements seemed to torture him even as he tortured her. He moaned and panted, his chest heaving. When she shot him a helpless, beseeching glance, she saw that his head was thrown back, his neck arched, his whole body rigid, as if he clawed at the edge of a precipice, struggling to maintain his grip.

Her body had begun to relax around his. The lightning bolt from the place he touched inside her had released a stream of wetness and eased the fit. She could almost breath normally now, as long as he didn't move.

But he did, suddenly, and with vehemence. He bucked his hips against her, driving his cock in deeper, making her whimper with the potent impact. Sparks struck somewhere near her womb, as tender, sensitive flesh was set aflame with keen pleasure. She gasped and cried out as the feeling crested and drove her down into dark spirals of ecstasy.

Even as her own body strained and jerked, she felt him reach his release. She wrapped her arms around his chest and pressed her face against his heaving shoulder, clinging to him as if they were two desperate drowning souls being washed downstream.

Then it was over and the awkwardness of their embrace became overwhelming. She sat up and slid from her perch on his lap. Wetness trickled down her leg, and she became aware of how uncomfortable the remnants of her costume were. Though her breasts and crotch were totally bare, she still wore the pieces of fabric over her shoulders and arms and around her hips and down her legs. She wanted to take off everything, yet she was somehow uneasy to reveal more of her body. Despite their intense coupling, the tension between them had not dissipated. He watched her with heavy-lidded eyes, and his face looked harsh and hungry. "Untie my hands," he said. It was not a request, but a demand, and abruptly, she was afraid.

The feverish wildness that had come over her as she danced was gone, and she could scarce believe what she had done. Had she truly had him drugged and taken to a bedchamber to await her pleasure? Had she really danced before him, exposing her body and flaunting her sex? And what madness had possessed her to make her push him back on the bed and straddle his raging erection?

Thinking about it made her want to do it again, but this time when his hands were unbound, so that he could touch her breasts and hold her buttocks and guide her up and down as she rode his big, heavenly cock. But faint unease kept her from indulging her desire. That he had allowed her to climb onto him and find her release did not mean his animosity toward her had eased. And he might be even angrier with her for what she had done, usurping his power in such blatant fashion.

She had controlled the encounter, chosen the herbs that scented his body and the strips of fabric that bound his hands. She had teased and seduced him, offering that which he could not reach out and take. She had kissed him, exploring his lips as he had once explored hers. Fondled her own body while he watched. Touched him, stroked him, inflamed him, then mounted him.

No mare ever mounted a stallion. Nor any female beast controlled the moment of coupling. But she had. The outrageousness of what she had done added to her apprehension, and she was suddenly aware of her heart pounding. *Sometime* she would have to free him. Then, what would he do?

"Untie me," he said again. His voice was softer this time, more coaxing. She did not trust him, but realized she had no choice. Better to free him now while the languorous heat of their pleasure softened his mood.

She moved near, smelling their mingled scents rising from the smooth, dark warmth of his skin. His gaze followed her as she slid behind him on the bed and began to unfasten the cloth strips securing his wrists. She'd tied his bonds herself, wanting to make certain they were not be too tight, lest they abrade the skin or make him uncomfortable. The strips of silk she had used were strong and soft, but it was no easy matter to untie them.

She concentrated, using her fingernails to undo the knots. Slowly, tediously, she gradually loosened them. When he was free, he sat forward and rubbed his wrists. She started to climb off the bed, but as one bare foot touched the floor, Fawkes suddenly whirled and grabbed her, then flung her down upon the bed and crouched over her.

Her head spun with the swiftness of his movements, even as her mind reminded her that this was a warrior she had sought to dominate, a man for whom quick reflexes were a matter of survival. How many enemies had he outmaneuvered in similar fashion?

Now she was helpless on her back. She stared up at him, panting with dread. He leaned back on his heels. "You would shackle me and have your way with me," he said. "Now it is my turn."

His eyes were hooded and unreadable, but as they perused her body with slow intensity, her thrilling arousal increased by leaps and bounds. She wanted him; violent, angry, even punishing, she desired what he would give her.

He touched one of the sleeves of the costume. "Take it off."

She sat up, feeling almost as lustful as she had during her dance. The remainder of her costume covered nothing erotic or intimate, yet as she removed it, she felt her nipples contract, a quivering heat spread between her thighs. She untied the lacing under one arm, then the other, finally stripping off the upper portion. The bottom piece was more difficult. She had to unfasten the bands that tied around her thighs, then work the fabric down off her legs.

At last she was utterly naked. She looked up at her captor

and saw the intent, raw look on his face. "Now," he said, nostrils flaring, "now we will tie *you* up." She thought he meant to secure her hands behind her, but instead, he placed his hands on her thighs and spread them wide. He moved down on the bed, then grabbed her ankles and pulled her, legs still splayed, down to the carved bedposts. He crouched between her legs, slid his hands under her buttocks and spread her even wider. She shivered with expectation. She was exposed, revealed, bared utterly to his gaze. He used his thumbs to stroke her, playing with the soft flesh on either side of the swollen outer lips. He teased her, milking moisture from her aching chasm, yet not touching the throbbing folds.

At last, he fingered the ring. Her body jerked with sensation almost too intense to bear. "How did you know?" he whispered. "How did you know I dreamed of you like this?"

"You told me," she said. "I wanted to make your fantasy real."

He stared at her, at the exotic glittering ring and the naked splendor of her sex. "Did it hurt?"

Nicola shook her head. "Not exactly. You see, it does not pierce the skin."

He reached out to touch the gold ring and saw what she meant. The little band of metal gripped her tender flesh loosely. "Does it stimulate you?" he asked, eyes on her face.

"Yea."

"Arouse you and make you wet?"

"Yea."

He slid the ring on his littlest finger and heard her breath catch. Her eyes grew glazed, and she looked as if she might faint. He withdrew his hand, breathing heavily himself.

He sat back. "Does merely wearing it make you ache with desire? Does every movement of your body make your cunny throb and your clit tingle?"

She nodded.

He touched her lightly then, using the tip of one long

finger to flick the ring back and forth. She panted, on the verge of screaming. Then he leaned forward and mouthed her again, sucking her clit, ring and all, deep into his mouth. She closed her eyes and gave a ravaged moan.

Then abruptly, he released her. She opened her eyes, shaken. While she lay limp and helpless, he searched for the strips of silk, then used them to secure her ankles to the bedpost. She watched as he climbed from the bed.

She felt a sense of helplessness, then realized it was no worse than what she had forced him to endure. Her femininity was displayed, revealed, as his manhood had been. There was no way to hide her need; he could choose to satisfy it or make her suffer.

He returned to the bed, and she saw that he had a piece of cloth in his hand. She also saw that he was aroused again, his erection blatant. She caught a glimpse of it, jutting out, as ruddy and big as ever, as he crouched between her outstretched thighs. Then he touched her with the cloth and she forgot everything else.

The cold wetness made her gasp, and the soft, sublime pressure against her aching flesh made her raise her hips and close her eyes. Yet this time he did not fondle or caress her, but used the cloth to clean her with smooth efficiency. It was agony to have him touch her and yet not give her what she needed. Her breathing came hard and fast, and she fought the urge to plead with him.

But she would not give up what little control she had left. She wanted to win him back, to make him admit that his desire for her was so overwhelming that he could not give her up, could not ignore her. She must be strong. She must not beg.

For a long moment, he simply stared at her from his vantage point between her thighs. She raised her upper body and stared back. He looked so fierce and male. His long hair framed his face like a lion's mane and his spectacular shoulders and chest shone tawny gold in the firelight. The burnished sleekness of his skin was broken by the shadow of black hair that swirled on his upper chest and trailed down to his groin.

And there were scars marring his skin, as well. Pale lines crisscrossed his forearms. A thick, silver streak slashed across his lower belly, and the raw, red wound from the crossbow bolt shone near his collarbone. The flaws did not detract from his formidable appeal, but enhanced it. They were the marks of a warrior, a seasoned knight, a man to be feared.

Her gaze went to his groin where that long, sleek, powerful staff of flesh thrust out. She had touched it, gripped it in her fingers, felt its heat, its fascinating vigor. So firm and hard, but cloaked in smooth, soft skin. She shivered with longing merely to think of how it felt inside her.

"Do you like it?" His voice was a harsh whisper. "Does my cock please you?"

Gazing at his face, she nodded.

"Say it."

She licked her lips. "Your cock pleases me."

"Do you want it?" His voice was strained, intent. She had the feeling that everything between them depended on her answer. And the answer he wished was the truth. She did want his cock, with a great, burning need that made her feel weak. She nodded again, then seeing his face, whispered, "Yea, I want it."

His smile was triumphant, dazzling, and the sense of power she felt as she said the words was also a revelation. If he did not believe she loved him, perhaps he would believe that she desired him more than any man in the world. "I want it," she said again. Bracing herself on her elbows, she thrust her breasts out and raised her hips, shamelessly offering herself.

His smile turned smug. "You shall have it, every inch. But first, I will do what I wished to do to you while you so coldly held me captive." He scooted up on the bed, and holding his cock in his hand, began to stroke between her outstretched legs. As the soft tip grazed her sensitive, swollen flesh and played with the glimmering ring, she wanted to scream with the aching need that washed over her. Her hips lifted and twisted of their own accord and she could not hold back the soft whimpers and moans that issued from her throat.

"You are even more beautiful when you are aroused," he said "Your skin glows with rosy fever and your mouth turns crimson." Abruptly, he ceased his torment and got down on his hands and knees over her. She had scarce caught her breath when he began to kiss her. Although he was gentle, she felt like he was devouring her. Her lips throbbed and tingled with sensation. But when she thought he might satisfy some of her craving by filling her mouth with his warm, sweet tongue, he moved to kiss her neck.

Hot breath and nuzzling lips sent waves of shimmering pleasure through her body. He licked the column of her throat, then nibbled on her earlobe. His tongue followed the whorl of her ear, then sought the sensitive opening. She gasped, and gasped again. He rubbed his lips over her neck, then repeated his provocative movements on her other ear.

She felt weak, almost dizzy with the urgent hunger that held her in its grip. He kissed her collarbone, then lower. "I have waited some weeks for this," he said. "I mean to enjoy myself to the fullest."

He kissed one of her nipples, then looked at her. She sank back and closed her eyes. Breathing deeply, she sought to control her desperate hunger.

He did so enjoy looking at her like this. Her body was primed, aroused to the fullest. The cool ice princess had vanished, and in her place was a wild-eyed creature with flushed skin, swollen lips and a heated, deliciously sensitive body. Her nipples were almost wine-colored and so taut they felt hard and firm in his mouth as he suckled her. Every inch of her was hot and melting, glazed with the faintest sheen of perspiration. There was nothing "ladylike" in her demeanor now. She was an animal in heat.

And what a magnificently beautiful animal. Her perfect features looked animated and sensual, and she glowed with passion. Her body felt strong and vital beneath his. The marbled-skinned goddess had never moved him the way this woman did.

And her arousal. He scarce dare look at the delectable, rosy sweetness of her quim lest he lose his own control. She had shaved for him, put a ring on her clit, frankly displaying herself for his pleasure, fulfilling his fantasies. It was a splendid gift, a gift of generosity and tenderness. How could he resist? This night, she was his most lustful dreams made real, his erotic fantasies incarnate. Nay, he would not think about that, not yet. There was so much left of her to explore.

He tasted her luscious nipples, stroking the soft curves of her breasts as he did so. He licked and rubbed her belly with his mouth. Then he shifted down to her ankles and began to stroke and knead her silky skin, moving upward. He felt currents of sensation tingle through her body, and she squirmed and wriggled, as if trying desperately to ease herself. But the center of her desire lay open and untouched, inflamed and provoked by his caresses. As he smoothed his hands up her slim, soft inner thighs, he finally allowed his gaze to rest upon her exposed sex.

A trembling, dusky rose surrounded by soft down like a willow catkin. "Pussy" some men called it, "bunny" or "coney," as if it were a docile pet. "Honeypot" or "pie" or "loaf" as if a satisfying treat. A woman's secret place, so beguiling and mysterious. But he would explore her hidden charms and sample the nectar of her brimming flower. He would have his fill of her.

He gently put his finger in the ring and pried it open, then removed it. "I don't want to hurt you," he said. "And I want nothing between you and my hands and my mouth." He took one finger and stroked it down the inner crease of her cunny, feeling her shudder. Then he dipped his head and began to mouth her tenderly.

His mouth felt sublime against her roused, sentient flesh. He licked her, tasted her, and she grew breathless with waves of sensation. He seemed determined to leave no part of her unexplored. And with each sucking kiss and probing caress, he possessed her, controlled her, more and more.

When he slipped his tongue inside her, all her restraint shattered, and she was nothing but a hollow reed buffeted by the wind of his hot breath against her skin. She could not control her moaning, wordless cries nor the way her body convulsed and shuddered. Then the bonds connecting her to reason seemed to snap altogether and she was thrown into mindless rapture.

When her breathing finally slowed and she opened her eyes, she saw him sitting between her thighs, smiling triumphantly. Who had won? she wondered. Had she succeeded in seducing him, or was it she who was hopelessly beguiled?

His mouth was wet, glistening with the proof of her violent peak. His dark eyes glowed with smug contentment, and he looked like a dark, beautiful beast licking its lips after a kill.

He placed his palm on her mound, as if seeking out the quivering aftershocks of what he had done to her. Indeed, she could still feel the ripples of her climax echoing in her womb, sending little tremors of delicious heat throughout her body.

"Untie me," she whispered.

"Why?" he asked.

"Because I want to wrap my legs around you when you come inside my body."

He gave her an intent, probing look, like a hawk sighting its prey, then moved to untie her ankles. When she was free, he moved up on the bed and kissed her. She could taste herself on his lips, piquant and heady, then she sampled the warm, sweet nectar of his mouth and gorged herself on the plush delight of his tongue.

When they were both breathless and gasping, he drew back. He appeared to examine her nakedness, then he stroked both nipples once with his callused thumbs. After spreading her legs again, he took his cock in his hand and pressed it against her wet opening. She yielded instantly to him, and he plunged deep.

She cried out at the first thrust and fought to catch her breath as he moved inside her, deep and slow at first, then with a faster rhythm. He braced himself above her and she reached up to glide her hands down his smooth, thickly muscled back, then to grip his solid, softly rounded buttocks. She could feel them tighten and pulse as he thrust into her. Even as her body responded to his driving rhythm with waves of pleasure, her fingers savored the feel of his strong, graceful body.

"Wrap your legs around me," he suddenly cried. "Pull me in, take it all!"

She obeyed him, feeling the pressure deepen and intensify until she could scarce bear it. She clung to him, merged, mated, joined with this frenzied beast who drove into her with such fury. His head suddenly thrust back and he gave an exultant cry, arching into her with one last savage lunge. Then he collapsed upon her, hot and slick with sweat.

She felt exhausted, drained, as a warrior might after a battle. A battle, but both of them had won, or perhaps they had both surrendered. Surrender—how sweet it felt with this man, her beloved. A rush of emotion and tenderness choked her throat. How close they were at this moment, as if they made one being. She wanted it to last, this sense of ease and peace between them.

Groaning, he lifted himself off her. She reached out for him. He grasped her fingertips and, smiling, kissed them. "Nicola," he said, "you are the stuff of dreams."

Epilogue

There were many things to celebrate, Fawkes thought as he gazed out at the crowded hall. It was, of course, All Hallow's Eve, a celebration that at Valmar marked the end of butchering and the final preparations for winter. Then there was the joyous fact that he was almost healed. Although sometimes his shoulder felt stiff, the pain was mostly gone. And then there was his wife. He watched Nicola across the hall, talking to one of their guests. She appeared magnificent in a rich, crimson velvet gown, her long dark hair covered with a veil of matching hue, held in place by a circlet of pearls. Her beauty never failed to enchant him. Cool, elegant, queenly Nicola. And yet she offered him her body with an abandon that made his knees go weak and his head spin. She was a thing of enchantment and dreams. And yet she was his, warming his bed, filling his life with beauty and comfort. How could he not surrender and give her his heart?

Over time, he'd come to understand what she'd done, the desperate measures she'd taken to protect her son. And *his* son. Most of the time, he believed that Simon was his. And even if he wasn't, he was happy to claim him. Simon made a most promising heir. He was clever and quick, traits that would serve him well in combat and many other endeavors. With his ready laugh and smile, and his angel's face, he'd already charmed everyone at Valmar.

As if sensing Fawke's thoughts, Simon suddenly escaped

from his seat by Old Emma and ran up to the dais, his mouth a sticky mess from eating some sort of sweet. "Papa, Papa!" he called. "Sir Adam's bitch had puppies. Can I have one, please?"

"We'll discuss the matter later." Fawkes laughed. "Your mother and I will, that is. Now, go sit down and eat your food."

He looked again for Nicola, wondering who she was talking to. He hated to keep everyone waiting. Peter Wazelin, the son of an old comrade from the Crusade, sat to his left, the prior of Malvern to his far right. Wazelin had arrived the day before, bringing with him the news that money for King Richard's ransom had finally been raised, and that Queen Eleanor and the archbishop of Rouen were on their way to Germany to make final arrangements for the king's release. Like everyone in England, Fawkes had contributed a fourth of the income from his estates to the ransom fund. But the cost would be well worth it, he thought, to put a rein on scheming, unscrupulous Prince John and the threat of greedy barons like FitzRandolph.

At last Nicola approached the high table, talking animatedly to the elderly white-haired man who limped at her side. Reaching the dais, she looked up at Fawkes. "This is Sir Gerald. He was a friend of my father's. I have not seen him in nigh on ten years!"

"Bring him up here," Fawkes responded.

She took Sir Gerald's arm and helped him up on the dais, and led him near to Fawkes's chair. "Sir Gerald," she said, "may I present to you my husband, Fawkes de Cressy, lord of Valmar, Mordeaux and Wilford." There was such pride and warmth in her voice, it made his heart swell in his chest.

"Milord." Sir Gerald bowed.

"Sir Gerald." Fawkes nodded in return.

Nicola introduced Sir Gerald to their other guests, then she took her place at Fawkes's right, with Sir Gerald next to her. Fawkes listened to the two of them reminisce for a time, then his attention wandered.

The meal was delicious. Huge sides of roasted beef, quail and doves, capons and pike, lamprey and trout served in a dozen different sauces, fresh manchet bread, garlic-flavored cheeses, stewed pears, apples and apricots spiced with honey and cinnamon, and for dessert, an almond-flavored subtletie, shaped like Valmar Castle, right down to the cunningly fashioned drawbridge over a moat of custard.

When they brought the masterpiece to the head table, Old Emma released her squirming charge and a wide-eyed Simon came running up to examine the subtletie. A rather tipsy Reynard appeared and cheerfully lifted Simon up so he could see, and even poke a finger into the custard to lick. "You spoil him!" Nicola chastised.

"I'm practicing so I can spoil my own son someday," Reynard retorted, grinning.

"Glennyth says this one is going to be a girl," Nicola said. "Do you dare to gainsay her?"

"Nay, never!" Reynard cried. "I only mean to suggest that there will be other babes. One of them will be a boy, surely."

"Maybe," Nicola said smugly. To Sir Gerald, she said, "That's our son, Simon. He celebrated his third birthday in September."

"I might have known he was yours," Sir Gerald responded. "The resemblance is striking. Takes me back near forty years, to when your father's youngest brother was a lad. Young Simon is the very image of William Oxbury, who would be his great uncle. Most comely child, William was. Sadly, he died in a fall from a horse when he was about twelve years."

"What?" Nicola said. "I had an uncle who looked like Simon?"

Sir Gerald nodded. "Very like. I remember that everyone remarked upon it, with your father being dark like their Welsh mother, and his brother so fair. But your grandsire

had Saxon blood, and though he wasn't as blond as young
Simon here, he had quite light hair in his youth."

Nicola shot Fawkes a strange look, and he knew instantly
what she was thinking. An odd sensation built in his chest.
Was this the reason for Simon's coloring?

Peter Wazelin joined the conversation, nodding fervently.
"Just like horses, traits in people don't always show up right
away. Often a man will look more like his grandsire than his
sire." He turned to look at Fawkes. "You, milord, you probably have some Saxon blood in you, too. Most people around
these parts do, though a lot like to claim their ancestors came
over with the Conqueror. Add that smidgen of Saxon blood
mixed with what Lady Nicola has of her uncle, and you end
up with young Simon, who looks little like either of you."

"Young Simon who is making a mess!" Nicola exclaimed.
While Reynard was busy listening to the conversation, Simon had reached out and was trying to pry off a piece of
subtletie. "Take him away, Reynard!" Nicola cried. "Before
he brings down Valmar Castle single-handedly!"

"That would be quite a feat," Fawkes said, laughing. The
warm bubble of happiness in his chest expanded. It was odd,
but it was suddenly clear to him that Simon really was his
son. It had taken an old man and a castle fashioned of mar-
zipan to set his doubts to rest.

"Glennyth dances as gracefully as ever," Nicola noted
sometime later when most of the trestle tables had been
cleared away and the hall rang with the sounds of tambor,
cryth and harp and the muted tones of laughter and merriment. "You'd never know she was four months gone with a
babe. I wonder if I will appear so healthy and energetic when
I am carrying. As I recall, with Simon I felt sick nearly the
whole time."

"Every babe is different, the women say," Fawkes said.

"And when the time comes that you conceive a child, I promise I will cosset and spoil you every moment."

"You would think that I would have conceived by now," Nicola said. "I mean, it only took twice with Simon. And we were . . . together a great deal this summer." She gazed at him suggestively.

"Indeed," Fawkes agreed, feeling the blood fill his cock. "But practice makes perfect. As soon as it is seemly, let us excuse ourselves and go upstairs."

"Hush," Nicola whispered. "Do you want Prior Ioworth to hear?"

"Nay, I do not. What I really want to do is . . ." He bent to whisper in her ear, telling her in graphic detail all the delicious activities he wanted to share with her. When she blushed near as red as her dress, he took pity on her and said, "Go fetch Reynard to keep an eye on Simon, and I'll meet you abovestairs."

She rose swiftly, either glad to be away from his teasing, or, perhaps she was simply as eager as he was.

A short while later, in their bedchamber filled with candles and warmed by a brazier against the autumn chill, they kissed tenderly. Finally, breathless, Nicola drew away. "What do you want to do first?" she asked.

"I want you to take off your gown, but leave on your garters and hose. Then I want you to dance for me while I sit on the bed, and finally, when I can endure no more, you will come over here and take me in your mouth while I kiss your cunny at the same time."

"Mmmm," she murmured, beginning to unlace her gown. "Sounds delicious."

"Oh, but that is just the beginning." He reached for her breasts. "I will suckle your nipples until they are as red as berries." Playing with the throbbing tips, he looked at her eyes, his eyes dark and wild. Slowly, he slid one hand down her body, pressing his palm against her groin. "Then I will lick your sweet quim until you cannot stand. Fill you with as many fingers as you can take."

"Mmmm," she moaned.

"And then"—he leaned near to kiss her neck—"then and only then, I will fuck you."

"How?" she whispered, rubbing her hand against the crotch of his braies. "How will you fuck me?"

"What have we not tried for a while? You leaning over the bed? Sitting on the table? Or do you want to straddle me with your slippery wet cunny and ride my cock while I thrust deep and hard inside you?"

"I will ride you," she whispered. "Off to fairyland." She sighed in expectation.

"Wherever you wish to go," he answered huskily.

The Queen of Romance

Cassie Edwards

Stella Cameron

"A premier author of romantic suspense."